He Won't Need It Now
The Dead Stay Dumb
By James Hadley Chase

Introduction by Rick Ollerman

Stark House Press • Eureka California

HE WON'T NEED IT NOW / THE DEAD STAY DUMB

Published by Stark House Press
1315 H Street
Eureka, CA 95503, USA
griffinskye3@sbcglobal.net
www.starkhousepress.com

HE WON'T NEED IT NOW
Originally copyright © 1939 by James Hadley Chase and published in
hardback by Rich & Cowan Ltd., London, as by James L. Docherty.
Reprinted in paperback by Panther Books, 1975, as by James Hadley Chase.

THE DEAD STAY DUMB
Originally copyright © 1940 by James Hadley Chase and published in
hardback by Jarrolds, London, as *The Dead Stay Dumb*. Reprinted in the
U.S. by Eton Books, Inc, New York, as *Kiss My Fist!*, published and copyright
© 1952 by James Hadley Chase.
This edition reprints the unexpurgated, unedited version of this novel.

"a.k.a. James Hadley Chase" copyright © 2016 by Rick Ollerman.

ISBN-13: 978-1-944520-07-6

Book design by Mark Shepard, SHEPGRAPHICS.COM

First Stark House Press Edition: May 2016

First Edition

a.k.a. James Hadley Chase
by Rick Ollerman

When we talk about genre fiction, a "thriller" novel is often a euphemism for "throwaway beach read" or "airport book," meaning a book picked up without much thought. It may or may not keep you from napping on the plane on your way to some place interesting. The books themselves are often not taken very seriously, whether they were ever meant to be or not.

In the seventies we had innumerable series of "men's action/adventure" books, like "The Executioner," "The Liquidator," "Killinger," and the like. These seemed to be linear descendants of the pulp magazines, with updated violence and a bit more sadism, a more "realistic" view of an exaggerated life. Many of today's "thrillers" feature these same larger than life heroes that can, with nearly equal aplomb, destroy just about anything standing, flying or floating, and likewise survive in any circumstance against the longest of odds.

Another kind of thriller came from more literary origins, novels from Graham Greene, Eric Ambler, or even John le Carré and Frederick Forsyth. These kinds of "thrillers" are often driven by a more sophisticated plot, with suspense carrying the reader through the books, and conflict relying more on character behavior and plot than a propensity for violent acts for their own sake, the literary equivalent of special effects.

A reliance on the term "crime fiction" has been resurgent, separating many of these types of books from the more modern connotation of the word "thriller." While it is easy to call le Carré or Ambler writers of "spy fiction," how do we label the works of others like Hammett or Chandler, books like Forsyth's *The Day of the Jackal* or *The Odessa File*?

More so, how do we classify the works of an enigmatic writer like René Brabazon Raymond, far better known as James Hadley Chase, author of some 90 novels that cross the boundaries of multiple sub-genres? Oftentimes he is said to have written "thrillers," but of what sort? What does that mean?

René Raymond was born on Christmas Eve in London in 1906, the son of an officer in the British Indian Army. Intended for a scientific career, Raymond left home at the age of 18 and tried his living selling children's encyclopedias door to door. He later worked for a book distributor and in 1938, despite have done little writing previously, published what has always been his most literate and best known book, *No Orchids for Miss Blandish*.

It is an American book written by Raymond, an Englishman using the name "James Hadley Chase," and satisfied the needs of Europeans cut off from American fiction by paper shortages and the ravages of war. The book itself sold millions of copies and was controversial in its time, and remains so today.

It is a tale of kidnapping and corruption, sadism and violence. George Orwell, in his 1944 essay entitled "Raffles and Miss Blandish," calls it not "the product of an illiterate hack, but a brilliant piece of writing, with hardly a wasted word or a jarring note anywhere." But Orwell was no fan, bemoaning the lost moral standards present in work not forty years old, where good must fight evil and bad men must pay for their crimes or loose morals somewhere by the end of the book. *Miss Blandish* was, in Orwell's terms, "American" fiction, and as such he found it objectionable as a book written by a British author.

American pulps and crime fiction used to cross the Atlantic as ballast in ships, giving people in Europe a source for books published in the States. But once the war started, this source of weighty material disappeared and perhaps this was one factor that drove Raymond to write his own "American" story, although there clearly was another. It was rumored that Raymond wrote the book over the course of six weekends but it actually took him more than a year to finish. Beyond Orwell's opinion, beyond the length of time it took to write, and beyond its possible moral effect on the masses, the book itself borrows largely from another. Orwell describes it as an "impudent plagiarism of William Faulkner's novel, *Sanctuary*."

This is a problem Raymond created for himself early in his career, indeed, right from his very first book, but one he eventually overcame, possibly through influence from his friend (and at one point, publisher) Graham Greene. If plagiarism is described as passing off one's work as your own, Raymond didn't do that in *Miss Blandish*. Instead, what he did was borrow the notion of the plot from *Sanctuary*, the kidnapping, holding and corruption of a society girl, and transplanted it to a much more complex and rich setting of rival gangs.

That may sound forgivable, and indeed, this type of inspiration is a constant happening throughout all of literary history, but Raymond took it one step further and modeled his character Slim directly after Faulkner's Popeye. In fact, you could argue that Slim is Popeye, down to the sociopathic personality and propensity for unpredictable violence, and especially in that Raymond gave his Slim Popeye's childhood incident of using rusty scissors to dismantle a kitten.

But again, as Orwell said, the writing is not a hack job but is deeply engrossing and well done. Raymond's version of Popeye is more functional as a crook, and is more fleshed out as a whole, as is his version of the society victim, Miss Blandish. The book is both hard-boiled and noir, bloody and emotionally ruthless, almost as hard on the reader as it is on the characters.

There's no main character or protagonist; instead we have a shifting cast moving in and out of focus, with individuals and groups taking the stage in turn. As the story moves along, so too does the cast of characters change.

At the time Raymond wrote *Miss Blandish*, he had never set foot in America. With an atlas and a dictionary of slang he created a novel as quintessentially American noir as anything by Thompson or Willeford. His characters aren't just acting bad, they *are* bad, pulling no punches for the sake of his readers' sensibilities, or anyone else's. This is no holds barred fiction at its most raw. Raymond shows us what could happen when amoral creatures take hold of an innocent like Miss Blandish, and the power and authenticity of what takes place is precisely what Orwell finds so objectionable. Is it bad to write about people like this, or is it *too bad* that these people exist to write about?

With *The Dead Stay Dumb*, Raymond's second book (also published as *Kiss My Fist!*), he delivers another raw-bitten noir, bleak and filled with the false hopes of the damned. It starts out as a stranger-comes-to-town story, then transforms for a while into a boxing story, the kind we don't see anymore this side of the '40s. After the stranger leaves town we get the rise and bloody fall of the petty gangster. There's a lot of punch here as the criminal is as much a cold blooded killer as he is a mobster.

Like *Miss Blandish*, we're back to a third person narrator and only a modestly shifting viewpoint. The book is raw and powerful, and there are plenty of surprises as it moves along, but the inevitable fall after the rise, once you come to expect it, dampens the plot and indeed, softens the main character, the once tough-as-they-come Dillon.

There are no two word names in this one, or very few. Almost exclusively we get a first or a last name and that's it. It pares down the narrative and gives an immediacy that is just right for the book. What it gives us is writing like this:

His broken, tortured face, those two horrible eyes, sightless, with a yellow blob in each pupil, looking like two clots of phlegm, the great square head, the overhanging brows, and the ferocious mouth made her shiver.

This description of the blind boxer Butch Hogan sticks in your mind, and leaves an impression. Unfortunately, it harkens directly back to Faulkner and *Sanctuary*:

> ...for he was both blind and deaf: a short man with a bald skull and a round, full-fleshed, rosy face in which his cataracted eyes looked like two clots of phlegm.

In 1939's *He Won't Need It Now,* written as by James L. Dochery, Raymond gives us the first person account of one Duffy, an honest guy with a chance to make a semi-honest shot at making it big. Unfortunately this means he has to go up against bigger and meaner fish and the optimism of his attempt to grab a bigger piece for himself is a classic bit of noir.

There are some wonderful touches of Raymond's mastery of the "American" novel, despite a number of British-isms that pop up throughout the book:

> The pale green wrap of heavy silk which she had changed into set her figure off sharply. Duffy appreciated his private view. He admired her skin, which was pale and lovely, and he told himself that a dame with eyes as large as hers was a menace to weak men. He felt mighty weak himself toward her.

Despite his mastery of this style, American or not, in this book there are a pair of minor characters who share a certain affinity toward each other, much like a pair of hoods in Raymond Chandler's first novel. And there's the notion—no more than that, but it is there—of a rich girl who may not be in her right mind, and you have a few of the touches that Chandler himself took issue with.

Raymond/Chase had clearly formed some bad habits. He was much too skilled of a writer to need to borrow or steal so directly, or even subtly. After his 1944 book, *Blonde's Requiem*, he was obliged to satisfy Raymond Chandler himself, who had nothing good to say about Raymond's/Chase's work. (In a letter to Cleve Adams, he called *Miss Blandish* "half cent pulp writing at its worst," where I might argue it is half cent pulp writing at its *best*.) With a notice in the British publishing magazine *The Bookseller* Chandler publicly asserted certain borrowings from his own work by Raymond/Chase, and then he let the matter be. In any case, the borrowings were not extensive and apparently with his friend Graham Greene's help, Raymond/Chase finally put this tendency behind him.

Greene and Raymond were to play significant roles in each others' lives although interestingly enough, it wasn't until well after the death of both men that it was known the two had even been friends. In a suburban area west of London called Ealing, the site of a bank of poisonous, black gas unleashed by H.G. Wells' Martians in *The War of the Worlds*, the Raymond family's papers were discovered in a basement. Young René had lived there for a time while his father was away in Calcutta.

Among the papers were a collection of over 500 letters that showed that Raymond had known Greene since the end of World War II and had a friendship that carried on for decades afterward. In Greene's life as a publisher, he worked with Raymond on the one and only book he wrote under the pseudonym "Ambrose Grant," *More Deadly Than the Male*. The book is notable for being unlike Raymond's other works, with a more measured pace and tone, and for the first part, its autobiographical description of the door-to-door selling of children's encyclopedias. The book is different enough that it has been speculated that Greene himself may have written the book, or large parts of it, but upon reading it that doesn't seem likely. Raymond was such a fine writer on his own, there wouldn't have been much point.

Whatever the influence on the book, Raymond's "borrowings," such as they were, certainly appeared to vanish from his work, quite possibly owing to Greene's influence. Interestingly, Greene's officially appointed biographer, Professor Norman Sherry, had been unaware of the exact relationship between Raymond and Greene. With Greene's background in intelligence work, he was naturally reticent with the details of his personal life, or at least less than wholly forthcoming.

Raymond was one of a group of acquaintances, including Noel Coward and Charlie Chaplin, who had invested with a mobbed up financier named Tom Roe. Roe and his partner, famed British actor George Sanders, set up companies in, among other places, Switzerland, to be used as tax shelters for wealthy Brits trying to invest out of the country as a way of saving tax dollars. When one of their domestic schemes went bad, a sausage company in England, Raymond took his money out of Roe's control and was saved from the eventual tax exile that eventually forced Greene out of the country.

Greene allowed Roe to talk him into staying with him, even letting him act as his agent and broker paperback rights to some of his books. Later, when Roe was pulled over on a Swiss highway after passing some counterfeit bills, the police found another $100,000 worth of the stuff in the trunk of his car. Roe's partner in this endeavor was a Hollywood producer by the name of Dennis Lorraine. Lorraine had Mafia contacts that ran through Hollywood and the entire scandal caused problems for the likes of Chaplin and Greene.

In Greene's case, he ended up moving to his flat in Paris and then settling in Antibes. In his old age, after a fall, he moved to the village of Corseaux-sur-Vevey where he was looked after by his wife, Vivien. Coincidentally, this is the same village where Raymond had passed away in 1985. Greene followed him six years later in 1991.

□   □   □

Raymond's view of the criminal element was that they were bad people, and bad people do bad things. Often very bad things. He neither glossed over nor glorified these acts, but he did use his clear and straightforward style to depict what he at least thought these bad people did. Indeed, it was this same dedication to his version of stark realism that brought such condemnation from the likes of Orwell even though the same praised the actual writing.

In 1941's *Miss Callaghan Comes to Grief*, this style caused new troubles for Raymond, who by this time was already one of the best-selling writers in England. Again borrowing some elements from another writer's work, this time his friend Graham Greene's *A Gun for Sale* (including naming his chief villain Raven, right out of Greene's book), *Miss Callaghan* tells the story of a depraved hood taking over the St. Louis vice racket.

The Miss Callaghan of the title appears just once, in the prologue. A trio of men, tired of the oppressive summer heat, get the idea of spending the night in a giant refrigerator. One of the men has a friend who works in the morgue, and despite feeling a little creepy, they all agree to go.

Here a bit of voyeurism takes place as they start randomly pulling drawers and looking at the corpses. The males were disappointing but they finally got to the women. The tag on one of those identified the deceased as Miss Julie Callaghan, 23 years old, 5 feet 4 inches. Cause of death was murder by stabbing. Her occupation was listed as "Prostitute."

When one of the men speculates the girl might have been one of Raven's, another of the men says he has no idea who that is. The Raven saga had been ended a year or so and the men settled in to tell him the story....

Raymond's Raven character had left Chicago on the run and, after spending time in Nevada, thought he knew just how to build up the city's prostitution business. Raven was an ambitious man and his plan called for more and more girls; he cared neither where they came from nor how his men got them. The novel is centered around the "slavery" angle, or the kidnapping and forcing of women into Raven's "houses."

Drugs, beatings, humiliation, and Raven's ultimate tool, the pouring of turpentine onto the stomachs of his restrained victims, were all matter-offactly detailed in the book. It's a difficult read, not for the sensitive reader even today. And in 1941 it caused an uproar.

In May of 1942 Raymond and his publishers were found guilty of publishing an obscene book and it was banned from that point on. Despite the scandal, Raymond received the support of other figures in the literary establishment and indeed, his papers show that he was on such good terms with the police that they had actually shared with him the details of the case against him. None of that stopped him from being vilified by those he had offended and we are left only to imagine what effect all this had on him as a writer, for of course he went on to write nearly eighty more books.

Greene himself had gone through something similar a few years before when he wrote a review in his magazine *Night and Day* of the John Ford directed Shirley Temple vehicle, *Wee Willie Winkie*. The picture was an adaptation of a Kipling story and Greene was appalled by what he thought were clear sexual overtones regarding the Shirley Temple character. Similar movies today cause some notice, especially given their even more graphic depictions of young women or girls in exploitative situations, but in 1937, the outcry from America against Greene's article was terrific. The resulting libel suit led to judgments against both *Night and Day* and Greene himself, although the magazine had already published its final issue prior to the verdict.

In 1948 Raymond did something remarkable: he published a sequel to the book that to this day remains his most famous, *No Orchids for Miss Blandish*. A very different book from the original, *Flesh of the Orchid* is the tale of a new Blandish, born of the first book but a very, very different novel. It is perhaps more of a "James Hadley Chase" book than *No Orchids for Miss Blandish*, with a much less psychological or literary aspect but with more of the unique Raymond "thriller" touch.

The book itself moves distinctly from style to style, with the first third or so reading as an edge of your seat horror novel. The book morphs smoothly into a crime story, then into a suspense thriller, and then finally a multi-layered revenge plot comes into play. This is the kind of a book that defies the concept of outlining but it is brilliant in its pervasive suspense and although quite a different book from *No Orchids*, it is not only a worthy sequel but a wonderful book on its own merits.

It takes place twenty years after the events in *No Orchids*, and has no characters in common, but the events as they happen are directly informed by the happenings in the first book. It is indeed Raymond at his best and the two books together make an impressive duology. The ease with which Raymond's walk-on characters take on lives and personalities all their own give a clue as to how this "thriller" writer can be so engrossing. No, these characters are not as deeply rich in background as they could be, but they are fleshed out and motivated beings, more than cardboard characters existing merely to advance plot. This may be Raymond's most impressive gift, that of giving us plot-driven stories populated by characters strong enough and individual enough to propel his books to the upper levels of his genre. They may stop short of being people we *care* about, most of them are simply too bad, but they are fundamentally real people, or at least people that we can understand in the real world.

□   □   □

There are strong sexual elements in his books, but the books aren't sexy or titillating. They are suffused with a sort of dark voyeurism, feats of unhealthy love, the kind best kept shut away behind heavily curtained windows and soundproofed doors. These relations are base and often tawdry, more likely to be the result of a strong man taking advantage of a weak woman. There is love in these books but it's not moonlight and roses; sex and love are tools, and in Raymond's world, they're depicted as used by the wrong kind of people. It makes for a gritty, gutter feel that may be in line with the story but often makes for uncomfortable reading. Put this together with good ol' American hard-boiled fiction and you have that unique James Hadley Chase synthesis.

Raymond wrote few short stories, released in his one collection, 1942's *Get a Load of This*. A veritable sampler of the kinds of kinks present in his novels, many of the stories are not for the faint of heart or easily offended. Raymond seems intent upon showing us the unhealthy effects of man's attraction to woman, sometimes out of nobility, sometimes out of lust. The ethical and emotional gamut is on display here and the book is perversely an interesting distillation of both Raymond's engaging writing and his shocking subject matter. If there are happy endings, they come on the collapsed backs of the characters within.

□   □   □

The man himself remains something of an enigma to this day. Perhaps because of the "borrowing" scandals earlier in his career, as a rule he shunned the media, disdaining interviews, saying, "There are authors who like to talk about themselves and their work. I don't. If an author's work sells steadily and well, worldwide, he should not need to waste time giving press interviews, writing introductions, or bothering about what critics have to say. My job is to write a book for a wide variety of readers. I do this job conscientiously. An introduction to my work would certainly not be of use to my general readers. They couldn't care less. All they are asking for is a good read: that is what I try to give them."

Raymond deserves to be known for better than that, perhaps better than as a "thriller" writer (at least by today's definition). At his best he is an intensely readable purveyor of those that live in the seamier sections of town, a chronicler of criminals and would-be movers and shakers, an uncompromising painter of the sins and vices that motivate the common man. Above all else, he is an entertaining and enterprising writer.

Perhaps one day someone will publish those found papers from Ealing, west of London, and we will learn more of the man behind the ninety novels. For too long we've been left with second hand paperback reprints, the kind with covers adorned by sexy lingerie models, books that may look appealing on the racks but that you wouldn't take home to mother.

In the end, Raymond didn't want his public to know him personally. Perhaps he was like a modern baseball player, dogged by rumors of using performance enhancing drugs to the point where he shuns the press and earns a reputation for being unfriendly to the media. Inevitably Raymond would be dogged by the same sort of questions regarding plagiarism and the earlier part of his career and it may simply have been most prudent for him to shy away.

Regardless, it's interesting that Raymond's "James Hadley Chase" identity is so strong that even the books written by his other pseudonyms, "Raymond Marshall," "James L. Docherty," and "Ambrose Grant" are reprinted as by "James Hadley Chase." The name of René Brabazon Raymond never emerges and that may be, in the end, precisely the way it should be. After all, it's James Hadley Chase that we know best.

Littleton, NH
November, 2011
Revised for this book April, 2016

References:
Faulkner, William, *Sanctuary,* Jonathan Cape and Harrison Smith, 1931
MacShane, Frank, ed., *Selected Letters of Raymond Chandler,* Columbia University Press, 1981
Orwell, George, "Raffles and Miss Blandish" from *Essays,* Everyman's Library, 2002
Reilly, John M., editor, *Twentieth Century Crime and Mystery Writers, 2nd edition,* St. Martin's Press, 1985
West, W. J., *The Quest for Graham Greene,* St. Martin's Press, 1998

He Won't Need It Now
By James Hadley Chase

For James Whittaker

Part One

IT BEGINS

Chapter One

The lounge of the Princess Hotel was crowded with stragglers, filling in time before going into dine. At the far end of the room, waiters hovered at the open doors of the restaurant, waiting patiently for someone to come on in and eat. It was just after seven o'clock, and the room was seething with movement as people pushed past small tables to greet friends, or shouted across, whichever way they felt.

William Duffy sat in a corner, drinking a Bacardi Crusta. The table before him held a number of bottles. The barman was a friend of his and let him mix his own drinks. There was a scowl on his face and he hadn't removed his hat. He just sat there drinking and smoking and scowling. Looking up suddenly, he saw Sam McGuire of the *Tribune* crawling by, muttering apologies as he lurched into small tables. Duffy reached out and touched Sam's cuff. Sam stopped at once.

"My God!" he said, "I'm goin' blind or somethin'."

"You ain't doing so badly," Duffy said, looking him over. "You ain't quite blind, but you're getting on."

McGuire hooked a chair with the toe of his shoe and pulled it towards him. He folded himself down and grinned.

"You goin' on a bender?" he asked with interest, looking at the collection of bottles before him.

Duffy signalled the barman, who brought another glass. The barman looked the two of them over with a practised eye. "Ain't goin' to overdo it, are yuh?" he asked in a pleading voice.

"Okay, don't you worry about us," Duffy said, picking up the rum and pouring it into the shaker.

"I hope not, boss." The barman took another long look and went back to his counter.

"Poor old George," Sam sighed, "he's forgotten us since he's moved in with the Big Shots. Listen Bill, make that a strong one. I guess I'm just about all in. If you notice a funny smell in a minute, go away, I shall've died on you."

Carefully Duffy added the absinthe, squeezed a lime and spooned in some sugar. He chased some crushed ice round with the tongs before getting a grip, then he sealed the shaker and went to work.

McGuire lit a cigarette and pushed his hat on to the bridge of his nose. He looked at Duffy carefully while he handled the shaker. Duffy met his eye and grinned. "Go on, I know what you're going to say."

"It ain't true, is it?"

Duffy nodded his head and poured the shaker's contents into the two glasses. McGuire took his in his hand and rested his nose on the rim of the glass.

"Mi Gawd!" he said, "you mean old Sourpuss has tossed you out?"

"Yeah, just like that."

Sam sat back and groaned. "What the hell—?"

"Listen," Duffy said. "Arkwright and me have been hating each other's guts for a long time. I never gave him a chance to bat me. Today I did. He'd been waiting for the chance and he grabbed it with two hands like a starving man would grab a dollar lunch. O boy! Did it make him feel good! He tossed me out so quickly, I'm still dizzy in the head."

"But why, for the love of Mike?"

"I was young and innocent and you know how these things go. I didn't think he was that sort of a boy, and look, mother, what's happened now."

"Skip the comedy." Sam was sitting up with a fierce look on his broad face. "Did you slip up on somethin'?"

"You know me, I don't slip on anything. Anyway, if I do, I cover it up all right. This was a frame. That heel Arkwright has been angling for an interview with Bernstein for weeks, and at last he got it. You know how difficult Bernstein can be. He said that art was out. Mind you, with a mug like that Yid's got on him, I ain't surprised he was a bit touchy. Anyway, Arkwright kept right at him until he gave way. I was sent along to get the pictures. I reckoned I had a nice set until I got 'em in the bath, then Mrs. Duffy's son had a shock. Those goddam' plates were fogged, the whole lousy lot. Sabotage, that's what it was. Some smart guy'd tampered with the stock. I tested the remaining plates and they were all duds." He paused for a pull at his glass. Sam said nothing. His face was flushed and his foot tapped against the leg of the table. Duffy knew he was getting mad. "Well, I explained to Sourpuss and do you think he'd believe me? Not likely! We exchanged a few words, and I guess I got tough, so he ran me inside and they ran me outside."

Sam helped himself to another Bacardi Crusta.

"This may put you in a spot," he said thoughtfully. "That punk's got the ear of most Art Editors in town."

"Sure, I know. Unreliable, fell down on a scoop!"

Duffy finished his drink and began to mix more Bacardis. "What the hell," he went on, "it's my funeral anyway. Come on in and feed with me."

Sam climbed to his feet. He looked worried. "Ain't possible, soldier," he said. "I've got to get back and put in some more sweat. Come over in the morning, will you? Alice's goin' to be sore about this."

Duffy nodded his head. "I'll be over. Tell Alice not to lose any sleep. I'll get somethin'."

"Sure." Sam clouted Duffy on the back, nearly jerking the shaker of his hands. "Keep 'em bouncin', brother, keep 'em bouncin'."

When he had gone, Duffy finished the last of the Bacardis and, feeling pleasantly drunk, sat back and considered his future with optimism. He glanced over to the far end of the room at the fat man who had been watching him all the evening. You can't go two hours or so with someone's eyes shifting all over your face without feeling it, and Duffy had been vaguely aware of intense scrutiny ever since the fat man had come in.

Feeling more interested now, he wondered indifferently who he was. In the past, he might have been unusually striking, but he had let himself go and he was running to fat in a big way. He had broad lumpy shoulders that might easily have carried a nasty punch, but he was getting thick in the middle, which told Duffy all he wanted to know. His face was big and fat, and his mouth turned down at the corners, giving him a dismal sneering look. His little eyes were restless and shifted about like black beads.

Duffy guessed he was on the wrong side of forty-five. He had dough all right. Not only were his clothes good, but they were cut right and he wore them right. There was an air of confidence that money brings; the look that tells you that the bank balance's fat.

Getting to his feet, Duffy began an unsteady journey to the restaurant, and he purposely made a detour so that he would pass the fat man's table. As he reached the table, the fat man climbed to his feet and stood waiting. Duffy stopped and looked him over. At close quarters he liked him a lot less.

"I'm Daniel Morgan," the fat man said as if he were saying Rockefeller instead of Morgan. "Mr. Duffy?"

Duffy squinted at him, astonished. "Sure," he said.

"Mr. Duffy, I want to talk to you. Will you dine with me?"

Duffy raised his eyebrows. He told himself that he wasn't spending his money, so he said that it was okay with him. Morgan led the way into the restaurant, and Duffy thought his guess that Morgan's wallet was well lined was a good one. He could tell by the way the waiters fawned on the fat man. He got a table in a corner, pretty secluded, and sat down. Duffy took a chair opposite him. Three waiters came bowing round them, and the wine waiter hovered outside the fringe. The *maître d'hôtel* came up smoothly as if he had been drawn along on wheels, and the other wops grouped themselves in a line at the back. Royal stuff, but even then Morgan wasn't satisfied. He wanted the chef. Well, of course he got the chef.

You either get a big kick out of tossing your weight around like that, or else you feel all hands and feet. Duffy felt all hands and feet.

The chef and Morgan got into a huddle with the bill of fare. He didn't ask Duffy what he wanted and Duffy was glad of that. He just kept talking in his deep harsh voice and the chef squeaked back at him in broken English until they had put a meal together that seemed to satisfy him. After they had done that, they got some elbow-room. Then Morgan remembered that Duffy was sitting opposite him.

"You'll excuse me for not asking you what you would like, but on these occasions I feel the choice of a good meal lies in the hands of the chef rather than in the hands of the diner. Consult the chef and you put him on his mettle. I think you will be satisfied."

Duffy shrugged. He began to want another drink.

"I should like to confirm a few details," Morgan went on; "forgive me if I seem inquisitive, but my questions will eventually be to your advantage, so I must ask for your patience."

This long-winded stuff gave Duffy a pain, but he hadn't had oysters for a couple of years, so he let himself go with them.

Morgan didn't seem to expect an answer, but went straight on. "I believe you resigned from the *Tribune* this afternoon?" he said casually.

Duffy grinned. "You're partly right there," he said. "I didn't resign, I was tossed out."

"Arkwright is a difficult man."

This bird seems to know all the answers. Duffy laid his oyster-fork on the plate and looked regretfully at the glistening shells. "So what?" he said.

"You may find it difficult to get a job again."

The soup and the sherry turned up then. Duffy looked at the sherry and then at Morgan. Morgan got it all right. "Perhaps you would prefer Scotch?" he asked.

"These sissy drinks upset my guts," Duffy said, apologetically.

The wine waiter was called and a bottle of Scotch materialized. Duffy felt he could cope with anything with that at his elbow. He gave himself a generous shot and dived into his soup again.

"As I was saying…" Morgan began.

Duffy raised his head. His eyes were hard. "You seem to know a hell of a lot," he said sharply, "who told you—?"

Morgan waved his hand. "Please," he said, let me continue. I was saying, you will find another job difficult to get."

Duffy laid his spoon down with a sharp clatter. "You know, pal," he said, "a guy with my experience seldom stands in the bread-line. I've got a swell equipment, I know my job, and if the worst comes, I could set up a studio. I guess you're being mighty pleasant with your sympathy, but I ain't worryin' and I'd hate to have you worry for me."

"I'm quite sure," Morgan said, rather hastily, "you'll get along all right, but I have a proposition that might be extremely useful to help you start that studio."

"What is it?"

"Before we come to that, I wonder if you would enlighten me on a few technical points of your work?"

"Sure." Duffy was getting bored with all this. "What'd you want to know?"

"Would it be possible to get pictures of a person who is unaware of you, in ordinary lighting, in an ordinary room, who probably would be moving about. I want good pictures, not just anything."

"It depends a lot on the room," Duffy said, pouring some more Scotch in his glass and forgetting to put the water in after it. "I wouldn't like to say without seeing the room. It depends so much on the walls, if they reflect the light. If you don't want real art, I could get you pictures all right. Pictures that would reproduce."

"You could do that?"

"Yeah, that wouldn't be so hard."

Morgan seemed satisfied with that and went off on another long-winded ramble about nothing at all. They went through the dinner without getting anywhere, and Duffy guessed Morgan was stalling until he had finished the meal. He was right, for when the coffee was served, Morgan lit a cigar for Duffy and one for himself and got down to business.

"This is a delicate situation," he said, pursing his thick lips, and letting the heavy smoke slide, almost hiding his face. "I don't want you to know too much about it. The less you know the better for both of us. My wife's being blackmailed and I want to help her out."

Duffy grunted. He was surprised, but then you never knew what was coming to you, he told himself.

"Unfortunately my wife and I don't get on as well as we might." Morgan fidgeted a little with his liqueur glass. "We don't live together. However, that does not concern you. She is being blackmailed and I'm going to put a stop to it. She won't come to me for help, but that does not alter the situation. I want to catch this blackmailer with the goods. This is where you come in. I want you to get pictures of her giving this crook money, then I can crack down on him. It is no use trying to cooperate with Mrs. Morgan, she wouldn't want me to help her. I can get you into her apartment and you must do the rest. I shall pay you well."

Duffy didn't like this. He thought there was a phoney smell that went with it. He shifted in his chair.

"This sounds like a job for a private dick," he said, without any enthusiasm.

Morgan seemed to expect opposition. "I want pictures," he said with emphasis. "To get them, I must employ an expert. You'll be wanting money pretty soon, and you're an expert. I think it fits, don't you?"

Duffy told himself that if he was going to pull this job, the dough had to be right.

"Now as to terms." Morgan spread his big hands on the tablecloth and looked at them. "I will give you five hundred dollars down, and a thousand dollars for every good picture you turn in."

Duffy got his nerve back with a long drink. He was getting pretty high by this time, but he was still cautious. "You must want those pictures mighty bad," he said, thinking that he could do himself well with fifteen hundred bucks.

"I do," Morgan said, "I want them fast too. Will you do it?"

Duffy waved a hand. "Take it easy," he said, "you're rushing me. I want to get this straight. You want me to go to your wife's apartment and take pictures of her and someone else and turn these pictures over to you, that right?"

Morgan was getting impatient, Duffy could see that, but he held himself in with an effort. "That's right," he said.

"What happens if she spots me and sends out the riot call?"

"She won't spot you," Morgan said shortly. "Let me give you the idea. She is crazy about music and she's rich enough to indulge herself. In her sitting-room she has a small organ loft. This loft's a kind of balcony about ten feet from the floor, looking into the room. It's reached by a special staircase and there is a back entrance to the staircase."

Duffy reached for the Scotch, but Morgan put his hand on the bottle. "Don't you think…?" he began, but Duffy took his hand away. He just lifted the fat man's hand and flung it back at him. His eyes looked annoyed. "Listen," he said tersely, "if you think I'm getting drunk, forget it. When I want a drink, I have a drink, see?"

Morgan shrugged. His face was pale and he gently rubbed his wrist. "Quite a grip you have there," he said.

Duffy grinned. "Sure," he said. He poured the Scotch into the glass and swallowed it. "Go on," he said.

Morgan tapped on the table with his thick fingers. "You see, my wife didn't want the musicians tramping through her room. They could come up the back entrance and get fixed without any fuss. All you have to do is to go up the stairs and lie on the floor in the dark and take photos of the room below. You can't be spotted."

When he put it like that, Duffy thought it certainly seemed easy. At the same time, something told him that this set-up was not quite on the level. For one thing, Morgan didn't give him any confidence. On the other hand, the dough was good, and he was going to need it. He had another go at him.

"Let's look on the dark side," he said; "suppose she takes it into her head to play the organ and finds me up there, what then?"

Morgan shrugged his fat shoulders. "There's no other way up to the loft, so all you have to do is to slip the bolt. Once you're there, you're safe." He took out his wallet and pushed five one-hundred-dollar bills over the table. "Besides," he said with a little oily smile, "you surely expect to earn this money and not just have it given you."

Duffy reached over and took the bills. He shoved them in his inside pocket. "Okay," he said, "when do I start?"

Morgan pulled out a gold watch and glanced at it. Duffy noticed that his hand shook a little. "It's just after ten now," he said, "you've got to get your equipment, and then go to the house. I think we could start now."

Duffy got to his feet and pushed back the chair with his legs. Morgan looked at him and said quietly, "I want to impress on you that this is important—"

Duffy raised his hand. "Skip it," he said, "you don't have to tell me all that again. A thousand bucks a picture is more than important to me."

Morgan climbed out of his chair. "You can do quite a bit with money like that," he said.

Duffy said, "You're telling me."

Chapter Two

Morgan had been quite right. The whole set-up was easy. Duffy sat on his heels in the organ loft and felt hilariously at home. The small camera hung round his neck by a strap and the lighting of the room gave him no misgivings. He was going to make some money, he told himself. The organ loft was just as Morgan had described. It had an uninterrupted view of the room below and it was partly screened by heavy magenta curtains. Duffy had bolted himself in, and with the help of a pint of Scotch that he had brought with him, his nerves were calm and he could take a professional interest in his work.

He set the camera, using a big stop and a fairly fast shutter. Then he settled himself down to wait. Morgan had driven him to his apartment to collect his equipment and then had driven him to the back entrance of the loft. Morgan seemed to have had the whole thing planned carefully and it ran on oiled wheels. He had arranged to meet Duffy at the Princess bar that night, and Morgan was prepared to wait until he came.

Duffy looked down at the room with appreciation. It was a pretty swell joint, he told himself. The decoration was in magenta and cream. A cream pile carpet on the floor, and the large leather chairs, half cream and half magenta, gave the room a smart modern appearance. Duffy thought he'd like to have a place like this for his own.

He glanced at his wrist-watch. It was getting on for midnight. He wished that he could smoke, but he thought that that would be too risky. He wondered how long he had to wait. Just then the door below opened and a woman walked in hurriedly. She crossed the room and disappeared through another door. She had moved so quickly that Duffy hadn't had a chance to see what she was like. He cautiously spread himself on the floor, so that he was lying full length, his elbows supporting his arms as he swung the camera into position. He found that he could aim the camera through the narrow slots of the balcony, and he knew that he was completely hidden from the room below. He made himself comfortable by taking out a pint bottle of Scotch from his pocket, which was digging into him, then he settled down to wait.

A quarter of an hour dragged past, and he began to get fidgety, but suddenly he heard a faint whirr of an electric bell. He stiffened and looked towards the door expectantly. The woman came out and crossed the room. He could see her now, and he thought, "O boy! O boy!" She was tall and slender. The pale green wrap of heavy silk which she had changed into set her figure off sharply. Duffy appreciated his private view. He admired her skin, which was pale and lovely, and he told himself that a dame with eyes as large as hers was a menace to weak men. He felt mighty weak himself towards her. Her scarlet lips promised passion, and he thought the red-gold hair was just the right finish to a mighty swell job. He thought Morgan showed a nice taste in women, but at the same time he wondered how a dame like that could have fallen for Morgan in the first place. It didn't surprise him in the least that she had given Morgan the air.

He watched her go to the door, and when she came back into the room again a man followed her closely. Duffy looked with interest at him. He was short and slight, with dark wavy hair. He seemed nervous and his face was unusually pale. The woman sat on the arm of a chair, quite close to a lamp standard. Duffy noted that the light fell directly on her. He focused his camera and gently pressed the release. The shutter slid with a faint click and Duffy pulled the trigger-like film-changer. The man below said in a low voice, "You got it?"

When she spoke, her voice came drifting up to Duffy in a soft cadence. She had that rather breathless voice with a very faint huskiness that make most men interested. Duffy was more than interested.

She said, "I have the money." She spoke with contempt, and the man squirmed under her gaze. "Did you bring the stuff?"

"I want the dough first," he said; "make it snappy, lady, it ain't too healthy for me being here."

Again she looked at him, then turning to the table she pulled out a drawer. Duffy saw her take out a thick wad of greenbacks. He again pressed the release. The faint click of the shutter seemed to roar in his ears. Down below, they noticed nothing. He saw the woman give the money and then the man, in his turn, hand over a small parcel. Duffy fired off his camera, pulling the film-changer rapidly, intent on what was happening below him. Then he lowered the camera, satisfied that he had got what he wanted. He reckoned he had at least twenty photos, and most of those would be nice ones. He calculated that five thousand bucks would be his by the morning, and he groped on the floor for the Scotch. He still kept his eye on the two in the room, but nothing was happening to get excited about, and he felt that a drink would help him along. At the back of his brain he was trying to place the short man down there in the room. He had seen him somewhere, but where it was, for the moment, escaped him.

The man was moving to the door now. He sidled like a crab, watching the red-headed woman closely. She followed him out of Duffy's sight and after a short delay she came back again. Duffy watched her. She relaxed into one of the chairs. Her green wrap parted and Duffy could see her long white legs. He raised himself slowly, so that he could see better. This dame was certainly a honey. He wondered if she had anything on under that wrap. The thought disturbed him, and he nearly wrenched his neck muscles trying to see more of her. He felt dispirited leaving her all on her own, but then, Morgan was waiting and so was the dough. He guessed that he wouldn't get to the first base with this dame without dough, and to get it he had to leave her. He rose quietly to his feet and took a step back. *Something hard dug him in the back.*

"Grab a little air, lug," said a voice in his ear.

In the ordinary run of things, Duffy's nerves were pretty sound, but this nearly ruined his heart. He felt his long limbs quiver with shock, and he raised his hands quickly.

"Take it easy," went on the voice, "don't start anything."

Duffy turned his head very slowly and looked over his shoulder. Standing behind him was a broad-shouldered man, wearing a black Fedora, pulled down low. In spite of Duffy's usual nonchalance, he felt his short hairs on his nape bristle. There was something utterly repulsive in the hard white face behind him. It gave Duffy the same feeling he might have got if he turned over a rotten log that had been lying in long grass for some time, and suddenly seen the foul things the log hid. The scurry of beetles and ants, the brown dead grass, and the white fungi, and particularly the long white slug that squirmed away from the sunlight. Down below he heard a door shut, and he guessed that the woman had left the room. Keeping his hands raised, he said, "For the love of Mike, where did they find you?"

The man's eyes were almost closed, but the light in the room was sufficient for Duffy to see that they were mean and hard. He dug the gun into Duffy hard.

"Stand still," he said again. His voice was hoarse as if he smoked too much. He put out a hand and snatched the camera hanging from Duffy's neck. The strap snapped, jerking Duffy's head forward.

"Hi!" Duffy said, in alarm. "You ain't pinching my outfit?"

"Shaddap," the man snarled at him.

A violent rage consumed Duffy. "A frame-up huh?" he snorted. "Mr. Sonofabitch Morgan wants his pictures for nothing?"

"If you don't stop yappin', I'll blast your guts," the other rasped. "What the hell do you think you're doin' in here?"

Duffy began to lower his hands, but the gun dug into him again. "Listen," he said, "I'm just doin' a job of work. Come to that, what about yourself?" All the time he was speaking, he was wondering if this tough would shoot him. He began to think he was in a bit of a spot.

"I guess we'll go for a little walk," the other said. There was a threat in his voice, but he took a step back, taking the gun from Duffy's side. Duffy didn't hesitate. He took a deep breath and suddenly kicked back with his heel. He hoped to connect with the other's leg. Maybe splinter his shinbone for him but his leg shot back meeting nothing, and before he could save himself he toppled over the low balcony and crashed into the room below.

He came down on his hands, breaking his fall by sliding a little on the carpet. For a moment the shock did things to him, then he sat up.

A door opened and he looked up gingerly, wondering if his brain had broken loose from its moorings. The red-head was standing there. She crossed her arms over her breasts and screamed. A breathless little scream that made Duffy want to put his arms round her and soothe her; not perhaps quite the same way as a mother might soothe her hurt child, but along those lines. When he saw the .25 in her hand he changed his mind.

Women with guns made him nervous. He could never believe that they were safe with them. Before now, a woman had held him up with a gun. He remembered one particularly irate blonde who had been so mad with him that she had squeezed the trigger a little too hard. The thought made him sweat a little, and he sat on the floor very still, giving her no cause for alarm.

Her eyes were large and scared, and her red lips were parted, showing her white even teeth. Duffy thought she was pretty good.

"Who… who are you?" she stammered breathlessly.

"Lady," he said, holding his head in his hands, "I'm asking myself the same question."

"What are you doing here?"

Duffy looked at her through laced fingers. "Would you mind very much putting that rod away? I've just fallen out of that loft and my nerves won't stand any more."

"Will you tell me what you are doing here?" She was getting her nerve back, and her voice was steady.

"For the love of Mike don't start getting' tough," he pleaded, "take a look at that hoodlum up there before you get that way."

She looked frightened again. "Is there anyone else up there?"

Duffy laughed shortly. "I should say so," he said, rubbing the back of his head gingerly, "he's just tossed me out, so I should know."

She took a step back hastily and looked up into the loft, then she shook her head. "There's no one there."

Duffy groaned. "The so-and-so's pinched my camera," he said wearily. "Do you mind if I get up? There's a draught round here that ain't doing me much good."

"I think you had better stay where you are," she said firmly. She held the gun steady as she reached for the telephone.

"Don't do that," Duffy said in alarm, "you ain't calling the cops, are you?"

"Isn't that what I ought to do?" she asked, her hand hesitating on the receiver.

"Listen, Mrs. Morgan, I can explain everything. It's all a big mistake," Duffy said; then he pondered and went on, "I've heard that crack before. My God! I must be losing my grip or somethin'."

She lowered the gun in her astonishment. "Why do you call me that?" she asked quickly.

Duffy stiffened a little. "Ain't you Mrs. Morgan?"

"No, of course not."

He scrambled to his feet and waved his hands at her as she jerked up the gun. "Okay, okay, skip it," he said impatiently, "this is important. Who are you?"

She tapped her foot on the floor. "What *is* this?"

"I'll tell you what this is," Duffy said furiously, "I've been taken for a ride. You've got to get this straight. Listen, Toots, I'm Duffy of the *Tribune*. Some guy who called himself Morgan spun me a yarn that you were his wife and you were being blackmailed. He wanted me to take photos of the crook who was putting the screws on you. I fell for this guff and came up to the hen-roost here and took photos of you and the guy you slipped the money to. Just as I am reaching for my hat and calling it a nice day's work, some thug hops up, pinches my camera, and heaves me out on my neck. You tell me you ain't Mrs. Morgan. In your own interests you'd better tell me who you are."

She stared at him and then said finally, "I think you must be mad."

"Use your head," Duffy was getting impatient, "can't you see that you're in a spot? Morgan wanted a photo of you with this other guy and he's got it. Ask yourself why."

She still stared at him and shook her head. "I don't understand… I don't believe.…"

He slid across to her in one movement and pushed the gun away. For Krizake," he said roughly, "will you listen to me? Who was the guy you gave that money to?"

His urgency touched her and she said quickly, "I don't know. I think his name's Cattley…."

Duffy stepped back. "Cattley… of course. By heck! I *must* be losing my grip. Cattley…." He swung round on her. "What the hell are you doing with a rat like Cattley?"

Her eyebrows came together. "Will you stop asking me questions—?" she began.

"Listen, baby." Duffy came close to her. His voice had a sharp edge to it. "Cattley's got a name that stinks in this town. Everyone knows him. Cattley the pimp. Cattley the dope. Cattley the slaver. I tell you he's poison to dames like you. You… you've let yourself be photographed with him… and someone's got those photos. Does that mean anything to you?"

"But—" She stopped and he saw she had gone pale.

"Yeah! That's made you think. Sit down and tell me quick. Make it snappy; I've got things to do."

She turned on him suddenly with furious eyes. "You started this," she stormed at him. "If it hadn't been for you—"

"Forget it!" he snapped at her. "I'm getting those pictures back all right. But you've got to wise me up a hell of a lot before I do."

The flash of temper was gone almost before it started. She sat down limply on the large settee and tossed the gun on the table. Duffy winced a little. Women were hell when it came to handling guns. He took a quick glance and saw that the safety catch was still down.

"Now come on, come on, let's get down to it," he said, sitting on the edge of the table. "What's your name?"

"Annabel English," she said, twisting her hands in her lap.

"What are you? Just a little dame with plenty of dough, running round lookin' for a good time?"

She nodded. Duffy lit a cigarette. "Yeah I bet you are, and bet you have a pretty nice time of it. What's this Cattley to you?"

Her face flushed and she hesitated. "I... I asked him to get material on the... the underworld...." She stopped. The colour in her face was deep.

Duffy groaned. "For the love of Mike, don't tell me you're writing a book or something," he pleaded; "a Society-dame-looks-on-the-underworld stuff?"

"I thought it would be amusing," she said. "It's about the White Slave traffic...."

He threw up his hands. "So you thought you would write a book on the White Slave traffic, did you?" he said, dragging smoke into his lungs and letting it drift from his nostrils. "And you've to pick on the worst hoodlum in town to help you. Well, I reckon you'd better change your ideas and write a book on blackmail. You're going to get a grandstand seat in this racket, and if you ain't careful you're going to pay plenty."

She looked up swiftly, her face resentful. "What am I to do?"

Duffy slid off the table. "You ain't doing a thing at the moment. I'm getting that camera back. That's the first thing."

He walked over to the telephone. "Take a look in the book and see if you can find Daniel Morgan in it," he said, spinning the dial. She got to her feet and began to rustle through the directory. While he was waiting for the line to connect he let his eye run over her as she leant forward over the table. "Annabel English," he thought. "A swell name and a nice little job."

A sharp metallic voice snapped in his ear, "*Tribune* here, what department do you know?"

"H'yah, Mabel," he said. "Dinny in?"

"Hold on an' I'll put you through."

McGuire came on the line. "Hello, pal," he said. Duffy thought he sounded a little drunk.

"Listen, soldier," Duffy said, keeping an edge on his voice. "This is important. Will you meet me at the Princess Hotel right away?"

McGuire groaned. "Aw, what you think I am? I'm goin' home. Listen bozo, what'll Alice say? I ain't been home all this week."

Duffy was certain McGuire was drunk. "I'll fix Alice," he said. "Get going and make it fast." He hung up as McGuire began to protest again.

Annabel English said, "There are ten Daniel Morgans in the book."

"That's okay," Duffy returned. "I'll find him." He walked over to her. "Now you forget about this... leave it to me. I'll give you a ring tomorrow and let you know how it went." He paused, looking into her blue smoky eyes. "You all alone here?"

She nodded. "I sent my maid out for the evening. I didn't want her to see Cattley—"

"You ain't scared?"

"Why should I be?" She looked startled.

Duffy shrugged his shoulders. "Why, I just thought…." He suddenly grinned at her. "If I get that camera, shall I come back an' see you tonight?"

Her eyes laughed at him, but her face was quite serious as she shook her head. "I shan't be alone—"

"Who's your boy friend…?"

She walked slowly to the door. He could see her smooth muscles moving under the green wrap. He knew that she hadn't anything on under that. She looked over her shoulder. "I think you had better go now," she said, "I've heard that you newspapermen get funny ideas when you're alone with girls."

Duffy looked round for his hat and found it near the settee. "Well, what of it?" he said, walking to the door. They stood quite close, facing each other. "What the hell's a girl got to beef about if he does? Ain't that a compliment to the girl, anyway? By heck! I can guess how they'd feel if we didn't get that way sometimes!"

She opened the door and he walked past her. Standing in the doorway, he faced her again. "Well, good night, Toots," he said with his wide grin, "sleep easy… I'm goin' to do things for you."

Pushing the door slowly to, she kept his eyes watching her. Then when the door was nearly shut she leaned forward. "Did you say your name was Duffy?"

"Yeah!"

"Anything else?"

"Bill Duffy, if you like."

"It's a nice name." She leant against the doorway, the door pulled against her fat hip.

Duffy stood there, putting his personality over on a short wave. "It's an old family name," he said modestly and grinned.

She raised her eyebrows. "So?"

Duffy moved a little her way until he leant against the wall, touching her shoulder. "We Duffys go for red-heads," he said.

She raised her chin. Her lips invited his. "Yes?" she said.

He touched her lips with his. A long green arm slid round his neck and pulled his head down. She did not close her eyes and when he looked into them he tried to jerk his head away, but she held him hard. Stormy, hungry wild eyes she had. He stood there, his mouth crushed on hers, startled by her fierceness. She suddenly drove her teeth into his top lip. The pain stung him, and he pushed her away violently, starting back with an angry oath. She stood looking at him, her red-gold hair wild, and her eyes big and dark, stormy with passion. She took a step back and slammed the door in his face.

Duffy stood there, dabbing his lip with his handkerchief. "That dame's gonna let herself go one day," he said to himself, "and when she does, she's going to make a meal of someone."

He walked slowly to the elevator and pressed the button. His lip was beginning to swell already. He stood before the grille, waiting for the elevator to come up. "My God," he thought, "what a hell of a night."

As the elevator came up slowly he saw, lying on the roof, the mangled body of a man. He watched the roof glide past him, carrying its grisly burden, then the empty cage came to rest at his floor.

He stood very still, feeling the sweat start out all over him. He said, "Well, well," for something better to say, then he walked back to the flat and hammered on the door.

Chapter Three

She didn't come to the door at first. It was only by keeping his thumb on the buzzer, while the minutes ticked by, that Duffy got her to come at all. When she did come, she had the door on the chain. Duffy thought it was a hell of a time to start playing around with door-chains, but he let it drift with the current.

She started to close the door when she saw who it was, but Duffy got the toe of his shoe in first.

"Listen, bright girl," he said, "open up, and be your age. You've got a corpse on your hands right outside."

"I honestly believe you're as mad as a coon," she said breathlessly, "or very, very drunk."

Duffy leant his weight against the door, his face pressed against the small opening. "Cattley's on the roof of the elevator. First glance, I'd say it was in the basement when he hit it."

He saw her eyes widen, and then she giggled. He'd have forgiven her if she had screamed, or even passed out, but the giggle made him mad. He took a step back.

"That suits me, if that's the way you want it."

She pushed the door to, slipped the chain, then opened the door and stepped into the corridor.

"Wait," she said, putting her hand on his sleeve. Her hand looked white against his dark suit.

"Someone'll want this elevator in a moment and then things are going to happen."

"Is he really… I mean, you're not just saying this to scare me?"

He got in the elevator, slid the grille and pressed the down button. He let the elevator sink half-way, then broke the current by opening the grille. He climbed out with a struggle, leaving the cage between floors.

"Does that look like a bedtime story?"

She peered at Cattley, not moving her body, but just craning her neck. One of her hands went to her mouth. "Is he dead?"

"Do you think he's catching some sleep up? Look at him, baby, look at his arms and legs. Could you sleep like that?"

She turned on him angrily. "Well, do something about it," she said.

He pushed his hat to the back of his head. "I'm beginning to wonder if you're as dumb as you seem to be. You wouldn't be dumber than a hophead, the way that brain of yours works. Do something about it? Well, what you want me to do? Send for the cops? Call an ambulance? What?"

She raised both hands and pushed her hair off her ears. She did it unconsciously. "But you must know what to do," she said.

Duffy stood looking at Cattley with a faint grimace, then he went over and took hold of him. He gripped his arm and shoulder. It gave him quite a turn when the arm bent back at the elbow. There were a very few bones in one piece with this guy. He pulled and slid Cattley off the roof and let him as gently as he could on to the floor. Cattley's legs folded up, but not at the knees, they folded up in the middle of his shins. Duffy felt himself sweating. Putting his hands under Cattley's shoulders, he dragged him into the flat and laid him out in the hall.

"What are you bringing him in here for?" Her voice was pitched half a note higher.

"Don't talk now," he said, looking with disgust at the blood on his hands. "This guy's going to make a mess in your joint, but it's better than making a mess of you."

He walked back to the lift and inspected the roof. The woodwork was smeared with blood.

"Get me a wet towel," he said.

She went into the apartment, carefully walking round Cattley. He stood by the lift watching her. She'd got a good nerve, he told himself. She came back again with a wet hand-towel. He took it from her and carefully mopped off the bloodstains. Then he wiped his hands on the towel and folded it neatly. He walked into her apartment and put the towel on Cattley's chest. She followed him in, again skirting Cattley, drawing her green wrap close to her.

"Will you see if he's got the money on him still?" she said.

Duffy looked at her hard.

"What makes you think the money ain't there?"

"It's the way I said it. I meant will you get the money from him."

Duffy grimaced. "I hate handling this bird. He's brittle."

She came and stood close to him, looking down at Cattley. "Isn't he going to get stiff soon?" she said. "Hadn't you better straighten him out a little before he gets that way?"

Duffy said, "For God's sake," but he knelt down and cautiously pulled on Cattley's legs. One of his shin-bones poked up through his trousers leg. Duffy got up and looked round the hall. He went over to the coat-rack and selected a walking-stick. Then he came back to Cattley and put the ferrule of the stick on the shin-bone and pressed. The leg straightened, and he did the same with the other one.

His face was a little yellow, and sweat glistened on his top lip. Cattley was making him feel a little sick. He hooked the handle of the stick round Cattley's arm and put his foot against Cattley's body then he pulled gently. The arm came out from under Cattley like a limp draught-preventer.

Cattley's head lay on his right shoulder. The skin round the neck had split a little. Duffy straightened the head too with the stick.

"Want me to cross his hands?" he said for something to say. All the time he was fixing Cattley, she stood at his elbow and watched. Then she said, "Get the money."

Duffy looked at her, his eyes narrowed. "Leave the money where it is," he said shortly, "get me a drink."

She went into the sitting-room and he followed her. He suddenly found that he was still holding the walking-stick. It had blood-smears on it. He went and put it beside Cattley. Then he walked back into the sitting-room again.

She stood by the table, fixing a Scotch. He took the glass from her before she could add a Seltzer and tossed the liquor down his throat. It was good Scotch. Silky and full of body, with no raw bite in it. He felt it in his belly, a round little knot of warmth. He took the bottle from the table and poured himself another glass.

"Did you kill him?" he said, looking at her over the top of the glass.

She spread her hands across her breasts, standing very quiet for a moment, then she said, "Was he killed?"

Duffy took another pull at his glass. "Use your head," he said shortly, "how could he have fallen down the shaft? He wasn't drunk, was he? Think a moment. He goes out of your apartment. The elevator is standing on the ground floor. He opens the grille to look at it, then he feels giddy and falls down. They wouldn't pass it in a nut factory."

She was going white again and she sat on the edge of the table. Her wrap fell open, showing her knees, but neither of them bothered with that.

"This is the way it went. Cattley goes out to the elevator and is smacked on the dome, then he is tossed down the shaft. That makes sense." Duffy put the glass down on the table and lit a cigarette. "You ain't answered my question. Did you kill him?"

"No," she said.

"There's only one person who's going to believe that," Duffy said, "and that's you."

She raised her head. Her big eyes were frightened now. "You don't think I killed him?" she said; her words ran into each other.

"Can't you see what a spot you're in?" he asked patiently. "Look, let me wise you up. Cattley calls on you to sell you something. You say it's material for a book; okay, it's material for a book. You show him the door and then, there he is on the elevator roof smashed to bits."

"That doesn't prove that I killed him," she said breathlessly.

Duffy shrugged. "It helps," he said; "let me have a look at that material he sold you."

She slid off the table and walked into her bedroom. Duffy sat down in an armchair. He gave her a few minutes, then he called, "I guess the killer pinched it."

She came out of the bedroom, her face white. She stood in the doorway, one hand at her throat, the other gripping the door-handle.

"I… I can't find it," she whispered.

Duffy pursed his lips. "I bet you can't," he said. Then he got to his feet. He walked over to her and took both her elbows in his hands, he drew her towards him. "You're a goddam silly little loon," he said evenly, "you think you can play this out on your own. Well, you can't. You've put on the thinnest act I've ever struck. That writing a book on the underworld went out with the Ark. Get wise to yourself, red-head."

She drew away from him. "What are you going to do?" she asked, her voice a little flat and toneless.

Duffy scratched his head. "This is a hell of a night," he said, then he stood very still, his fingers spread through his hair. "I wonder…" he broke off, looking at Annabel. "It looks to me that Morgan wants you to take the rap for Cattley's murder," he said, speaking rapidly, "it fits, by God!" He was getting quite excited. "Listen, baby, how's this for a theory? Morgan gets me to photograph you and Cattley. Cattley gets smacked down by one of Morgan's mob just outside your door and tossed down the shaft. I get my camera pinched containing the photos. All Morgan has to do is to threaten to turn the pictures over to the cops for you to dive into your deposit account and fork out plenty."

Annabel was scarcely breathing. "Will you help me?"

Duffy said, "I can't help myself, can I?"

"You're being nice, aren't you?"

"Nice, hell! I took the photos, didn't I? I've got to do something to square that."

She dropped into the arm-chair, and held her hand over her eyes. Duffy looked at her and then fetched another glass from the wagon. He poured in three fingers of Scotch and then filled his own glass. He came over to her. "Can you drink this stuff?" he said.

She took the glass from him. "I don't want it," she said.

"You'd better get a little drunk," he said, "you've got a nasty job on your hands."

She looked at him and he jerked his head at the door. "I guess we've got to get rid of Cattley."

She said, "Can't you do it?"

He grinned mirthlessly. "You're in on this, too, sister," he said. "I'm helping you, but I ain't taking any rap."

She drank the whisky neat and he gave her a cigarette.

"In a couple of hours that bird's going to get as stiff as a board. I guess he won't be too nice to handle like that. Now, we could pack him in a bag without much fuss."

She shuddered.

"It beats me where the hell we're going to plant him." Duffy began to pace the floor. "He's got to remain planted and he ain't going to be found. As soon as they turn him up, then those photos will come into the market. It's the only way we can beat their game."

He looked at her. "Go and get dressed," he said.

She got out of the chair and moved over to the bedroom. "Give me a trunk, if you've got one," he said.

She paused. "There's one in here," she said.

He followed her into the bedroom. She pointed to a large wall cupboard and he opened the door. In the corner was a small black cabin trunk. It was covered with labels. There seemed to be every hotel under the sun advertised on its black shiny sides. He looked at it and then he said, "You've got about." She didn't say anything. He hauled the trunk out and dragged it into the sitting-room.

"You got a sheet of mackintosh that I could wrap him in?" he called.

She came to the door. "Mackintosh?"

"He's going to mess this trunk without it."

She went across to another door and disappeared. He could hear her rummaging about, then she came out with a large luggage wrap. "Will this do?"

"Yeah." He took it from her.

"Don't say 'yeah,'" she said.

He stood holding the mackintosh. "What's it to you?"

"It's tough."

He stood staring at her. "Suppose it is tough," he said, "isn't this a hell of a time to start a crack like that?"

"Do you think so?"

He let the luggage wrap slide out of his hands on to the floor. He could see her eyes were completely blank. She was hissing a little through her teeth. She fumbled with the girdle round her waist until she had it undone. The green wrap fell open and he saw she was naked. She stood a little on her toes, her hands clenched at her sides.

"Take me," she said, her voice just above a whisper, "take me, take me, take me."

Duffy smacked her face. He could see the marks of his fingers on her white skin. Then he smacked her face again. She blinked twice. Her eyes became human again, and she stood looking at him, a surprised and frightened look on her face.

"Get dressed," Duffy said thickly. He could only think of Cattley.

She turned away from him and walked limply into the bedroom, then she shut the door.

Duffy blotted his face with his handkerchief. He picked up the mackintosh sheet and walked into the hall. All the time he was telling himself what a sweet spot he had got himself into. It was bad enough to have to handle Cattley in the state he was in, but a dame as screwy as Annabel flattened him. He looked at Cattley in disgust. "If you weren't going to stiffen on me, I'd be having fun right now," he said viciously.

He spread the sheet flat by Cattley's side, then he picked up the walking-stick and hooked hold of Cattley's armpit. He couldn't quite bring himself to touch him with his hands. With a little manoeuvring he rolled him on to the sheet. Then he knelt down and made a neat parcel of the body.

By the time he had done that he felt so low that he went back into the sitting-room and gave himself another shot of Scotch. His legs were feeling light, and he guessed he was getting pretty high. His head was clear, and he felt just reckless enough to go on with it.

He poured out a stiff dose in Annabel's glass and went into the bedroom. When he got in the room, he nearly dropped the whisky. She was lying on her side on the bed. She was in her birthday suit, and it was a pretty good birthday suit at that.

He put the glass on the small table by the bed, and then he backed out of the room. There was only one driving thought in his mind. He had to plant Cattley before his muscles went like a board. Once he got that way,

Duffy knew he'd be sunk.

He went into the kitchen and flicked on the light. The kitchen was large, with white tiles half-way up the walls, and yellow varnished paint on the other half. The floor was covered with large black and white checks. He thought it was a swell kitchen. He hunted about until he found a length of cord, then he went back to Cattley, lying snug in his parcel. He knelt down and made the parcel secure with the cord. Then he walked back to the sitting-room and dragged the trunk into the hall and wedged Cattley into it.

Half-way through he had to stop and sit on a chair. There was no re-sistance in the parcel at all. Cattley was just pulp. He sat there staring at the trunk and at the bulge of the mackintosh that overlapped the sides of the trunk. Then he got up and wedged the overlapping parts in with the stick. The lid wouldn't quite close, so he stood on it. That made him feel bad, but he got the locks fastened somehow.

He took out his handkerchief and wiped off his palms and patted his face.

While he was standing there Annabel came out of the bedroom. She was wearing a black skirt, a white silk blouse, and a black three-quarter coat. She held a pair of magpie gauntlets in her hand. She moved slowly, with just a little sway on. He could see that the whisky was hitting her.

She peered at him

"He's packed up," he said harshly.

She said nothing, but he was surprised to see how her eyes hated him. He thought about it for a moment, then agreed that she had reason to be sore.

"I never was good with a corpse lying around," he said.

She ignored that and stood, her head turned away from him, by the table. "What now?" she said.

"Can you get your car?"

"The garage is in the basement."

Duffy went outside and pressed the buzzer for the elevator. It came up steadily and he found himself looking for more corpses. There weren't any. He slid the grille, then walked into the apartment. She made no move to help him drag the trunk into the cage. It was heavy, but he did it all right.

She followed him into the elevator and they both stood beside the trunk. Neither of them looked at it. He put his thumb on the basement button and the cage sank. He counted the floors as they went by. By the time they got to the basement, he counted twelve. He thought Cattley was lucky to have any skin left at all.

The attendant came up with a run. He was a little runt, with wire-like black hair. When he saw Annabel he nearly fell over himself. He looked just like an excited puppy.

"You takin' the bus out tonight?" he asked, wiping his oily hands on a bit of waste.

She managed to look fairly bright, and to say, "Yes, please," nicely, but it cost her a lot.

Duffy stood just inside the elevator, watching. The little runt bounced off into the darkness, and they heard him start up an engine. Duffy told himself that the engine was powerful all right. A minute later, the attendant brought round a big Cadillac, just with the parkers on. He brought the car round in a sweep, nailing it just where Annabel was standing. Duffy thought it was a nice piece of driving. It was.

The attendant dusted off the seat and held the door open for Annabel. Duffy might not have been there. He polished the wind-screen.

Annabel got in and slammed the door to. Duffy took hold of the trunk and looked at the attendant.

"Lend me some of your muscle," he said.

The little runt was willing enough, but he was not much help. Duffy was sweating by the time they had fixed the trunk to the grid.

"She goin' away?" the attendant asked.

"Nah," Duffy returned, testing the straps. "Just getting rid of some books."

"It's mighty late."

Duffy looked at him sharply. Perhaps he wasn't so dumb as he looked. "You mind?" he asked curtly.

The attendant blinked. He hastily said, "I didn't mean anythin'."

Duffy gave him a couple of bucks, then he went round the car and got in beside Annabel. She engaged the gear and the Cadillac rolled up the slip-way.

"Where are we going?" she asked.

Duffy had already thought that one out. "There's a little burial ground on the East side, beyond Greenwich Village," he said, "we're going there."

She shot a quick glance at him. "That's cute," she said.

Duffy leant back against the leather. "You're a swell kid," he said quietly, "this is my unlucky day."

She didn't say anything.

"I'll never bring this up again," he said, "but I can't leave it like that. I want you to know that I appreciate what you offered me, but that guy would have stiffened up by the time we were through, so I had to pass it up. You got plenty of reason to be sore at me."

She said nothing for a few moments. "I'm not sore at you," she said at last. "I think you're cute to throw me back at myself."

Just like that. Duffy sighed and groped for a cigarette. "Let's not fight," he said, "we've got enough on our hands."

"I'm not fighting," was all she said.

They rode the next three blocks in silence, then Duffy said, "You turn right here."

She swung the wheel. Duffy thought she handled the big Cadillac as if she were part of it. She judged distance to the closeness of the paint on her fender and the car threaded its way through the traffic without losing speed at any time. By uncanny anticipation she beat the lights most times. The Cadillac had plenty under the hood, and a touch on the pedal was enough to make it sweep forward like an arrow.

They came upon the burial ground as the clocks were striking two. Duffy leant forward. "Take it easy," he said, "this is a lonely burg, but someone may be here."

She stopped the car by the iron gates. Duffy opened the off door and got out. There were no lights to be seen in the burial ground; it was a pretty dark night.

Duffy was glad he wasn't Irish. The place was creepy. He turned to the car. "You wait here," he said. "I'm just going to take a look round."

She opened the door and stepped into the road. "I'm not staying here alone," she said.

Duffy wasn't surprised. He walked to the iron gates and pushed, they yielded, and swung open.

"Suppose you back the bus in," he suggested, "then we'll be off the road."

She got in the Cadillac again and started the engine. Duffy let her run the car well down the centre lane of the graveyard and then signalled her to stop. He closed the iron gates again. When she got out of the car, she was holding a small flashlight. The night air was close, and Duffy hooked a finger in his collar and jerked at it. He looked round the dim place. He didn't like it at all. She stood quite close to him, and he felt her shivering when he touched her.

Up above, the moon hung like a dead face, just visible through the mist. Duffy thought it was likely to rain any time.

"I want to find an old mausoleum," he said. "If we can park Cattley in one of them, he ain't likely to be turned up for some time, if ever."

He began to walk slowly down the lane. Annabel kept close beside him. The white stones on each side of them looked ghostly. "What a spot to be in," Duffy thought.

As they penetrated further into the burial ground it got darker. The trees overhead began to get more dense.

"Nice spot this, ain't it?" Duffy said.

The heavy scent of graveyard flowers hung in the air. Underfoot the cinders crunched, and sounded to Duffy like fire-crackers.

"I wish we could get away from here," Annabel said nervously, "this scares me."

"Me, I'm quaking," Duffy said. "I guess we're far enough off the road to chance having a little light."

He swung the beam of the flash-light. It lit upon the tombstones, making them look startlingly white in the darkness.

"I think this looks like it." Duffy paused and pointed the beam.

Over on the left stood a mausoleum in black marble. It was almost invisible until the beam showed it up. They went over and examined it carefully. The marble door was locked.

"This is Cattley's new home," Duffy said, running his hand down the smooth cold door. "But how the hell do we get him in?"

He put his shoulder against the door and heaved. He made his shoulder sore, but the door remained solid.

"What's that number there?" Annabel asked. She was holding the flash so that he could push against the door.

Duffy followed her eye. There was a small plate let in on the side of the door with a number 7 printed on it. Duffy said he didn't know.

"Do you think they keep the keys of these places at the porter's place?" she asked.

Duffy grinned at her. "That's a grand idea," he said. "Let's go an' see."

The porter's lodge, by the gates, was locked and deserted, but Duffy got a window open without much difficulty and looked round. He found a rack of keys by the front door, each key had a wooden tab hanging from it, with a number burnt into the wood. He looked for number 7 and found it.

"I believe you've got something," he said. "Suppose you drive the car up to the crypt while I go on and test the key."

She got into the Cadillac and began to back it down the lane. He had to come back and help her with the flash, as she ran off the lane once or twice. They got back to the mausoleum at last and Duffy tried the key. The lock turned all right with some heavy pressure from Duffy, and he forced the door back. The air was bad down there, and he stepped away from the open door.

"That guy's going to have good company," was all he said.

He went to the back of the car and wrestled with the straps that held the trunk. Annabel stood, holding the flash steady. He got the straps off and then levered the trunk to the ground. It was heavy, but he managed to get it down without making any noise. Then he stood up and wiped off his palms with his handkerchief.

"I guess I could do with a drink," he said heavily.

"There's a pint flask in the driving-pocket."

Duffy slipped round to the door pretty quick. He belted that pint hard. He thought it would be safer not to give Annabel any of it. Whisky seemed to take her in the wrong way. He didn't like to think of turning her down again.

"I guess I can tackle anything now," he said, putting the flask in his hip pocket.

He took off his coat and undid his collar, pulling his tie loose. Then he walked over to the trunk and dragged it into the mausoleum. Annabel stood just outside the door, shining the flash. The beam jerked about. Her hand was shaking like a barman at work.

Duffy got the trunk inside and then paused.

"For God's sake gimme that light," he said.

She seemed glad to do so. "I'm going to be sick," she said.

"No you ain't," he said sharply. "Go and sit in the car quick."

When she had gone he opened the trunk and turned it on its side. The mackintosh parcel was jammed tight and he had to pull at it. The sheet suddenly tore in his hand and he went over backwards. He landed against a shelf, and his hand touched a cold metal strip. He fingered it, then he snatched his hand away. It was a handle of a coffin. His face oozed water as if it had been squeezed.

He went to the door and took a deep breath of the dank air, then he went back to the trunk. Savagely he pulled Cattley out, pulled away the cord, and jerked off the mackintosh sheet. Cattley sprawled at his feet. He didn't look at him. Dumping the sheet into the trunk, he pulled the trunk out of the crypt.

The whisky was hitting him all ends up now, and he lurched as he walked. He went back to get the flash, but he still didn't look at Cattley. Then he pulled the door of the mausoleum shut and shot the lock.

His shirt was sticking to his chest, and his legs were a little wobbly. Annabel called from the car, "Are you all right?"

Duffy said he was fine, but that was because he was drunk. He didn't feel so good. He'd have liked to get so drunk right now that the whole of the evening could be washed out in sleep. He had had enough of it for one night.

She came out of the car and stood near him.

"What about the trunk?" she asked.

"Back at the lodge, there's a tap and hose for filling cans. I noticed it when I went in. I'll take these things over and wash 'em up, then we can go home."

She sat on the running-board of the car and smoked a cigarette. She sat there the whole time with her eyes tight shut. She was so scared of being alone, that if it hadn't been for the cigarette between her lips she would have screamed and screamed.

On his way back, Duffy called to her when he was some distance away. He didn't want to come on her suddenly.

"It's okay," he said, hoisting the trunk on to the grid again. "There ain't no mess now. Cattley's planted good, so I guess that lets you out."

She got into the Cadillac and drove slowly down to the gates. He walked beside the car. Opening the gates, he looked cautiously up and down the road, but it was dark and deserted. He shut the gates when she had driven into the road and climbed in beside her.

She drove at a furious pace without a word. Her eyes were fixed on the road ahead, and Duffy leant back, breathing heavily, his eyes heavy with sleep.

When they began to run into traffic again he raised his head. "You can drop me off here," he said. "I'm going home."

"I'll drive you there," she said.

"No."

She stopped the car.

"I'm sorry I…" she began.

"I'm going home," Duffy said firmly. He had had a bellyful. "Tomorrow, perhaps. Tonight, no."

He opened the door and lurched on to the street. He stood there, holding the door in his hand. "I've got to get those pictures back," he said. "I'll see you then."

He slammed the door hard. He had a swift vision of her great eyes, wide with hate, her white teeth gleaming in the dark, then the Cadillac shot away from him.

He looked up and down the street for a taxi.

"I guess that honey hates my guts," he said sadly, as a yellow taxi slid up to him.

Chapter Four

Duffy's place was a three-room affair on the top storey of an old-fashioned apartment house.

The taxi-driver drew up at the curb, just under the street light. Duffy got out of the cab, letting the door swing on its hinges.

"This it?" the taxi-driver asked.

"Yeah, that's right."

The taxi-driver looked at him. "You been havin' a good time?"

Duffy shifted his head a little so that he didn't breathe over the taxi-driver. He said, "You don't know the half of it."

The taxi-driver said, "The first half's good enough for me." One of those smart guys.

Duffy paid him off and slammed the door for him. He slammed the door so hard that the cab rocked. The taxi-driver scowled, but said nothing. He was smart all right, but he wasn't dumb. He rolled the cab away.

Duffy walked up the steps, fumbled for his key and fumbled at the lock. "Jeeze, that Scotch was dynamite," he said, as he poked at the lock. The key sank suddenly, and he turned it. The hall was in darkness, but he knew his way up. He started to climb the stairs as the wall-clock struck four. The wall-clock hung in the hall. It had a little brittle chime that always irritated Duffy. Treading carefully, one hand on the rail and the other just touching the opposite wall, he went up silently. He had to go up four flights, but he was used to that. When he reached his landing he paused. A light was burning in his apartment. He could see the bright light coming from under the door.

Two things crossed his mind. First, the cleaner had forgotten to turn the light off; and second, McGuire was waiting for him. It gave him quite a shock when he remembered McGuire. He had forgotten all about the poor guy. Too bad. He wagged his head. Maybe he'd be as sore as hell. He fumbled for his key again, and opened the door. The light quite blinded him for a second.

Two men were sitting in his room, facing the door. Another one was standing by the window, looking into the street, peeping round the blind.

Duffy jumped.

"I bet you've been stealing my whisky," he said.

The man who was looking out of the window turned his head quickly. He was big. He had Mongolian eyes and a loose mouth. He had that battered, brutal face of an unsuccessful prize-fighter.

Duffy looked at him, then he looked at the two sitting in the chairs. The nearest one was a little guy with tight lips and cold, hard eyes. His face was white as cold mutton fat, and he just sat, with his hands folded across his stomach.

The other one, sitting on the little guy's right, was young. He had down on his cheeks and his skin had that peculiar rosy tint that most girls want, but don't have. He looked tough, because he had screwed up his eyes and drawn down the corners of his mouth. Duffy thought he was just movie-tough.

The little guy said, "He's here at last."

Duffy shut the door and leant against it. "If I'd known you were coming," he said, "I'd been here sooner."

The little guy said, "Did you hear that? The bright boy said if he'd known we were coming, he'd been here sooner."

The other two said nothing.

Duffy said, "Now you're here, what's it all about?"

"He wants to know what's it all about," the little guy said again.

Duffy slowly closed his fists. "Must you repeat everything I say?" he asked. "Can't these two birds understand what I say?"

The little guy eased himself back in his chair. "You understand him, don't you, Clive?" he said to the youth.

"Clive?" Duffy was getting annoyed. "That's the name for a daffodil, ain't it?"

The youth sat up. "Listen, you long stick of—"

The little guy giggled. "How do you think of such things?" he said.

"What *is* this?" Duffy demanded. He looked across at the tough bird by the window.

"Come on, come on," the little guy said, suddenly looking bleak again. "Give it up."

"Give what up, for God's sake?" Duffy demanded.

"Did you hear him, Clive, he wants to know what to give up?"

The youth called Clive slouched out of his chair. He stood over the little guy, his face viciously angry. "You won't get anywhere with this stuff," he said. "Turn Joe loose on him."

The big bird on the corner took a step forward. He seemed to be holding himself in with difficulty. The little guy waved his hand at him. Not so fast," he said, "we ain't *got* to get rough with this lug."

Duffy thought they were all screwy, and he wished he hadn't socked that pint away. Clive stood away from the little guy and glared at Duffy.

The little guy looked at Duffy with stony eyes. "Get wise, bright boy," he said. "We've come for the camera."

Duffy pushed his hat to the back of his head and blew out his cheeks. So that was it, he thought. He wandered over to the wagon and picked up a bottle of Scotch. "You gentlemen want any of this?" he asked.

Clive had a gun in his hand. Duffy looked at it surprised, then he said to the little guy, "Tell that fairy to put his rod away, he might hurt someone."

The little guy said, "I should care. What's it to me?"

Duffy said very sharply, "Tell that punk to put his pop-gun down, or I'll do it for him, and smack his ears down."

Clive made a high whinny sound like a horse. He looked as though he was going to have some sort of a fit. He stood there, his face white, and his eyes dark with hate. Duffy went a little cold at the sight of him.

The little guy said, "Put it away."

The youth turned his head slowly and looked at the little guy. "I'm going to pop him…" he said shrilly, all his words tumbling out of his mouth in a bunch.

"I said, put it away." The little guy was quite shocked that he had to speak twice.

Clive hesitated, blinked, then pushed the gun into his hip pocket. He stood undecided, his hands fluttering at his coat. Then quite suddenly, he began to cry. His face puckered up like a little indiarubber mask that someone had squeezed. He sat himself on a chair and covered his face with his thin bony hands and cried.

The little guy sighed. He said to Duffy, "See, you've upset him now."

Duffy threw his hat on the settee and ran his fingers through his hair.

The big tough came over from the window and patted Clive's head. He didn't say anything, but just patted the youth quite heavily on his head.

The little guy shifted uncomfortably. "Aw, I didn't mean anything," he said. "We ain't supposed to pop this guy, so I couldn't let you do it, could I?"

Clive took his hands away and said with a snivel, "But look how you spoke to me."

"Sure, sure, I know," the little guy smiled with his tight mouth. "I'm sorry. There, I can't say more, can I? I've said I'm sorry, that's pretty generous."

Clive looked at the little guy earnestly. "It wasn't what you said that upset me," he said, "it was how you said it."

"I know, it was the way I said it, wasn't it?"

Clive began to cry again. He didn't cover his face this time, but screwed up his eyes, and wiped his nose with the back of his hand. "Yes," he said, "it was the way you said it."

"Quite a big shot, ain't he?" Duffy said, leaning against the wall, watching with extraordinary interest.

"You leave him alone," the little guy said. "He's all right, but he upsets himself."

Clive stopped crying and shot Duffy a look of hate. The other two followed his glance, as if just remembering Duffy.

The little guy said to Clive, "You all right now?"

Clive said he was fine.

"Come on," the little guy said to Duffy, "we're wasting time."

Duffy said, "I'm disappointed. I thought we were all going to let down our hair and have a good cry."

The little guy giggled, then stopped and looked annoyed. "Let's have the camera, we got to blow soon."

Duffy lit a cigarette and blew a cloud of smoke to the ceiling. "I ain't got it," he said.

The three stayed very still.

"Listen," the little guy said patiently, "we've come for the camera, and we're going to have it, see?"

Duffy shrugged. "I can't help that," he said shortly, "I ain't got it."

The little guy said, "You ain't got this right. I said we want that camera and we are going to have it."

"Sure, I heard you the first time. I tell you I ain't got it."

The little guy said, "You ain't got this right. I said we want it."

The youth drew his top lip off his teeth. "I told you you weren't getting anywhere with this bastard."

Duffy pushed himself away from the wall. He began to wander slowly round the room. He didn't take his eyes off the three, watching him.

"You be careful," he said to Clive, "you'll be getting some false teeth mighty soon."

Clive looked at the little guy. "Turn Joe on him," he said excitedly. "Go on, beat the sonofabitch to hell."

Duffy was quite close to him now. He seemed to be carelessly looking for something. "Don't call me that," he said viciously, and his right fist came up from his waist to slap in Clive's mouth. Duffy was nervous of the big bird. He thought with the other two out of the way, he might stand a chance with him, but he wasn't sure.

Clive went over, taking the chair with him. He lay on his side, hissing through his hand, that he had clapped to his mouth.

The other two were too startled to move. Duffy hit the little guy on the bridge of his nose. It was an awkward punch because the little guy was sitting but it had plenty of steam behind it. The little guy tossed back in his chair and went over with a crash. He lay there completely stunned.

Duffy stood, his hands a little advanced, his elbows pressed into his waist.

The big bird looked at Clive and then he looked at the little guy. Then he grinned, showing very white even little teeth. "Jeeze!" he said hoarsely, "you're going to get it now."

He came in, weaving and bobbing. Duffy saw at once that he was right out of this fellow's class. He jumped away, and retreated until his heel thudded against the wall. The big bird came flat-footed but sure. His head was down, with his chin well tucked into his shoulder. Duffy let one go. It was a good one, coming up with a whistling sound. The big bird shifted a little, not much, but just a little, and Duffy's fist hit the air. Then the big bird hit Duffy under the heart. It sounded like a cleaver going into a side of beef. Duffy thought the house had fallen on him. He felt his knees sag and the big bird let him come into a clinch. Duffy wound his arms round him, holding him so he couldn't hit him.

The big bird let him recover. He said, "That was a good smack, huh?"

Duffy broke from the clinch, stepped back quickly, collided with a small table and went over backwards. He scrambled to his feet, hurriedly. The big bird gave him plenty of time, then he came in with that flat-footed shuffle, slipped Duffy's punch and banged Duffy in the ribs again. That punch hurt like hell. Again Duffy sagged at the knees; this time the big bird swung one to the side of his head and Duffy went over on his side and lay there. He landed quite close to the little guy, who was just sitting up. The little guy took a gun from inside his coat, holding it by the barrel, he leant forward and hit Duffy in the groin, hitting very hard.

Duffy curled into a ball, but he didn't yell. He bit his lip right through, but he didn't yell. Then he felt his inside coming up into his throat and he vomited.

The little guy shifted hastily. "Look," he said, "the bastard nearly had me." He got quite excited about it.

Clive said with approval, "Now you're doing something."

They stood round Duffy, watching him. The little guy pressing the bridge of his nose tenderly with his fingers, his eyes watering. Clive knelt on the floor with his lips swelling. He could feel that his front teeth moved a little when he touched them with his tongue. Joe stood with his hands hanging loose, like a dog deprived of its bone.

Duffy raised his head slowly. His face glistened with sweat. The shaded light from the ceiling lit his greenish skin. He was feeling awfully bad, but he held on to himself low down and rode with the pain. The blood ran down his chin from his lip. He could feel the salty taste in his mouth.

The little guy said, "Give."

Duffy didn't say anything. He didn't trust his voice. He lay there, his eyes on the little guy, hating him.

The little guy said, "Ain't you had enough?"

Duffy still said nothing.

The little guy raised his hand. "Soften him a little," he said to Joe.

Joe smiled. He really took a pleasure in being tough. He put out an arm and his hand closed on Duffy's shirt front, then he heaved a little. Duffy came up, like a cork out of a bottle. He gave a little grunt of anguish. His open hand smacked Joe across the eyes. Joe blinked. "Did you see what he did to me?" he said.

The little guy said, "Full of fight, ain't he?"

Duffy swung at Joe feebly, his punch wouldn't have knocked down a child. Joe grinned. "Get wise to yourself, bright boy," he said. "You ain't hurting no one."

The little guy said, "Just pat him around a bit, will you, Joe? We ain't got much time."

Joe said, "Sure." He held Duffy at arm's length and hit him between the eyes. His fist travelled at a tremendous speed. Duffy could see it coming, but he couldn't avoid it. Something exploded in his brain, and a bright flash of brightness blinded him. He wanted to lie down, but something was holding on to him.

The little guy said, "Now don't hit him too hard, just pat him around." His voice sounded a long way away to Duffy.

"I know just what you want," the big bird said, and he started to slap Duffy's face with heavy resounding blows with his open hand.

The little guy said to Clive, "If this makes you feel bad, you can turn your head."

Clive said, "I'm feeling fine. I wish I was as big as Joe."

The little guy patted his arm. "I don't," he said.

When Joe got tired, he said; "Shall we try him now?"

The little guy said, "I think so."

Joe let go of Duffy, who fell in a heap on the floor. His face was a sight. The little guy knelt down. "Where's the camera, bright boy?"

Duffy mumbled something, but his mouth was so swollen that the little guy couldn't hear what he said.

"Lay him up on the couch, Joe, we'll have to get him into shape!" Joe pulled Duffy across the floor by his arm and dumped him on to the overstuffed couch.

"Get some water, Clive, and a towel," the little guy said.

Clive went out of the room into the bathroom. Duffy lay with his eyes shut, his breath coming in shuddering gasps.

Joe went over to the wagon and poured himself out a drink. He took it neat, then punched himself on the chest with his fist.

Clive came back with a wet towel. The little guy held out his hand, but Clive walked over to Duffy. "Let me do it"

"Well, well, did you hear, Joe?" the little guy was surprised. "Clive wants to do it."

Clive went on one knee beside Duffy and mopped his swollen bruised face with the towel. Duffy looked at him through a puffy eye. Then Clive put his hand on the side of Duffy's head, made his fingers into claws and dragged his nails down Duffy's face.

The little guy ran across the room and pulled Clive away. Clive had flecks of foam at the sides of his mouth. "That'll teach him," he said shrilly. "He won't hit me again in a hurry."

"You might have broken your nice nails," the little guy said sharply. "That ain't the way to go on."

Duffy pushed himself up on the couch and lowered his legs to the floor. Joe watched him, a big grin on his face. "Ain't he a pip?" he said, admiringly.

The other two turned and watched him too. Duffy was sitting up now, his head sunk on his chest. He remained like that for several minutes, then he put both hands on the couch and levered himself to his feet. His face was a mask of blood. Swaying, he made a little tottering run at Clive, who hastily got behind the little guy.

Joe stepped in front of Duffy. He said, "Still looking for trouble?"

Duffy swung a leaden arm, but Joe hit him in the ribs again, stepping in close and driving at Duffy a jarring jolt. Duffy opened his mouth and said "O!", then he fell on his knees.

Just then the telephone bell rang. The three started and looked at the telephone. It continued to ring.

"That's bad," the little guy said, looking worried.

They waited, all concentrated on the sound of the bell. It rang for several seconds, then it stopped.

Joe dragged Duffy on to the couch again. He heaved him up and looked at the little guy.

"Bring him round," the little guy said.

Joe pulled Duffy's ears. He took them in each hand and tugged as if he were milking a cow. Duffy groaned and tried to get his head away.

"He's here now," Joe said.

The little guy stood quite close to Duffy. "Come on," he said loudly, "spill it. Where's that goddam camera?"

"Somebody stole it," Duffy mumbled only half conscious.

The little guy stood back. "Christ!" he said. "Did you hear that? He said someone stole it. This bird must be nuts to hang on so long."

The telephone bell began to ring again. Clive said suddenly, "Perhaps it's Mr. Morgan."

The little guy said, "Quiet," and looked at Duffy. Duffy lay with his eyes shut, but he had heard all right. His brain wouldn't think, but he remembered all right. The little guy hesitated, then went over to the 'phone. He unhooked the receiver from its prong.

"Hellow?" he said in his tight voice.

He stood listening. Then he said, "You got a wrong number, buddy," and hung up. He shook his head. "Some guy wanting this bird," he jerked his thumb at Duffy. "Suppose you try him again, Joe?"

Clive took a step forward. "Why don't you burn him a little?" he demanded. "This is wasting time."

The little guy looked at Joe. "Do you think you can shake him loose?" he said.

Joe grinned. "Yeah," he said; "give me a little time. This pip thinks I am playing with him, don't you, bright boy."

Duffy was getting light-headed, but he felt a little strength stealing into his legs. "Wait a minute," he said with difficulty. "Can't you believe what I tell you? Some bird stole that camera before I left the dame's house. I've just come back. I ain't got it on me, have I?"

The little guy put his hand on Joe's arm.

"Maybe he's telling it straight," he said.

Joe shook his head. "That guy couldn't tell it straight to a priest," he said.

The little guy looked at the clock on the mantelshelf. "Look at the time," he said.

Clive said, "It's all talk… talk… talk… talk!"

The little guy patted him on his arm. "If he ain't got the camera, what can I do?"

Duffy sat up slowly and passed a hand over his face gently. Near by, on the arm of the couch, was an ash-tray. One of those affairs with a leather spring that gripped the arm. It was quite a heavy thing. Duffy put his hand on it, then with one movement, he picked it off the arm of the couch and tossed it through the window. The glass shattered, making a high tinkling sound. Some of the glass fell in the street below.

The little guy said, "Clever, ain't he?"

Clive ran to the door. "Let's skip before the cops come up," he said.

The little guy said, "Sure we'll go." Then he looked at Duffy. "We'll be back, bright boy."

He followed Clive out of the room.

Joe clouted Duffy on the side of the head. The blow knocked him off the couch on to the floor. "We'll get together by'n by," he said, and went to the door hurriedly, then he paused, looking at Duffy lying there. He came back and kicked Duffy very hard in the ribs.

The little guy put his head round the door.

"Come on, Joe," he said, "we gotta get out of this."

Joe followed him from the room, shutting the door quietly behind him.

Duffy lay on the floor, his knees drawn up to his chin. After they had been gone some time, he began to sob a little.

Chapter Five

A voice said, "What a guy!"

Duffy forced one swollen eyelid back and tried to see who it was. A blurred figure was standing over him. He thought it might be Joe again, so he shut his eye and lay still.

"Bill!"

That wasn't Joe, he thought; it sounded like McGuire. Duffy raised his head painfully. "I think you've come a little late," he said with a faint groan.

McGuire said, "My Gawd!" and meant it. "What the hell have you been doing with yourself?"

Duffy turned a little to the wall. He wasn't quite ready for any bright talk. "Gimme a break," he said faintly.

McGuire was so upset and astonished, he just stood gaping at Duffy. Then he looked round the room, seeing the overturned furniture, the mess of the blood, and the blood-smears on the wall. "What's been going on round here? Jeeze! This looks as if a massacre came off not so long ago."

Duffy said through his clenched teeth, "Me, I'm it."

McGuire took another look at him, then hurried into the bathroom. He found a small bowl and a towel. He filled the bowl with tepid water, and came back to Duffy again.

"Come on, soldier," he said. "Let's make you look a bit ship-shape."

"Suppose you go take a pill," Duffy said with difficulty.

"Now come on." McGuire put the bowl on the floor and dropped the towel into the water. He squeezed the towel and began wiping Duffy's face with awkward care. He was as tender as a woman to Duffy.

Duffy said suddenly, "Hi, you rat, be careful of my nose."

McGuire said, "You don't call that a nose any more, do you?"

When he cleared the dried blood away, he took the bowl into the bathroom and changed the water. Deep down, a burning anger smouldered against those who had done this to Duffy. McGuire was one of those guys who made few friends, but when he had picked one, he stuck. He was, on the surface, casual and a great kidder, but he'd stick like a burr and fight once he had found a friend. Duffy and he had knocked along together on the *Tribune* for some little while. They had quarrelled, kidded, and double-crossed each other, but let anyone else start anything then they'd side up together and beat hell out of the intruder.

He filled the bowl with water again and walked back to Duffy.

"For God's sake, you must be losing your grip or something," Duffy mumbled from the couch.

"What now?"

"Listen, dimwit, instead of pulling this Flo Nightingale act, what the hell's wrong in giving me a drink?"

McGuire put the bowl down on the table. "You're right," he said. "This business startled me." He went over to the wagon and poured out two stiff Scotches. He was going to hold the glass to Duffy's mouth, but Duffy took the glass from him roughly. "For the love of Mike," Duffy said, "don't you think I can help myself to Scotch?"

They both felt better after the drink. McGuire said, "Was that some woman you brought home who set about you like that?"

Duffy put his glass on the floor and sat up very slowly. He put his hands over his groin and his mouth twisted. McGuire watched him uneasily. "You all right?"

"Sure, I'm all right," Duffy said. "I'm fine."

"All right, tough guy, but you can take it easy for a moment. Here, lie back, will you?"

Duffy swung his feet over the side of the couch, then he stood up. As soon as his legs had to take his weight, he bent in half. He would have fallen forward if McGuire hadn't taken his arm.

"I'm getting soft, I guess," Duffy said, sweat starting out on his face.

McGuire led him back to the couch and sat him down.

"Quit this stuff," he said impatiently. "Lie down, or I'll smack your ears for you."

Duffy sank back on the couch. He was glad to.

McGuire poured him out another Scotch, and after that he felt his strength coming back.

"Suppose you tell me what happened?"

"Sure. I ran into three toughs who pushed me around."

McGuire shook his head. "Do you want me to call in the cops?"

"This ain't for the cops."

"Okay, what now?"

"What's the time?"

"It's getting on for ten o'clock."

Duffy groaned. "What a hell of a night I had," he said, resting his head on his hands.

McGuire went over to the telephone and dialled a number. Duffy watched him curiously. He heard the line connect with a little plop, then McGuire said, "Sam here, honey." Then, after a pause he went on. "This crazy loon's got himself into a jam. You ought to see him. Gee! He looks terrible. Yeah, someone pushed him around. Well, I don't think he's capable of taking care of himself, so I'm bringing him right round to you. Fix up the spare bed for him, will you?" He stood listening for quite a while, then he said, "Coming right now," and he hung up.

Duffy said heatedly, "If you think you're going to turn that wife of yours loose on me—"

"Pipe down," McGuire said sharply, "you're doing what you're told. Listen, you small-time prizefighter, you come on your feet or you come on your ear, it's all the same to me."

"Okay, I'll come."

McGuire had quite a job getting him over to his place, but he did it. The taxi-driver who brought them took an extraordinary interest in Duffy. He helped McGuire get him out of the cab and up the steps. Then he stood there, shaking his head.

McGuire got a little heated about it. "All right, all right," he said; "ain't you seen someone pushed around before?"

"He ain't been pushed around," the taxi-driver said, looking Duffy over, "someone's been making love to him."

McGuire shut the door in his face.

On the third floor Alice was waiting for them in the passage. A tall, dark girl, with black hair dressed low that set off her olive complexion, and gave her just a slight foreign look. Her large eyes, alight with life, were now large and scared.

It didn't matter how low Duffy felt, Alice always made him feel good. When she saw him, she put her hand quickly to her mouth. Her skin went a little paler, so that it looked almost oyster colour in the sunlit corridor. Her eyes filled with tears, but that was as far as she would show her feelings.

"Bill Duffy!" she said, "how could you?"

McGuire said, "A real fighting drunk, ain't he?"

Duffy tried a grin, but it was so painful to him and to look at, he hastily took it off his face. "This ain't anything," he kidded; "you ought to've seen me when I put Dempsey to sleep."

"He's light-headed," Alice said, but she put her hand on his arm. "Get him inside quickly, Sam."

McGuire said, "I'll be glad to. The way he's leaning on me, you'd think he's hurt."

They took him into McGuire's little flat. A pleasant four room box of a place, bright and comfortable. Everywhere, Alice had left something of herself. The neatness, the sweet-smelling flowers, the shine of the stained boards, showed the woman's hand. Duffy looked round the sitting-room regretfully. When ever he saw it, he felt a faint hunger. He had never made a secret about it. If McGuire hadn't married Alice, he would have. The three of them were close linked.

When McGuire got him undressed and into the cool sheets, he relaxed, and the pain that was riding his body gradually began to ease. Alice came in a moment later, fixed his pillow, fussed round him with a scent bottle, and Duffy loved it.

McGuire looked at his watch. "Let the animal sleep," he said to Alice. "I gotta go and work. Keep away from him. If he gets fresh, call a cop." Then looking at Duffy, he said, "Take a nap, soldier, I'll have a little chin with you later."

Duffy said, "I'll steal your wife from you."

Alice and Sam exchanged glances, Duffy watched them through his swollen eyes. He thought they looked a swell pair. He shut his eyes for a moment, then found it was too much trouble to open them again.

Alice looked down at him. "What can have happened to the poor dear?" she said, keeping her voice very low.

McGuire put his arm round her and they left the room together. "He said three toughs set about him," he said, when they were in the living-room. "Let him have a good sleep, then we'll hear something more. I'll get back early tonight."

"Sam!" Duffy's voice was urgent.

McGuire went back into the bedroom. "Go to sleep, you big loon," he commanded.

"Listen, Sam." Duffy raised his head. "I want you to find out all you can about a girl called Annabel English, a guy called Daniel Morgan and who-ever works for him. Dig in and get the lowdown on them. Don't miss a thing. Also find out what you can about Cattley the dope-peddler. Get that, and I'll rest all right."

McGuire took out a note-book and jotted down the names. "All right," he said; "it all sounds screwy to me, and I'm bursting with curiosity, but I'll get you the dope, but in the meantime, take it easy."

When McGuire got back in the evening, Duffy was still sleeping.

Alice said, "He's been that way all day!"

"Sure, that's the best thing that could happen to him. Suppose we eat, and then maybe he'll be ready to talk."

While Alice was serving up, Duffy woke. He got into a dressing-gown and came out into the sitting-room. He looked a lot worse than he felt.

Alice said, "Bill Duffy, go straight back to bed!"

"I wish you two wouldn't pick on me," Duffy said, sitting in an easy chair, "I'm feeling good. Hi, Sam, what about a drink?"

The other two looked at each other helplessly.

"A hopeless soak," Sam said sadly. "You better go back."

Duffy shook his head. "You two birds had better be careful," he said, "I've just had a little fast training, and I'll get tough."

McGuire settled the argument by producing a bottle of rum, a squeezer, some fresh limes, and a bottle of absinthe. He set about making up some Bacardi Crustas.

"Make 'em big and strong," Duffy said, "I want to get cockeyed tonight."

Alice looked round the kitchen door. "I've been waiting for that all day," she said.

"My wife's an awful drunkard," Sam said.

"You're telling me?" Duffy stood up to look at himself in the mirror. He took one glance, grimaced and sat down again. "I remember, before you knew her, when she got so stewed that it took ten cops to handle her."

Sam poured out the drinks. "That's old stuff," he said, "you don't know what she's like now. Give her a few shots of rum, and it takes an army to handle her."

Alice came in. "When you two loafers've finished pulling my reputation to bits, come on in and eat."

They followed her into the kitchen, Duffy walking slowly, careful not to touch anything, and Sam with the big shaker in his hands.

They sat round the table. Duffy found it was difficult to eat, but he made a good show. They talked about general things until the meal was over. Both Alice and Sam were burning with curiosity, but they let Duffy have his head. When they had finished, they went back into the sitting-room. Alice sat herself on the arm of Duffy's chair, and McGuire stood in front of the empty fire-grate.

Duffy said, "I'm sorry to keep you waiting. I guess you'd better have it from the start, and then we'll go into the whys and whats after."

He told them everything. How he met Morgan, what Morgan wanted him to do, how he went to the house and took the photographs, how the camera was stolen, how he found Cattley in the lift-shaft, how he got rid of the body, the meeting with the three toughs. He gave them the whole works.

When he had finished, there was a long silence. Then McGuire said, "You've started something this time."

"I've not only started something, but it's something I'm going to finish."

Alice ran her long fingers through his hair. "I know it's no good me saying anything, but don't you think you've done enough?

Duffy put his fingers tenderly on his face, his eyes were suddenly very bleak. "No one can push me around like this and not know something about it," he said softly.

Alice got off the arm of his chair and walked over to the fireplace. She stood looking down at Duffy, her big eyes were sad. "You men are all alike," she said; there was a faint undertone of bitterness in her voice. "All tough guys, who come home hurt!"

Duffy looked over at Sam. "Suppose we forget that for a moment," he said; "tell me what you found out about Annabel English."

Sam began to fill a pipe. "That dame's going to get herself into trouble one of these days," he said, fumbling around for some matches. Alice took a box off the mantelshelf and gave them to him. "One of these days, she's going to be stuck for a sucker, and then she'll be landed in the cooler."

Duffy said, "I want facts, not an extract from *True*."

"Well, in brief, she's Edwin English's daughter. I supposed you guessed that?"

Duffy looked startled. "No," he said seriously, "I should have thought of that, but I didn't."

"Do you mean Edwin English, the politician?" Alice asked.

Sam nodded shortly. "Yeah," he said, "Annabel's the wild one of the family. English stands for anti-vice, you know all about his racket. Annabel's his big thorn. I guess she about crucifies the old man. About three years ago they agreed to part. He set her up in a swell apartment, and gave her a big allowance, on condition that she behaved herself, and didn't give him any cause for getting in bad with his voters."

Duffy said, "I'd just hate to be an anti-vice candidate with a daughter like that."

Sam nodded. "You bet," he said, "this little dame's a nymphosomething or other, I forget the word. You know, she's hot for anything in pants."

"You mean nymphomaniac?" Alice said, "isn't that rather strong?"

"Strong?" Duffy broke in. "Say listen…." He paused, changed his mind, and went on, "never mind. It ain't too strong. Go on, Sam."

"The old man's for ever steaming himself in case she breaks out, and stains the family name. You know the type of thing. The other politicians are just praying that she does start something. They all hate English like hell. I don't wonder at it. That guy's mind is so narrow, he overbalances every time he uses it."

"Anything more?"

Sam shrugged. "A lot of hushed-up scandal that won't help you much," he said. "English has paid plenty during the last two years, keeping her out of jail and out of the papers. She goes to every smut night-club in town. She's on the list for getting smut cine-films for private exhibition. She's had three or four fancy boys who've been mixed up in shady business. And so on. Not a nice little girl."

Duffy brooded. "Somehow," he said, "I guessed as much."

"Now you know all this," Alice said quietly, "you are not going to do anything further?"

"You're a swell kid." Duffy got up and went over to her. "Quit worrying, can't you? I don't care how bad that dame is, I started this damn' business. I was sucker enough to take those photos, and I guess I'm getting them back."

Alice sighed. "Worthless women always seem to get help from men," she said. "I suppose it is so easy to fool a really fine man."

Duffy exchanged glances with Sam. "Skip it, Alice," Sam said. "You know what Bill is. You're holding us up."

Alice forced a little smile. "I'm sorry," she said and sat down in Duffy's chair. Duffy came and sat on the arm.

"What about Morgan?"

Sam blew out a cloud of smoke. "Now Morgan, he's a cagey bird to nail. He's got some racket in connection with a chain of night-clubs. I'd say at a guess, he's a boss behind the scene, and he's controlling vice in a big way.

Anyway, I can't get a proper line on him, except rumours. They know him down at headquarters, but they've never pinned anything to him yet. Still, they're always hoping. He's got plenty of dough, runs a big house, and has a tough mob working for him."

"If Morgan's got that sort of a background, I guess he'd want those pictures of that girl. It might give him enough pull to scare English off closing his joints." Duffy was looking thoughtful.

Sam nodded. "That's just it," he said. "Morgan would be sitting very pretty if he could close English down."

"Cattley? Did you find out anything fresh about him?" Duffy asked.

Sam shrugged. "There's not much you don't know about that rat," he said, "you know what he did. Dope, women, and white slaving. Cattley's certainly been making plenty of dough these last months. No one's sure of where he got it. He's moved up a lot since we knew him. Does, or rather did, everything on a big scale. The cops can't get a line on him, but they watch him from time to time."

"Is he going to be missed?"

Sam shrugged. "Not unless someone who knows him gets worried and blows to the police. That ain't likely."

Duffy brooded some more. "You done a swell job of work," he said at last. "What I want to know, is where do I go from here?"

Sam said, "I'd take it easy for a bit."

Duffy shook his head. "I got to get those pictures," he said, "and I've got to get 'em fast."

Alice said, "Has Morgan got them, do you think?"

"No. Morgan hasn't got them. It was Morgan's crowd who pushed me around. It looks to me that some other party has horned in and helped themselves. Just as long as Cattley remains in that vault, trouble will stay still. As soon as he pokes up his head, the balloon will go up."

"Don't you run a risk of being made an accessary after the fact or something?" Alice asked, her brow wrinkled.

Duffy said, "I guess I've been in worse spots than accessory charges."

Sam got up and began to pile the plates in the kitchen. Alice went out to help him. Duffy sat in the arm-chair and brooded. His body was one dull ache, but he wouldn't let his mind dwell on it. There was a bitter angry feeling smouldering inside him. Furious with Morgan, revengeful against those three toughs, and determined to get those photos back, he thought of Annabel. Then he got up and went over to the telephone. He dialled a number, after consulting the book.

He recognized her voice at once.

"This is Duffy here," he said.

"Have you got them?" Her voice was eager.

"Listen, baby," he said, speaking low and fast, "you don't know half what happened last night."

"What is it?"

"For one thing Morgan ain't got those pictures. For another, he wants them mighty bad. When I got home last night, three birds were waiting for me and they beat me silly when I couldn't give them the camera."

She was silent for a moment. "But who has got it?" she said at last.

"I don't know," he had to admit it; "this is a line up against your Pa. Why the hell didn't you tell me who you were?"

"Well, who am I?"

"You're Edwin English's daughter."

"I prefer to say I am Annabel English."

He laughed. He couldn't help himself. "I've been looking up your record, baby, it ain't so hot."

"You think so?" She sounded very cool. "I thought you'd appreciate me."

"I think you ought to go very slow for a bit," he said, "you just lie low, and don't start anything. It wouldn't be a bad idea for you to get out of town for a little while."

"Oh no," she was very definite, "I won't do that."

"Okay, but watch your step from now on."

"When am I seeing you?"

He grinned, but he felt no mirth. "Sooner than you think," he said quietly, and hung up.

Chapter Six

It took Duffy two impatient days to shake himself loose. Sam and Alice, their nerves frayed, were at last forced to give way to his insistence.

In a new suit, his face still battered, his temper vile, Duffy walked into the street. Sam came along at his heels.

"I feel," said Sam, "that you're going to run into trouble so fast we ain't going to have any time to stick you together again."

Duffy was walking fast. "You don't know nothing," he said shortly; "I feel fine, and I ain't going to find trouble."

Sam swung along at his side. "What's the hurry, for God's sake? You got a date with someone?"

"No, but I got to get me some exercise. Come on, get going."

"You ain't said where you're going," Sam said.

"First I'm going back to my joint, then I'm going to find out something about Cattley."

"Why Cattley, for the love of Mike?"

"Just that; I don't know. Maybe, I've got a hunch. Cattley's at the bottom of this, and I want to find out quite a bit about him. I want to find out why he was rubbed out. When I find that out, I guess I'll be pretty close to his killer. Okay, when I find his killer, I'll find the camera."

Sam stopped at the corner. "Well, I can't run around with you all day. I've got a living to make. Now, soldier, you're coming back to us tonight, ain't you?"

"Listen, Sam, you're swell, and Alice's swell. You're both swell, but from now on, you keep out of this. I'm going my own little way, without you two popping your heads into anything I might stir up."

Sam groaned. "I love you like this; just a big selfish playboy. You have the fun and we're just to sit round to put on the adhesive tape. Listen, mug, we're both in this, get it?"

Duffy grinned. It still hurt him to grin, but he grinned. "I'll be along," he said, "I get it."

Sam looked pleased. "Bounce 'em brother, bounce 'em," he said.

"They'll take some bouncing," Duffy said ruefully, as he watched McGuire's long frame disappearing through the crowded traffic.

He walked down the street, conscious of quick furtive glances at his battered face. He felt suddenly angry, his eyebrows coming down, making his face even more unattractive.

When he reached his apartment he was glad to find the place had been cleaned up. He made a little grimace at the faint stains on the walls. He wandered through the rooms, looking at everything carefully. Then he returned to the sitting-room. He sat on the edge of the table and thought a little while.

Cattley must have an apartment somewhere. The telephone directory gave him the information. He dialled the number opposite Cattley's name, but there was no answer.

Going down once more into the street, he flagged a taxi and gave an address on the East side. After he had gone a little way, he glanced out of the small rear window. A big Packard was rolling along behind him. He thought, "Maybe I'm just jumpy," but he watched the Packard closely. After he had been riding for several minutes he leant forward. "A bird's sitting on our tail," he said abruptly. "It makes me nervous."

The taxi-driver was a big beefy Irishman. He turned his head and grinned. "Watch me shake 'em," he said.

Duffy gave him five minutes, then said again. "You'll have to do better than that."

The driver pushed the cab until it began to rattle but the Packard just sat behind them.

Duffy said, "He's too big for you."

"What do you want me to do, boss?"

Duffy fumbled for some money. He gave the driver a couple of bucks. "Drop me at the first boozer you see," he said; "don't stop, just slow down. If they come after you, you don't know where you were taking me."

"Like the movies, huh?"

"Sure, you got it. Like the movies."

The driver suddenly crowded on his brakes and swung to the curb. Duffy bundled out, slamming the door. He stood on the pavement, watching the cab drive on. The Packard slowed down, hesitated, then shot away at right angles, turning a corner, disappearing quickly. Duffy didn't see who was in it. He flagged another cab and told the driver to drive on for a while. When he was sure that he hadn't got the Packard on his tail, he gave the apartment address again.

Cattley's apartment was big and showy. It was on the second floor of a large block. Duffy didn't take the elevator up, he walked. On the front door, was a small metal plate bearing Cattley's name. Duffy rang the bell. No one answered. He stood waiting. Then he rang the bell again. While he was standing there, he heard the elevator coming up. He stepped away from the door quickly and went up three stairs of the next flight. He was just out of sight from the elevator. He heard the grille slide back, and he looked round cautiously. A woman was standing in front of Cattley's door. He couldn't see who she was, but he watched her closely. There was something very familiar in her slim figure. She took a key from her handbag and opened the door. He came down the three stairs silently and walked into the room behind her.

"Hello, baby," he said.

She stood quite still for a moment, then turned and faced him. Her face was a little drawn, and her eyes big.

"You frightened me."

Duffy thought she had an iron nerve. "Nice to see you again," he said.

Annabel English looked at him. Then she put a hand quickly on his arm. "But your face," she said, "what has happened?"

Duffy touched his face with his finger-tips, then smiled; it was a very bleak smile. "I told you," he said, "some toughs pushed me around."

"It's horrible." She came closer to him. "They must have hurt you so."

Duffy shrugged. "Forget it," he said; "what brings you up here?"

She turned from him and wandered away across the room to the window. It was a shabby room. Duffy was quite surprised. The address was good enough, but Cattley had let the place run to seed. The furniture was old and battered and the walls needed attention. There was dust everywhere.

Duffy stood watching her. "What brings you up here?" he repeated.

When she reached the window she turned, so that the light was behind her. "I wanted to look round," she said; "why are you here?"

He lit a cigarette. "You know, baby," he said, moving further into the room and sitting on the corner of the table. "I don't think we're going to get along so well together."

"Oh, but yes."

He shook his head. "I guess I got you into a spot the other night, but you ain't doing anything to help me get you out of it. You're holding back on me."

She came over to him. "May I smoke?" she said.

He took out his case and she took one. He lit it for her. "Your poor face," she said softly.

"Quit stalling," he said impatiently. "You know, if you don't play ball, I'm going to ditch you."

"Please don't get that way." She went and sat down in a low, overstuffed chair. She crossed her legs, and Duffy grinned.

"You women," he said, "you think you've only got to show what you've got, and a man will roll over on his back, with his paws raised. Now, listen, this is important. What are you doing up here? How did you get a key to this joint?"

She studied her red finger-nails. "Suppose I said that I can't tell you?"

"Okay, you can't tell me. Well, those photos can take care of themselves."

She raised her heavy lashes and looked at him. "Honest, Bill, just now I can't tell you."

He slid off the table. "I'm going to look round this joint," he said shortly, "you sit there."

He went into the bedroom and began a systematic search. Patiently he went through every drawer, examined the sides of the arm-chair, looked behind the few pictures of doubtful taste hanging on the walls, took the grubby bed to pieces, but he found nothing to interest him. He went into the small kitchen and hunted about there. Then he stood still and scratched his head. He didn't know what he was looking for, but he had hoped that he would have found something to give him a lead. He went to the kitchen door. Then his eyes narrowed. Annabel was sitting quite still, but he knew that she had moved from the chair whilst he was in the kitchen. Her elaborate calmness, her frank smile when he came into the room, told him.

"Have you found anything?" she said, with a great show of interest.

He began wandering round the room. "Not yet," he said, "but I'm getting hot."

She got out of the chair. "Where's the Johnny?"

He stood quite still, then he jerked his head.

"Just through the bedroom," he said.

"I won't be a minute."

He didn't say anything, but watched her go into the bedroom, then he heard her shoot the bolt on the bathroom door.

He saw that she had left her bag on the table, and he went over quickly and scooped it up. He pressed on the paste diamond clasp and opened it. Quickly he emptied the contents on the table. There was the usual collection of junk that most women carry. A powder compact, cigarette-case and lighter, a lipstick in a gold case, a small phial of scent, some letters, and a roll of greenbacks. Nothing to interest him.

Making a little grimace of annoyance, he pushed the stuff back into the bag.

Then he began to examine the room carefully. The drawers yielded nothing, but on the sideboard he noticed a cigarette box had been moved. He could see the outline of dust had been disturbed. He opened the box, but it was empty. He took it over to the window and examined it carefully. Putting his fingers inside, he gently pushed. The bottom of the box suddenly sprang up. There was nothing in the false bottom. He took the box back and put it on the sideboard again.

Annabel came into the room again, touching her red hair with her finger-tips. She was quite calm. He looked her over thoughtfully.

"Finished?" she asked, going over to the table and picking up her bag. "Suppose you come and have some coffee with me?"

Duffy mashed his cigarette out in the tray. He held out his hand. "Give," he said.

She raised her eyebrows. "Now don't start being silly," she said, there was a faint note of anger in her voice.

Duffy walked over to her. "Come on," he said roughly. "Hand it over."

"What *is* this?" She turned impatiently to the door.

Duffy said evenly, "Wait a minute, sister, you and I are going to have a little talk."

She looked over her shoulder at him. Her eyes were stormy. "We're going right out of this place," she said. "I'll talk to you over coffee."

Duffy wandered over to the door and set his broad back against it. "We'll talk right here," he said briefly.

She shrugged and leant against the table. "Well, what is it?"

"I want you to get this business straight," he said; "up to now you've been acting like a dimwit all along. Well, you gotta wake up to things. You and I are in a murder mix-up. You stand a sweet chance of getting fried, and I'm in line for an accessory rap. You're playing it like an afternoon tumble with the curtains drawn. Get wise to it, Redhead."

She tapped on the floor with her shoe. "I know all that," she said, "but that gets me nowhere."

The smile on his face was hard. "You're holding back on me, baby, and you know it," he said. "If I weren't in this as an accessary, I'd let it ride. I'm in this for two reasons. One, I'm in it, if you get pinched, and two, I've got a little score to settle with Morgan. I'm easy enough if you play ball, but I'll get goddam' hard if you don't."

She said suddenly in a sharp voice, "Let me out of here."

Duffy didn't move. "You're in a spot, sister," he said, "there is only one way you can get out of here. You can open your pretty mouth and start squawking, and that'll bring the cops arunnin', asking questions. You'll have a sweet twenty minutes, explaining why you're here, and how you got the key to this joint. Then they'll start looking for Cattley, and suppose they find him, what then?"

She looked at him thoughtfully, then a little smile broke on her lips. "All right," she said, "if that's the way you feel, let's talk."

Duffy shook his head sadly. "My, my," he said. "You're like an eel, ain't you? Tough one minute, then the soft pedal. It ain't getting you anywhere, sister. You came here to find something and you've found it. Okay, you and me are going to share it."

She swung herself on the table, so that her skirt rode above her knees. Duffy looked at them, and thought they were nice. "You know every-thing," she said; "you're quite right, I did come here to find something. I suppose I'd better tell you all about it."

Duffy grinned. "And with perfect grace, she confessed the truth," he said.

"Well, I've been a fool," she said, studying her nails; "naturally, I wanted to keep it to myself. You've guessed by now that I lied to you about writ-ing a book?"

Duffy said, "You'd be surprised how much I do know."

"Cattley was blackmailing me," her voice was suddenly weary; "I've had to pay and pay. I did something crazy once and Cattley was there. My fa-ther would have been in a hopeless position to run for election if it got out, and Cattley was smart enough to know this. He put the screws on, and I had to pay. It's awful of me to say this, but his death was a great relief to me."

Duffy said, "You're giving me a grand motive for his killing."

She slid off the table and came over to him. "You know I didn't kill him," she said, "you believe that, don't you?"

"Go on," he said, "it don't matter a damn what I think, it's what the jury would think that counts."

She moved away again, and began wandering round the room, finger-ing the furniture aimlessly as she moved. "Cattley was a brute. He made me visit him. He gave me the key of his apartment. I had to go to him whenever he called. I knew he had some proof of what I did, so when he was killed, I came down to find it. That's the truth, you do believe that?"

"Sure," Duffy beamed, "a hophead would believe it."

She sat down suddenly in the arm-chair and hid her face in her hands. "I'm so unhappy," she said, her voice breaking; "please be kind to me."

Duffy came over and sat on the arm of her chair. "When you went into the Johnny just now," he said casually, "you smuggled something in your pants or some place. You can now go right back to the Johnny and dig it out again. Then you can give it to me."

She took her hands from her face and leant back. Her face was set. "You've got no right to ask for that," she said, "it is nothing to do with you. It is entirely personal."

Duffy put his arm round the back of the chair and patted her shoulder. "Go into the Johnny," he said.

She got out of the chair. Her eyes were very angry. Duffy thought she looked swell. "I've had enough of this," she said, speaking very fast; "I've told you the truth, and I'm not giving you anything. Now, understand that."

Duffy still sat on the chair-arm. He looked her over slowly, his mouth pursed, and his eyebrows raised. "You don't seem to understand," he said; "I want whatever you found in this joint, and I'm going to have it."

She started to say something, but he held up his hand. "Quiet," he said, "if you don't like to give it to me, I'll take it, how's that?"

Slowly, she began to back to the door. He could see that she was getting scared. He left his seat quickly as she reached the door, and swung her round. She struck him across his nose with her clenched fist. Duffy was quite hurt. He put his hand to his face, felt his nose gingerly, looked at his fingers to see if his nose was bleeding, then he grinned. "Well, of course," he said, "if that's the way you want it."

She struck at him again, but he caught her wrist, then she closed with him, a kicking, biting, scratching handful of outraged loveliness. For a moment, Duffy was busy keeping her nails out of his eyes. He smothered her arms with difficulty, turned her. Crossing her arms across her chest, and holding them tightly by the wrists behind her, he ran into the bedroom and slammed her face down on the bed.

"You Redhead," he said, panting a little with his exertion. "You going to play ball, or do I have to get rough?"

She said, her voice muffled, "Oh! How I hate you!"

"Come on."

She remained silent for a minute, then she said, "All right, I'll give it to you."

"That a promise?"

"Yes… yes, you beast."

He grunted and released her. She sat up, her face white and drawn. Her eyes were glittering with hate. He was quite startled to see how vicious she could look.

"Get going," he said, suddenly losing his good temper. She said, "Get out of the room. I have to undress."

He shook his head. "Be your age," he said, "I don't trust you."

She got off the bed, and stood, her hair ruffled, her green silk dress crumpled, and battle in her eye.

"I'm not getting undressed with a heel like you looking on," she said.

Duffy went over to the door and turned the key. He took the key out and put it in his pocket

"You surprise me," he said, "fancy you being coy. Sure I'll turn my back, but get going."

He went and looked out of the window. A very faint sound made him jerk round again. She was almost on top of him. In her hand she was holding an empty carafe by the neck. The look in her eyes made him catch his breath. He slid along the wall away from her fast, as she smashed the carafe at him. The glass exploded all round him. The paper on the wall split, where the carafe had struck, sending a stream of plaster running to the floor.

Her face was contorted with murderous fury. He saw tiny white flecks of foam on her lips. She began to call him filthy names. Hurling them at him, through her twisted mouth.

Duffy thought she must be in a kind of fit. He was so startled that he backed away from her. She advanced slowly towards him, her hands held out in front of her, opening and closing. Every time she closed them, her knuckles stood out white. Then she came at him, like a coiled spring unleashed. Her body struck him with her full weight, and he went back, reeling, off his balance. Her hand shot out and gripped his throat. He could feel the hot burning pain as her long nails dug into his flesh.

Swinging his fist up hard, he hit her on the side of the jaw. He didn't put any weight behind the blow, but it was a nice smack, all the same. She sagged, fell on her knees, her hands running down his coat front, feebly trying for a grip, then she went forward on her face.

Duffy stepped back and took out his handkerchief. He carefully wiped off his palms, then put the handkerchief back. "For crying out loud," he said.

He picked her up and put her carefully on the bed. She lay limp, her eyes closed, breathing hard. He made sure that she was right out, before he began to search her. He didn't like the job, it made him feel like a snake, but he went through with it. Pushed down the top of her girdle, he found what he was looking for. A little red leather note-book. He didn't wait to examine it there and then, he just put it carefully in his inside pocket, rearranged her dress and left her. He let himself out of the apartment, and brought the elevator up from the ground floor. While he waited for it to come up, he kept an ear cocked for any sound from the flat. It was only when he got into the street that he felt at ease. He noticed, across the road, a big Packard was standing. No one was in it. He crossed the road and glanced inside. He recognized the car as the one that had followed him. It belonged to Annabel English.

"Well, well," he said. This was getting quite beyond him. He walked a little way down the road, then he flagged a cruising taxi. He gave McGuire's address. When the cab jerked off, he settled himself back on the shiny leather, and took out the notebook. It was very neat, each page covered with minute writing. Just names and addresses, and against each name was a number of small denominations. He turned the pages, carefully reading each name, hoping to get some clue. At the fifth page he realized that he was reading down a list of New York's top-liners. He went on. There was no doubt of that. Well-known names began to jump out of the pages. Wives of bankers, stockbrokers, rich playboys, daughters of millionaires, actors and actresses, councillors, a judge here and there, quite a complete list of people in the public eye and who mattered. Duffy looked for Annabel English's name, but he couldn't find it. He held the book in his hand and scratched his head. He thought probably the key lay in the numbers against the names. But it had him beat. He counted the names for something better to do. They totalled just over three hundred. At the end of the book, written faintly in pencil, was a name and address, set apart from the other names. He made it out with difficulty: "Olga Shann, Plaza Wonderland Club." He put the note-book in his pocket, and leant back brooding. Perhaps, he thought, he'd get a line from this Olga dame.

The taxi swung to the curb, and he got out. There was something familiar in the taxi-driver's face. Duffy looked at him hard. The taxi-driver grinned at him.

"You must love that dame," he observed. "The last time I brought you to this joint you had to be carried, and now, God love me, she's scratched you to hell again."

Duffy gave him some money. "One of these days," he said evenly, "someone's going to take a dislike to you."

The taxi-driver grinned some more. "I should worry," he said.

Duffy left him and walked up the steps to the apartment.

Chapter Seven

When McGuire got in from work, he found Duffy and Alice in the kitchen. Duffy was standing over the stove, a heavy frown on his face, watching a large steak grilling.

McGuire took one look at him and said, "For God's sake, he's been at it again."

Alice looked up with a mischievous smile. She was peeling potatoes at the sink. "He won't say a word."

Duffy scowled. "For the love of Mike, pipe down," he said. "What if my girl friend did get tough?"

McGuire shook his head sadly. He leant himself up against the wall. "I never met such a guy," he said. "Can't you take care of yourself once in a while?"

Duffy said, "Know the Plaza Wonderland Club?"

Sam shot a look at Alice. "I've heard of it."

Alice said, "I knew you would. You know all the low clubs."

Sam protested. "You got me wrong there," he said violently; "I've never been there. I just heard of it from the boys."

"I know."

Sam groaned, "She's always imagining things," he complained to Duffy. "As if I'd be seen dead in one of those burgs."

"You're going to this one tonight," Duffy said, turning the steak carefully.

Sam cocked his head. "Is that so?" he said. Again he looked at Alice.

She shrugged. "I suppose I'll have to say yes," she said.

Duffy went over and gave her a pat. "Be nice," he said. "This is strictly business. You got to stay home."

"You men," she said, but she wasn't mad. Duffy knew she'd take it all right. She was like that. "Don't get him into trouble," she said, looking at Sam.

"Me?" Sam laughed. "I like that. Get him into trouble? It's me that's going to run into that, I bet."

Duffy shook his head. "You're just window-dressing," he said. "You'll see."

After the meal, McGuire pushed his chair back and looked inquiringly at Duffy. "You want to get going?" he said.

Duffy nodded. "Yeah," he said. "Might as well."

Sam lit a cigarette and went over to get his hat. He slapped it on the back of his head and turned to Alice. "We ain't going to be late," he glanced at

Duffy, who shook his head. "Keep the bed warm for me, honey."

She raised her face to his for a kiss, and Duffy looked on with approval. "You rnust've been screwy to marry a tramp like that," he said to Alice.

Sam grinned. "There was a shortage of men at the time."

Alice threatened him with a roll of bread, and he ducked out to get the car.

She said in a small voice, "You'll be careful?"

Duffy turned his head, and said with elaborate astonishment, "Why, sure, we're going to have a good time."

She got up from her chair and walked over to him. "Save it, Bill. You're poking your nose into this murder business."

Duffy shrugged. "This won't amount to much," he explained. "I've got a line on Cattley's girl friend. She might turn in some information. This business puzzles me. There is a lot I don't get. Maybe I've been a bit hasty, hiding up that rat. I don't know. This Annabel broad ain't nice. She's dangerous."

"I wish you hadn't anything to do with it. Sam's worried too."

Duffy put on his hat. "I gotta see it through now. Don't you worry about Sam, I won't get him into anything."

"I'm worrying about you."

"Forget it," he pleaded; "it's going to come out okay."

She went with him to the door. "I don't want to be a fuss."

He patted her shoulder. "You're swell," he said. "It'll be all right."

He found Sam sitting at the wheel of a small tourer that had seen better days. Duffy climbed in beside him. "Where's this joint, anyway?" he asked.

Sam let in the clutch with a bang, the car jerked forward, and then stalled. Duffy didn't say anything, he was used to it. Sam pulled the starter, reversed the engine, and let the clutch in again. The car pulled away from the curb, making a noise like a beehive.

"The Plaza?" Sam said; "it's near Manhattan Bridge."

"Know the place?" Duffy asked.

"Sure," Sam said. "This is a hot joint. I used to go there a bit in the old days." Sam always called the time he was single "the old days." "It's tough, and packed with hot pants. You wait."

Duffy leant back. "Sounds all right," he said.

Sam drove two blocks in silence, then he said, "You telling me the news?"

Duffy gave him a cigarette. "I looked up Cattley's dump today. Annabel turned up. She was looking for something. She found it, and so did I." He touched the scratches with his fingers and grinned. "I bet that honey's as mad as a hornet right now."

Sam swerved to avoid a big Cadillac, grabbed his handbrake and shouted, "You street pushover," to the fat driver.

Duffy took no notice; he had driven with Sam before. "What did you find?" Sam asked.

"It's a little note-book, full of ritzy names, and it don't mean a thing to me."

"So?"

"Yeah." Duffy frowned at his reflection in the driving-screen. "It's important. I know because I had to get tough with Annabel to get her to part. That dame scares me. She ain't normal."

"I thought you liked 'em that way." Sam looked at him in surprise.

"Watch the road, dimwit," Duffy said shortly. "You ought to see that dame. When she gets mad, she foams at the mouth."

"Yeah?"

"She tried to knock me off," Duffy said. "She's screwy. There can't be any other answer."

Sam went past the City Hall slowly, then he swung into Park Row and pushed the pedal down again. "She needn't be nuts to want to knock you off," he said. "Suppose we stop for a drink?"

Duffy glanced at the time. It was barely nine o'clock. "You'll get a drink when we get there," he said.

The Plaza Wonderland Club was situated on the second floor, over a hardware store. The entrance was down an alley, lit with neon lighting. They parked the car and walked up the alley and went in. At the top of the stairs tickets were being sold for the taxi-dancers. Duffy bought half a dozen, then they pushed aside the bead curtains and went into the hall.

There was nothing original about the place. It was dirty and shabby. The dance floor was small, and you had to step down to get on to it. Round the floor, tables were crammed together, and at the far end the girls sat behind a pen. Sam looked across the room at them and thought they were a pretty swell bunch.

There were very few people at the tables. Just a handful. They all looked up as Duffy squeezed himself past the tables and got on to the floor. They watched him cross the floor, with Sam behind him, and select a table against the wall, opposite the entrance. He sat down and Sam took the other chair.

The band of three were playing swing music without much enthusiasm. They plugged away staring with vacant eyes into space.

"You call this a hot joint?" Duffy said.

"Maybe the depression's hit 'em," Sam said.

Duffy made frantic signs to a waiter who came over to them with a flat-footed shuffle.

"Let's have a bottle of rum," Sam said.

"Yeah." Duffy thought that a good idea. "Make it a bottle of rum."

The waiter went off. Duffy said, "Take a look at this," he slid the little note-book across the table.

Sam picked it up and studied it carefully. After a little while he handed it back. "No," he said, "that don't mean anything to me. There's plenty of money in that list. I'd say at a guess that little lot's worth a million each. They all belong to the hot set, but that's all I get from it."

Duffy put the note-book back in his pocket. "Maybe I'll get a line on it later," he said.

The waiter brought the rum and set it down on the table with a crisp bang. Sam said, "This joint's changed."

The waiter glanced at him. "Buddy," he said, "it's early yet."

Sam turned to Duffy. "See?" he said; "it's early."

"Okay, it's early. Let's grab a couple of girls, and show them how it's done."

There was no one dancing on the floor. Sam poured himself out a shot of rum and drank it hurriedly. "Heck!" he said, "I believe I'm nervous."

Duffy looked at him. "You're kidding yourself, you want to get stewed."

Sam got up from his chair and wandered across the room to the pen. He stood looking at each girl carefully, until they began to giggle at him. He found a blonde that pleased him and he began to rush her round the empty floor. Duffy picked his girl from where he was sitting, then he went over and dated her up. She was a chestnut red, with a pert little nose and a big, humorous smile. She had a plump, hard little belly that he could feel against his vest. He thought she was cute.

Duffy could dance when he liked, and the rum had made him fairly happy. He swung her round in big smooth circles, and she just seemed to float with him. They didn't say a word through the dance, but when the band cut out, he said, "You're good."

She gave him her flashing smile. "You ain't so bad either." She got an accent like a heap of tins being tossed downstairs.

He said, "Come on over and get tight."

Sam was already there with his blonde. Duffy fancied she smelt, and he sat away from her. Sam liked her a lot. He was showing signs of considerable interest.

Duffy said, "You girls like rum?"

They both began to protest. They wanted champagne.

Sam shook his head. "Listen," he said. "We're God's gift to womanhood; if rum won't keep you, you can both take a walk."

Duffy said it was okay with him too.

So they had rum.

The place was crowding up. People kept squeezing between tables. One big chestnut, with large curves, tried to pass Sam, but she couldn't quite make it. Sam looked up, gaped and said, "Hi, Bill! It's the covered wagon."

Duffy started to sweat. He guessed Sam was getting drunk.

The chestnut screwed her head round and took a look at Sam, then she laughed. "You're cute," she said.

Sam got up and made an elaborate bow. "Sister," he said, "you've got it all."

The chestnut squeezed by, now that Sam stood up. Her escort, a little runt, glared at Sam, who raised two fingers of his right hand.

Duffy said, "Can't you behave yourself?"

Sam looked grieved. "She liked it," he said.

His blonde was looking across the room, tapping her foot. She was annoyed.

Duffy said to the girl with the big mouth, "Let's dance."

When they got on the floor he said, "Olga ain't here tonight?"

She looked up at him, a little frown creasing her brow. "Olga?" she said.

"Sure, Olga Shann. I'd like to meet her again."

"She's not here tonight."

Duffy said, "Hell, I wanted to talk to that dame."

They danced in silence for several minutes, then he said, "Would you like to earn twenty bucks?"

"It's going to cost you a lot more than that."

Duffy said, "We're on a different set of rails. I'm offering you twenty bucks for Olga's address."

She looked disappointed. "Gee!" she said with a pout, "I thought we were getting on fine."

"I'm out on business. I just gotta talk with her."

She went the length of the room before she said, "I'll get it for you."

At the end of the dance she left him. Duffy glanced over at Sam, who was making up to his blonde, so he turned into the toilet. He ran the water and washed his hands. The toilet was empty. It was a small room with cracked tiles half-way up the walls. He dried his hands and dropped the towel into the basket. The door pushed open and a tall man came in. The first thing Duffy noticed about him was his hair. It was jet black, with a broad white streak, running from his forehead to his right ear. It gave his hard face a look of distinction. He wore a close-clipped moustache, and his skin was grey.

Duffy just glanced at him, then made to walk out of the room.

The man said, "Wait a minute."

Duffy paused. "You speaking to me?" he said, surprised.

The man held out his hand. Duffy looked and saw he was holding a .25 automatic.

"You just bought it or something?" Duffy said, suddenly very cautious.

"You got the note-book on you, hand it over." The man had a curious voice. It was deep-pitched with a little buzz in it.

Duffy said, "I did have, but it's in the mail now."

Just then the door opened and Sam came in. The man put his gun away. He didn't seem to hurry, but the gun just disappeared.

Sam said, "There you are."

The man looked at Duffy. His pale eyes were very threatening. Then he walked out of the toilet.

Duffy said, "Who's that guy?"

Sam shrugged. "Search me," he said, "my girl might know."

Duffy stepped to the door quickly and Sam, a puzzled look on his face, followed him. "Did you see that guy come out just now?" Duffy asked the blonde.

She said, "Sure I did. That's Murray Gleason. Ain't he cute?"

Duffy blotted his face with his handkerchief. "I couldn't say," he said, "we were a bit shy with each other."

Sam put his arms round the blonde. "Ain't this a grand place?" he said. He was pretty drunk.

Duffy said, "I want to get out of here."

A white-headed little guy came through the hall, heading for the toilet. Sam took the blonde over to him. "Take care of this baby," he said. "Show her round. She's learning in a big way."

The blonde wrapped the little guy in her arms and began to cry. The rum had her all ends up. Duffy walked out with Sam. The little guy's face was a picture.

Outside, Duffy said, "You're just hell to go places with."

Sam waved his hands. "I guess I'm a little tight," he said. They walked into the dance-hall again. Sam said suddenly, "Did that blonde smell a little, or is my nose wrong?"

Duffy said his nose was fine.

The girl with the big mouth was standing by the entrance looking for them. Duffy went over. "Did you get it?" he asked.

She nodded and gave him a slip of paper, on it was an address. Duffy gave her twenty bucks, She rolled the notes and tucked them in the top of her stocking. Sam leant forward with interest. "I'm having a swell time," he said.

Duffy said to the girl, "I'll be back one of these nights. We'll have a fine time."

She looked at him wistfully. "I've heard that before."

Sam said, "You're young yet. You'll hear it dozens of times."

They went downstairs into the street. Duffy stopped at the end of the alley.

"Go home, Sam," he said. "Be careful how you drive."

Sam blinked at him. "The fun over so soon?" he asked.

Duffy nodded. "I said you were just window-dressing," he said briefly. "I gave you a break. Now go home and look after that wife of yours."

Sam scratched his head. "She's probably feeling a little lonesome right now."

"Get going."

"Ain't you coming?"

"I'm calling on this Shann broad."

Sam leered. "Three being a mob?"

Duffy nodded. "You got it, soldier," he said. He watched Sam go over to the parking-place, and then went to the subway on Frankfort Street. Olga Shann had rooms in Brooklyn. He'd never heard of the address, so when he'd got over Brooklyn Bridge he left the subway and flagged a taxi.

He got to the address just after eleven o'clock. He hesitated to ask the taxi to wait. Then making up his mind, he paid him off.

The house was a two-storey villa, with identical models either side, stretching right down the street.

He unlatched the gate and walked up the short gravel path. There was a light showing from one of the second-floor windows. He pressed the buzzer with his thumb, and leant against the wall. He hadn't the vaguest idea what he was going to say.

About three minutes ticked off, then a light sprang up in the hall. He could hear the chain being slipped and then the front door opened. A woman stood there, holding the door only partly open. He couldn't make out her features, she was standing squarely with her back to the light.

"Miss Shann?" he said, taking off his hat.

"Suppose it is," she said. Her voice had a Garbo tone.

He thought it was a hell of a welcome, but he let it slide. "It's late for a call," he said, trying to put his personality across, "but you'll excuse me, I hope?"

"What is it?"

"I'm Duffy of the *Tribune*." He took out his Press pass and flashed it, then he put it back again. "I wanted a word with you about Cattley."

He saw her stiffen, then she said, "Let me see that Press card."

He dug it out again and handed it over. She pushed the door to and examined the card in the light. Then she opened the door wide, and said, "You'd better come in."

He followed her into a small sitting-room. It was modern, but the stuff was cheap. He looked at her with interest. The first thing he noticed about her was her eyebrows. They gave her face an expression of permanent surprise. She was lovely in a hard way. Big eyes with long lashes, a scarlet, full mouth; the top lip was almost bee-stung. Her thick chestnut hair was silky and cared for. Duffy liked her quite a lot.

She was wearing a chocolate-brown silk dress, tight across her firm breasts and her flat hips.

"Why Cattley?" she said.

He put his hat down on the table. "This is most unprofessional, but I'm dying for a drink."

She shook her head. "Nothing doing." She was very emphatic. "Say your piece and get going."

"My, my," he said, "you babes get tougher every day."

She moved impatiently.

"Okay," Duffy said hastily. "I'm looking for Cattley."

"Why should I know where he is?"

"Why, you're his girl friend, ain't you?"

She shook her head. "I haven't seen him for months."

"He thought enough of you to have your name and address in his pocket-book."

She shrugged. "Lots of men have girls' names in their pocketbooks. It doesn't amount to anything."

Duffy thought she was quite right. "Well, well," he said, "I guess I've come out of my way."

She went to the door and opened it. "I won't keep you," she said.

Outside, Duffy heard a car drive up. "You got visitors."

He saw a startled look come into her eyes, but she said, "Then you'd better go."

The buzzer rang loudly. She started a little.

Duffy said, "Can I go out the back way? I'm feeling I might run into trouble."

She stood hesitating, then she said, "Wait here." Her voice implored him. The buzzer went again, long and insistently. Duffy said, "You want me to stay?"

"Yes—I don't know who it is."

She went out of the room, leaving the door open. Duffy glanced round, saw another door and went over and opened it. He found himself in a small kitchen. He pushed the door to, and stood looking into the sitting-room, through the small opening.

He heard her at the front door; then he heard her say, "Why, hello, Max."

"You alone?" the hoarse voice that spoke made Duffy stiffen. It was familiar. First, he thought it was Joe, but then he knew it wasn't quite like Joe's voice. He'd heard it before.

She said, "Yes… what is it?"

Duffy heard footsteps in the hall and he heard the front door close. "What do you want?" her voice was nervy and breathless.

A broad-shouldered man, wearing a black slouched hat, walked into the sitting-room. Duffy had him at once. *It was the man who had stolen the camera.*

Duffy clenched his fists. Just the bird he was looking for. Olga came in and stood by the table. Her face was white and a muscle in her throat fluttered.

"But, Max...."

The man glanced round the room suspiciously, then looked at her. His hard eyes raked her from head to foot. "I ain't seen you for a long time," he said. "You're looking swell." There was no animation in his voice. He sounded as if he were reciting.

She tried to smile, but her lips were frozen. She managed to say, "That's nice of you."

He sat himself on the edge of the table and looked at his hands. "You know Cattley's been knocked off?" he said.

She put her hand to her throat. "No... no, I didn't know that," she said.

Max raised his head a little and stared at the kitchen door. Duffy stiffened. Then Max said, "You were sweet on that guy at one time, huh?"

She shook her head. "He meant nothing to me."

"So?"

"We went around together, but that's all."

"You went around together?" He pushed his hat over his eyes. He wouldn't look at her.

"That's right... but why... why are you asking me?"

"Just curious." With the flat of his hand he rubbed the short hairs on his nape. "Did he ever tell you things?"

Duffy could see what a panic she was in. "He didn't tell me anything... he didn't tell me anything."

Max got off the table and went over to the mantelpiece. He examined the photos and fingered the small ivory elephants there. He seemed utterly bored. Then he shrugged. "I thought maybe he had talked to you," he said indifferently. He put his hand in the inside of his coat and took out a short silk cord. It was dark red in colour. He dangled it in his fingers.

Olga watched him like a rabbit would watch a snake. He said, "This is a pretty thing, ain't it?"

She said, "What is it?"

"This? Hell, I don't know. I found it." He continued to swing it in his hand.

She said, "Did you?"

"I guess I'll scram." He wandered to the door.

"But… but don't you want—?"

"I'll scram," he said, pausing at the door. "I thought maybe you'd be interested to hear Cattley's washed up. I see you ain't."

Her relief was obvious. "Of course, I'm sorry," she said, "but I haven't seen him for so long—"

"That's all right," he said. "I liked seeing you." The flat tone of his voice made the whole thing sound like a badly acted play. He stood on one side at the door and she went ahead to open the front door. When she passed him, he tossed the silk cord over her head with the rapidity of a snake striking, and twisted it round her neck. His knee came up in the small of her back and he threw all his weight on to the cord.

Duffy slipped out of the kitchen like a shadow, and hit Max on his ear with a roundhouse swing. Max, being only on one leg, went over like a felled tree. Olga went on her hands and knees, making a sort of honking sound in her throat.

Max rolled over twice until the wall brought him up, then he dizzily clawed inside his coat for a gun. Duffy whipped up a hall chair and smashed it down on Max. The wall took most of the force, and the back of the chair snapped. Max kicked out at Duffy with a long leg, and his boot caught Duffy on the shin. Duffy dropped on one knee, his face twisted, and then Max hit him on the side of the head. The blow had no weight behind it, as Max was lying on his shoulder, but it upset Duffy's balance and he went over.

Max again went for his gun and this time he got it out, but Duffy lashed out with his foot and caught Max under the chin. The gun went off with a violent noise. The bullet hit the ceiling, bringing a shower of plaster down on the floor. Max dropped the gun and flopped on his face.

Swearing wildly, Duffy grabbed hold of the gun and scrambled to his feet. He backed away from Max, but the big tough seemed right out. Cautiously, Duffy went over to Olga, who was going blue in the face. He jerked the silk cord loose and helped her to her feet. Her breath still rattled in her throat. He pushed her into the sitting-room.

"Okay, baby," he said, "you're all right now."

He dropped her into an arm-chair. The slamming of the front door brought him out of the sitting-room with an oath. Max had vanished. Outside, he heard a car start up, and by the time he had got to the front door he just caught a glimpse of a tail light vanishing round the bend of the road. He banged the front door to, and went back into the sitting-room. Olga was sitting up feeling her throat. She was crying a little.

"You got any liquor here?" he said.

She pointed to the kitchen. "It's in the pantry," she said hoarsely.

Duffy found a big earthenware bottle of apple-jack after a hunt round.

He found two glasses and came back into the sitting-room. He filled both glasses and gave her one. "Put it down," he said. "You need it."

He drained his glass. The apple-jack went down his throat and then when it reached his stomach it exploded. He had to hold on to the table while his head was spinning, and he caught his breath. Just for a moment, he thought he was going to die, then all of a sudden he felt fine.

He looked at the bottle in amazement. "That's panther's spit okay," he said.

He filled up his glass again, but this time he was more cautious. He did it in three. He looked at her with a little squint. "Sister," he said, "you're coming home with me. This spot ain't going to be healthy any more."

The apple-jack was bringing her round. He could see the faint colour coming back to her face. Again she touched her bruised neck. "I can't do that," she said.

Duffy went over to her. "Pack a bag and get going," he said; "you gotta make it fast. That bird might come back again."

Her eyes widened with fear and she got up quickly. He had to help her to the door, her legs were weak. Then, when he saw she could make it, he left her to go upstairs. He went back and gave himself another drink.

By the time she had come down again, he was half cocked. He waved the bottle at her. "This is the best drop of phlegm-cutter I've run into for some time."

She stood hesitating on the bottom stair. "Will you get me a taxi?" she said. "I'll go to some hotel."

Duffy went over and took her bag. "You're coming home with me," he said. "For the love of Mike, don't argue."

He went out in the road and looked up and down, but he couldn't see a taxi. "We can walk to the end of the road," he said; "we'll get a lift there."

She turned out the lights and slammed the door. They walked down the street together. Duffy felt his feet were pressing into cotton wool. She said nothing until they reached the end of the road, then she said in a small voice, "Thank you."

Duffy flagged a cab. He helped her in and gave the driver McGuire's address. Then he got in and sat beside her. He still had the apple-jack in one hand and her suit-case in the other.

"Don't you worry about that, sister. I was so scared I didn't think about you." He uncorked the bottle, and took another long swig. Then he looked at her suspiciously and said, "This stuff won't give me Screaming-meemies, will it?"

She turned her face away from him and began to cry.

Duffy fell asleep.

Chapter Eight

When Sam opened the door and saw them, his eyes popped.

Duffy came into the room, pushing past Sam. Olga hesitated, then followed Duffy. Sam shut the door and stood there scratching his head. He was in green pyjamas and a yellow bathrobe.

Duffy said, "Don't mind him. He ain't so sissy as he looks."

Olga gave Sam a scared glance, but said nothing.

Sam said, "Introduce me, you drunken rat."

"Miss Shann, this is Sam McGuire."

She still said nothing.

Alice came out of the bedroom, her dressing-gown wrapped tightly round her. Duffy went over to her. "This is Olga Shann," he said. "She's in a spot of trouble, so I brought her along."

"Why, of course." Alice put her hand on Olga's arm. "Bill can sleep on the couch, you can have his room."

Olga said, "But don't you—?"

Duffy put the apple-jack on the table. "Wait a minute," he interrupted. "A nice sleep is what you want, but I've got just a little question to ask you before you go."

She turned to face him.

"Who was that guy that tried to get tough with you?"

"Max Weidmer. He and Cattley used to work together."

Duffy nodded. "Okay; put her to bed, Alice, and be nice to her."

As Alice led her from the room, Olga said, "But his face? How did he get so knocked about?"

Sam jerked his head. "She was talking about you."

"Know where this Weidmer hangs out?"

Sam frowned. "Now what?" he asked.

"Come on." Duffy's face was set.

Sam went to the telephone and spun the dial. While he 'phoned Duffy went into the bathroom and washed his face and hands. Sam came in a moment later. "He's got a room at the Lexingham Hotel."

Duffy said, "Thanks," then he walked into the sitting-room again.

Sam came in looking lost. "What's breaking now?"

Duffy said, "Lend me your rod."

"Hey! You ain't going to mess around with a heater, for God's sake."

"Don't talk; I'm getting action. Come on, give me the gun. I want to get going."

Sam sighed and began taking off his dressing-gown. "Okay," he said, "but I'm coming with you."

Duffy touched his arm. "You ain't," he said. "Things might happen round this burg. You gotta stay and keep an eye on things."

Sam screwed up his eyes. "What *is* this?" he demanded.

"Weidmer tried to twist that dame's neck. He thinks she knows too much. I fancy he might try and get at her here. That's why you stay put."

Sam's eyes grew big. "You want to take my gun?" he said "What about me?"

"Get going," Duffy said impatiently, "give me the gun before Alice starts on me. If you drink enough of that panther's breath, you won't need any gun."

Sam went over to the hall table and came back with a .38 automatic. Duffy took it, looked at the magazine, then stuck it down the waist-band of his trousers. He adjusted the points of his vest to hide the butt.

"I may be late," he said.

Alice came out just as he stepped into the hall. She just caught a glimpse of him. "Where's that crazy coon going now?" she asked.

Sam put down the apple-jack hastily. "He's going to get another dame," he said wildly. "He's going to fill the whole goddam house with 'em."

Alice took his arm. "You come along," she said. "What you need is a good night's sleep."

She didn't see the worried look in his eyes, as he followed her into the bedroom.

Outside in the street, Duffy flagged a taxi. He gave the driver instructions and then got in the cab. He thought he was spending his life in taxis.

The drive was a long one, and it was just after twelve o'clock when the driver pulled up outside a shabby building.

Duffy paid him off and walked up the steps. The place looked more like a boarding-house than a hotel. He saw a row of letter-boxes and he examined them carefully. Weidmer's name was on the fourth one. Duffy rang the bell at the top of the row, furthest away from Weidmer's. A moment later he heard the catch being pulled on the front door and he walked in. The hall was lighted by a small gas-burner, and he had just enough light to grope his way upstairs.

On the second floor, he found Weidmer's rooms. He put his hand on the butt of the gun, and then turned the handle. He was surprised to feel the door give. He looked carefully over his shoulder to right and left, then drawing the gun, he stepped quietly into the dark room. He stood in the darkness, listening. There was no sound, except the ticking of a clock somewhere in the room. He just stood, holding his breath, listening. Then, when he was satisfied that the room was empty, he struck a match and lit the gas-burner.

It was a large room, full of shabby furniture. Across the far end stood a bed. Duffy jerked up his gun. There was someone lying face downward across the sheets; it was Weidmer. Duffy moved across the room, his gun steady. But Weidmer was dead. Duffy guessed that before he touched him. He turned him over, and then caught his breath; a big gaping wound showed in Weidmer's throat. Someone had certainly made a job of it, Duffy thought. He released Weidmer, and let him slump back on the bed.

For several minutes, he stood there thinking furiously. Then he began a systematic search of the room. He guessed it would be useless, but he made his search just the same. He couldn't find the camera anywhere. He found one thing that made him blink his eyes. At the bottom of a drawer, he dug out a large glossy photograph. At first glance he thought it was some movie star, then he recognized Annabel English.

"Well, by God," he said.

Across the photo, scrawled in large sprawling writing, was: "To dear Max, from Annabel."

Duffy folded the photo and stuffed it in his pocket. Then he slipped the gun once more down the front of his trousers, and quietly let himself out of the room.

Once more out in the street, he again flagged a taxi and gave Annabel's address. Lying back against the hard seat of the cab, his eyes closed a little wearily, but his mouth was hard and set. He was going to bust the business right on the chin, he told himself.

With the key Morgan had given him, he entered the door leading to the organ loft, and quietly walked up the spiral staircase. When he reached the loft, he found the sitting-room was brightly lit, although no one was visible. He swung his leg over the balcony and lowered himself quietly to the floor.

From across the room he could hear the sound of running water. He thought maybe she was taking a bath. Quietly he began to circulate round the room, opening and shutting drawers. When he came to the wine cupboard he had to kneel down to examine inside. At the back of the cupboard, behind a row of sherry bottles, he found his camera. He took it out and examined it carefully. The first thing he noticed was that the film had been removed. He put the camera in his pocket and shut the cupboard doors carefully.

The bath water had ceased to run, and there was a heavy silence in the apartment. Walking across to the door, he put his hand on the knob and gently turned it, then he walked in.

Annabel was lying in the bath, her eyes closed, smoking a cigarette. Duffy thought she looked swell. He shut the door very gently, and put his back against the panels.

She opened her eyes and looked at him. The only surprise she showed was the way the cigarette slipped out of her mouth. It fell into the water with an angry hiss, then floated down the bath until it rested on her knee. It lay on her knee, looking like some peculiar birthmark. Duffy eyed it with interest.

She shifted one of her feet, causing the water to ripple. "This calls for a foam bath, don't it?" Duffy said. He went over and sat on the bath stool, that was quite close to the bath. From there he could see the small bruise where he had hit her.

"Get out of here," she whispered.

He said, "We're going to have a little talk." He took from his pocket the camera and showed it to her. Then he produced the photo and showed that to her as well. She lay quite still, her eyes black with hate.

"I know who killed Cattley now," he said. "Whoever had the camera rubbed Cattley, I knew that. I had only to find the camera to burst this open. You played your hand very badly, didn't you?"

She said, "Get out of here, you sonofabitch."

Duffy's mouth set in a hard grin. "When I do," he said, "the cops are moving in."

She sat up suddenly in the bath, slopping the water over the edge with her violence. "You can't pin this on me," she said; her breathless voice was shrill. "Find Cattley and see."

Duffy raised his eyebrows. "So you shifted him, have you?" he said.

He watched her hand moving slowly over to a transparent bottle, standing on a shelf just above her. He saw it contained ammonia. He took the gun from his waist and showed it to her. "I'd like to give you another navel," he said softly. "Make a move like that and you'll be able to play the penny whistle on yourself."

Her hand dropped into the water again. He stood up. "Come out of that," he said. "There's lots we got to talk about."

She climbed out of the bath and grabbed a bath-robe, which she hastily wrapped round herself. Her eyes were like pinpoints. Duffy said. "I'll give you five minutes to fix yourself up, then come out quietly. Don't start anything. I'm leaving the door open."

He stepped out of the bathroom backwards. A new voice said, "Drop that gun."

Duffy stood quite still. The voice said, "Go on, put the gun on the floor. Don't turn round yet until you've got rid of the gun."

Duffy put the gun down carefully on the floor at his feet and turned his head. Murray Gleason was standing quite close to him. His hard grey face was cold. He held a Luger in his hand.

Annabel said, "He knows too much."

Gleason nodded. "So it seems," then he said, "hurry up and come out. I want you to help me with this bird."

Duffy stood there, his hands half raised, cursing himself for being so careless. The little note-book burnt in his pocket. It looked as if he were getting into a mighty tight jam.

Gleason said, "Come away from that gun."

Duffy turned slowly. "You don't mind if I sit down?" he said, moving over to an arm-chair. "Something tells me that I'm going to need a little rest."

Gleason watched him. "Don't pull anything," he said.

Duffy took a cigarette from the box on the table and thumbed the table lighter. He sat down, keeping his hands on the chair arms. He thought Gleason was a trifle jumpy. There was a little twitch going on at the corner of his mouth.

"You've pointed a gun at me before," he said.

"That was unfortunate. We were interrupted." Gleason sat on the corner of the table, swinging a long thin foot.

Annabel came out of the bathroom. She stood near Gleason. Her face was very hard, and her eyes were frightened.

Duffy looked at her, then he said, "What now?"

Gleason said, "I want that note-book."

Duffy nodded. "Sure, I can understand that. I told you before, it's in the mail."

Annabel said breathlessly, "He's lying."

Duffy shrugged. "You think so? Ask yourself, what would you do? I guessed it was important, so I put it in an envelope and posted it to an address in Canada. When I want it, I just write for it."

Gleason's eyes narrowed. "Maybe we could persuade you to write for it."

Duffy mashed the cigarette into the tray. "Meaning what?"

"We've got ways...."

"Be your age. You can't scare me. Do you think anything you can do to me would pry me loose from something I want? If you want to have that book, talk terms."

Gleason let the barrel of the Luger fall a shade. It pointed at Duffy's waistcoat. "How much?" he said.

Annabel said, "You mad?"

Gleason frowned at her. "Let me handle this."

Duffy studied his finger-nails. "What's it worth to you?" he said at last.

Gleason showed his teeth in a little grin. "I'd pay five hundred dollars for it," he said casually.

Duffy got to his feet slowly. "Okay," he said, "if that's all you rate it, why bother?"

Gleason jerked up the gun. "Sit down," he said, his voice suddenly harsh.

Duffy just looked at him. "Wake up, louse," he said evenly. "You've got nothing on me. That heater don't mean anything now."

Annabel said with a little hiss, "Shoot him low down."

Duffy glanced at her. "Hell," he said. "At one time I got a kick out of looking at you, you murderous little bitch."

Gleason got to his feet and stood hesitating. His face was almost bewildered. Duffy said to him, "I'm on my way. When you want that note-book back, give me a ring. I'm in the book."

Gleason said, "Wait."

Duffy shook his head. He wandered to the door. "You don't get anywhere by letting the gun off. You'll never find the book without me being around."

Gleason's arm dropped to his side. "Well, five grand," he said with an effort.

Duffy shook his head, he opened the door. "Don't rush it," he said, "take your time. Think about it. I'll wait." He pulled the door behind him and walked to the elevator. He suddenly felt very tired and his brain refused to think. He slid the grille and stepped into the elevator and pressed the ground-floor button.

Outside, he beckoned to a yellow cab, and in a short time he was again climbing the stairs to McGuire's apartment. He opened the door with his key and went in. The clock on the mantelpiece stood at 1:45. He tossed his hat on the sofa and wandered over to the apple-jack, that was still standing on the table. The bottle was light; it was nearly empty. He made a little face. Then he drained the bottle and put it down on the table again. He held his breath for a moment, then gently puffed out his cheeks. The stuff was good.

He stood perfectly still and listened. The apartment was very silent, except for a faint rumbling of Sam's snores. He lit a cigarette and tossed the match into the fireplace, then remembering Alice, he went over and picked it up, putting it carefully in the ash-tray.

With legs that felt rubbery with fatigue, he walked to the spare room and gently opened the door. The room was in darkness. He could hear Olga breathing softly.

He felt his way cautiously to the bed and flipped on the small reading-lamp, then he sat down on the bed gently.

Olga started up, her fists clenched and her lips formed into an "O." Duffy put his hand gently on her mouth. "Okay," he said softly. "Take it easy."

She looked at him and then lay back. "You scared me silly," she said.

"Quiet," he said, "I don't want the others to wake."

She looked from him to the clock and then back at him again. "It's so late… what is it?"

"Things are happening," he said. "I gotta talk to you. You know the spot you're in, don't you? Max has been knocked off. Someone paid him a visit and slit his throat for him."

The pupils of her eyes became very big. "You mean—?"

"I'm going to start from the beginning. Then you gotta fill in the gaps." He lay back a little, resting on his elbow. His battered face was drawn with fatigue. She suddenly felt a little pang of compassion for him.

"Take off your shoes and lie here beside me."

He shook his head. "I'd go to sleep," he said. "Now listen. There's a redhead called Annabel English, she's the daughter of Edwin English, the politician. She's wild and bad. One of her boy friends is this guy Weidmer. She has dealings with Cattley. This punk called on her and she tossed him down the elevator shaft. Right, before we go any further, you gotta tell me all you know about Cattley."

She said in a low voice, "Cattley was mixed up in a big dope traffic. He started off in a small way, peddling the stuff and taking a rake-off. That was when I knew him. Then he got big and began to make money. Weidmer was his boss. Gleason was the big shot. Cattley got tired of taking orders and he stole the list of customers—"

"Stop!" Duffy's voice sounded like the snap of a steel trap. He took the little note-book from his pocket and put it on the coverlet before her. "Is this the list?"

Her startled face told him. "So that's it," he said. He thumbed the book through. "Why, these guys can't operate without this list… the dope buyers must be hopping mad." He shut his eyes and tried to think.

"How… how did you get that?" she asked.

He opened his eyes. "I got it from Cattley's joint. Annabel came down to look for it, and I took it off her. This makes things pretty clear. Hell! They certainly operated in a big way. Look at those names, for God's sake."

She put her hand on his arm. "They'll get it away from you," she said, fear coming into her eyes. "It means millions to them."

Duffy turned on his elbow and looked at her. His tired eyes searched her face. "You know," he said, speaking slowly, "years ago, I used to think of being in a spot like this. To have the chance of grabbing a million dollars from a bunch of toughs. Well, I've got my chance. I'm going to play the ends against the middle."

"What do you mean?"

"If they find you've squawked, you're going to be washed up. I like you, honey. Will you come in on this with me?"

Her eyes became shrewd again. "How?"

"This guy Morgan," Duffy said, "you ain't heard about him. I can't quite see how he fits, except he's looking for easy dough."

She looked blank. "Morgan?"

Quickly and with economy, he told her about Morgan and the three toughs. "They thought they'd blackmail Annabel. It'd be good enough to publish a photo of Cattley and Annabel to upset old man English. I thought it was deeper than that. Gee! I gave her the benefit and thought they killed Cattley to pin it on her. All the time she had killed Cattley herself, and I was sucker enough to help her shift the body. Anyway, that's her funeral now. I'm selling the book to the highest bidder."

Olga said, "Why should Morgan want to buy it?"

Duffy grinned. "Use your head," he said. "This crowd here," he tapped the note-book, "is lousy with dough. They'd pay anything to hush up scandal. How'd it look if it got round that they traded in dope?"

She leant back in the bed and brooded. Then she said, "I believe you've got something."

Duffy put the note-book away. "You bet I've got something," he said. "Why not? Why the hell shouldn't I make a little dough out of these punks? Why shouldn't you?"

"How much will it be?" she asked.

"Fifty grand, hundred grand, anything."

She lay back flat, and ran her fingers through her thick hair. Duffy thought she was a very nice broad indeed. "We could do a lot with that money, couldn't we?" she said, her voice thrilling.

Duffy patted her hand. "Yeah," he said, "we could do a lot." He glanced at the clock and got stiffly to his feet. "I'm going to have a little sleep. There's action coming."

She put her hand on his arm. "You look so tired," she said.

He dug up a grin. "You're dead right, sister."

She lay there, her eyes very bright, and he could see the sudden rising and falling of her breasts under the sheet. She said, looking into his eyes, "I could make you better. Won't you come?"

He sat down on the bed again. "You're swell," he said. "Not tonight. Tomorrow we'll get out of here." He paused, then he nodded his head to the next room. "They're nice people. It wouldn't be fair on them. To-morrow."

He put his hand against her face. "Didn't you think Alice was swell?" He stepped away from the bed. "They mustn't know about this. This is between you and me."

She watched him go from the room, then turned out the light. She lay in the dark a long time, before she fell asleep.

Part Two

IT FINISHES

Chapter Nine

Duffy stepped into Ross's garage and looked round the dim shed. Ross came out of the little office at the far end of the shed. He was big and fat, with a glistening rubbery face. He plodded over the oily concrete, waving a short thick arm.

"Don't tell me," he wheezed when he saw Duffy. "Let me guess."

Duffy drew his lips off his teeth in a mirthless grin. "Ain't seen you for years," he said.

"I bet you're in a jam."

Duffy shook his head. "You're wrong," he said. "It ain't anything like that. I want to spend some dough with you."

Ross put his broad hand on Duffy's arm. "Well, well," he began, leading Duffy to the office. "I've got a bottle in there that'll suit you."

Duffy sat down in a basket chair and looked round the small box-like room. Ross nearly filled it.

"Getting' mighty hot, ain't it?" Ross said, bringing out a black bottle from his desk cupboard. He wiped the mouth of the bottle on his shirt-sleeve and pushed it over to Duffy. "You be careful of that liquor," he went on, "that's Tiger's sweat okay."

Duffy took a swig, rolling the liquor round his mouth before swallowing. Then he grunted a little. "Yeah," he said, "it's fierce."

Ross took the bottle from him and raised it to his lips. Duffy watched his Adam's apple jump in his fat throat. Ross put the bottle on the table, wiped his wet mouth on the back of his hand, and hitched his chair forward a little. "Now, what's the business?"

Duffy lit a cigarette and rolled another across the table to Ross. "You still got that old Buick around?" he asked.

Ross's little eyes opened a trifle. "You mean the armoured one?"

"That's it."

Ross nodded. "Sure I've got it."

"Does she run?"

Ross grinned. "Does she run? Listen, all my cans run. That bus's as good as new."

Duffy said, "I want to rent her for a bit."

Ross shrugged. "That's okay," he said simply. "Why not have my Packard? Now that's a swell job."

Duffy shook his head. He got to his feet. "I want the Buick," he said. "I might need a little protection from now on, and I'd feel a lot safer in the Buick."

Ross said, "I knew it, you're in a jam."

"Show me the wagon."

Ross led him out into the shed again. "That's her."

The Buick was just an ordinary-looking car, slightly shabby in the body, although she had been freshly washed down. Duffy looked her over thoughtfully. "Sell her to me," he said at last.

Ross took a quick look over his shoulder, then plodded over. "She looks the berries, don't she?" he said. He opened the door. "You try that."

Duffy had to make a strong effort to get the door to shut. "That's steel," Ross said. "Good thick stuff, see?" He opened the door again and climbed inside. Duffy leant against the door and put his head forward.

"The guy that threw this bus together knew all about it," Ross said, settling his hindquarters firmly on the padded seat. "The roof is armour plate. Take a look at the windows." He rolled one down. "Looks all right from the outside, but see how thick they are."

The glass was at least three-quarters of an inch in thickness.

"That'll bounce a .45 slug back at the guy who sent it," Ross said. He touched a spring in the dashboard and a small panel slid back. He put his hand inside and took out two Colt automatics. "You won't need these," he said. "I'll clear them out for you."

"Let 'em stay, they can go with the bus," Duffy said quietly.

Ross looked at him, pursed his fat mouth, then shrugged. He put the guns back. "Under the seat there's four hundred rounds."

Duffy said, "For the love of Mike."

Ross grinned. "I ain't had time to shift the stuff. It's been in there some time."

"It's a fine job. Anything else?"

Ross climbed out of the car again. "The radiator grill is bullet-proof. The engine is protected with plate. The rear window rises from the bottom, so you can operate a gun if you wanted to. And the tyres are filled with puncture-healing liquid which fills any holes immediately if a slug finds its way there. That cab is certainly a swell job for trouble."

Duffy pushed his hat to the back of his head. "Yeah, I guess it's right up my street. What you want for her, Ross?"

Ross scratched his bald head. "What you got, buddy?" he asked. "You done things for me in the past...."

Duffy said, "I'll give you thirty bucks a week for her."

Ross shook his head. "Too much," said. "I'll take twenty."

Duffy took forty dollars from his pocket-book and handed them over. "I'll take her for a couple of weeks," he said. "Fill her up, will you?"

Ross pushed the money into his trouser pocket. "She's ready to go."

Duffy opened the door and got in. "I'll be seeing you, pal," he said.

Ross put his fat face through the window frame. "Take it easy with the cannons," he said anxiously. "They ain't registered, but take it easy all the same."

Duffy nodded at him and engaged the clutch. The Buick rolled out into the street. Duffy drove to his bank, cashed a cheque for a thousand dollars, checked his deposit and went back to the car again. With the thousand on him, and three thousand in the bank, he could last a little while, he thought.

Olga was waiting for him at "Stud's Parlour," a quiet little bar just off East 164th Street. When he drove up, she ran out and he pushed open the off door for her. She got in, and he had to lean over her to slam the door shut. "That's stiff," she said.

"It's steel," he grinned, pulling away from the curb. "This tub's from Chi. They know how to build 'em there."

She was silent for a half a block, then she said, "You expecting trouble?"

"Trouble'll blow up sooner or later in a racket like this. I like to be prepared for it." He pushed the Buick past a big truck, then he said, "You ain't going to get scared?"

She shook her head. "I don't scare easily." She put her neat gloved hand to her throat. She was wearing a high-necked blouse. "Your friends were swell," she said as an afterthought.

Duffy nodded. "I'm a heel all right," he said. "I told Alice I was seeing you on the train for your home."

Olga said, "You couldn't let them in on this?"

Duffy shook his head. "They've got each other. They don't give a damn for money; why should they? It's punks like you and me that ain't got anchors that think money's the tops."

She shot a quick glance at him. "You're not feeling sore?" she ventured.

Duffy shook his head again. "No, not sore. I've started this, so I'm finishing it. If I don't get away with it, it don't matter. If I do, well, I'll spend what I get, and think I'm having a swell time."

She said in a low voice, "And me?"

Duffy put his hand on her knee. "You're okay, baby, you'll get what you want."

He pulled up outside his apartment. "Come on in and see how you like your new home."

They went upstairs, and she stood waiting for him to open the door. Inside the small apartment they stood and looked at each other, then she turned her head quickly and walked over to the window. "I like this," she said. "It's nice, isn't it?"

Duffy threw his hat on the chair and brought out a bottle of rum. "You like Bacardi?" he said.

"Yes, but it's early yet, isn't it?"

Duffy took two glasses and poured out the rum. He went over to her and put the glass in her hand. "To you and to me and to dough," he said.

The Bacardi went down smooth, leaving a hot ball of fire burning inside them.

"Take your hat off, honey," he said, "this is your home now."

She said, "Is that the bedroom over there?"

"That's it. Go ahead and have a look." He was surprised to find his hands were trembling. He watched her walk slowly across the room and into the bedroom. Her long legs and flat hips had a lazy movement, but there was an electric tension that radiated from her.

He followed her and stood just behind her, looking at her in the mirror. She raised her eyes, studied his face, then she turned quickly.

He put his hands on her hips and drew her to him. "You're swell," he said. "I've known you twenty-four hours, but it seems a lifetime. I bet you're bad. I bet you've loved, but I don't care."

She said, "I've been all that and more." She took his hands in hers, held them for a moment, then pushed them away from her. She went over to the bed and sat down.

Duffy shifted away from the mirror and leant over the back of the bed. "We've got to get together," he said. "Tell me about yourself."

She turned her head and looked at him. "Isn't it unwise?" she said.

Duffy shook his head. "I want to know," he said.

"I was born in a small Montana town." Her voice was flat and expressionless. "Living there was like living in a morgue. Nothing ever happened. The sun shone, the dust collected on the dry roads, carts came and went, nothing ever happened. I used to get fan magazines and read about Hollywood. Millions of other girls have done the same. I thought if I got to Hollywood, I'd get a break. I dreamed Hollywood, lived Hollywood, and I guess I even slept Hollywood. Well, one day I took my chance. I waited until my Pa had gone into the fields, then I took all his money—it wasn't much—and I blew. I never got to Hollywood. My dough gave out when I hit Oakland. I got a job as a hostess in a dance hall there."

Duffy came round and sat on the bed close beside her.

"I had to be nice to the men at the bar. Talk to them, kid them along, and get them to buy drinks. They paid me commission on the drinks. It didn't last long. The boss called on me one night, and then I hadn't anything to take care of after he had been over me. Well, you know how it is, once on the slide, you can't stop."

Duffy said, "How long ago was this?"

"About eight years. I was seventeen then. I ran into a guy named Vernor. How that guy kidded me! He certainly could paint a picture. He showed me how I could make money so fast that I'd get dizzy. Pretty clothes, motor-cars, jewellery, and all the rest of it. Just by selling myself three or four times a night. I fell for it. What did it matter, so long as I could get enough dough to get out of the game in a year or so?

"He got me into a house in Watsonville, one of the northern Californian towns, and once I was there I knew what a sucker I'd been. I just couldn't get away. They never gave me any money. They kept my clothes from me. They threatened me with the police; in fact, they had me."

Duffy grunted, "A sweet life you've had."

She was silent for a moment, then she went on. "I didn't see a white man for three years. Filipinos, Hindus and Chinks, yes, but no white man."

Duffy moved restlessly. He didn't like this.

"Just when I was giving up, along came Cattley. Can you imagine that? Cattley came into my room, and I was expecting another of those fierce little brown men. Cattley fell for me, and I gave him everything I had. He thought I could be useful to him, so he got me out of the place and set me up in that little house."

Duffy said, "How could you be useful to a guy like Cattley?"

Her face hardened a little. "I'm telling you everything, aren't I?" she said.

Duffy leant back on his elbows. "Sure, and it don't sound so good."

She lifted her shoulders wearily. "It isn't good. In Cattley's business he had to have a woman around. He got me to play hostess to his suckers. I got him introductions to the upper set. It was through me that he made so much money. Cattley was on the level with me. He gave me plenty." She sighed, twisting her hands. "Now the poor mug's dead."

In the other room the telephone began to ring. Duffy made no move to answer it.

Olga said, "What's the matter? Don't you want to answer it?"

"Let it ring," he said, looking at her.

The telephone stopped ringing.

She stood facing him, then she said, "Yes… yes… yes."

He reached out and pulled her roughly to him. "I'm crazy about you," he said, his lips hard against her throat.

The telephone began to ring again. It rang for a long time, then it stopped. A fly buzzed busily from room to room, hitting the window with distinct little plops.

On the bed, Duffy lay, his eyes half shut, feeling the muscles of his body running into liquid. Olga went to sleep. Duffy watched her. Time meant nothing to him. He was quite content to look at her. Her body was strong and white. Her flesh was firm. He thought she looked good.

He put out his hand gently and touched her hair. She stirred and opened her eyes. She smiled at him.

Duffy said, "You've got me. You've got me hard."

"I want to go away with you," she said, putting her hand on his arm. "I want to get away from all this. You won't let me down, now?" She said "now" very urgently.

Duffy shook his head. "It'll be all right, you'll see."

The telephone began to ring insistently.

Olga sat up. A little shiver ran through her. She said, "No, don't go. Leave it."

Duffy hesitated, then got off the bed. He looked at her for a moment, smiled, then went into the other room. He took the receiver off the prong.

"What is it?" he said sharply.

"Gleason talking," came the harsh purring voice.

Duffy pulled a chair up and sat down. His eyes and mouth were suddenly hard. "Okay," he said, "I didn't expect you so soon."

"I've been ringing for some time." There was just a hint of nerves in Gleason's voice.

"Well, you got me now."

"I'll buy that thing from you for fifteen grand," Gleason said with a rush.

Duffy grinned into the 'phone. "I must be getting deaf," he said. "It sounded like you said fifteen grand."

Gleason was silent for a minute, then he said, "I can't go higher than that. Fifteen grand."

"What the hell kind of a cheap punk are you? Ain't you aching to get that list back? The list is worth that much as State evidence."

"Now listen," Duffy could almost see Gleason squeezing the telephone with excitement, "I can't lay my hands on any more dough. I'll make you a fair offer. Fifteen grand and five per cent cut on the business."

"Aw, use your head," Duffy shifted forward in his chair a little. "I ain't so dumb. What's five per cent cut to a corpse? I wouldn't trust you, Gleason, for a second. Once you had that list, you'd bust your guts to iron me out. No, it's cash or nothing."

Gleason said, "You goddam sonofabitch."

"Skip it. You don't know what you're up against. I've got another buyer in the market. You're going to pay plenty for that list, or the other guy gets it."

There was a heavy silence at the other end, and Duffy reached over for a cigarette. He had nothing to do, and plenty of time to do it in.

Then Gleason said, "That's the way you're going to play it, huh?"

"You got it. Ends against the middle. I ain't in a hurry, but you'd better start revising your ideas."

"You're going to find yourself in a heap of trouble," Gleason said. His voice was suddenly steady. He seemed no longer excited. "I'd play ball on the level, Duffy, or…."

"Listen, you yellow punk, you can't throw a scare into me. I know just where I've got you. Start the bidding at fifteen grand if you like, but the price is going to the roof." He dropped the receiver back on the prong and sat back.

Olga came out of the bedroom. She was still nude. "Are you handling this right?" she asked.

Duffy went over to her and put his hands round her back. "This is the way it's going to go," he said. "It'll take a little time, but it'll yield the most dough."

She looked up into his face. "Can't you trust him?"

Duffy shook his head. "It's going to be tricky getting away with the dough," he said, "but you watch me, we'll beat 'em."

She leant against him. "I didn't care what happened, but I do now. I don't want you to get into a jam after this."

He led her back into the bedroom. "Put on a wrap," he said. "I can't think with you like that."

He watched her undo the small case she had brought with her, and find a wrap, then he helped her put it on.

They went back into the sitting-room again. Olga lit a cigarette, drawing down the smoke and holding it. She said, "You're hatching something, what is it?"

Duffy took from his inside pocket a little note-book and put it on the table. Then he brought out another book, identical with the first. He laid it beside the other.

Olga looked at them closely, then released a cloud of smoke down her nostrils. "A double-cross," she said.

"You've got it." Duffy drew up a chair and sat down. I'm showing you how dough's made." He took out a fountain-pen and began to copy the list of names from the first book into the second.

She sat on the edge of the table and watched him. "Someone's going to get mighty sore about this," she said at last.

Duffy didn't look up. He went on writing, but he said, "We won't be there to see 'em."

When he had finished the list, he went back again to the beginning and studied the pages. "You know what these numbers stand for? Look, Max

Hughson 5. Johnny Alvis 7. Trudie Irvine 4."

She leant over his shoulder. "Payments," she told him. "Hughson used to pay five thousand dollars a month for his dope and protection."

"That's plenty. Why protection?"

Olga swung her long legs. "That was Gleason's way. These birds aren't real hopheads. They just play at it. Gleason sold them the dope, then warned them that someone was on to them, and it would cost them so much to hush it up. He only had to put the screw on a little, scare them to hell, and show them that he could warn off all comers, to get himself put on their pension list."

Duffy did sums, then he looked up. "This little book is worth five hundred grand to a cool million, if they all pay."

Olga nodded. "When I was with Cattley and he was working it, they mostly did pay," she said.

Duffy grinned. "It's easy to make money, if you know how," he said, getting to his feet. "Well, we'll see what Morgan's got to say."

She slid off the table. "What are you doing with the books?" she asked.

"You shall have one and I'll have the other." He gave her the copy. "Be careful with that."

She held the book in her hand for a moment, looking at him very hard, then she smiled and put the book in his hand.

"What's this?"

She said, "I hoped you would do that. I just wanted to see if you trusted me. It's screwy to keep this where it could be lifted. Keep it."

He said, "Well, I'll be goddamned." But she looked so pleased that he took the book and put it with the other in his inside pocket.

She said, "You're not going to Morgan alone. I'm coming with you."

He thought for a moment, then he nodded. "Oke, but you stay outside in the bus. We'll plant the lists at my bank on the way down."

She ran into the bedroom to change. Duffy called to her. "I'll get Morgan's address from the *Tribune*. They'll be bound to know it."

While he 'phoned, he vaguely heard her in the bathroom, and when he had got the address from the reporters' room, he wandered in. She was standing under the cold shower, holding her face up to the tingling pinpoints of water. Her eyes were closed, and she held her breasts cupped in her hands.

Duffy leant forward and turned the wheel on hard. The cold water struck her fiercely, and she ducked away, gasping. Duffy grabbed a towel and wrapped her in it.

"Get busy," he said, "we ain't got all day."

She mopped her face, then stepped out of the bath. "Try it," she said, "it's nice."

Duffy shook his head. "Later," he said. "I've got the money itch."

She took off the rubber cap that protected her hair and threw it at him. The drops of water splashed his face. Duffy aimed a smack at her, then he jerked her to him and kissed her.

He thought, "We're behaving like a couple of kids."

She said, looking up at him, "Will you always be kind to me?"

He gripped her arms suddenly, hurting her. "Let's go," he said, "there's work to be done." And he left her, standing quite still, holding the towel round her, with a little bewildered look in her eyes.

Chapter Ten

Duffy left the Buick at the curb and climbed the five flat steps to the front door. Morgan's house was in a big way. Duffy was quite surprised. He expected something good, but this was a lot better than good.

The front door was a plate-glass affair, plastered with wrought iron. The bell had to be reached for and pulled down, like the plumbing in an old-fashioned toilet.

Duffy called back to Olga, who was sitting in the car, "Some Joint." He self-consciously jerked the bell-pull hard.

Clive opened the door.

Duffy said, "Tell your Queen I want to see him."

Clive threw up his hands and backed away from the door. He said in a shrill voice, "You get out…." Duffy pushed the door wide open, but he stayed where he was. He said in a level voice, "Get going or I'll start on you."

Clive slid his hand inside his coat, and Duffy took a quick step forward and smacked Clive across the face.

The little guy said from the head of the stairs, "Don't hit him again. He'll be all right."

Clive took his hand away from his coat and backed farther away. A high whinnying sound was coming from his mouth. Duffy said, "Why don't you take this bum away?"

The little guy came down the stairs. He wore his hat pulled down. Duffy couldn't imagine him without that hat.

Duffy said, "Where's Morgan?"

The little guy was very cautious, he did not get too close to Duffy. He said with a thin smile, "You surprised him."

Duffy said, "I don't care about that. I came to see Morgan."

The little guy turned his head to speak to Clive. "You heard him?" he said. "He came to see Morgan."

Duffy reached forward and grabbed the little guy by the coat-front. His eyes were like granite. "Cut this circus stuff of yours out."

The little guy pushed an automatic hard into Duffy's vest. "Don't get tough, Mister," he said.

Duffy took his hand away, and stepped back a little. He said, "Put that rod up and use your head."

The little guy said to Clive, "Tell Morgan."

Duffy stood there watching the little guy thoughtfully.

The little guy said hopefully, "You ain't going to start trouble, are you?"

Duffy shook his head. "Your daffodil went for her gun," he said. "I wouldn't stand for a thing like that."

The little guy giggled. "You'd like Clive once you got to know him," he said.

Duffy still stood motionless. "Suppose you put that heater away," he said evenly. "This ain't the time for pop-guns."

The little guy shoved the gun into his shoulder-holster. "I get nervous sometimes," he said, waving his hands apologetically.

A door at the end of the hall opened and Morgan came out. He called, "Come in here."

Duffy walked the length of the hall slowly. Then he entered the room. Morgan was standing just inside. Across the room, Joe leant against the wall, chasing holes in his teeth with a wooden pick.

Duffy nodded at Morgan.

Joe said, "Why, for the love of Mike, here's the pip back again."

Morgan half raised his hand, stopping Joe. He said, "Have you brought the photos after all, Mr. Duffy?"

Duffy said, "Clear your thugs out, I want to talk to you."

"Shall I pat him around?" Joe asked. "He likes it, and can he take it?"

Morgan said, "Wait outside."

Joe shrugged, but he went out, passing close to Duffy. As he passed, he pushed his flat face into Duffy's and grinned. "Nice boy, ain't you?" he said.

Duffy didn't move. "Your breath's bad," was all he said. Joe shut the door behind him, then Duffy walked over to a big arm-chair and sat down. He didn't remove his hat. Morgan leant against the overmantel and waited.

"We're due for a talk, ain't we?" Duffy said.

Morgan took out a cigar case, selected a long thin Havana, put it between his small teeth, bit off the end neatly and spat the end into the empty grate. He put the cigar case back in his pocket.

Duffy said, "I'll smoke too."

Morgan looked at him. His hooded eyes were very hostile. "Not mine, you won't. You talk."

Duffy shrugged and took a cigarette from his case. "If that's how you feel…."

Morgan hid his face behind thick smoke as he lit the cigar. "You've still got five hundred bucks of mine," he said.

Duffy nodded. "Sure," he took his wallet out and counted out five one-hundred bills, then tossed them on the table. "I've been keeping them for you."

Morgan's face was quite blank. He looked hard at the five bills, then he put his hands behind him, and raised himself slightly on his toes. "That came as a surprise," he said, "I thought you were taking me for a ride."

Duffy said, "That's scent money; buy your nance a present."

Morgan stiffened. "You watch your mouth," he said in a thick voice.

"Let's skip this, and get down to things. I've been wanting a talk with you for some time. When you sent me out on that phoney photo stunt of yours, I fell right into trouble, and I've been that way ever since. I'm getting to like it, and I'm seeing quite a bit of dough hanging to it. You play ball with me now, and you're going to get into something that's going to make your ears flap. Let's get this straight. You wanted to put the screws on Edwin English, through his daughter, ain't that the way it goes?"

Morgan stared at him for several minutes, his eyes expressionless, then he said, "Suppose it was?"

"If I'd turned in those photos of Cattley and the girl together, you could have cracked down on English. You could have warned him off your rackets, and he would have had to like it."

Morgan wandered over to a chair and sat down, but he didn't say anything.

"You know Murray Gleason?"

A flicker of surprise went over Morgan's face. "Yeah, I know him."

"What do you know about him?"

"Where's this leading?" Morgan was suddenly impatient.

"I'll tell you. Gleason is running a big dope racket amongst some of the real big shots in the upper circle. He's got them so short that they're screaming murder. That guy has a pension from them of nearly a million bucks. Did you know that?"

Morgan shook his head. His thick lips curled a little. "That ain't true," he said. "Gleason is only a cheap peddler—was when last I knew him."

Duffy laughed. "You're out of date," he said. "Gleason's moved into the big-shot class, but he's smart enough to keep it to himself. He stands no chance of having any political boss smacking his ears down for him."

Morgan said at last, "I ain't interested in Gleason."

Duffy nodded. "Sure you ain't," he agreed, "but you'd like his racket, wouldn't you?"

"When I want his racket I'll take it," Morgan said, tapping the long ash into the tray.

Duffy leant back and studied the ceiling. "Gleason's had a list of all his customers and the amounts they pay for protection," he said.

Morgan looked up sharply. "You said 'had'?"

Duffy still didn't take his eyes from the ceiling. "Sure, that's right. I've got it now."

Morgan sat silent, then he said, "I see."

Duffy said, "It's in the market right now."

Morgan became elaborately casual. Duffy nearly laughed at him. "It might be useful," he said.

Duffy said, "You ain't got the idea quite." He spoke carefully, as if to a child. "This English girl is tied up with Gleason. She's as wild and crazy as a loon. These two are working this racket between them. And they're making plenty out of it. With the list, you can smash their little game, put English on the spot, and have three hundred big shots pouring their dough into your lap, just to keep out of it."

Morgan chewed on his cigar. "The way you're putting it, it sounds good," he said.

"It is good. That's why I'm offering it to you."

"What have I done?"

"You got the dough."

"How much?"

"Fifty grand," Duffy said. "I don't mean thirty, or forty. It's worth fifty, and it's fifty I want."

Morgan shrugged his shoulders slightly. "I guess you'd never peddle that for that amount of dough," he said.

Duffy stood up. "Okay," he said, "I'll get the money from the other side. Why should I worry?"

"Wait. You've overlooked something." Morgan looked foxy. "You've given me some nice information. I don't doubt that. Think, would you pay that much money? You forget, I've got three guys who're eating their heads off for a job. I ain't paying fancy prices for a thing like that. Do you know what I'd do if had a list like that?"

Duffy said, "What would you do?"

Morgan grinned. He looked like a wolf. "What you've done. Make a duplicate and sell it to both sides."

Duffy's face was quite blank. "It's an idea," he said, considering it.

Morgan shook his head. "It was a pip of an idea, but not now. When you've sold that list to Gleason, I'll call on him and take it away from him."

Duffy said, with a hard smile, "You're pretty sure of yourself, ain't you?"

Morgan raised his fat shoulders again. "And I'll tell you something else," he went on, flicking his ash into the tray, "I'll send Joe to collect that fifty grand off you, when Gleason has paid it. That ought to show you."

Duffy moved to the door. "I guess you and I won't get on so well in the future," he said sadly. "I'm sorry about that."

"You will be," Morgan said very gently.

Duffy opened the door. Joe was standing just outside. Duffy looked over his shoulder at Morgan. "There ain't anything more now, is there?"

Morgan shook his head. Then a thought crossed his mind and he said, "Wait."

Duffy stood still. He didn't turn his back to Joe, but stood three-quarters, so that he could watch Joe from the corner of his eye. "Yeah?" he said.

Morgan picked up the five bills from the table. "Suppose you take these and give me the list?"

"What for?" Duffy was quite startled.

"You can't break into the game," Morgan said. "You're soft. What've you got that'll stand up against an outfit like mine? Get wise to yourself, you little heel. Where's the dough coming for your protection? Who's going to work for an out-of-work button-pusher? You must be nuts to come to me with a proposition like that. Here, give me the list and take the five hundred bucks. That's what you're worth, and save yourself a lot of grief."

Duffy's expression didn't change, but his eyes went suddenly frosty. "Soft? Was that it?" he said.

Morgan shrugged. "I've wasted enough time with you. Scram, I'll do the job myself." He put the five bills into his pocket. Then he looked up quickly. "I want that list tonight," he said evenly. "You can't buck the rap. The list tonight, or I'll turn Joe loose on you."

Duffy nodded; he stepped past Joe carefully, who grinned at him, then he walked to the front door and down the steps. Olga looked at him and said, "So it didn't work."

Duffy engaged the gear and drove the Buick down the block. He began to swear softly under his breath, without moving his lips. Olga laced her fingers round her knees and stared ahead. Duffy swung the Buick into Seventh Avenue and went with the traffic. He cut right at Longacre Square and drove into Central Park. When he reached the lake, he stalled the engine and stopped.

Olga said, "Don't get mad."

For a moment he said nothing, then he took off his hat and tossed it at the back of the car. "Those birds certainly got me going," he said. A grim little smile came to his mouth, and she liked him a lot better.

"Tell me," she said.

He screwed round in his seat, so that he was facing her, and took her gloved hands in his. "This is going to get tough," he said. "You'd better skip before the war starts."

Her eyes narrowed slightly. "Suppose you cut out the hysterics and tell me."

Duffy said, "Morgan wants the list. I'm to hand it over tonight or else…."

Olga said, "No dough?"

Duffy nodded. "That's right. No dough."

She was silent for a minute. "And then…?"

"Morgan's got big ideas. He thinks he's the only big shot round here. He told me to lay off the big dough with a few compliments on the side."

Olga took her hands away and began to pull off her gloves. "I expected it, didn't you?" she said. "Does this dough mean anything to you?"

Duffy said, "How do you mean, anything?"

"High-pressure bastards like Morgan can't imagine you're serious. You've got to have a reputation as a killer to get away with a proposition that you've put up."

Duffy said, "For God's sake, what can I do?"

She leant forward, touched the spring on the dashboard, and took out the Colt automatic. "A rat less won't make any difference. Pop him, before he pops you."

Duffy looked at the gun with distaste. He shook his head. "No," he said, "I guess I wouldn't go that far."

For a moment she sat very still, then she said, "He's right. You're soft and you're yellow."

Duffy took the gun from her and put it back into the panel. He sat looking at the knife-edge crease of his trousers. "No dough's worth murder," he said. "If you and me are going to get along, we got to think the same way."

She put her hand on his arm. "I guess I'm a heel," she said.

"Forget it," he said. "You're fine."

"You go ahead. The next move's yours."

"Let's take Gleason for a ride. If we get some dough out of him, we can scram to the coast. Would you like that? Some nice hot place with plenty of yellow sand. With a sky a real blue and just you and me?"

She leant back. "It sounds pretty good."

"It would be a lot better than having the cops chasing you and getting that nice little bottom of yours burnt. Come on, honey, let's look Gleason up."

He started the engine and drove out of Central Park, down Second Avenue.

She said, "Go along the river. It's nice there."

He turned left when he could and came out at Bellevue Hospital. They drove with the traffic as far as the Williamsburg Bridge, then Duffy spun the wheel and they headed East.

They got back to his apartment just as the evening sun was dropping behind the roofs, throwing long, starved shadows.

They left the Buick at the curb and walked up the stairs together. Duffy said, "It seems a mighty long time since I had my last drink."

"How about putting on the glad rags and taking me out?" she asked.

He put his hand on her back and pushed her a little. "These stairs are hell, ain't they? Sure, we'll go places, but I want Gleason first."

He opened the door of the apartment and they walked in together. Then Duffy said, "Well…."

The room was a complete shambles. The furniture was overturned, drawers had been jerked out and left piled on the floor, the contents strewn over the carpet. The overstuffed furniture had been ripped to pieces and the stuffing dumped in piles. Pictures had been taken down from the walls and were lying with their backs cut. A tornado had certainly hit that room.

Duffy said gently, "Gleason trying to save himself some dough."

Olga wandered round the room, stepping carefully. "That was a swell idea of yours about the bank."

Duffy nodded. His face was hard and cold. "I'll fix that smart bastard," he said.

She said, "There's time for that. You'd better move over to my place."

He looked round the wreckage. "I guess it don't really matter. We're due to pull out tomorrow, so what the hell." He wandered into his bedroom and looked round with a grimace. The room had been searched as thoroughly as the sitting-room. There was a lot more mess, because the mattress and the pillows had been ripped.

Olga peered round the door. "Our love-bed's been destroyed."

"To hell with that," Duffy said. "They've stolen my whisky." He dug about under the bed and dragged out two battered suitcases covered with feathers. "Get going," he said. "Do some work for a change."

Just then the telephone bell began to ring, and he went over to answer it, leaving her sorting his shirts and things from the wreckage.

It was Sam at the other end.

"Why, Sam," Duffy was pleased. "I'm glad you 'phoned."

"Listen, you bum," Sam sounded excited. "Don't tell me you let that hot mamma go home to her people."

Duffy said softly into the 'phone, "She's in the other room."

Sam groaned. "That dame'll get you into trouble. Look, Bill, for God's sake chuck this thing, will you? I've heard the *Post* will give you a job, right up your street, and a swell equipment on the side."

Duffy said, "Thanks, pal, but I'm on to something big. Not peanut money, but the right stuff. I'm getting out tomorrow and I'm hitting the coast. When I've spent it all, I'll be back. Olga and me are getting on fine."

Sam said, "Alice'll kill me if I don't bring you back tonight. She told me to drag you by the short hairs."

"It's time you left Alice, if that's the way she's talking." Duffy grinned. "No, I'm going ahead. When we're in the money, we'll invite you over."

"It's on the level?" Sam sounded worried.

"Is any big dough on the level?" Duffy asked. "Don't you sweat about me, I'm okay."

Sam said, "I'm going to have a sweet time with Alice tonight."

"Tell her about Olga. She'll understand. Tell her Olga's swell. She won't expect me then."

"Is she?" Sam sounded curious.

"Is she what?"

"Swell."

"O boy! Listen, that honey's—" Duffy broke off as Olga walked into the room. "Well, Sam, I'll be seeing you. Don't do anything you wouldn't like me to know about." He dropped the receiver on to the prong.

Olga smiled at him. "I heard. I'm glad."

"You packed my things?"

"Just finished. There's so much junk."

"Leave it. We ain't coming back."

He put his arms round her. "I like you a lot," he said.

She pulled his face down to hers hungrily. "Was I really good for you?" she whispered.

He said, "Huh-uh."

She put her mouth against his neck. "Best of all?" she asked, taking a little of his skin between her teeth.

He pressed her to him and said, "Sure, best of all."

They stood there for a long time, just holding each other. Duffy liked the feel of her hair against his face. Then he pushed her away gently, holding her at arm's length. "I wonder if we've been crazy, going for a gang like Morgan's," he said. "I could get a job right now, and we could settle down."

"Play Gleason and we'll skip," she said.

Duffy shrugged. He walked over to his bags and closed them, pulling the straps down hard. "Yeah," he said, "you ain't Alice, are you?"

She looked puzzled. "Alice?" she said. "Who's Alice?"

Duffy grinned at her, but his mind was not with her.

"Oh, nothing—she's a sucker. Dough don't mean a thing to her. It's love in a poorhouse with her."

Olga shrugged. "That type's nearly dead," she said a little scornfully, "but you find 'em sometimes."

Duffy stood looking round the room, holding the bags in either hand. He stood there so long that Olga touched his arm.

"Let's go, hophead," she said.

Duffy said, "Sure." He walked to the door and then stopped again. "I ain't ever going to see this joint again," he said.

Olga pushed past him into the corridor. "Who cares?" she asked, walking down the stairs.

Duffy looked after her, put one of the bags on the floor, shut the door, picked the bag up again, and followed her down.

Chapter Eleven

Back at Olga's villa, Duffy immediately put through a call to Annabel. While he was waiting for the connection, Olga began packing. Duffy could hear her moving about in the bedroom, overhead, singing in a husky monotone, but with plenty of swing with it.

The line connected with a little plop, and he said, "Hullo."

Annabel's breathless voice floated to his ear. "Who is it?" she asked.

Duffy said, "Your boy friend there? This is Duffy."

"You're going to make a bad move soon," she said fiercely, "and I'm going to get a big laugh when you fall down."

Duffy said, "I ain't got time to talk to you just now, hot pants. Get Gleason."

She said very evenly, "They put smart guys like you in a gasoline bath and drop in a match."

Gleason must have taken the 'phone from her. Duffy heard him say, "Pipe down, for Gawd's sake."

"Gleason?" Duffy asked.

"Yeah. You ready to play ball?"

"Sure, I'm ready to trade. Competition wasn't so hot. They offered forty grand, no more, no less. It's yours for fifty."

Gleason raved, "How the hell can I get fifty grand together?"

Duffy's mouth shaped into a smile, but his eyes were mirthless. "I'm moving out tomorrow first thing," he said. "I don't care who has the list, but I want somebody's cash tonight. Fifty grand ain't all that big, for an outfit like yours."

Gleason said, "You're going to pay for this, you sonofabitch."

Duffy said, "Not until I get the dough and you get the book. After that, we'll all have to watch out."

Gleason was silent for a moment. Then he said, "I can't bring cash; I'll make it a certified cheque."

"Cash," Duffy's voice was hard. "I'm feeding at the 'Red Ribbon' tonight around eighty-thirty. If you ain't there by the time I'm through the deal's off. And it's gotta be cash." He dropped the receiver back and went upstairs.

Olga was kneeling before a large cabin trunk. The floor was strewn with her clothes.

Duffy said, "For God's sake…."

She turned her head and smiled at him. "Come and help," she said.

He looked at the small clock on the mantelshelf. From where he stood he could just make out the tiny hands. It was six-thirty. He put his hands under her elbows and brought her to her feet.

"Listen, baby," he said patiently, "this is going to be a quick journey. Leave all this junk. Just pack a bag. I'll buy you the world when we're out of this."

She made a little face. "They're so lovely." She turned and looked at the things lying about.

"Come on," he urged, "time's moving."

Together, they packed two large grips. Then Duffy went downstairs. He went into the kitchen and found a full bottle of Scotch. Taking two glasses, he went upstairs again. Putting the bottle on the small table by the bed he said, "Let's have a drink."

Olga came over and tore off the tissue wrapping round the bottle and flipped up the patent stopper. She splashed three inches of whisky into each glass.

Duffy said, "To us," and they drank. "We're feeding at the 'Red Ribbon' tonight."

She added some ginger ale to the whisky.

"And then…?"

"Gleason might bring the dough. I think he will. If he does, we get in the Buick and get out of town quick."

"And the lists?"

He nodded. "Sure, I ain't forgotten them. I'm going to collect right now. I'll be gone about half an hour. You change. Put on something you can travel in."

She came over to him and put her arms tightly round his neck.

"What's this?" he asked.

She raised herself on her toes and whispered urgently in his ear. He looked at the clock, then he shook his head. "Not now," he said gently.

Her cool arms tightened, pulling his head down. "Please…" she said, very low. "Now."

He put his lips gently on hers and pressed her to him, but his mind was elsewhere. He was thinking of Gleason, of Morgan, of the money, of how he was going to slip out of town. He was surprised at her. He thought this was a hell of a time to start a thing like this.

Then he put up his hands and took her arms from his neck, and pushed her away, still holding her arms.

"Tonight," he said firmly. "Look at the time. I've gotta get to the bank."

A faint colour came to her face, and she didn't look at him. She turned away. "The bank will be shut, won't it?" she said, still keeping her back to him. He noticed how toneless her voice was.

"Yeah, but I fixed that. There's an audit that's keeping 'em late. The teller there's a pal of mine. I warned him I might want the list late."

He wandered over to her. "You ain't sore with me?" he said gently, putting his arms round her.

She turned her head. She was still flushed. "No. I'm not sore." Then she said fiercely, "If only it were all over. If only we were out of this with the money, and safe."

Duffy said, "Now don't go into a spin. It's going to work out okay, you see."

"But you don't know," she said, her breasts suddenly rising and falling. "Bill, you don't know. I've been through so much… and—and now I've found you. I'm frightened it won't be all right."

Duffy said, "Hey! You don't want to get worked up. I tell you, we'll get away with it. We're going to have a fine time. We're going to be in the dough. You and me. We're going to have dough to burn… you see."

She said quite quietly, "I feel something horrible's going to happen."

Duffy said, "Skip it, honey. The Scotch's got hold of you." He kissed her and he had to push her gently from him. Then he walked to the door. "I shan't be long," he said over his shoulder, and shut the door behind him.

She stood motionless where he had left her, then she suddenly said in a low voice, "Come back, I'm scared. Bill, come back…."

Out in the street, Duffy paused to light a cigarette. He threw the match from him and climbed into the Buick. As he started the engine he saw in his driving-mirror a big Packard turn into the street and drive slowly towards him. He glanced at it and then engaged his gear. His mind was still brooding on his future plans.

Pushing the pedal down, he drove the Buick fast. The Packard vanished from his mirror, and he thought no more about it.

At the bank there was a slight delay. Duffy had trouble in convincing the watchman that he had arranged to speak to the teller. The watchman was a stolid Irishman, with a big, beefy face, and not much brain.

Duffy took him through the explanation slowly again. "Sure," the watchman nodded his head, "But this joint's closed, see?" He said the last word with obvious triumph.

Duffy said bleakly, "Listen, punk, get going and tell Anscombe I'm here, or I'll get you fired."

The watchman blinked at him, then thinking it wouldn't hurt him to inquire, he grumblingly left Duffy to cool his heels in the street. He came back again, after a delay that infuriated Duffy, and opened the iron-studded door.

"Come in," he said shortly. "This is mighty irregular."

Duffy stepped in and stood waiting. A flustered clerk came over to him and Duffy nodded at him. "I want that note-book I deposited," he said shortly.

"Sure," the clerk said. "Mr. Anscombe's getting it for you."

Anscombe came out of his office at the end of the hall and waved. He walked towards Duffy with a springy step. In his hand was the note-book.

"This is what you want, isn't it?" he said. "I got it out as soon as the janitor brought me your name. Take it and give me a receipt. I'm doing you a favour. We oughtn't to do business as late as this."

Duffy took the note-book, glanced at it, put it in his pocket and scribbled his name on the slip of paper Anscombe held out to him.

"Much obliged," he said. "I want this in a hurry, and it's worth something."

Anscombe came with him to the door. He seemed in a hurry to get rid of him. Duffy stepped into the street. The air was very close. He cocked his eye at the sky. "Looks like a storm," he said.

Anscombe said it did; then he said good night, and shut the door. Duffy grinned a little, found that he was sweating, and blotted his face with his handkerchief. Then he walked over to the Buick and climbed in. He pressed the spring in the panel that held the guns, took one of the automatics out, glanced at the clip and shoved it down the waist of his trousers. He took out the note-book and put it in the panel. Then he pressed the spring and snapped it shut. It would be safe there, he thought.

The clock on the dashboard stood at seven twenty-five when he pulled up again at Olga's villa. He got out of the car and noticed that the light was still burning in her bedroom.

He said, "I bet she's fretting over those dresses still." He walked up the path, feeling the gravel through his thin soles. Then he opened the door with the key she had given him and entered the hall, shutting the door behind him.

He said, raising his voice, "You dressed yet?" He didn't wait for her reply, but went into the sitting-room to get some cigarettes. He stopped at the doorway, feeling suddenly cold. Then he said, "For God's sake...."

The room had been torn to pieces in the same way as his apartment had been. He just took one quick glance, then he blundered up the stairs, his legs curiously weak. At the top of the stairs he hesitated, then he called, "Honey!" The sound of his voice quite startled him. It was hoarse and quavering.

"If those lugs have touched her," he thought. He took a step forward, then stopped again. "Honey," he shouted. "You there?"

The silence in the house mocked him. He put his hand on the gun butt and pulled the gun out. Then he began to slide forward silently, his feet making no sound on the carpet. He reached the bedroom door and put his hand on the knob. Then he gently turned the handle, holding the gun waist-high. He walked in.

Olga was lying on the floor, with a knife in her left breast. The knife had been driven in so hard that it had sealed the wound. She hadn't bled at all. The wrap she had put on just before Duffy had left had been torn from her, and was lying at the other end of the room, where it had been thrown. Her large eyes were open and her lips were parted, showing a little of her small white teeth. She didn't look scared, just surprised.

Duffy stood looking at her for a long time. The only sound in the room was the sharp busy ticking of the clock. Duffy didn't have to touch her to know she was dead.

For a moment the only thing that Duffy could think of was that she had offered herself to him not an hour ago, and he had refused.

A little trickle of sweat ran from under his hat, down his nose to his chin. He still stood looking at Olga. The telephone began to ring downstairs insistently. Duffy raised his head and listened. Then he turned and went down into the sitting-room. He pulled the telephone to him and said, "Yes?"

The dry, brittle voice of the little guy said, "We're waiting for that list. Zero hour's eleven o'clock. Then we come and get it."

Duffy said through his teeth, "Go and — yourself," and hung up.

He climbed the stairs once more and went into the bedroom. He picked up the wrap from the floor and covered Olga with it. His hands shook when he touched her flesh. He said, "I am sorry about this, honey," just as if she could hear him, and he picked her up and carried her to the bed. Then he touched her hair very gently with his finger-tips, letting them move slowly down her face. "You've had all the bad breaks, ain't you?" He stooped and kissed her full lips, feeling them growing cold against his. Then he stood up, examined his clothes for bloodstains, satisfied himself that there weren't any, and walked to the door.

"Take it easy, buddy," a hard voice said.

Duffy raised his eyes. He felt no shock. Standing in the door was a cop, holding a gun in his hand. Just behind him, Duffy could see another flat cap.

Duffy said, "I'm glad you've come. They've killed my girl friend."

The first cop said, "Keep your hands still." The other cop came round and walked slowly towards Duffy, watching him carefully.

Duffy said, "What's this?"

The first cop said, "Frisk him. He'll have a rod."

Duffy said, "You're dead wrong." He had left his gun on the settee, when he had carried Olga to the bed. It was lying there, half hidden by a cushion.

The second cop stepped round him cautiously, just as if he were a wild animal that might snap any time. When he got behind him, he ran his hands down Duffy's clothing, patting firmly. Then he stood back and shook his head. "He ain't carryin' one," he said.

Duffy said, "Listen, you're wasting time."

"Just a minute," the first cop said, "you're Duffy, ain't that right?"

Duffy said, "Sure."

They both looked at him as if surprised that he admitted it. Then the second cop wandered over to the bed and had a look at Olga. He pulled off the wrapper and gaped at her.

Duffy said savagely, "Cover her up, you heel."

The second cop jerked round. "Keep your trap shut, punk," he snarled. "Another crack like that and I'll smack you down."

The first cop said, glancing at the bed, "She dead?"

"Yeah, this guy used a knife."

Duffy said, "I came back and found her like that."

"You hear that? He came back and found her like that!" The first cop grinned. "You're coming with us... come on."

"You ain't charging me with killing her?" Duffy was incredulous.

"Get wise to yourself." The first cop liked the sound of his voice. "We've been tipped off."

Duffy felt a restricting band across his chest. "I don't get that," he said slowly.

"That dame had a hidden roll salted away in this joint, and you knew it. You made up to her and tried to get the roll away, but it didn't work. So you rubbed her out, and took the joint to pieces. The roll is on you, now, ain't that right, Gus?"

The second cop nodded. He walked over to Duffy and put his hand in Duffy's inside pocket. He pulled out a flat packet of currency.

Duffy said, very evenly, "A frame-up, huh?"

Gus looked at him and grinned. "Between you and me, you're right. You're bucking the wrong outfit, mug," he said.

Duffy said, "You ain't making this stick."

The first copper shrugged. "You don't know the half of it. You're going for a little ride right now."

"There's a bottle of Scotch somewhere," Duffy said, looking round the room. "Mind if I cut the phlegm?"

Gus passed the end of a thick finger round the inside of his collar. "We'll cut it, too."

Duffy walked across the room, conscious of the hard unwavering watchfulness of the cop with the gun. His brain was ice-cold. If they were ready to frame him by such a clumsy method of palming money and planting it on him, they might even knock him off resisting arrest.

He picked up the whisky and filled the two glasses that Olga and he had used, half full.

As he turned, he intercepted a quick glance between the two cops. He felt himself go very cold. It told him what he suspected. He gave Gus one of the glasses and then wandered over to the other. "I guess I can use the bottle," he said carelessly.

The gun looked as big as a cannon trained on his vest, but he showed no sign of jumping nerves as he held out the glass. He was just about five feet away from the cop. Then he moved with incredible rapidity. He stepped quickly aside. At the same time he tossed the whisky into the cop's face.

The cop gave a howl, clapped one of his hands to his eyes, stepped back, and blindly pulled the trigger. The gun crashed. Duffy jumped in, threw himself on the cop's gun arm, and jerked the gun out of his hand.

The next sound he was conscious of was the breaking of glass. The cop was behaving like a madman, trying to get the whisky out of his eyes. Duffy had no time. He hit the cop, holding the gun by the barrel, between the eyes. Then he whirled round, expecting to run into a blast from the other cop.

Gus was standing with his hands on his belly, staring at his highly polished boots. Duffy saw blood oozing between his fingers. Gus fell on his knees, hesitated, his body swaying. Then he straightened out on his face.

Duffy said, "Hope you liked it." He went quickly to the luggage that was piled on the floor, selected a long strap from one of the grips, and bound the first cop's arms tightly. Then he went over to Olga, picked up the wrap, and covered her with it.

He moved silently and swiftly. All the time at the back of his brain he could see the jam he was in. He went back to the cop who was coming round. Duffy hauled him on to the settee, retrieved his gun from under the cushion, and stuck it down his waist-band. Then he slapped the cop across the face twice with his open hand.

The cop opened his eyes, gave a grunt, and then tried to sit up. Duffy said, "Who's behind this frame-up?"

The cop glared, but didn't say anything.

Duffy drew his gun and put it close to the cop's face. "I'm in a hurry," he said, his eyes like chips of ice. "Spill it quick, or I'll hook your eyes out with this gun-sight."

The cop suddenly went limp and began to sweat. He mumbled, "Miss English tipped us off. She gave us a nice slice to knock you, resisting arrest. We've worked for her before."

Duffy said, "Her father in this racket?"

The cop shook his head. "He don't know nothing."

Duffy went over to Gus, turned him over with his foot, searched in his pockets, and found the roll of notes. He counted them carefully. Then he looked up. "There's ten grand here," he said. "Was that your cut?"

The cop shook his head. "That was evidence against you," he said. "That dame sure wants you out of the way."

In the street, Duffy heard a car draw up. He ran to the window in time to see four uniformed police officers tumbling out. Two quick steps took him to the door. Then he slid down the flight of stairs, darted into the kitchen as the front door burst open. Quietly, he let himself out the back door. He could hear the cop upstairs yelling his head off. He told himself that he'd got to make the Buick. He ran round the small garden, paused when he reached the front, and peered carefully round the corner of the house. He could see the police car, and a little way further on was the Buick. He ran hard, not caring how much noise he made. As he reached the Buick and pulled open the heavy door he heard a shout; but he didn't stop. He scrambled into the car, swearing softly and continuously. The cold sweat ran down his face, and he expected to feel the jagged pain of a hot slug smash into him. As he slammed the door to, a gun roared from the bedroom window.

He started the engine, revved hard, engaged his gear, and shot the Buick down the road. He heard three distinct thuds on the back of the car before he jerked round the corner.

He said, "It's going to be a grand finish." And his face stiffened into a hard mask as he swung the quivering car to the bends.

Chapter Twelve

Ross was having a snack when Duffy drove in. He waddled out of the office, his little mouth tight with food. He nodded at Duffy, gulped, then said, "Anything wrong?"

Ross always expected trouble. Duffy got out of the car and said, "The wagon's hot. Gimme new plates."

For his size, Ross moved amazingly quickly. He went back to the office, and returned with a new set of plates. Duffy helped him change them. Ross said, "You jammed?"

"Listen, pal, ask nothing and hear nothing. I'm buying this box. Maybe, you won't see me any more."

Ross raised his eyebrows and put his hands on his enormous buttocks. "Okay," he said, "keep her, you've looked after me before now."

Duffy took out the roll of notes and peeled some off. He stuck them in Ross's belt. "Buy yourself a yacht with that," he said. Then he climbed back in the car. Ross put his head through the window. "If you want a good hide-out," he said, "go to the Bronx on Maddiston and tell Gilroy I sent you."

Duffy repeated, "Bronx on Maddiston."

Ross took his head from the window, glanced out into the street. "It's clear," he said. "I'm sorry about this."

Duffy showed his teeth. "Me too," he said. "Others are going to share our grief."

He raised his hand in a salute, then rolled the Buick into the street again. He drove carefully up Lafayette Street, cut across Broadway to Washington Square and headed for Greenwich Village. He parked outside a drug store and went in.

Several men were eating at the quick-lunch bar, and Duffy sat on an empty stool. He had a chicken sandwich. He washed it down with three quick drags from the pint flask he had taken from the car. The whisky was rough, but there was plenty of life in it. When he had finished the sandwich, he crossed over to the telephone booths and shut himself in. He dialled the *Tribune* number and asked for Sam. When Sam came to the 'phone, Duffy said, "Sam? Got any news?"

Sam said in a low voice, "I gotta see you."

Duffy said, "Can you come out to Dinty's? I'll go straight there."

Sam said, "Yeah," and hung up.

Duffy walked out of the drug store, looked up and down the street before he crossed the pavement, then climbed into the Buick. He let in his clutch and drove over to Dinty's. He parked the car in the underground garage, took the lift to the top floor, asked for a private room.

The waiter who served him said, "A lady is coming?"

Duffy shook his head. "Get the room ready, have some rum, absinthe and dressing up there, and some Club sandwiches. I'm waiting downstairs for a friend."

Sam came in the hall a little while after. They went up together in the lift. Neither of them said anything, but Sam kept wiping off his hands and face with a large handkerchief. They went into the room and Duffy shut the door.

Sam said, "You gone crazy?"

Duffy went over to the table and began to fix the drinks. "Has it broken yet?" he asked.

"They're printing it now. I was down at the station when the report came in." Sam was trying to be casual, but he was as jittery as a hophead.

Duffy poured the drinks from the shaker, and silently pushed one of the glasses over.

Sam said, "You're in a hell of a spot."

"Annabel's playing this," Duffy said savagely. "She's pulling strings behind the scene."

"What happened, for God's sake?"

Duffy drained his glass, and immediately filled up again. "We were set to pull out. I went down to the bank to get the book out. When I got back, I found the joint in pieces and Olga dead. Some rat had stuck a knife in her. I must have been crazy. Instead of grabbing the 'phone and reporting it right away, I ran round in circles. Then a couple of cops moved in. They had the story pat. I'd killed Olga for her roll. They even found the dough on me. One of 'em palmed it, put his hand in my pocket and seemed surprised to find it clinging to his hand."

Sam stared. "Why the frame? They had you sewed up tight enough without that."

Duffy shrugged. "You telling me? The sweet part of the setup was they intended to iron me out. I could see them getting set for it. Resisting arrest, closing the case, and slapping the murder rap on a corpse. Save the State plenty. It was nice planning, but they were slow on it. One cop shot the other, and I ducked out as the patrol wagon arrived."

Sam fidgeted with his glass. "You're it," he said.

"Annabel knocked her off." Duffy sat on the edge of the table, he held his glass a little on one side, so that the liquor slopped slightly on the carpet. "They thought they'd get the list without paying. Well, they won't. It's going to be just too bad for them."

"You better skip while the goin's good. You can't stand up against this outfit. It's too big for you."

Duffy said evenly, "I'm finishing this. They've had all the fun up to now. Olga said I'd never get anywhere with those rats till I took a gun, and by God, she's right."

Sam said, "You liked that jane, didn't you?"

Duffy's mouth set in a thin line. He kept his eyes on the floor. "I was getting used to her," he said at last. "She had all the bad breaks."

"I still say skip. You can't buck the cops, as well as Morgan. They're too big for you."

Duffy said, "You keep out of this, Sam. I'm going out to the Bronx on Maddiston. Ross's got a hide-out there. If things begin to break wrong, you can find me there. I'll wait until the heat cools off, then I'll start something."

Sam said, "I got to go. I'm on my way to the Villa. All the boys are down there."

Duffy went over to him. "Tell Alice to keep her pants on. I guess this's bound to happen sometime. I wasn't cut out for a soft life."

Sam moved to the door. "If you want some jack, I can stake you."

Duffy grinned. "You'd be surprised just how much dough's coming my way."

They didn't shake hands, they just looked at each other. Sam gave a worried smile, it hadn't much heart in it, but he smiled. Duffy nodded. "You'll hear from me," he said.

He waited until Sam had gone downstairs, poured himself another drink, lit a cigarette, then went out and down to the Buick.

Rain was beginning to fall in heavy drops. Duffy leant over and rolled up the off-side window, then he drove the Buick on to the street. As he threaded his way through the traffic, the rain drummed hard on the car roof. It was splashing knee-high off the pavement.

Duffy drove carefully. It took him quite a time to get to the Bronx, which was a basement club, with a convenient garage over the way. Duffy left the Buick at the garage and walked down into the club.

"Gilroy around?" he asked.

The thin man who opened the door looked at him suspiciously, said, "Who wants him?"

"Tell him a friend of Ross."

The thin man pulled the door open. "Come in," he said. When Duffy stepped into the dimly-lit passage, the thin man ran his hands down Duffy's suit. He stepped back. "You can't bring a rod in here," he said.

"Tell Gilroy," Duffy snapped, "and shut up."

The thin man looked at him, hesitated, then walked down the passage. He disappeared through a dirty green baize door, and Duffy leant against the wall, waiting. After a short delay the door opened again and a very light-coloured negro came out. He was tall and slender, with a heavy wave in his oily hair. He gave Duffy a hard look. "You want me?"

Duffy said, "Ross sent me here. I want to keep under cover for a few days."

Gilroy passed a long thin hand over his hair. "Okay," he said. "A hundred bucks a day."

Duffy sidled close. "Forget it," he said. "You don't make profit out of me."

Gilroy looked at him, then his large lips smiled. "No," he said, "that was bad. Ross's a good friend of mine. Make it twenty-five."

Duffy took out his roll, peeled ten saw bucks and handed them over.

"That'll hold you for a few days," he said.

Gilroy moved near the light, counted the bills, put them in his pocket, and grinned some more.

He said, "How low do you want to stay, mister?"

"When you read the papers, you'll see," Duffy told him. "I want a meal, plenty to drink and a telephone."

Gilroy led him through the baize door, down three stairs, past a bead-curtained door and through another door at the end of a dimly-lit passage. The room was small. It contained a bed, table, two arm-chairs, and a small radio.

"I'll get you some chuck right away."

Duffy said, "How safe's this joint?"

Gilroy rolled his eyes. "It's okay. I'm paying plenty for protection. The bulls won't worry you here."

He left Duffy and shut the door behind him. In the corner of the room, standing on a small table, was a telephone. Duffy looked at it, his mouth pursed thoughtfully. Then he walked over and dialled.

He recognized Gleason's voice. "Too bad you didn't get the list when you knocked my girl-friend off," he said, biting off each word.

There was a startled gasp as Gleason caught his breath. "Why, you dou-ble-crossing rat," he jerked out. "What's the big idea? I'm just back from the 'Red Ribbon.' I had the dough and you never showed up."

Duffy said, "Cut the comedy. You killed Olga and you pinned it on me. Okay, wise guy, you ain't getting away with it...."

Gleason broke in. "What the hell is this? Who's Olga?"

Duffy stared at the wall for a full minute, then he said, "I'm coming over. You got that dough still?"

Gleason said, "Sure."

And Duffy hung up.

Gilroy walked in with a bottle of whisky, three bottles of ginger ale and a glass. "Your chuck's coming right now."

Duffy took the whisky from him and poured out a long shot. He shook his head at the ginger ale, and drank quickly. Just then a knock came on the door, and the thin man came in carrying a tray. He put it on the table, and glanced at Duffy before going out.

Duffy sat down and began to eat. Gilroy hung around, fidgeting by the radio. He said at last, "I knew that dame."

Duffy looked up, a fork full of food suspended before his mouth. "Huh?"

Gilroy said, "I guess you'd better get moving."

Duffy laid the fork down. "What the hell's this?"

"Olga Shann, I knew her."

Duffy picked up the fork again. "She was a swell kid," he said. "I didn't kill her, if that's what's biting you."

Gilroy stirred restlessly, beads of sweat hung on his top lip. "It looks that way," his voice was exceedingly hostile.

Duffy went on eating. "A little judy called Annabel English shoved that knife into her," he said. "This is a frame-up. I'm it."

Gilroy took out a handkerchief and carefully wiped his mouth. He stood still, looking at his bright yellow shoes.

Duffy finished the meal in silence. Then he drank some more whisky and sat back. He lit a cigarette, and forced two thin jets of smoke down his nostrils. "If you like that dame as much as I did," he said, "I know how you feel."

Gilroy relaxed a little and came over to the table. "Ross's never sent me a bum yet," he said. "I guess I was wrong."

Duffy nodded. "Sure, that's okay."

"I'd like to make this a personal matter." Gilroy studied his pinkish nails. "If you want any help, I've a nice little outfit."

Duffy grinned. "I've gotta see this through myself."

"Sure, sure," Gilroy nodded his head. "Still, you can't always beat the rap."

Getting to his feet, Duffy said, "I'll file that offer away. I might have to use it."

He moved to the door, then looked over his shoulder. "It's on the street now?"

Gilroy nodded. "Yeah, the heat's on good."

A hard little smile came to Duffy's lips. "I ain't starting anything just yet," he said. "I'll be back some time."

He went over to the garage, got into the Buick and drove over to Annabel's apartment. He parked up a side street and walked back. At the entrance to the organ loft, he paused. At the corner he could see a flat cap, standing under a street light. He turned quickly and walked once more back to the Buick. He got in and sat there, watching the cop. The rain had ceased, but the pavements were still wet and shiny in the street lights. The cop moved on after a bit, and Duffy went back to the entrance. He opened the door with the key he still had with him, and silently went up the stairs.

When he got into the loft, he saw Gleason sitting in the room below nursing an automatic. Sinking on his knee, so that his head did not appear over the balcony, he watched Gleason for several minutes. Then he said in a hard voice, "Put your rod on the floor, or you'll get it."

Gleason started, hastily put the gun at his feet, and looked up.

Duffy stood up and leant over the rail. He kept the Colt steady. "Where's

Annabel?" he asked.

Gleason said in a dry, strangled voice, "She ain't in."

Duffy swung his legs over the balcony and sat there. "I'm coming down," he said. "Don't start anything. I'm itching to blast you."

He pushed himself off, breaking his fall with one hand. Gleason's face was a little drawn. He kept both hands folded in his lap.

Duffy walked over and sat on the edge of the table. He held the Colt down by his side. He reached out a foot and kicked Gleason's gun under a chair, away from Gleason. He said, "I gotta lot to talk to you about."

Gleason looked at him, twitched his mouth a little, but said nothing.

Duffy said, "You've double-crossed me once. You've pulled a fast one at my joint, and another at the Villa. You tried to slap a murder rap on me. Well, you've had fun. Now I'm going to have some."

Gleason said in a thin voice, "I don't know what you're talking about."

His face was so blank that Duffy stopped talking and stared at him. "Okay, you don't know anything about it," he said. "What do you know?"

"I'm dealing it off the top deck," Gleason said. "I want the book, you got it, and I'm paying for it. I went to the 'Red Ribbon' with the dough as arranged, but you didn't show up. I came back here and you 'phoned. That's all."

Duffy rubbed the short hairs on his nape with the flat of his hand. Then he said, "Who killed Weidmer?"

Gleason shifted his eyes. "That doesn't get you anywhere."

"You're wrong. Who killed him? Come on! If you know you'll let yourself out of this."

Gleason said, "But I don't know."

Duffy raised the Colt. "This is my first killing." He spoke very harshly. His face had gone oyster colour. Two thin lines ran down the sides of his mouth. "I hope I do it right."

Gleason's skin went a little yellow, and he opened his eyes very wide. He said, running all his words together, "It was that damned little judy."

Duffy pushed his hat to the back of his head. His face glistened in the diffused light. "You damned louse," he said, "you nearly made me kill you."

Gleason lay back in the chair. He looked bad.

Duffy said, "What's this dame to you?"

"She's my wife." Gleason put his hands on his coat lapels to stop them from shaking. "I wish to God I'd never seen her."

"So that's it, is it? She killed Cattley and Weidmer and Olga?"

Gleason shifted. "Who's this Olga you keep bringing up?"

"Never mind." Duffy got to his feet. "You ought to watch that dame, she's dangerous."

Gleason tried to cross his legs, but couldn't quite make it. He stared down at the carpet. "She's hop screwy," he said. "I can't shake her. She'd stick a knife into me."

"How much jack have you got?"

Gleason looked up sharply. "You said fifty grand. I got twenty-five here." He took a long sealed envelope from his inside pocket and laid it on the table.

Duffy looked at the seal, then he said, "Open it."

Gleason tried twice, but his fingers bothered him. Duffy leant over, took the envelope from him, put his gun down on the table, and tore off the end of the envelope. He shook the contents on to the table and looked at it. Then he picked up the thin sheaf of notes and put it in his pocket. He took the notebook out and tossed it into Gleason's lap.

Gleason looked at him in complete astonishment. Duffy shook his head. "You expected a double-cross, ain't that right? I guess you ain't keeping it long."

Gleason thumbed through the book as if he couldn't believe his eyes. Duffy went over and picked up Gleason's gun, took out the clip and then tossed the gun back on the floor. He put his own Colt down his waist-band and adjusted the points of his vest.

Gleason looked up at him. "This is the first level deal that's happened to me," he said.

Duffy's eyes were still hard. "You don't know a thing. You ain't going to keep that list long. Morgan's after it."

Gleason stiffened and got to his feet. "Morgan? How the hell did Morgan know?"

Duffy shrugged. "I guess I talked too much," he said. "Anyway, that's your funeral."

He walked to the door. "I gotta few things to fix, then I'm blowing."

Gleason stood in the middle of the room, the note-book in his hands, staring at the floor. Duffy took one look at him, shrugged, and opened the door. *Annabel was standing there pointing a .38 at his belly.*

Duffy raised his hands just above his waist very quickly. She said, "Reach up, punk, the roof's not high enough."

Gleason came across quickly and jerked Duffy's gun out. Then he said in a low voice, "Walk backwards."

Duffy obeyed. Annabel came into the light. Her face was very pale, and it had a scraped, bony look. She looked a hundred years old, standing there hating him with her eyes. Gleason put Duffy's gun into his hip pocket and then went across to Duffy and took the sheaf of notes from him. He gave a little grin. "Too bad," he said.

Duffy continued to look at Annabel. He said very evenly and through his teeth, "You'd better let that heat off. I'll kill you if I get the chance."

She said, "Sit down."

Duffy sat down because he wanted to, not because she told him to. She said to Gleason, "Put the radio on."

Gleason looked at her, puzzled, then walked over to the radio, that was a little to the right and behind Duffy. When Gleason turned his back, Duffy saw Annabel stiffen. Her eyes seemed to film over, and her lips came off her teeth. Not understanding, he stared at her, then he suddenly guessed and gave a shout. Annabel shot at Gleason twice. The gun barked, then barked again. Gleason swung round, his face twisted, his eyes startled, unbelieving, frightened, then he crashed over, taking the radio with him.

"Don't move," Annabel said to Duffy, swinging the gun round to him.

Duffy sat very still, looking at Gleason. Then he said through stiff lips, "You poor devil."

Annabel said, "I've been waiting a chance to get rid of that punk for some time." She spat each word at him.

"They'll burn you for this," Duffy said coldly.

"Think so?" she laughed. "Can't you see? Watch me pin it on you."

She went over to Gleason's gun, lying on the floor, and picked it up. Then she backed away from Duffy. "I'd like a chance of shooting you," she said. "So start something if you're tired of life."

She wiped the .38 carefully on her skirt, then she tossed the gun beside Gleason. "That's your gun," she said, covering him with Gleason's automatic.

Duffy grinned. "So what?"

She said, "Don't you get it? I'm going to shoot you now. The police will find you. I shot you in self-defence after you killed Gleason. Don't you think I'm cute?"

Duffy got slowly out of his chair. "You're nutty," he said evenly, and began to walk towards her.

She waited until he was within two yards of her, then she pulled the trigger. Her lips were off her teeth and little white specks of foam touched her mouth. The automatic went click—click—click. Then Duffy put his hand on the automatic and jerked it out of her hand. "I took the clip out before you showed up," he said quietly, then he smacked her across her face with his open palm as hard as he could hit her. She bounced against the wall, slid down, and rolled on her side. She began to scream in a thin reedy tone that sent hot wires into Duffy's brain.

From the organ loft, a tight voice said, "Pipe down, he ain't hurt you. It was just a slap."

Chapter Thirteen

The little guy said, "How the hell does one get down from this nest?"

Duffy looked at him, then he looked at Clive, and then he looked at Joe. Clive and Joe were carelessly holding guns. Duffy said, "You jump." He went over to the sideboard and began to pour himself a drink.

Annabel sat up, pressed herself against the wall, and stared up at the three in the loft.

The little guy swung his short legs over the balcony and let himself drop. He landed on his shoulders with a thud. He sat up carefully and cursed. Then he said, "You come down, Clive; but Joe, you watch these birds and pop 'em if they get tough. You heard that, didn't you, Joe? I said pop 'em if they get tough."

Joe leant over the balcony and looked down. He looked a little tired. "Yeah," he said, "I heard you. I'm watching okay."

Clive scrambled over the balcony, making black marks with the toes of his shoes on the wall.

Duffy drank a little of the Scotch and felt better. He said, "You ain't met these two before, have you?" to the little guy. "The stiff over there was Murray Gleason, and the red-head sitting on the floor showing all she's got is Annabel."

The little guy giggled, then said, "My, my, you go places, don't you?"

Duffy said, "Sure. Well, now you're here, what's next?"

Clive went over to Gleason, turned him over, and searched him. He found the sheaf of notes and the little pocket-book. He came over with them to the little guy. They both examined the note-book carefully.

Duffy lost interest in them, he went over to Annabel. He said very quietly, "When you killed Olga you started something. I'm going to pin that on to you, if it takes me a hundred years."

She drew back her lips and spat at him. He raised his hand, looked at her, then stepped away. "It's time you were dead," he said.

The little guy held the note-book and said to Clive, "Would you like to watch this?"

Clive said he would.

"Give him a hoop as well," Duffy said.

The little guy looked at him with disapproval. "I told you before not to make fun of him."

Clive said, "I'm going to rub this heel out."

The little guy scratched his head, then looked up at Joe. "You heard that?"

Joe grinned. "Why not? It's some time since Clive knocked anyone off."

The little guy said, "Yes, that's right. It is some time. Yeah, okay, you knock him off."

Clive turned slowly on Duffy, who was standing near the wall. Duffy's face was tense, he pushed out his chin a little, the muscles in his neck suddenly going hard.

Annabel said from the floor, "Give it to him low down."

Clive and the little guy both jerked their heads in her direction, and Duffy snapped up the light switch, then he dropped to his knees and shot away to the left. In his mind he could clearly see the wires that fed the two standard lamps. He groped for them, found nothing, groped again, touched them, and then pulled sharply. He felt them come away loose.

The little guy said in a sharp voice, "Don't start shooting. We don't want the cops here. Clive, stand by the door. I'll put on the lights."

Duffy grinned. He stood up, listening for the slightest sound. The darkness made him feel like a man.

Joe said, "I'm coming down."

The little guy said, "Wait; I'll tell you."

Duffy moved softly towards the little guy. When he got near enough as he could judge, he stopped. Quite close to him, he heard a rattle of matches. He balanced himself, and as the match flared up he hit the little guy right in the middle of his face. The match fell on the carpet and went out. Duffy took three quick steps away from the little guy, who was lying on the ground, collided with a chair. Joe fired just once. It was close enough. Duffy felt the bullet against his sleeve as it passed.

Moving to the door, he ran up against Clive. Clive gave a high scream, but Duffy's questing hands found his head, and he banged it back against the wall hard. Clive went limp.

The little guy said in a sudden panic, "Quick, Joe! He's got Clive."

Joe said, "What the hell do you think I can do? I can't see."

Holding Clive by the shirt-front, Duffy jerked the door open, and stepped into the hall, dragging Clive with him. The hall was in darkness. Duffy threw Clive on the floor, sprang back to the door, found the key on the outside, and turned it. Then he struck a match and flicked on the electric light switch.

Clive was lying in a heap, dazed. He stared up at Duffy with unseeing eyes. Duffy searched his pockets, found the notes and the little book and transferred them to his pocket, then he stood up.

"I guess I owe you something," he said softly, and put his heel on Clive's upturned face, pressed down hard, turning the heel slowly. Clive clawed at his foot, and began to scream. Duffy said, "Here it is, Nance, it's been coming to you for a long time." He put his entire weight on his right leg and twisted his heel sharply. There was a cracking sound, and under his heel it felt soft. Clive stopped screaming. Duffy stepped away, dragged his heel once, then twice on the soft carpet, leaving two long smears of red. He opened the front door and stepped into the passage, and ran downstairs, not waiting for the elevator. Faintly, he could hear the thudding of Joe's shoulder against the locked door.

He reached the street. It was raining again. The air was heavy and very warm. He ran on to the Buick, pulled open the door and got in. Then he drove away very quickly.

The streets were less congested. He took half the time in getting back to the Bronx. Leaving the car in the garage, he walked down the steps of the basement and rapped on the door.

Gilroy opened it. The negro showed his big white teeth. "You okay?" he asked.

Duffy nodded. He said, "Come and have a drink."

Gilroy followed him down the passage into the little room. Duffy sat on the bed and pushed his hat to the back of his head. Gilroy fixed the drinks, came over and gave Duffy a glass. He stood waiting. His thin face sleepy, but interested.

Duffy looked him over thoughtfully from the bed, scratched the side of his face, making a little rasping noise. Then he said, "Perhaps you might like to come in on this."

Gilroy lifted his shoulders. "Maybe," he said, "it's nothing to me now."

"Gleason was knocked off tonight," Duffy said, swirling the whisky in the glass. "I was there, so was Morgan's gang and Gleason's wife. She popped him and tried to pin it on me."

Gilroy rolled up his eyes. "They're slapping it on you all right," he said at last.

Duffy nodded. "Sure, they got a reason. I'm holding up a million-dollar racket." He took the note-book out of his pocket and tossed it on the table. Gilroy picked it up curiously and examined it. Duffy could see it meant nothing to him.

He explained.

Gilroy sat listening, his black eyes half closed. He pursed his lips together. He said, at last, "You gotta be careful."

Duffy said, "I know that." He got to his feet and wandered round the small room. "If Olga were here, I'd pull out, but where the hell can I go now?"

Gilroy thumbed the book over. "You wouldn't get far," he said.

Duffy shrugged. "I don't know," he said. "I might."

"You thinking of playing this further?"

Duffy stopped walking and stood very still. He looked hard at Gilroy. "That depends a lot on you."

Gilroy said, "Where do I come in?"

"A while back, you offered me your outfit; I guess I can use it."

Gilroy smoothed down his crinkly hair with his hand. "How?" he said. He was being very cautious.

Duffy leant forward and tapped the top of the table with his index finger. "I'd like to run Morgan out of town."

Gilroy drew his breath in with a little hiss. "You're nuts," he said. "You gotta have dough for a job like that."

Duffy took from his pocket the thin sheaf of notes and put it on the table. Then from his side coat pocket he took the ten grand he had lifted off Gus, and laid it on top of the other money. Gilroy watched him fascinated.

"Thirty-five grand enough?" Duffy asked.

Gilroy eased his collar with a thin black finger. "It helps," he said slowly. "Where the hell did that come from?"

Duffy scooped up the money and put it back in his pocket. "It fell in my lap," he said. "What say? You on?"

Gilroy sat down, poured out more drinks and lit a cigarette. "Let's talk about it. What's your idea?"

Duffy came over and sat down too. "I don't know," he said. "I just want to run this Morgan louse out, and his gang with him."

Gilroy screwed up his eyes, then said, "Why?"

Duffy's mouth set. "He thinks I can't do it. He's told me so. Well, I'm going to show the palooka he's bucking the wrong horse."

Gilroy nodded. "That's the way it goes, is it?"

Duffy said, "Yeah, that's it."

"You won't get far with the cops after you."

"I've got that on the line. First thing tomorrow I'm getting protection."

"Protection? Where do you get that from?"

"English." Duffy leant back in the chair and took a long pull at his glass. "I'm blowing the whole works to that guy, and then watch him cover me up."

Gilroy said, "You've got something there."

Duffy said, "Sure, I have. Once I get protection, I'm a big shot. I can handle Morgan with protection and an outfit like yours."

Gilroy said, "There's me, there's Shep, and there's Schultz."

"Okay. Suppose we all get together, after I've seen English."

Gilroy nodded and stood up. "The boys get in around about one o'clock. If you can make it, we'll be here then."

He wandered to the door. "It ain't going to be easy," he said.

Duffy was watching him cross the room. "You ain't gone into it," he said.

"It's a cinch."

Gilroy nodded and went out, pulling the door behind him. Duffy got up and took off his coat. A knock came on the door and the thin man put his head round. "There's a jane asking for you," he said.

Duffy said, "Sure, and I suppose you told her I was right inside?"

The thin man said, "I told her I'd never heard of you, but it won't shift her. She says, 'Tell him it's Alice,' like that. So I come back, and here I am."

"Well, for God's sake!" Duffy put on his coat. "Shoot her in quick."

The thin man shrugged and went away. He came back with Alice at his heels. Duffy went over to her and took her hands. He said, "Why, honey…" then he stopped.

"Sam told me," she said breathlessly. "I had to see you. What is all this, Bill? The papers say you killed that woman. It's all in headlines."

Duffy patted her arm. "Swell of you to come," he said, leading her over to the bed. "Sit down, baby. Take the weight off your feet."

"What are you going to do?" she said. "Sam won't tell me anything."

Duffy grinned. "He's told you too much as it is," he said. "Listen, I didn't kill Olga. It was a frame-up. Look baby, I've got dough." He took the money from his pocket and tossed it in her lap.

She gave a little shiver and put her hands behind her. She just sat and stared at the money. "Take it away," she said quickly.

Duffy stared at her. "Look," he urged, "There's thirty-five grand there. Did you ever see so much dough all at once?"

She said again in a tone that was just off-pitch, "Take it away."

He picked up the money, a sulky look in his eyes. "If that's the way you feel," he said.

She put her hand on his arm. "Oh, Bill, you're heading for trouble. Can't you see? For your own sake, please, stop it."

Duffy put the money carefully in his side pocket. "Now listen—" he began.

She interrupted him. "Money isn't everything. You know it isn't. Please Bill, give yourself up. I know it'll be all right. We'll get someone to help you… get back to your job. Don't go on with this business."

Duffy raised his hand. She took one look at the hard glint in his eyes, and she sat away from him and began to cry. Duffy said, "I'm going through with this. I've been a little shot for years. I've been 'Come here, you bastard,' 'Do this, you heel,' 'Get that, you punk' all my goddam life. I'm through with it now. I'm bucking an outfit that's supposed to be tough. Okay, I'm bucking 'em. I'm going to get an outfit twice as tough. Do you get that? Twice as tough! When I've got it, I'm going to be the big shot around here from now on. How do you like that?"

Alice got to her feet. She said in an unsteady voice, "For God's sake, keep

Sam out of this."

Duffy said, "I'm sorry, honey." He felt a sudden tenderness for her. "I'm just shooting off my mouth. I'm just wild. A no-good out of work. Forget it, will you?"

She looked at him for several seconds. "You're going through with this, I know," she said. "You're going to hurt people and you're going to get hurt. Just to satisfy a little pride, a little ego in you. I can't stop you. When you're tired of this, come and see us. But stay away until you've got it out of your system. I've loved you a lot in the past; don't make me hate you ever, will you?"

She patted his hand that rested on the table, then she walked out of the room. Duffy stood looking at the closed door. Then once more he took off his coat, went over and shot the bolt on the door, kicked off his shoes, and lay down on the bed. He reached up and turned off the light.

In the dark, he lay for a long time thinking. Then he said in low voice, "Some nice hot place with plenty of yellow sand. With sky a real blue and just you and me." He put out his hand to the empty pillow at his side and let his fingers lightly touch the cool linen.

The room felt suddenly cold and empty.

Chapter Fourteen

Edwin English was a tall, thick-set guy, with a round fleshy face, blue-white hair, and cold, fishy eyes. He sat at a big flat top desk, a cigar burning slowly in his short white fingers, staring with blank eyes at Duffy.

He sat there for maybe twenty minutes listening to Duffy talk. He examined with no sign of interest the note-book Duffy threw on to the desk. Then he put the cigar back in his mouth and half-closed his eyes. He sat there for some time looking through Duffy at something hanging on the wall behind Duffy's head.

Duffy was satisfied that he had told him everything, concisely and clearly. He thought he had made a swell job of it.

English took the cigar out of his mouth and tapped the top of the desk with a well-manicured finger-nail. "I could turn you up for a murder rap, it seems," he said.

Duffy grinned mirthlessly. "Ain't you working from the wrong angle?" he said. "You ain't got to worry about me. It's your daughter that you gotta concentrate on."

English said, "I'm always concentrating on my daughter."

Duffy nodded. "Sure, but not half as hard as you gotta work now. Look, suppose you let me handle this?"

English said, "You'll be picked up by the police. No, I don't think you would be any good."

Duffy got to his feet. He still carried the thin smile on his mouth. "Well, well," he said, "I guessed you'd feel like that. If you think I'm taking the rap for her, you got it all wrong. I'm going right down to headquarters and I'm going to squawk so loud you'll hear it right up here."

English said, "You haven't got any proof."

Duffy shrugged. "That's what you think," he said. "I've got enough evidence to get that jane fried three times over."

English raised his hand. "Wait," he said. "Perhaps we can think up something."

Duffy came back to the desk. He leant over and stared hard into English's eyes. "You're playing it wrong. Can't you see how they'd fall over themselves to get Annabel indicted for a first-degree murder rap? They're snapping round your heels already, English, and you know it. One false move from you, and you're out. Your policy ain't popular. I don't like it myself. Let me tell you, it's a goddam awful policy with a daughter like yours around."

English pushed his chair back and stood up. Just for a second Duffy saw the fishy eyes look uneasy, then they went bland again. Duffy grinned to himself. He knew he had slipped in a hot one.

"What do you propose?" English said.

"Cool the cops off me, for a start. You can do it. Once I've got protection, I can go after Morgan and run him out. I can pick up Annabel and get her into a nut-house… that's the place for her."

English brooded. "You've got to have more than protection. You want money and you want help."

Duffy said, "Gilroy's mob's backing me."

"Gilroy? Yes, I know him. He's all right, but he's not big enough."

Duffy sat on the edge of the desk. "With me around, he'll be big enough."

"And money?"

"Suppose you put up some dough? It's worth a lot to fix this mess, ain't it?"

English walked to the door. "We'll see about that," he said. "Suppose you come down to headquarters and we'll talk things over with the right man."

Duffy looked at him hard. He shook his head. "You gotta fix that," he said. "This is too important to me to risk a double-cross. I'd look a grand mug walking into headquarters, if you were losing your grip."

English shrugged. "You have a strange way of expressing yourself," he said. "But have it your own way. I'll ring you."

Duffy looked at the clock on the desk. It was just after eleven o'clock.

"I'll do the ringing. I'll come through after one o'clock. I'll expect to get moving right away by then."

English nodded, then, as if a thought had struck him, he said, "Where's Annabel now?"

Duffy shrugged. "The last time I saw her, she was telling a little nance to shoot me in the guts. You've got a grand daughter, ain't you?"

Leaving English, Duffy picked up the Buick and drove slowly back to the Bronx. He left the car at the garage and then went to his room.

He sent the thin man out to get the newspapers. While he was waiting for them he mixed himself a strong Scotch and lit a cigarette. He let his mind wander as he sat there, but he kept coming back to Olga. He could see her lying naked with the dagger in her breast. He tried to think of other things, but his mind kept switching back to that picture.

He was glad when the thin man came in and dumped several tabloids on the table. Duffy gave him some small change. Then he went through the papers carefully. When he had finished them, he sat back and lit another cigarette. There was nothing in any of the papers about Gleason's murder.

He got up, went to the telephone and dialled Annabel's number. He sat for a minute or so listening to the buzz, and then hung up. Well, anyway, she had skipped all right.

Then he wandered about the room, thinking. He wondered if Morgan's gang had wiped her out and got rid of both bodies. He thought that was an idea, but he couldn't do anything about that for the moment.

Just before one o'clock, Gilroy came in with two other men. Gilroy said, "This is Shep," to Duffy. Duffy looked at Shep and nodded. He thought Shep was an extraordinary-looking man. He had a very small head perched on a long neck, and the rest of his body was grossly fat. His head just didn't fit his body. Duffy thought it looked like the maker of Shep had run out of the right size, and had just slapped on the first head that came to hand. Schultz was a tall, wiry bird, with a thick mop of black hair, that stood up like a wire brush.

Duffy said, "Sit down, boys, and have a drink."

They sat down self-consciously, looked at the empty table and then at Duffy. The thin man put his head round the door and Duffy said, "Let's have some Scotch."

Gilroy stood by the window. He said, "I've put the general idea up. They'll go for it okay."

Shep said in a gritty voice, "Ain't you the guy the cops are looking for?"

Duffy glanced at Gilroy, who nodded. Then he said, "That's right, but not for long." He got up and went over to the telephone and dialled. While he was waiting for the line to connect, the thin man came in with the drinks.

Schultz reached out a bony hand and began to fix them.

Duffy said into the 'phone, "English?" then he said, "You fixed it yet?"

English said, "It wasn't easy, but you're in the clear now. You gotta pin this rap on someone, but it's not to be you know who."

Duffy grinned. "That's okay. I only want a stiff or two, and that's who's done it."

English grunted. "You've got to have your stiffs first," he said.

"If you could see this outfit sitting right here, you wouldn't worry about that. I want some dough, don't I?"

English said, "If you run Morgan out and Annabel where I don't have to see her again, you're going to get plenty."

"It's got to be better than that. I want some on the nail."

English was silent for a moment. "I'll open an account for you at the National. You can draw up to five thousand dollars."

Duffy said, "You do that," and hung up.

Gilroy came over from the window and took a glass from Schultz. He said, "Let's go."

Duffy sat down. "English is covering me. He's lifted the heat for the moment. He'll back me for dough if we give him action. I guess we might start right away."

Schultz said, "What's my split?"

"Five grand each," Duffy said, doing sums in his head.

Shep nodded. "I could use that," he said.

"Your first job is to find Annabel English," Duffy said, folding his arms and resting his elbows on the table. "That jane is dangerous, and she's got to be put where she won't be."

Gilroy said, "Knock her off?" He said it with distaste.

Duffy shook his head. "I don't want any killings. I can fix her. She's as crazy as a coon."

Shep said, "We'll find her, but the nut angle is not up our street."

Duffy said, "You find her. I'll do the rest."

"Where do we start?"

"The last time I saw her, she was with Morgan's mob. They will know what happened to her."

Shep clambered to his feet. "That's easy," he said. "I know that gang. Leave it to me."

Duffy waited until he had lumbered out, then he looked at Gilroy. "Give me the lowdown on Morgan?"

Gilroy said, "He's running three clubs. He's got offices on Transverse Avenue by the river. That's where he does his business."

"What business?"

"All his rackets. Calls the place the Morgan Navigation Trust Co. It's his headquarters for vice, smuggling, getting girls over from Cuba, you know, the whole works."

Duffy went over to the book and turned up Morgan Navigation Co. He dialled and waited. Then he said, "Mr. Morgan there?"

A pert voice said, "What's it about?"

Duffy said curtly. "I'll ask him to tell you, if he wants you to know."

She connected him. Before she plugged, he heard her say, "Some day these sharp punks will cut themselves with their own wit."

Duffy grinned. Morgan's voice came over. "Yes?"

Duffy said, "Listen, Morgan. Your mob let you down."

Morgan said very evenly, "You had the breaks that time, Duffy, but watch out."

"Gleason's out of the bidding," Duffy said, looking with blank eyes at the wall in front of him. "That little book's going to cost you fifty grand."

He heard Morgan draw his breath in, then he said, "My boys are collecting that free of charge. I've warned you. They're coming gunning for you."

Duffy said, "On second thoughts, I'll turn the book over to the State."

"I shouldn't do that." Morgan said it just a little too quickly. There was no punch in the threat.

"I'm turning it over, just the same. Then we'll see what happens. I got twenty-five grand out of Gleason, so I should worry."

"Wait." Morgan raised his voice. "I'll give you five grand."

Duffy said, "Make it twenty-five and its yours."

"Okay," Morgan's voice was very soft. "You bring the book over, and I'll have the money here."

"I'm not that screwy," Duffy said. "Turn it over in the open. I'll be in the lobby of the Belmont Plaza at six o'clock tonight. We'll make the exchange."

There was a short pause, then Morgan said, "Okay," and hung up.

Gilroy had been listening, his eyes on Duffy's back. He said, "You're going to have a sweet time bringing that dough home."

Duffy picked up his hat. "Come on," he said, "let's go."

They followed him over to the garage. Duffy said to Schultz, "Can you handle this bus?"

Schultz nodded. "You bet," he said, faintly surprised.

"Well, drive it then. Gilroy and me want to talk."

Gilroy and Duffy got in at the back and Schultz climbed in under the wheel. "Where to?" Schultz asked, jerking the starter.

Duffy gave him the address of his bank, and Schultz nosed the car carefully down the narrow alley into the main street.

Duffy said to Gilroy, "We'll double-cross this louse right away. I'm turning the list over to English and he can get busy on it. It's too big for us to handle. Next, we give the copy to Morgan and get his dough. Then we fix Annabel, and after that we'll call on Morgan's office and collect any evidence to run him out. If we don't turn any up, we'll have to run him out on our own."

Gilroy leant back against the cushions and closed his eyes. He said sleepily, "You got quite a programme, ain't you?"

Duffy said, "I want to get shot of this, then you boys can spend what you've earned."

Schultz ran the car to the curb and Duffy went into the bank. The other two stayed in the car, waiting. When Duffy came out he glanced up and down the street, then stepped hastily into the car. Schultz pulled away at once.

Duffy gave English's address. He said, "Make it fast." Schultz glanced at him in the driving-mirror, nodded, and swung to the side streets.

Gilroy said, "Seems a shame to turn that list over to the cops."

Duffy shrugged. "You ain't thinking of handling a thing that big?" he asked.

Gilroy shook his head. "I don't handle dope," he said. "I just don't like to give those punks a break."

Duffy grinned. "It'll wash up Morgan, so what the hell?"

English was surprised to see him. He took the book from Duffy, glanced at it, then said, "So this is the first step, eh?"

Duffy nodded. "You turn that over to the Narcotic Squad. It ain't evidence, but it might stampede some of those hopheads. Anyway, it'll stop Morgan running the same game."

English nodded. "Have you found Annabel yet?"

"It won't be long." Duffy went to the door. "I'll get in touch pretty soon."

Out in the street once more, he went over to the Buick. Gilroy said, "Ain't it time to eat?"

Duffy climbed in. "Go ahead," he said. "I've got time on my hands till six."

Schultz swung the car in a half-circle, reversed her back again, then spinning the wheel hard round, he turned her completely, heading rapidly east.

Chapter Fifteen

Shep came in just after five o'clock. Duffy was cleaning his Colt. Gilroy and Schultz sat in chairs, watching him.

Duffy looked up sharply and said, "Found her?"

Shep waddled in, sat down and blotted his face with his handkerchief.

"Yeah," he said. "Guess where?"

Duffy put his gun on the table. His mouth became a thin line. "Where?" he said.

Shep smiled happily; he said, "It's rich. She's gone hot pants for Morgan's nance."

Duffy's eyebrows rose. "Clive?"

Shep nodded. "She's over at the little rat's apartment right now. He's in bed, screaming hell, because someone trod on his pan."

Duffy got to his feet. "We'll go right over and pick her up," he said, slipping the gun down his waist-band.

Gilroy said, "All of us?"

Duffy shook his head. "Suppose Shep and me go," he said.

Shep said, "Sure." He mumbled something to Gilroy and gave a loud tinny laugh.

Duffy said, "I'll go on to the Belmont Plaza after. Suppose you two boys get down there and watch the lobby. We ain't going to take any chances with Morgan."

Gilroy nodded. "Okay," he said.

Duffy and Shep went out and climbed in the Buick. Duffy took the wheel. As he pushed the Buick down the street, he said, "If that jane gets tough, knock her off."

Shep nodded. "She's a grand looker, ain't she?" Then he said sadly, "It's tough being fat."

Duffy shot him a side-glance. "You don't know when you're getting the breaks," he said shortly. "That jane's poison."

Shep gave him some directions, then said wistfully, "I guess it'd be good, going places with a honey like that."

Duffy said nothing. He drove fast. After a ten-minute run, he said, "This the street?"

Shep stuck his little head out of the window and peered. "That's right."

Duffy drew into the curb. They both got out. "What number did you say?"

Shep hunted in his pockets, found a scrap of paper, screwed up his eyes, then said, "1469."

Duffy checked the house near him. "It's on the other side farther down."

Together they crossed the street and began walking casually down. Duffy said, "They're both dangerous; you got to watch 'em, Shep."

Shep grinned. "Me… I'm scared to hell… like hell," he said.

1469 was a tall, gaunt apartment house. Duffy ran up the steps and checked the list of names. "Clive Wessen," he said. He rang the next bell, waited until the latch gave, pushed open the door and walked in. Shep shuffled behind him. "Third floor," Duffy said, keeping his voice down.

They climbed the stairs slowly. The place was clean and bright. Duffy said, "These punks live well, don't they?"

Shep said nothing, he was saving his breath. On the third floor, Duffy took the Colt out; he held it loosely in his hand, hanging down by his side.

He nodded to a door at the far end of the passage. "There it is," he said. "Can you open it?"

Shep said, "I can open any door. Watch me." Moving very quietly, he went to the door, examined the lock, then turned his head and beamed. "It's a cinch," he said.

"Get going," Duffy murmured.

Shep felt in his pocket, took out a little tool, fitted it in the lock and turned. Duffy heard the lock slip with a faint click. He said in Shep's ear, "Give me two minutes, then come on in."

Shep nodded and stood aside. Duffy gently turned the handle, pushed open the door, and walked in. He found himself in a small hall, about twelve feet by sixteen. Facing him were two doors. He trod quietly over and listened. He thought he heard someone talking behind the right-hand door. Holding his gun waist-high, he pushed open the door, stepped in quickly. Then he said in a cold voice, "You seduced him yet?"

Annabel spun round. She was standing by a divan, on which Clive was lying. Clive's face was beautifully bandaged with plaster. Someone had made a very neat job of it. All Duffy could see of Clive's face was two eyes that hated him.

Duffy said very sharply, "Don't start anything. Keep still."

Clive said in a curiously adenoidal voice, "Get out of here."

Annabel ran her fingers through her hair. She smiled at Duffy. "I think you're cute," she said.

Duffy said, "Sit down."

Shep wandered in. He looked first at Clive, then at Annabel. He puffed out his cheeks, then took off his hat.

She had sat down on the foot of the divan. She said in her breathless voice, "Who's your gentleman friend?"

Shep beamed and fingered his necktie. He glanced at Duffy. "What a honeypot!" he said.

Duffy had his eyes on Clive. Although Clive was dressed, he had a rug over him, hiding his hands. Duffy said, "Put your hands where I can see them."

"Suppose we be friends…?" Annabel broke in.

Duffy turned his head a little. "You're coming with me," he told her. "We've got a home for you to go to."

She said, "Now?"

Duffy said, "That's it. Right now."

She stood up. "Home?" she said suddenly. "What do you mean… home?"

Duffy said, "You'll know. Say good-bye to your boyfriend, you ain't seeing him any more."

She looked at Clive, then she shrugged a little. "I don't mind," she said. "He's not quite in one piece. He's a waste of time."

Shep grinned. "A jane like you ain't got no right running with a nance," he said seriously.

Clive said in a low voice, "Get to hell out of here, all of you."

Annabel said, "May I get my things?"

Duffy shook his head. "You can come as you are," he said. "I want to talk to you… come on."

She giggled. "I love you when you get like that," she said. "Let's talk; I've got lots to tell you." She waved her hand at Clive. "About him and Morgan. You'll eat it up."

Clive drew his lips off his teeth, then he shot her. Duffy just caught the slight movement under the rug as the gun roared. The rug began to smoulder.

Duffy fired at Clive, but the big Colt kicked up and the bullet smacked against the wall two feet above Clive's head. Moving with incredible rapidity, Shep flung himself on Clive.

Duffy walked cautiously over to Annabel, looked at her, then shoved his gun in his hip pocket and knelt down beside her. She lay on her back, one hand clenched tightly to her right side. She opened her eyes and looked at him, then she began to cry.

Duffy said, "Take it easy. You'll be all right."

He picked her up. Shep said, "Bring her here." He had tossed Clive on to the floor. Clive lay flat. Shep had smacked him hard on the chin.

Duffy put her on the divan. He said urgently, "Get some water and dressing. She's bleeding like hell."

Shep went out of the room. Duffy could hear him pulling drawers open and hunting about in the next room. He took his pocket-knife and ripped away her clothes round the wound. "Hurry, damn you," he shouted to Shep when he saw where she was shot.

Shep came back in a lumbering run. He had a handful of small towels and a jug of water. Duffy took them from him. "Phone English, and tell him," he said. "Get going, this is urgent."

While he was fixing the wound, she opened her eyes again. She looked at him. She saw the sweat glistening on his face and she said, "Am I going to die?"

He couldn't do anything to stop the bleeding. He said rather helplessly, "It's the best way for you, I think."

She said, "I think so, too," and she began to cry again.

He tied a pad over the wound, but he knew it was useless. She said, "Give me a drink."

He had to hold her head to give her the Scotch. She said, "I'm sorry about everything."

Duffy's face was very hard. "You little girls are always sorry when it's too late."

She said, "It was your fault that I killed your woman."

Duffy said, "It's best you should go like this." He couldn't bring himself to say anything else.

"No other man's ever turned me down," she said. "Remember I offered myself?"

"Yeah, I remember. I guessed you'd want to settle that score."

"If you wrote down everything, I could sign it," she said. "I'd like that."

Duffy took a quick step to the writing-desk, found a pad and came back. She said, in a low voice, "You'll be quick?"

Duffy said, "Sure. You killed Cattley, didn't you?"

"Yes, Cattley was double-crossing Gleason, who was my husband. No one knew about that. Gleason was bad, but he was making money. I had to have that. I learnt that Cattley was taking half, so I pushed him down the lift shaft. He was a little man, it was quite easy. You came along and covered me on that. Then Max. You see, they all bothered me. I tried once just to see, but none of them were any good. So after that I didn't want them again. Max was always pressing me. Then he got the photos, and asked me up to his flat to trade them in the usual way, so I went and I killed him too."

Duffy wrote quickly. He gave her another drink. Shep came in and stood behind him. He said, "English is coming." Duffy raised his hand for silence.

Annabel went on, "I hated you. When I went out to the Shann woman's villa to find the book, I thought you'd both be out. I saw you drive the car away, and I thought she was with you. Then I went inside and she started getting excited, so I killed her too."

Duffy said, "It got you nowhere, did it?"

She said, so faintly that Duffy had to lean forward, "Was so tired of… Murray… when you came… I… thought I could… put it… on you."

Duffy scribbled quickly, put the pen in her hand. "Can you do it?" he said anxiously.

She said, "I… can't… see."

Duffy held her hand and put the nib on the paper. "Sign," he said loudly and roughly. The pen slipped out of her fingers and her hand dropped out of his. He turned and looked at Shep. "Can you beat that?" he said savagely. "This confession lets me out, and I'm damned if she doesn't die on me before she signs."

Shep said, "That's tough."

Duffy stood up. "Look at her, Shep," he said. "You ain't likely to find a worse woman in the country."

Shep shrugged. "What's the matter, as long as she looks right?"

Duffy said impatiently, "Clive okay?"

Shep nodded. "He'll be out for another hour."

Duffy glanced at the clock. He saw it was quarter to six. He said, "Come on, we got a date. Let English fix this."

Shep followed him out of the apartment and down the stairs. Duffy said when they got into the street, "Morgan'll just hate me for this."

Shep grinned as he climbed into the car. "Yeah," he said. "Will they burn the nance?"

Duffy shrugged. "Maybe English'll hush it all up. But you bet they'll pin something on that nance to keep him busy."

It was just after six when Duffy swung the Buick to the curb outside the Belmont Plaza. "Come with me," he said.

They walked into the busy lobby. Across the lounge he saw Schultz reading a newspaper. Schultz made no sign that he had seen him, but by the way he folded the paper and laid it down Duffy knew he had.

The little guy and Joe came in. Joe was looking mad, he scowled at Duffy. The little guy said, "You're going to get into trouble one of these days."

Duffy said, "Skip the talk. Let's get down to business." He walked into the bar. The little guy followed him, leaving Joe in the lobby. Shep beamed at Joe, but said nothing.

The little guy said, when they got to the bar, "What you doing with Gilroy's mob?"

Duffy stared at him coldly. "You'll know before long," he said. "Come on, let's get this over, you stink."

The little guy giggled. He put his hand inside his coat and took out an envelope. He opened it and drew out a sheaf of notes. Duffy watched him count them. Twenty-five grand. Then Duffy took the note-book out and they exchanged. The little guy said, "And the duplicate?" Duffy smiled. His eyes were like ice. "The State's got that."

The little guy shook his head sadly. "You shouldn't have done that," he said. "Morgan's going to get mad when I tell him that."

Duffy said deliberately, "Morgan can—himself."

The little guy giggled again. "I'll tell him that too." He put the note-book in his pocket. "Those notes are phoneys," he said, as an afterthought.

Duffy took the envelope out of his pocket, examined one of the notes carefully. It looked all right to him. "You don't say," he said.

The little guy nodded cheerfully. "Sure, Morgan wouldn't pay a punk like you in real dough."

Duffy put the notes away. He had an idea.

The little guy said, "Well, for God's sake, you're taking it quietly, ain't you?"

Duffy said, "Take my tip, scram."

The little guy looked at him, then nodded. "You'll see me again, of course," he said apologetically.

Duffy said, "Before you think."

He watched the little guy walk out, followed by Joe, then he beckoned to Shep and called for two ryes. Shep came over. "You got it?" he said.

Duffy slipped one of the notes out and gave it to him.

Shep glanced at it, beamed and said, "As easy as that, huh?"

Duffy pushed the glass over to him, drained his quickly and nodded at the barman. "One more," he said.

Shep said, "You drink too quickly."

"So long as I don't drink too much, why should I worry?"

Shep frowned, then said, "It amounts to the same, don't it?"

He gave Duffy back the note reluctantly. Duffy put it with the others. He said, "Let's go."

Gilroy and Schultz were sitting in the Buick waiting for them. When the Buick was rolling, Gilroy said, "No fuss?"

Duffy handed the notes over to him. "There they are," he said.

Gilroy counted them and whistled. "This don't seem natural," he said.

Duffy stared out of the window. "Maybe, it ain't."

Gilroy examined the notes carefully, then he said, "Phoneys."

Duffy nodded. "Yeah, he told me as much before he left."

"So what?"

Duffy turned his face, so that he looked at Gilroy.

"I guess we're going to frame Morgan with those. It'll be worth twenty-five grand to clap him away. English'll pay as much as that for the job."

"How… frame?"

"We'll go out to his place and plant that stuff tonight. There's a nice little rap for making notes as big as these. Once we get those planted, then we tip English, and he does the rest."

Gilroy said, "The dough would've been better."

Duffy shrugged. "You can't have everything," he said.

Shep had been listening to the conversation. He turned his head. "Say, those notes sure made a sap of me. Why not put 'em on the street? We'd pass 'em okay."

Duffy said, "No, that's not the way to play it. You'll get the dough all right, but it'll take a little longer. When you get it, it'll be safe."

When they got back to the Bronx, Duffy 'phoned English. English said, "We've got Wessen."

"How about Annabel?"

"Never mind about her. I've paid another five thousand dollars into your account. That should hold you for a bit."

Duffy grinned to himself. "Listen, English," he said. "Are you holding Clive Wessen on a murder rap?"

"Murder?" English seemed surprised. "No, he's in for cocaine smuggling."

Duffy grinned and winked over his shoulder at Gilroy.

"I bet that guy had his pockets full of the white stuff," he said.

"The police found enough incriminating evidence to justify an arrest," English said smoothly.

"I bet they did," Duffy said. "And Annabel?"

There was a pause, then English said in a faintly hostile voice, "You know about that. My unfortunate daughter was killed by a hit-and-run motorist."

"That's too bad," Duffy said. "I'll be having some more work for you in a little while." He hung up. "That bird's cagey," he said to Gilroy. "They framed Wessen, smothered Annabel's murder. It's a hit-and-run case."

Gilroy shook his bullet head. "You gotta watch him."

Duffy shrugged. "We're playing on his side." He went over and helped himself to a drink. "It's nice to have a guy like that behind you."

Gilroy nodded and left him. When he had gone, Duffy sat down and did some thinking. Then he got up and went over to the small bureau, unlocked the top drawer, took out the bundle of money he had left there, and looked at it. Then he went to the door and turned the key. He sat down at the table and counted the money carefully. He'd got thirty-four grand and some small notes. He counted on the table three piles of five thousand dollars. That left him nineteen thousand dollars. He split the nineteen grand into four parts. One went into his hip pocket, another in his side pocket, and the third in his trouser pocket. The fourth, three thousand dollars, he folded carefully and put in his shoe. He had to take his shoe off and put it on twice before it was comfortable.

He went over and unlocked the door, picked up the money on the table, and wandered into the bar.

Gilroy was talking to Schultz and Shep. They were drinking beer. They all looked up, a faintly expectant expression on their faces.

Duffy leant on the bar. "Here's your split," he said gently. He gave each man the money rolled in a tight ball. "Five grand," he said. "Don't count it now."

Shep picked up his glass and poured the beer on the floor at his feet. "Gimme champagne," he said to the barman. "I'm goin' to launch myself."

Schultz fingered his cut, then shoved it in his trouser pocket. He looked vacantly at Duffy, nodded, and went out.

Gilroy turned his head, watching him walk across the floor. "That guy's mighty careful with his dough," he said. "I wouldn't say he's tight. He's careful."

Duffy glanced at the clock. "I'm going to snatch myself a little sleep," he said. "We'll get going about eleven."

Gilroy said, "Any dough hanging to this job?"

Duffy nodded. "Sure," he said. "I want you boys to make money while you can."

Shep took his short fat nose out of his glass. "That's a hell of a way to talk," he said.

Duffy grinned. "You expect to earn this dough, don't you?" he said.

"Sure, but we won't work that hard."

Back in his room, Duffy rang Sam. He said, "Do you feel like doing me a favour?"

Sam said, "Aw, forget it, will you? Alice's only a little dumb; she don't know what it is to want things."

Duffy's mouth twisted. "You lay off Alice. She's right. See? Alice is god-dam right. If I'd got the sense of a louse, I'd be doing a job of work instead of trying to be a big shot. Well, I ain't got the sense, and what's more, I'm getting a kick out of this. What I want you to do is to keep your ear open down at headquarters. I want you to keep an eye on English. That bird's been pulling too many fast ones to make me sleep easy. Will you do that, Sam?"

Sam seemed puzzled. "Sure," he said. "I'll do any little thing like that."

Duffy said, "You'll keep me in touch. If anything starts popping, gimme a buzz?"

Sam said, "Sure," then he said, "You know what you're doing?" He sounded worried.

Duffy said, "I'm bucking something that thinks it's too big for me, but ain't." He added, "'Bye, soldier," and dropped the receiver on its prong.

Outside, he could hear the rain beating down. He went over to the bed and lay flat, one leg hanging over the side. He scratched the side of his face gently with his nail. "I wonder…" he said to himself, then he heard some-one walk past his door. He heard Gilroy say, "She don't wear 'em. It saves time." Shep said something in his tinny voice, but Duffy couldn't hear. In time, the sound of the rain lulled him.

Chapter Sixteen

Somewhere a big clock chimed half past twelve as the Buick slid to the curb. The rain drummed on the roof hard.

Shep said, "Heck! What a night!"

"You should worry, no one about," Duffy said, rolling down the window and putting his head out. The rain touched him, cold and sharp. He looked up and down the deserted street, then he rolled up the window again, opened the door, and stepped out. Gilroy followed him.

"Fat, you stay in the car," Gilroy said.

Shep nodded his tiny head. "Suits me," he said. He pulled a Luger from his overcoat pocket and laid it across his knees.

Then Schultz got out. The three hurried across the pavement to a block of offices.

"Round the back," Duffy said.

They walked on, turned a narrow alley, and then stopped. Just above their heads was the fire-escape. Gilroy put his back against the wall, folded his hands in front of him, and nodded at Schultz. Schultz put his foot in Gilroy's cupped hands, and Gilroy hoisted him up. Schultz just touched the fire-escape with his fingers. He said, "Higher."

Gilroy gave a little grunt, shifted his feet and raised Schultz a few inches. Schultz's fingers curled on the iron rung, and then he put his weight on it. The fire-escape creaked and slowly came down.

Duffy went up first, then Gilroy, then Schultz. On the first landing, Duffy stood aside, whilst Schultz opened a window. He did it very easily. They all climbed into a dark corridor.

Duffy said, "It's on the first floor."

They walked quietly forward, Duffy a little ahead, the other two on either side of him, a few steps in the rear. Duffy held a powerful flash directed on the floor. He kept the beam down, but the reflection lit up the frosted panelled doors. At the end of the corridor Duffy read, "Morgan Navigation Trust Co."

"Here," he said.

Schultz examined the lock, bent over it, then stepped back. He said in a low voice, "Go ahead."

Duffy pulled the Colt from his waist-band and gently opened the door. Then he walked in.

The office was big. Steel files lined the walls. There were three large flat-topped desks. Three typists' desks, holding typewriters. The centre desk had a number of telephones.

Duffy said, "Morgan's room is over there, I guess."

He wandered over to a door at the far end of the office and went through. The room was smaller than the outer office, but it was more luxurious.

Duffy went round the desk and sat down. He tried the drawers, but they were all locked. He looked over at Gilroy. "I guess we won't disturb anything. Morgan might tumble. I'll just plant the notes and we'll blow."

Schultz said, "Maybe there's a heap of dough in this joint." He said it wistfully.

Duffy took the roll of counterfeit money from his pocket, spread them flat. He leant forward, picked up a framed calendar and took off the back. Then he put the notes in the calendar and replaced the back.

"You like that?" he said.

Gilroy nodded. "That'll be difficult to find."

"You'll be surprised." Duffy pulled the telephone towards him and dialled a number.

While the line buzzed, the three stayed motionless. Only Gilroy showed he was anxious. His big eyes rolled continuously.

The line connected. English said, "Who's that?" He sounded sharp.

Duffy drawled into the 'phone, "I've got Morgan sewed up," he said. "If your boys make a call at his office early tomorrow, they can safely slap a charge on him."

"Where are you?"

"It don't matter. Look, this is a tip off. Morgan's got twenty-five grand in phoney notes hidden in his desk calendar. Could you make that stick?"

English was silent for a moment, then he said, "You certainly get action, don't you? We'll make it stick all right."

Duffy said, "Morgan Navigation Trust Co."

"I know." English hung up gently.

Duffy pushed the telephone away from him and stood up. "Let's go," he said.

They walked out of the office, carefully relocking the door, down the fire-escape, into the pouring rain.

Shep was still sitting there, fondling his gun. They climbed into the Buick, and Schultz started the engine.

Shep said, "All right?"

"Easy," Duffy returned, lighting a cigarette. "Morgan's going to get a mighty big shock tomorrow."

Gilroy said out of the dark, "English has got to be pretty leery to pin anything on that bird."

Duffy forced a thin stream of smoke down his nostrils. "English can handle him all right," he said. "You'll see."

Schultz said, "We go back, don't we?"

Duffy nodded. "Yeah," he said, "the hay wants hitting."

As Schultz headed East, Shep said in a confidential whisper to Duffy, "I thought I'd have a woman tonight. You know, just to celebrate the five grand."

Duffy nodded sleepily. He began to think about Olga.

"It's a hell of a night to look for a woman, ain't it?" Shep went on gloomily.

Duffy grunted. He wished Shep would shut up.

Schultz had been listening. He said, "For God's sake, Fat, what you want with a woman?"

Shep giggled self-consciously, and Gilroy joined in. "He's got the dough, why shouldn't he enjoy himself? Lay off him," he said.

They drove two blocks in silence, then Shep said to Duffy, "Ain't you got a woman?"

Duffy turned his head slightly. He could just see Shep's face, stuck like a turnip on his shoulders, as the street lights flashed past, lighting Shep at regular intervals. "Think about your own troubles," his voice was cold. "I'll think about mine."

"You bet," Shep said hastily. "I didn't mean a thing."

Gilroy broke in, "Did English say anything about dough, when he talked to you?"

Duffy shook his head, then remembering that Gilroy couldn't see him, he said, "No."

The Buick ran along the curb, slowed, and came to a stop outside the Bronx.

Schultz said. "Hop out. I'll take her over to the garage."

They climbed out and hurried down the basement steps, the rain beating down on them.

Gilroy unlocked the door and they entered quickly. The passage was dark. Gilroy swore softly. "Where the hell's Jock got to?" he said, speaking of the thin man. "He ought to be still up."

"Maybe he's got himself drunk," Shep said. "I gave him ten bucks out of my split."

Gilroy groped around and switched on the light. "You come and have a drink?" he said to Duffy.

Duffy said, "Sure, my feet are wet. I could do with a shot of Scotch."

Gilroy led the way down the passage, and walked into the bar. The first thing that caught his eye was the thin man. He was lying on his back, his hands and legs sprawling and his face a mask of blood.

The little guy said sharply, "Reach."

Gilroy and Duffy raised their hands. Shep dropped on his knee, drew his

Luger and fired at the little guy all in one movement.

Joe, stepping behind the door, tapped Shep with the butt of his gun as he fired. Shep gave a little cough and fell on his hands and knees. He looked like a stricken elephant.

Duffy said between his teeth, "Don't touch him again." Joe looked at him in wonder, then he grinned. "My, ain't you a pip?" he said admiringly.

The little guy said apologetically, "Take it easy. Don't move. I'd hate to pop this heater, but I gotta do it if you crowd me."

Gilroy said, hardly moving his rubbery lips: "What you want?"

"We want the pip," Joe said. "Ain't he hung a rap on Clive? Well, sure we want the pip. I wanta bounce him a little, don't I?" He looked triumphantly at the little guy. Then he walked over to Duffy, grinning from ear to ear. He feinted with his left, and hit Duffy on his ear, with a tremendous swinging punch that started from his ankles.

Duffy saw it coming a split second too late. A bomb burst inside his head. A bright light blotted the room out.

"Spill his guts," the little guy said with a snigger. "Go on, Joe, burst him open."

Joe walked over to Duffy quickly with long, sliding steps. He put his hand down on Duffy's body, seized Duffy low and swung him off the floor. He lifted him quite easily and smashed him down on the boards, as if he were dumping coal.

The little guy said, "Let's get him out of here."

Joe said, "Sure." He dragged Duffy to his feet and began pulling him to the door.

Gilroy stood like a waxwork, only his great eyes rolling in terror. The little guy looked at him, curling up his tight mouth. "Here it is, nigger," he said, and squeezed the trigger. The gun crashed. Gilroy stood with his hands folded over his belly, gradually sinking at the knees. His curiously coffee-coloured skin glistened with sweat. He went down very slowly. First on his knees, then a little on one side. His hip-bone struck the floor hard, and his face followed, cutting the flesh on the boards.

The little guy stood over him, looking at Joe. "Shall I finish him?" he asked.

Joe paused in the doorway, holding Duffy by his shirt-front. "Let the punk bleed," he said, with a snarl. "It takes longer that way, don't it?"

The little guy giggled and pushed his gun back in his holster. "You get ideas," he said.

Joe admired himself. "Don't I?" he said, walking down the passage, pulling Duffy with him. He said over his shoulder, "I'm going to give myself a grand time with this bum."

The little guy followed him closely. He opened the front door, and together they stepped out into the driving rain.

The sudden cold driving shower of water brought Duffy to his senses. He placed his legs firmly against the step and arched his body. Joe was brought up short. He swore at Duffy, who swung a punch blindly into the darkness. He hit Joe on the nose. He so startled Joe that the big tough let him go and reeled back, took a false step and almost went over.

Duffy scrambled away hastily, just as Schultz began blazing away from across the road. Schultz's .45 roared three times. Duffy felt a slug thud into the wall above his head.

The little guy fired twice at Schultz, his gun cracking like dry wood snapping, only much louder. Duffy fumbled at his waist, and pulled out his Colt. He crouched in the shadow, trying to see where Joe was. The rain blinded him, and the solitary street light, about fifty feet away, threw only black shadows.

Holding the gun, Duffy began to back further into the dark. He wanted to cross the road and get over to Schultz. Further down the road, the blackness was intense. He thought, if he could get there, he could cross in safety. He felt his heart beating hard against his ribs, but he wasn't scared. He felt a strong sense of exhilaration flooding through him.

Schultz began firing again. Three sharp sounds. Duffy could see the flash from the gun. He crossed the road, running bent double.

Faintly, somewhere at the far end of the street, came the faint blast of a whistle, then a low drumming of a nightstick being beaten on the pavement.

Schultz called to him, "The cops."

Duffy ran forward again, keeping to the wall, hugging the dark shadows. Schultz from a doorway pulled him into the shelter.

He said, "I've got to get out of here quick. The bulls know me."

Duffy said, "Gilroy's dead." He spoke as if he had been running a long way. "The cops can't touch you. I've got protection."

Schultz snarled in the darkness. "My rod's hot," he said.

Duffy held out his hand. "Change," he said. "They won't look at mine."

Schultz passed his over, and took Duffy's. They heard the wail of a siren, and a fast, closed car came swinging round the corner. Duffy stepped out into the street and waved. The car skidded to a standstill.

Four beefy faces looked at him from the car, suspiciously. He felt the hidden menace of guns, unseen in the dark, threatening him. He stood quite still.

Then one of them said, "It's okay. I know this guy."

Duffy stepped up to the car. "Morgan's gang've just knocked Gilroy off," he said slowly, putting his foot on the step. "I was there. You've come along at the right time."

Hesitatingly, three of the cops got out of the car and stood undecided in the rain, then they turned and walked over to the Bronx.

Duffy jerked his hand, signalling to Schultz, and followed them. Schultz, walking with elaborate caution, crossed the road and caught up with Duffy.

Inside, the three cops stood and looked at Gilroy, then walked over and stirred Shep with a foot.

One said, "He'll be okay. Just a rap."

The Sergeant caught sight of Schultz, and his face clouded. Duffy could see the sullen hostile expression blotting out indifference. The Sergeant said, "Where were you?"

Duffy broke in, "He's okay. He was putting my car away."

The Sergeant looked at Duffy, scowled, then said, "You're in the clear now, but watch your step." There was an ominous threat in his voice. It puzzled Duffy.

Shep began to move. Straightening his great limbs, and grunting. He raised his head painfully. Duffy thought he looked like a stranded turtle, lying there.

He said, "It's all right."

Shep looked at him blankly, sat up and rubbed the back of his head. He began to swear softly and vilely. When he saw Gilroy, he stopped. He turned his head and looked at Duffy. Then he got to his feet.

The Sergeant had given instructions for an ambulance; he was wandering round the room, sniffing suspiciously at everything.

Duffy said to Shep, "They beat it in the rain."

Shep put his hand across his eyes and squeezed his temples, as if trying to force his eyes back to normal. He said in his tinny voice, very low and hoarse, "I'll square those rats, you see."

Schultz was watching the cops uneasily. He said out of the corner of his mouth, "These birds ain't acting friendly."

Duffy went across the room and fixed drinks. He said, "You boys want something while you're waiting?"

The two cops looked up, their stupid faces brightening. The Sergeant said, "Skip that. You know better."

Duffy held the glass in his hand, astonished, but he said nothing. The ambulance came up then. They could hear the siren, and two white-coated attendants scooped Gilroy up and took him away.

The Sergeant came over to Schultz. "You got a rod?" he said.

Schultz pulled Duffy's Colt from his holster and handed it over. The Sergeant examined it, his eyes narrowed, and his lips thin red. "We'll look this over," he said. "It might have a record."

Duffy moved forward and took the gun out of the Sergeant's hand. He said in a hard voice, "Tell English I took it from you," he said. "I want this cannon for a while."

Thick red veins knotted at the Sergeant's neck. His watery blue eyes bulged. He didn't say anything, but walked out, jerking his head at the other two.

When they had gone, Schultz said uneasily, "Those guys seem to hate us."

Duffy stood frowning at the floor. Then he said, "I don't like this. Maybe English's losing his grip."

He went to his room and dialled. When English answered, Duffy said, "We've had a shooting here." His voice was tense and sharp. "Morgan's mob knocked off Gilroy and tried to iron me out. They got away."

English said, "You got to be careful."

Duffy grinned mirthlessly at the mouthpiece. "You telling me," he said. "What I want you to know is the cops seemed kind of unfriendly. You're giving me protection. I don't like to have it come back on me. These birds were only keeping their hands off me with an effort."

English said softly, "You're wanted for a murder rap. You can't expect too much."

Duffy stared at the opposite wall. "How long's your protection going to last, once Morgan's out of the way?"

English said immediately, "You've got nothing to worry about. I'm getting the papers to run the whole case tomorrow, clearing you. You see, you'll be in the clear tomorrow."

Duffy said, "We've fixed Morgan. You'll pay twenty-five grand into my bank tomorrow?"

English said, "Sure, tomorrow. When they got Morgan I'll do that."

Duffy said, "Bye," and hung up. He walked across to the window and looked out, lifting the blue blind away from the window. He could only see faintly the street light. He dropped the blind and went once more to the telephone. It began to ring. Its sudden violence startled him. He sat on the edge of the bed and pulled the receiver towards him.

Alice's voice said, "Oh, Bill."

He said, "Why, for God's sake. It's nearly two o'clock. What makes you call at this time?"

She said, her voice uneven, "Sam just heard. They say there's been shooting at the Bronx. I was so frightened. I thought something had happened to you."

"Where's Sam?"

"They called him up. He's gone down to headquarters. You are all right?"

"Sure, I'm all right. There's nothing to worry about." He paused and then went on, "Listen, honey, you're right. This is getting me nowhere. I'm quitting. I got nineteen grand salted away, and another little packet tomorrow, then I'm through. English is taking the heat off, and it's going to turn out swell."

She said, "I'm… I'm glad. It is all right, isn't it, Bill?" He thought she was crying.

"You see," he said, "tomorrow we'll have a party. You and Sam and me. It's going to be fine. And listen, I'm coming round in the afternoon, and you and me will go shopping. You can buy yourself the world. Doll yourself up and surprise Sam. How do you like that?"

She said, her voice still anxious, "I shan't rest until you're with us."

"Good night," he said. "You're worrying about nothing."

When he hung up, he sat on the edge of the bed thinking. A little shiver ran through him suddenly, and he got up impatiently. "Hell," he said. "I guess my feet are damp."

Chapter Seventeen

Duffy woke with a start. Across the room, the sun leaked round the side of the blind, throwing ragged lines of light on the walls.

The telephone was ringing, grinding shrilly.

He said, "Goddam it," and turned over in the bed. Pulling the blanket over his ears, he tried to ignore the jarring noise, but the bell went on ringing, insistently.

He turned over again and climbed stiffly out of the bed. Scooping up the telephone, he shouted, "What the hell is it?"

Sam was yelling at the other end. He was so excited that Duffy couldn't understand a word. He said, "I can't hear you. What is it?"

Sam choked, then came over quieter. "For God's sake, Bill," he said. "Hell's broken loose this end. English's double-crossing you. He's slapped every rap he can lay hold on you."

Duffy stiffened. "Tell me," he said.

"They arrested Morgan on some counterfeit charge. Then English got on to headquarters and withdrew his protection. I was there when he did it. He's thrown you to the wolves. They're indicting you for Olga's, Gleason's and Annabel's murder."

Duffy sat limply on the bed, still holding the telephone. "The lousy rat," he said.

Sam said urgently, "You've got to go carefully. They can't hope to make all those raps stick."

Duffy's mouth twisted. "They'll carry me to the station, that it?"

Sam said, "English is pulling wires. They're waiting for you to run, then they'll come after you with gunpowder."

"That'll let English right out of this, won't it? Me stiff, he can pin all his lousy scandal to my tombstone."

"What the hell are you going to do?"

Duffy said, "Skip, I guess I might make it in the Buick."

Sam said, "They'll be watching your joint by now. The news came over ten minutes ago. They started right away."

Duffy said, "Do they know you're in this?"

"No. They don't even know I know you."

"If I can't make it, can I hide up at your place?"

"Sure," Sam spoke without hesitation. "Why not come on over and lay up, until the heat's cooled?"

"I'll try a getaway first." Duffy said gently, "Thanks, soldier, you've been a swell help. My love to Alice. Don't tell her more than you need." He hung up and looked quickly at the clock. It was just after ten o'clock.

He dressed with cold unhurried haste. He made sure that he had his money safely distributed in his pockets, then picking up his hat he walked to the door, shot the bolt and stepped quietly into the passage.

As he walked into the deserted bar, he heard the faint wail of a siren, approaching rapidly. He smiled, without being amused, turned back and ran to the front door. He stepped into the street and walked across the road fast, but without any panic. He walked like a man about to start a day's work, who knows he's a little behind the clock.

He could see a long closed car swinging round the bend at the far end of the road. The siren was silent. He stepped hastily into the shadow of the garage and walked over to the Buick.

Schultz said, "Wait!" His voice had an edge to it.

Duffy peered and saw him standing in the dim light, half hidden by a big Packard.

"The cops are moving in," Duffy said in a low voice. "I'm skipping. Want to come?"

Schultz shook head. He was standing very still. Duffy looked again, then stiffened. Schultz was holding a shotgun in his hands; he was pointing it directly at Duffy.

Duffy said with stiff lips, "What's the idea?"

"Put that dough on the floor," Schultz said, "then you can skip."

Duffy said, "The cops are just across the road. You can't start anything."

Schultz's face was white, beads of sweat stood out on the backs of his hands. He said, "Don't talk. Put the dough down quick."

Duffy slowly put his hand inside his coat. The Colt-butt felt cold under his touch. Something was forcing him to pull that gun. A hidden instinct to keep what was his. His fingers closed over the butt and he braced himself. Then he jerked at the butt, at the same time he threw himself to one side.

There was a sharp choked roar from the shotgun, and something bit into

Duffy's side, sending him over on the oily concrete. White-hot wires of pain shot to his brain, making him feel sick and dizzy. He couldn't think of anything, just the jagged pain eating at his chest.

Faintly he heard someone cursing him, and then hands roughly jerked him this way and that. When the blinding light went away from his eyes, he saw Schultz run out of the garage, holding a gun tightly in his hand.

Duffy pulled himself to his feet by holding on to the wing of the Packard. He heard Schultz fire once, then twice. The noise of Schultz's gun was followed by a sharper report, as the cop in the car began shooting. The other cops were still in the Bronx.

Walking unsteadily over to the Buick, Duffy got in and started the engine. He tasted blood on his tongue, and he began to cough. Hard, tearing cough, that made his brain rattle in his skull. He could feel the blood running down his side, down his leg, into his shoe. Holding hard on to the wheel, he started the engine, slammed in the gear and shot out into the road. Schultz was still firing carefully at the cop from behind a stationary car. As Duffy swept past, both the cop and Schultz fired at him. The bullets made a cobweb on the window, but that was all. In his driving-mirror, he saw Schultz suddenly throw up his hands, and go over, like the felling of a tree. He had no time to see anything else, as the main road was ahead of him.

He drove fast, holding the wheel in both hands very hard, and sitting forward, his back clear of the seat. Hammers beat inside his head, and his chest seemed as if someone were stripping the flesh off his bones. He bit on to his underlip, and drove. His one fixed thought was to get to Sam's place. It wasn't far and it was safe. He thought if he held on a little longer, he'd make it.

Twisting and doubling, he felt that he had shaken off pursuit for the moment. The cop in the car hadn't much chance, with Schultz blazing away at him, to spot the Buick's plates. Anyway, that was what Duffy hoped. He came to McGuire's apartment round the back, pulling up in the narrow alley that skirted the fire-escapes from the block.

He felt strangely hot and weak, sitting there, and he wondered how the hell he was going to get up to the apartment. His wound seemed to have stopped bleeding now, and he looked down at the blood-caked suit with a little grimace. Then he reached over the back of the car and pulled his light dust-coat off the back seat. The effort made the sweat start out all over him, and he had to shut his eyes, as the building reeled drunkenly before him. He sat like that for several moments, then he began to cough again. Deep, tearing coughs that hurt.

It took him a long time to open the heavy door. He was surprised to find how weak he was. Then he stepped to the ground and immediately fell on his knees. He pulled himself up by the door, swearing softly. Obscene words, lodged deep in his subconscious, came tumbling from his lips. He steadied himself and put on the coat, hiding his bloodstained suit. Then he began to walk with uneven, hurried steps round the front.

He had to stop three times before he made it, but he got into the automatic elevator, shut the gates, pressed the button, and folded up on the floor.

The cage groaned and creaked on its upward journey. Duffy just sat there on the floor, breathing with little short gasps, frightened of the pain when he breathed normally. The elevator came to rest after an interminable time. He pulled himself to his feet by hooking his fingers in the grille. He stayed there, hanging on, like a man uncertain of his strength, breasting a gale. Then he balanced himself on the balls of his feet and took away his hands. Pulling open the grille, he lurched into the corridor.

Across the way was McGuire's apartment. He shuffled over and rapped on the door. Almost immediately Alice came. Her face lit up when she saw who it was, but almost at once her expression changed to alarm. "Bill, what is it?"

Before he could speak, the cough caught him again, and he folded up, his shoulder against the door.

She said, "O God," very softly, and put her arm round him, pulling him inside. She thrust the door to with her foot, and supported him through the sitting-room, into the bedroom.

He said thickly, "The flowers look good."

She lowered him to the bed, putting a pillow under his head. "What is it?" she asked.

"Get me a drink, honey," he mumbled, his mouth suddenly very dry.

Unsteadily, she ran into the other room, and returned with a bottle and glass. She poured him a stiff whisky, and held his head while he drank. The spirit knitted his will, and he managed to grin.

"Get my things off, baby," he said. "I ran into a handful of slugs."

Undressing him took time. She had to let him rest every now and then, but she finally got down to his shirt, and the caked blood nearly made her faint. Duffy said, "Don't get scared." He felt a lot stronger. "I don't think it's bad. It just hurts a lot."

She ran into the bathroom and came back with dressing, water and towels. She had to cut away his shirt. He had six pellet-holes down his right side. They had ceased to bleed. She stood looking at them, her eyes big and scared.

He said, "Listen, baby. You gotta get them out."

"I can't," she said. "I don't know how."

"Got some tweezers? You fix your eyebrows, don't you?" His mouth twisted into a little grin. "Try with those."

She looked at him, and shook her head.

He said, "It's important, baby."

When he said that, she drew a sharp breath and went over to the dressing-table. He reached for the bottle and gave himself a long pull.

She came back, holding the tweezers.

He said, "Burn a match round 'em."

While she was doing that, he drank some more whisky. By the time she started on him, he was pretty high.

Wires of pain clutched him, and sweat ran down his face. But he lay quite still, with his eyes shut, giving no sign that she hurt him.

He heard her say at last, "I've got them all." She sounded so far away that he turned his head slowly and looked at her. She was white, her large eyes sunk far in her head. Holding on to the edge of a small table, she seemed to sway before his eyes.

He said, "Get a grip on yourself." He tried to speak sharply, but just couldn't make it. "Have a quick drink, you're going to faint or something."

She sat down on the floor. "I'll… be… all right," she said, forcing her head down. "Don't worry. Just… give me a minute."

With a shaking hand he slopped some whisky into the glass and thrust it at her. "Go on, drink it," he said. The effort made his head swim.

He heard the glass rattle against her teeth as she drank. Then she got up unsteadily and put the glass on the table. "I'm all right now," she said.

Duffy said, "Put some dressing on this, and let me lie easy."

She sat down on the bed. "Would it be safe to get a doctor?"

He shook his head. "No, I'm on the run now, baby."

She began cutting a pad, biting her lips to stop her tears. He lay on his back, staring at the ceiling, slightly dazed by the alcohol.

She said, "I'll fix it with tape."

Duffy said, "You're swell."

With inexperienced hands, she strapped him, making a fair job of it. He lay watching her, and when she was done, he said, "Get me one of Sam's suits."

Her eyes opened. "What do you mean?"

"I'm getting out of here."

"Oh no, you're not," she said; "you're staying."

He shook his head impatiently. "I ain't getting you mixed up in this. There's a rap for you, if they find me here."

She said, with determination, "Don't get tough. You're staying."

He shut his eyes. "Okay," he said weakly. "Just for a little while."

She bent over and kissed his hot forehead. "I'm so sorry," she said.

He lifted his lids with an effort. "I started this… I guess it had to finish like this." Then, remembering, he said urgently, "Look in my coat. There ought to be some dough there."

She went over and gingerly examined the coat. "Nothing here," she said.

His mouth twisted. "Schultz got it," he said. The effort to worry was too much for him, and he closed his eyes.

She said, "Try and sleep."

"My right shoe. There's three grand hidden in it. It's for you."

She said, "Never mind that."

He raised his head, his eyes feverishly on her face.

"Take my shoe off and get the dough," he said urgently. "It's all I got out of this mess… it's for you."

She undid his shoes and took them off. She found the crumpled notes wedged in one of them. Holding the little ball of money in her hand, she stood there, tears running down her face.

He dropped his head back on the pillow again. "You're right, baby," he said slowly. "Money don't mean a thing."

She said, keeping her voice steady, "I'll leave you now. You must sleep. If you want me, call. I'll be right outside."

He said drowsily, "Sure, don't get Sam. I'm going to be okay. I'm feeling fine, only tired."

She pulled a light blanket over him, and he reached out and took her cool hand. "I've been a mug," he said.

Alice clenched her teeth hard to stop the sob that rose in her throat. She looked down at his white, drawn face, and forced her trembling lips into a smile. "You… you're okay now," she said. "Forget about it. You see, it's going to be all right."

She left him lying there on the bed. The heat of the street filtering through the window made him feel heavy and lifeless. The throb in his side was not bad. He just wanted to sleep.

How long he slept, he never knew. It might have been a few minutes, or a few hours, but he woke suddenly, his brain clear and full of strange urgent alarms. He raised his head and looked round the room, then over to the window. When his eyes reached the square of glass, he knew why he had awakened.

Joe and the little guy were standing on the fire escape, watching him. Even as he saw them, Joe pushed up the window, and stepped into the room. He said in a low voice, "We saw the bus, so we just dropped in."

The little guy sat on the sill. He nodded at Duffy. "We've been looking for you," he said.

Duffy turned his eyes to the door. "You wouldn't hurt her?"

Joe showed his teeth. "Not if she stays out," he said, keeping his voice down, "but if she comes in, she'll get a surprise."

Duffy dropped his head back on the pillow. He said, "Lock the door."

The little guy said, "Leave it, Joe. He won't squawk if she can get in easily." He smiled at Duffy, a tight little smile.

Joe wandered over to the bed and jerked off the blanket. His brutish face lit up when he saw the strapping. "You hurt?" he said. "Ain't that too bad."

Duffy said nothing; he just fixed Joe with hot, burning eyes. Whatever Joe did to him, he musn't let Alice hear.

Joe reached out a hand. Duffy stiffened, then realizing how futile it was, just kept his eyes on Joe's face. Joe took the pad in his fist, and ripped it and the strapping away.

The little guy giggled.

Duffy sank his teeth into his lower lip. He was very pale. The six little wounds began to ooze blood, running down Duffy's ribs on the sheet.

Joe sat down on the bed beside him. "Listen, pip," he said. "First you got Clive, then you fixed Morgan. You got a lot coming to you, ain't that right?"

Duffy said through his clenched teeth, "Go ahead… only quickly."

The little guy said, "Yes, Joe—get going."

Joe said, "I wanta take this guy apart an' see what makes him tick."

"That jane'll be in," the little guy said.

Joe grimaced. "I'll spill her insides all over this punk," he said.

Duffy lay flat on his back, looking up at the ceiling. His face and chest glistened with sweat. He was afraid, not for himself, but for Alice.

Joe put his big hand on Duffy's throat and squeezed. The little guy got off the window-sill and came over to watch. His mouth hung open a little. He stood on the far side of the bed, his eyes screwed up, watching.

Joe said, "Have a little air, lug," and eased the pressure, then he tightened his grip again.

The little guy suddenly cocked his ear. He said, "Listen."

Joe sat very still. His hand slightly relaxed. The only sound was the soft thrashing of Duffy's legs on the bed. A muscular reaction he had no control over. From the other side of the door they could hear Alice moving about, and they could hear the faint sound of crockery being moved.

"She's getting him a meal," the little guy said.

Joe grinned. "He's losing his appetite, ain't you, bright boy?" The effort of keeping his grip tight was making his face a little red. Then, drawing his lips back in a snarl, he threw his weight on his arms, savagely squeezing.

The little guy moved restlessly from one foot to the other. The room was absolutely silent now, except for Joe's heavy breathing. Then Joe got off the bed, flexing his thick fingers.

The little guy stepped to the window, then he jumped back quickly.

"Joe—"

Forms darkened the window, as three policemen, guns in hands, raced up the fire escape. They slipped into the room with paralysing speed.

Joe stood there, his mouth open, and the whites of his eyes suddenly yellow with terror. "Don't you shoot," he said with a jerk, putting up his hands.

The Sergeant pushed forward. His small eyes startled. "Quite a party," he said.

The little guy giggled. He stood close against the wall, his hands high. "You ain't got nothing on us," he said through white lips.

The Sergeant walked over to the bed, and stood looking. The other two officers remained motionless, their guns menacingly still.

The Sergeant said, "Well, for God's sake."

He walked over to the little guy and hit him in the middle of his face with his gun butt. The little guy's head thudded against the wall, and his legs spread, sliding him to the floor. He put his hands over his face, but he couldn't make a sound; he seemed to go into a fit.

Joe buckled at the knees. "Okay, boss," he quavered. "We didn't mean anything by it."

The Sergeant hunched his shoulders. "Sure, you didn't, you dirty rat," he said. "I've been waiting to nail you for a long time. Well, you've got it coming to you." He jerked his head to the other two. "Get the bums outa here."

Just then the door jerked open, and Alice stood there. The Sergeant stepped in front of her, and crowded her into the kitchen. She retreated, her eyes growing big.

She said, "You can't take him away… he's too ill… Please.…"

The Sergeant said, "That guy on the bed—Duffy?"

Alice nodded dumbly. "He's been shot… he's bad… please leave him there. Look, I'm getting him some soup. It's ready… you'll let him have that?"

The Sergeant pushed his cap to the back of his head, and blew out his cheeks. Her terrified face embarrassed him. "It don't matter about the soup," he said. He fumbled with his gun, pushing it into his hip pocket. Then he added, "He won't need it now."

The End

The Dead Stay Dumb
By James Hadley Chase

PART ONE

The Roughneck and the Shopkeeper's Daughter

There were three of them. The bigness of the room hid them from the sun burning up the road outside. They sat round a table, close to the bar, drinking corn whisky.

George, behind the bar, held a swab in his thick fingers, and listened to them talk. Every now and then he nodded his square head and said, "You're dead right, mister." He just "yessed" them along—that was all.

Walcott uneasily fingered a coin in his vest pocket. It was all the money he had, and it was worrying him. Freedman and Wilson had stood him a round, and now it was coming to his turn. He couldn't rise to it. His weak, freckled face began to glisten. He touched his scrubby moustache with a dirty thumb and moved restlessly.

Wilson said, "Cain't go no place these days but there's some lousy bum lookin' for a free flop an' a bite of somethin' to eat. This town's lousy with bums."

Walcott said quickly, "Ain't it gettin' hot in here? Seems like it's too hot to drink even."

Freedman and Wilson looked at him suspiciously. Then Freedman drained his glass and set it on the table with a little bang. "Ain't never too hot for me to drink," he said.

George leant over the bar. "Shall I fill 'em up, mister?" he said to Walcott.

Walcott hesitated, looked at the two blank, coldly suspicious faces of the other two, and nodded. He put the coin on the counter. He did it reluctantly, as if the parting with it was a physical hurt. He said. "Not for me... jest two."

There was a heavy silence while George poured the liquor. The other two knew it was Walcott's last coin, but they wouldn't let him off. They were determined to have everything they could from him.

George picked up the coin, looked at it, spun it in his thick fingers, and flipped it into the till. Walcott followed every movement with painful intensity. He screwed round a little in his chair, so that he couldn't see the others drinking. He put his hands over his eyes.

Freedman turned his red fat face and winked at Wilson. He said, "It's only the storekeepers that have the dough."

George said ponderously, "Yeah, you're right, mister."

"Sure I'm right," Freedman said, sipping his corn whisky. "Take a look at Abe Goldberg: ain't he got most of the dough in town?"

Walcott turned his head. His pale eyes lit up. "That guy's stinking with it," he said. "Hell of a lot of good it does him, too."

Wilson shrugged. "His fat wife sews up his pockets," he said. "He don't drink, he don't smoke, he don't do nothin'."

Freedman winked again. "You're wrong there," he said. "But what he does do don't cost him anything."

They laughed.

The three-quarter swing doors of the saloon pushed open and a girl came in. She stood hesitating in the patch of sunlight at the door, trying to see in the dimness of the room. Then she came over to the bar.

George said, "'Morning, Miss Hogan, how's your Pa?"

The girl said, "Gimme a pint of Scotch."

George reached under the counter and slapped down a bottle in front of her. She gave him a bill, and while he was getting change she looked round the room. She saw the three sitting watching her. They sat like waxworks, suspended in everything but her. She looked slowly from one to the other, then she tossed her head and turned back to the bar.

"I ain't got all day," she said. "Stir your stumps, can't you?"

George put the money on the counter. "Aw, Miss Hoga —" he began.

She picked up the money and the bottle quickly. "Forget it," she said, and walked out.

The three turned in their chairs as she went, their eyes fixed in a bright, unblinking stare. They watched her push the swing doors and disappear into the hot, sunlit road.

There was a lengthy silence.

Then Freedman said, "She ain't got a thing on under the dress, did you see?"

Walcott still stared at the door, as if hoping she'd return. He nervously wiped his hands on a cap he held on his knee.

Wilson said, "If I were Butch I'd take the hide off her back."

George said, "Ain't she a looker? There ain't another skirt in this dump like her, ain't that right?"

Walcott dragged his eyes away from the door. "Yeah," he said. "See the way she came in? Standin' in the sunlight like that. That girl's a tease. She's going to get into trouble one of these days, you see."

Freedman leered. "You don't know nothin'," he said. "You can't teach that babe a thing. I'm tellin' you. I've seen her at night with one of those engineer fellows in the fields."

The other two jerked their chairs forward. They leant over the table. George looked at them. They had suddenly lowered their voices. He couldn't hear what they were saying. He hesitated, then, feeling himself excluded, he moved further down the bar and began to polish glasses. Anyway, he told himself, it wasn't too healthy talking about old Butch Hogan's daughter. Old Butch was still dangerous.

A long, starved shadow of a man fell across the floor of the saloon, making George look up sharply.

The man stood in the doorway holding the swing doors apart with his hands. A battered, greasy hat pulled over his face hid his eyes. George looked at him, saw the frayed, stained coat, the threadbare trousers and the broken shoes. He automatically reached forward and put the cover on the free-lunch bowl.

"Another dam' bum," he thought.

The man came in with a limping shuffle, He looked at the three at the table, but they didn't see him. They were still wrangling about the girl. George leant forward a little over the bar and spat in the brass spittoon. Then, having expressed his attitude, he straightened up and went on polishing a glass.

"The name's Dillon," the man said slowly.

George said, "Yeah? Ain't nothin' to me. What's yours?"

"Gimme a glass of water." Dillon's voice was deep and gritty.

George said, his face hostile, "We don't serve water here."

"But you'll serve me an' like it," Dillon said. "D'you hear me, punk? I said water."

George reached under the counter for his club, but Dillon suddenly pushed up his hat and leant forward.

"You ain't startin' anything," he said.

The cold black eyes that looked at George made the barman suddenly shiver. He took his hand away with a jerk. Dillon continued to stare at him.

There were no guts in George. He was big, and every now and then he had to smack someone down with his club. He did it without thinking. This bum was different. George knew he'd get nowhere being tough with a guy like this.

"Here, take the water, an' get the hell outta here." He pushed a bottle of water across the wood in Dillon's direction.

The three at the table stopped talking about Hogan's daughter and turned in their chairs. Freedman said, "Well, here's another bum blown in."

George began to sweat. He walked down the counter to Freedman, shaking his head warningly.

Dillon took a long pull from the water-bottle.

Sure of himself, because of his two companions, Freedman said, "This punk stinks. Get him outta here, George."

Dillon put the bottle down on the counter and turned his head. His white, clay-like face startled Freedman. Dillon said, "You're the kind of heel that gets slugged some dark night."

Freedman lost some of his nerve. He turned his back and began talking to Walcott.

Just then Abe Goldberg came in. He was a little fat man, maybe about sixty, with a great hooked beak and two sharp little eyes. His mouth turned up at the corners, giving him a kindly look. He nodded at George and ordered a ginger ale. Dillon looked at him closely. Abe was shabby, but he wore a thick rope of gold across his chest. Dillon eyed that with interest. Abe met his eye. He said, "You a stranger around here?"

Dillon began to shuffle to the door. "Don't you worry about me," he said.

Abe looked him over, sighed, and put the glass on the wood. He walked over to Dillon, looking up at him. "If you could use a meal," he said, "go over to the store across the way. My wife'll fix you something."

Dillon stood looking at Abe, his cold eyes searching the little man's face. Then he said, "Yeah, I guess I'll do that."

The three at the table, and George, watched him shuffle out of the saloon. Freedman said, "That's a bad guy all right. There's sornethin' about that guy."

George mopped his face with the swab. He was mighty glad to see Dillon go. "You gotta be careful with those bums, Mr. Goldberg," he said. "You don't know how tough hoboes are."

Abe drained his glass, then shook his head. "That guy's all right. He's hungry," was all he said. He crossed the street and went into the store.

Abe Goldberg was proud of that store. It was all right. It was a good store. You could get most things from Goldberg's Stores. Maybe you did have to pay a little more, but it was convenient. All under one roof. It saved a walk in the heat, so you expected to pay a little more. Anyway, Abe made a good thing out of it. He didn't toss his money about, nor did he yell about it. He just socked it away in the bank and said nothing. Most people liked Abe. He was a little sharp, but then you expected that, too, so you haggled with him. Sometimes, if you haggled long enough, you got what you wanted cheaper. Abe's joint was the only one in town that you could haggle in. And sometimes people like to haggle.

Abe walked into his shady cool store, sniffed at the various smells, and smiled to himself. His wife, who came a little older than he, shook her black curls at him. She was fat, and she had big half-circles of damp under her arms, but Abe loved her a lot.

"Goldberg," she said, "what's the big idea, sending bums into my kitchen?"

Abe lifted his narrow shoulders and spread out his hands. "That guy was hungry," he said. "What could I do?"

He lifted the trap on the counter and passed through. His small hand patted his wife's great arm. "You know how it is," he said softly; "we've been hungry. Give him a break, Rosey, won't you?"

She nodded her head. "It's always the same: bum after bum comes into this town and they all make tracks for you. I tell you, Goldberg, you're a sucker." Her big, fleshy smile delighted him.

"You're a hard woman, Rosey," he said, patting her arm again.

Dillon was eating in the kitchen, intent and morose, when Abe went in. He glanced up, keeping his head lowered over his plate, then he looked down again.

Abe stood there, shifting his feet a little in embarrassment. He said at last, "You go ahead an' eat."

With his mouth full, Dillon said, "Sure."

Sitting there, his hat still wedged on his head, the knife and fork dwarfed in his big hairy hands, Dillon impressed Abe. There was an intense, savage power coming from him; Abe could feel it. It scared him a little.

For something to say, Abe remarked, "You come far?" Again Dillon raised his cold eyes and looked. "Far enough," he said.

Abe pulled up a chair and carefully lowered his small body down. He put his hands on the table—clean, soft hands of a child. He said, "Where you headin' for?"

Dillon tore a piece of bread from the loaf and swabbed his plate round, then he put the bread in his mouth and clamped on it slowly. He pushed his plate away from him and sat back, hooking his thumbs in his belt. He still kept his head slightly lowered, so Abe couldn't see him very well. "As far as I can git," he said.

"Maybe a drop of beer'd come nice?" Abe said.

Dillon shook his head. "I can't use the stuff."

In spite of himself, Abe's face brightened. The guy could have a drink on him with pleasure, but maybe he was getting a little generous. He said, "A smoke?"

Again Dillon shook his head. "Can't use that either."

Outside, in the store, Rosey gave a sudden squeal. Abe sat up listening. "What's up with my Rose?" he said.

Dillon explored his teeth with a match-end. He said nothing. Abe got to his feet and walked into the store.

Walcott was leaning over the counter, glaring at Rosey. His thin, bony face was red.

Abe said nervously, "What is it?"

Walcott shouted, "What's up? I'll tell you what's up, you dirty louse. She ain't givin' me no more tick, that's what's up."

Abe nodded his head. "That's right, Mister Walcott," he said, going a little white. "You owe me too much."

Walcott saw he was scared. He said, "You gimme what I want, or I'll bust you." He closed his hand into a fist and leant over the counter, swinging at Abe. Abe stepped back hastily and banged his head hard against a shelf. Rosey squealed again.

Dillon shuffled slowly out of the kitchen into the store. He looked at Walcott, then he said, "Lay off."

Walcott was drunk. The corn whisky still burnt in a fiery ball deep inside him. He turned slowly. "Keep out of this, you bum," he said.

Dillon reached forward and hit Walcott in the middle of his face. The blow came up from his ankles. A spongy mass of blood suddenly appeared where Walcott's nose had been. Walcott reeled away, holding on to his face with both hands.

Dillon stood watching him. He rubbed his knuckles with his other hand. He said, "Scram... get the hell outa here!"

Walcott went, his knees buckling as he walked.

Abe and Rosey stood motionless. The little man's hands fluttered up and down his coat. He finally said, "You shouldn't've hit him that hard."

Dillon said nothing. He began to move. to the door.

Abe said, "Wait. Don't go. I guess we gotta thank you for that."

Dillon turned his head. "Save it," he said, "I got to get goin'." Rosey plucked at Abe's sleeve. "Give that boy a job, Goldberg," she said.

Abe looked at her in astonishment. "Why, Rosey..." he began.

Dillon looked at them suspiciously. Standing there in the dim store, his great shoulders hunched, he frightened Abe.

Rosey said, "Go on, Goldberg, give him a break. You gotta get a hand some time, so make it now."

Abe looked timidly at Dillon. "Sure," he said uneasily.

"That's dead right. I was goin' to hire me a hand. That's right. Suppose we talk it over?"

Dillon stood hesitating, then he nodded.

"Sure; go ahead an' talk about it."

Myra Hogan walked down the main street, conscious of the turning heads. Even the colored men hesitated in their work, frightened to look up, but peeping, their heads lowered.

She clicked on, her high wooden heels tapping a challenge. The men watched her, stripping her with their eyes as she passed them.

The women watched her, too. Cold, envious eyes, hating her. Myra rolled her hips a little. She put on a slight strut, patting her dark curls. Her firm young body, unhampered by any restraining garment, moved rhythmically.

Her full, firm breasts jerked under the thin covering of her cheap flowered dress.

At the end of the street a group of slatternly women stood gossiping, ripping people to pieces in the hot sunlight. They saw her coming and stopped talking, standing there; silent, elderly, bulging women, worn out by childbirth and hard work. Myra stiffened as she approached them. For a moment her step lost its rhythmic swing. The wooden heels trod softer. Her confidence in herself had no solid foundations; she was still very young. In the company of her elders she had to force herself forward.

With an uneasy smile on her full red lips she came on. But the women, as she came nearer, shifted like a brood of vultures, turning their drooping shoulders against her, their eyes sightless, not seeing her. Again the wooden heels began to click. Her face flushed, her head held high, she went past.

A buzz of talk broke out behind her. One of the women said loudly: "I'd give her something—the dirty little chippy."

Myra kept on. "The sluts!" she thought, furious with them. "I've got everything, and they hate me."

The bank stood at the end of the main street. Clem Gibson was standing in the doorway. He saw Myra coming, and he nervously fingered his tie.

Clem Gibson was someone in the town. He ran the bank, he owned a car, and he changed his shirt twice a week.

Myra slowed down a little and flashed him a smile.

"Why, Miss Hogan, you are lookin' swell," Gibson said.

This line of talk pleased Myra. She said, "Aw, you're kiddin'."

Gibson beamed behind his horn glasses. "I wouldn't kid you, Miss Hogan, honest."

Myra made to move on. "Well, it's nice of you to say so," she said. "I've just got to get goin'. My Pa's waitin' for me."

Gibson came down the two steps. "I was going to suggest—that is—I wanted to ask you..." He paused, embarrassed.

Myra looked up at him, her long black lashes curling above her eyes. "Yes?"

"Look, Miss Hogan, suppose you an' me go places sometime."

Myra shook her head. She thought he'd got a hell of a nerve. Go out with him and have his horse-faced wife starting a beef? He was crazy. Myra had enough sense to leave the married men alone. They were only after one thing, and she wasn't giving anything away. "Pa just wouldn't stand for it," she said. "He don't like married men takin' me out. Ain't he soft?"

Gibson stepped back. His face glistened with embarrassment. "Sure," he said, "your Pa's right. You better not tell him about this. I wasn't thinking." He was scared of Butch Hogan.

Myra moved on. "I won't tell him," she said.

He watched her hungrily as she went, then turned back to the bank.

It was quite a walk to her home, and she was glad when she pushed open the low wooden gate that led to the tumbledown shack.

She stood at the gate and looked at the place. She thought, "I hate it! I hate it! I hate it!"

The garden was a patch of baked, cracked mud. The house was a one-storeyed affair, made throughout with wood that wind and rain had warped and sun had bleached. It stood there—an ugly, depressing symbol of poverty.

She walked up the path and climbed the two high steps leading to the verandah. In the shadow, away from the sun, Butch Hogan sat, his great hands resting on the top of a heavy stick.

He said, "I've been waiting for you."

She stood there and looked at him. His broken, tortured face, those two horrible eyes, sightless, with a yellow blob in each pupil, looking like two clots of phlegm, the great square head, the overhanging brows, and the ferocious mouth made her shiver. He startled her by suddenly regurgitating violently into the mud patch a sodden wad of chewing-tobacco.

He said, "Say somethin', can't you? Where in hell've you been?"

She put the bottle of whisky on the table beside him. "There it is," she said, and she put beside it the rest of the money. With fumbling fingers he checked the money before slipping it into his pocket. Then he stood up and stretched. Although he was tall, his great shoulders gave him a squat look. He turned his face in her direction. "Go on in. I wantta talk with you."

She went into the living-room, leading off the verandah. It was a large room, untidy and full of aged and decaying furniture. Hogan followed her in. He moved with quick, cat-like steps, avoiding in some extraordinary way any obstacles that lay in his path. Blindness had not anchored him. He had been like that for ten years. At first the darkness had suffocated him, but he had fought it, and, like all his other fights, he had beaten it. Now it was of little hindrance to him. He could do most things he wanted to. His hearing had intensified and served him for his eyes.

Myra stood sulkily by the table. She made patterns with her flimsy shoes on the dusty floor.

Hogan went to a cupboard, found a glass, and poured himself out a stiff shot of whisky. Then he went over to the one overstuffed chair and folded himself down in it. He took a long pull from the glass.

"What's your age now?" he asked abruptly. The two yellow clots fixed on her.

"Seventeen."

"Come here," Hogan said, reaching out a great thick arm.

She didn't move.

"If I come an' get you, you're goin' to have grief."

She moved over to him reluctantly, and stood just by his knees. "What is it?" she asked, her face a little scared.

His hand closed on her arm, the big thick fingers pinching her muscle, making her squirm.

"Stand still," he said. With his free hand he touched her lightly. Then he let her go, and sat back with a grunt. "You're growing up," he said.

Myra stepped back, a little flush of anger on her face. "You keep your paws off me!" she said.

Butch pulled at the coarse hairs growing out of his ears. "Sid-down," he said; "I'm goin' to talk to you."

"Supper ain't ready," she said; "I ain't got time to listen to you."

He left his chair with incredible speed, and before she could dart away from him he struck her shoulder with the flat of his hand. He was aiming at her head, but he misjudged. She went over on hands and knees and stayed there, dazed. He knelt down beside her. "You're getting big ideas, ain't you?" he snarled at her. "You think I can't hold you, but I can. Do you get that? Maybe I've lost my peepers, but that ain't goin' to mean a thing to you. So get wise to yourself, will you?"

She sat up slowly, nervously feeling her shoulder. A smack from Butch meant something.

"I gotta hunch you're goin' to take after your Ma. I've had my eye on you for some time. I hear what's been said. You're after the punks already. Like your Ma. You're showing yourself off, an' you're working up a hot spot for yourself. Well, I'm watchin' you, see? I'm going to crack down on you, once I catch you at it. You leave punks alone, and make 'em leave you alone."

She said uneasily, "You're nuts! I don't go around with fellas."

Butch sneered. "I'm tellin' you before you start. You're ripe. You're ready to go ahead. Well, start somethin' an' see what you get."

She climbed to her feet. "You gotta catch me at it," she thought.

"Okay, go an' get somethin' to eat. You get the idea now, huh?"

She turned to the door, but he reached out and jerked her back. "You get it?"

"Oh, sure!" she said impatiently.

Butch tapped the broad belt round his waist. "If ever I catch you with a man, I'm goin' to lift the hide off your back."

She snatched her arm away and walked out of the room, her knees trembling a little.

Outside, a ramshackle car drew up, and three men got out.

Myra sped to the door, looked out, then ran to her bedroom. Her eyes were bright with excitement, and a little smile flickered on her lips. Gurney was coming in, with his ham boxer. Gurney made Myra's heart flutter. He was some guy, this Gurney.

Sankey the boxer walked up the broken path, his head on his chest, his big hands hanging loosely by his side. Hank, his trainer, watched him anxiously. He caught Gurney's eye, and jerked his head. He looked worried. Gurney was looking for Myra. Sankey gave him a pain.

The three of them paused on the verandah. Butch came out of the room. He said, "You ain't been around here for some time. How're you makin' out?"

Gurney made signs to the other two. Sankey took no notice, but Hank nodded briefly.

Butch was glad to have them. He said, "Sit down, for Pete's sake. How's your boy shapin'?"

Under cover of the noise made by the other two dragging their chairs up, Gurney slipped into the house. He knew Myra's room. He opened the door and put his head round. Myra was painting her lips. She jerked round, seeing his face in the fly-blown mirror.

"You get out!" she said.

Gurney found his mouth suddenly dry. He stepped in and shut the door, putting his back against the panels. Gurney was big. He had a bent nose and a big slit of a mouth. His eyes were always a little shifty. He dressed in a loud, flashy way, wearing black suits with a yellow or pink stripe. His shirts were mostly red or yellow cotton. He thought he was a swell dresser.

Myra, suddenly anxious, said, "Nick... blow; the old man won't stand for it... please."

Gurney came round the bed and reached out for her. She skipped away, her eyes suddenly large and scared. "If you don't get out, I'll yell," she said.

"Aw, honey, that ain't the way to talk." Gurney was crowding her the whole time. "You're lookin' swell. I ain't goin' to start anythin', honest." His hand touched her arm, and she suddenly felt weak. She said feebly, "Don't, Nick, the old man'll kill me—"

Gurney said, "Don't worry about him." He pulled her into his arms, his hands burning through her dress.

She searched for his mouth with hers, gripping him round the neck, half strangling him. Gurney grinned to himself. He said to her, "I'm comin' out to see you one night soon. You're goin' to like that, ain't that right?"

Outside on the verandah, Butch punched and pummelled Sankey. Sankey stood there, with his head on his chest, like a horse on the way to the knacker's.

Butch said, "He's all right, ain't he?" He said it anxiously, looking in Hank's direction.

Hank said, "Sure." But it wasn't impressive.

"I'm goin' to need a lot of luck with Franks," Sankey mumbled.

Butch stiffened. "That guy ain't no use. He can't hit you."

Sankey shifted. "I wish you're right."

"That punk couldn't hit you with a handful of gravel."

"He ain't got to hit me with gravel, has he?" Sankey turned to the rail and sat on it. He still kept his head down. Butch rubbed both his hands over his bald head. "Listen, this is crazy talk. When you get in there, you're goin' to give this punk the works, see? You're goin to left-hand him till you've pushed his nut off his neck. Then over with your right, an' lay him among the sweet peas."

Sankey didn't say anything.

Butch was getting the jitters. "Where's Gurney? Ain't he here?" he asked suddenly.

"Sure," Hank said quickly. "He's fixin' the auto. She ain't so good as she was. He'll be along."

Butch said, "I want him now."

Hank went to the edge of the step and. yelled, "Hi, Gurney! Butch wants you." He put a lot of beef in his voice.

Butch said suspiciously, "Why d'you yell like that?—he ain't deaf."

Hank began to sweat. He shouted again.

Gurney came round the side of the shack at a run. He'd got a lot of red smears on his face from Myra's paint. That didn't matter. Butch couldn't see them. He was quite cool when he came up the steps.

Butch said, "What've you been doin'?"

Hank put in quickly, "I told you, he's been fixin' the bus."

Gurney grinned a little. "Yeah, that's right. That auto's sure goin' home."

Butch said, "Where's Myra?"

Gurney was elaborately calm. The old fellow was sharp, he thought. "Just what I was goin' to ask you. I gotta soft spot for that kid."

Butch chewed his underlip. He sat down in the chair, his great fists clenched. "You leave her alone," he growled.

Gurney grinned again, but he made his voice smooth. "What's biting you, Butch? You know kids ain't my racket. When I have a woman, she's gotta be a tramp."

Butch said, "Okay, but leave Myra alone."

There was a little pause, then Hank said: "Will you be there, Butch?"

His mind brought back to Sankey, Butch began to look worried again. "Your boy ain't got no confidence," he said to Gurney.

Gurney lit a cigarette and tossed the match into the mud patch. "He's okay. He's just nervous. It don't amount to anythin'."

"Yeah?" Butch levered himself forward. "You crazy? That guy's carrying my dough. That guy's gotta win."

Sankey shifted. "Forget it," he said. "Can't you gab about somethin' else?"

Butch turned his head. "Take him away," he said to Hank. "Lead him round the place. I wantta talk to Gurney."

Hank got up and jerked his head. "Come on," he said to Sankey. They went down the path and sat in the car.

Butch leant forward. "What's this?" he snarled. "That palooka's out on his feet already."

Gurney scratched his chin. "What can I do about it? Franks has scared him, got him jittery. They ran into each other at the boozer the other night. You know Franks, he got on Sankey's nerves."

Butch got to his feet. He raised his clenched fists above his head. "The yellow punk," he said, his voice suppressed and strangled. "You gotta do somethin', Gurney. I've got too much dough on that bum to risk. I tell you, you gotta do somethin'."

"I've got a hundred bucks on him myself," Gurney said uneasily. "He's a trifle over-trained, I guess."

"You've got a week to fix things," Butch said slowly. "Use your head."

Myra came out on the verandah. Her eyes were fixed on Gurney. Butch jerked his head round. "Where've you been?" he demanded.

"Your supper's ready," she said.

Gurney got to his feet. "Okay, Butch, I'll see what I can do."

Very softly he walked across to Myra and kissed her. Kissed her right under Butch's nose. Myra didn't dare stop him, but she went so white that he held her arm for a second.

"What you doin'?" Butch asked. He stood there, his head on one side, straining his ears.

"I'm on my way," Gurney grinned. " 'Bye, Myra; take care of your Pa."

He went away, grinning.

Myra slipped into the kitchen. Her heart was thumping hard against her ribs. The crazy loon, she thought, to do a thing like that. She stood quite still, in the middle of the untidy kitchen, her eyes half closed, thinking of him.

The town took an interest in Dillon. Abe noticed that trade picked up when Dillon was in the store. The women came in to look at him. They had heard about Walcott. A guy who could hit like that must have plenty of steam. Any guy with steam made the women in Plattsville a little light-headed.

They got a shock when they saw Dillon, but they wouldn't admit they were disappointed. They had hoped to see a Clark Gable, and Dillon's clay-like face and cold, expressionless eyes startled them. They told one another that he was a bad man, and they kept on coming in to have another look at him.

The men in Plattsville got sour about it. They said anyone could have smacked Walcott down; he was a cheap punk and didn't amount to anything.

They were talking about Dillon in the saloon when Gurney came in. They broke off. Gurney stopped most talk wherever he went. They wanted to know how Sankey was shaping.

Freedman pushed his way forward. "H'yah, Nick," he said, "what you havin'?"

Gurney was used to this sort of thing. He couldn't place Freedman, but that didn't worry him. He said, "Rye, straight."

George lumbered along the counter with the bottle and glass. He left it at Gurney's elbow.

Freedman said, "Your boy okay?"

Gurney poured himself out a shot and tossed it down his throat. He said, "Sure, he's all right."

"I got my money on him," Freedman said. "I'd like to see him win."

"He's goin' to win, you see."

Wilson lounged to the bar. "Franks ain't so bad," he said; "I guess I fancy Franks."

Gurney looked him over. Just a small-town wise-guy, he thought, maybe not so small-town. He said, "Someone's got to back him."

The others laughed.

Wilson's face reddened angrily. "Yeah?" he said. "Sankey's gettin' nerves. That guy's goin' to be stiff before he gets in there. Franks'll beat hell out of him."

Gurney turned to fill his glass. He thought this line of talk wouldn't get him anywhere. He tapped Wilson on his coat-front. "Get wise, sucker," he said. "Ain't you heard of a front? Sankey's full of tricks. This is one of 'em. Listen, Sankey could whip Franks blindfolded. He's springing a surprise for that palooka. Get your dough on the right man."

Wilson began to lose confidence. "That straight?" he asked; "that on the level?"

Gurney winked at Freedman. "He asks me if it's straight? Me! Take him away someone an' bury him."

Freedman said, "I'd like your boy to push this Dillon around. That's what that punk wants."

Gurney raised his eyebrows. "Dillon? Who's he?"

They jostled one another to tell him. Gurney stood, his shoulders against the wall, a glass in his hand, and listened. He said at last, "Abe ain't no fool. This guy can't be so bad."

Freedman said, "He's got Goldberg fooled."

Gurney was getting sick of Freedman. He straightened his coat, leant forward over the counter, and adjusted his hat in the wall mirror. "I gotta see Abe; I'll look this guy over."

Freedman made as if to go with him. Gurney checked him with a look. "This is a little matter of business," he said.

Freedman said, "Sure, you go ahead." He said it hastily. He didn't want to get in bad with Gurney.

Crossing the street, Gurney entered the store. It was the slack part of the day, and the place was empty. Dillon came out from the back, and stood with his hands resting on the counter, framed by two towers of tinned foods. He was wearing one of Abe's store suits that fitted him in places, and his face was close-shaven. He didn't look the hobo that had come into Plattsville a few days back. He looked at Gurney from under his eyelids. A cold, suspicious stare. Gurney thought he might be a mean sort of a guy.

"Abe about?" he asked.

Dillon shook his head. "He's out," he said briefly.

"Too bad. I wanted to see Abe." Gurney fidgeted a little. Dillon made him a little uneasy.

"Will he be long?" he said after a pause.

"Maybe." Dillon began to edge away into the darkness of the store.

Gurney thought he'd try a little probing. He said: "You're new around here."

Dillon rubbed his forearm. He still looked at Gurney from under his eyelids. "You're the guy who's runnin' Sankey, ain't you?" he said.

Gurney swelled a little. "That's me," he said.

"What's the matter with him?"

"Matter? Nothin'. What d'you mean?"

"You know. That guy's gone yellow. What's eatin' him?"

Gurney paused, uncertain. Then he said, "Listen, I don't like that line of talk."

Dillon wandered out from behind the counter; he still rubbed his forearm. "Don't 'big shot' me," he said. "I said what's the matter with him?"

Again Gurney felt uneasy. The dangerous, savage power in Dillon conveyed itself to him.

"Franks got him jittery," he said reluctantly.

Dillon nodded. "He's goin' to win?"

"Sankey? I guess not." Gurney frowned. "I gotta lotta dough on that boy."

"I guess I could fix it," Dillon said, watching him closely.

"You?" Gurney looked incredulous.

"Sure, why not?" Dillon lounged to the door and looked into the street, then he came back again.

"What d'you know about fixin' fights?" Gurney asked suspiciously.

"Plenty," Dillon told him, then, after a pause, he added: "I'm lookin' for a chance to break into the dough again."

Gurney was getting more than interested. "Suppose you come on out an' see Butch tonight? I'd like you to meet Butch Hogan."

"Hogan?" Dillon thought a moment. "That the old ex champ?"

"That's the guy. He lives just outside the town now. Blind he is—a tough break for a guy like that."

"Yeah," Dillon nodded his head, "a tough break."

"Will you be along?"

"I guess so. Any other guys interested in Sankey?"

"There's Hank, he trains him, an' there's Al Morgan, who manages for him."

"Tell 'em both to come. Not Sankey; he'd better keep out of it."

Gurney said, "I'll take you along tonight."

Dillon nodded his head. "I'll be there," he said; "you ain't got to worry about me."

He walked back behind the counter leaving Gurney standing uncertain in the middle of the store. Then Gurney walked out into the bright sunlight. This guy Dillon got him beat. There was somethin' phoney about him. He was no hobo, he could tell that. This guy was used to handling men. He said a thing and expected the thing done. He scared Gurney a little.

He was so busy thinking about Dillon that he didn't see Myra walking down the street. Myra hastened her steps, but Gurney was already climbing into the car, and before she could call to him he had driven away.

Myra was quite pleased he hadn't seen her. She had taken some trouble in dressing. Her flowered dress had been washed and ironed. Maybe it had shrunk a shade, but that didn't worry her. She knew it showed off her figure. Her thick black hair glistened in the sunlight, and was dressed low in her neck. The seams of her imitation silk stockings were straight, and her shoes shone. She was going to have a look at Dillon.

She'd heard about Dillon the day he had moved in, but she had purposely waited until he had seen all the women in Plattsville. She thought it was time now to give him an eyeful. Walking down the street, she knew she was good. She knew the men turned their heads, and she guessed that she was going over big with this Dillon.

She walked into the empty store, clicking her heels sharply on the wooden floor. Purposely, she stood in the patch of sunlight flooding the doorway. She'd seen that trick worked before, and with her thin dress she knew she was an eye-opener.

Dillon looked up. "I've seen it before," he said; "it ain't anythin' new. Come out of the light."

If he had struck her she couldn't have been more furious. Automatically she moved a few paces into the shadow, then she said, "What kind of a cheap crack do you think that is?"

Dillon shifted a wad of gum from one side of his mouth to the other. "What a you want?" he said.

"A real live salesman, ain't you?" she said, gripping her purse hard. "If you want to keep your job you gotta do better than that."

Dillon said, "Skip it. I ain't listening to big-mouth talk from a kid like you. Get what you want and blow."

Myra took three quick steps forward and aimed a slap at Dillon's face. She was nearly sobbing with rage. Dillon reached up and caught her wrist. "Be your age," he said; "you ain't in the movies."

She stood there, helpless in his grip, loathing his hard eyes. "I'll tell my Pa about you," was all she could say.

He threw her arm away from him, spinning her into the center of the store. "Scram, I tell you," he said.

She screamed at him. "You dirty heel! My Pa will bash you for this!"

Abe stood in the doorway, his eyes popping out of his head. "What's going on?" he asked.

Myra spun round. "You're crazy to have that bum in here. He's been insulting me—"

Dillon came round the counter with a quick shuffle. He took hold of Myra and ran her to the door, then he swung his arm and smacked her viciously, sending her skidding into the street. Myra didn't stop—she ran.

Abe tore his hair. "What do you think you're doing?" he squeaked. "That's Butch Hogan's daughter. The old man'll raise the dead about this."

Dillon came back into the store. "Forget it," he said. "I'm about sick of these women starin' at me. Maybe they'll leave me alone for a while."

Abe, bursting with impotent fury, forgot his fear of Dillon. He spluttered, "An' what about my business? What are people goin' to say? They ain't comin' here to be roughed around. This is goin' to ruin me."

Dillon pushed him away and walked into the kitchen. Abe followed him, still shouting.

"Aw, forget it," Dillon snarled. "This ain't goin' to hurt your business. I bet that little chippy is as popular in this burg as a bad smell. This ain't goin' to get round the town. A kid like that ain't goin' to let on she's just been smacked. Forget it."

They all sat on Butch's verandah and waited for Dillon to come. The moon was just appearing above the black silhouetted trees, throwing sharp white beams on the windows of the house.

Upstairs, Myra crouched by the window, also waiting for Dillon. Her eyes, red with weeping, remained in a fixed stare on the road below. Her whole being curled with hate. Her mind seethed.

Butch shifted a little in his chair. "Who's this fella?" he asked suddenly, asking the same question that the others were pondering about in their minds.

"I don't know," Gurney said. "Maybe he can get us outta this jam. I thought it might be worth tryin'."

Hank said from the darkness: "Sankey's in a terrible state. He don't say anything, but just sits around an' broods. Franks's got him tied up."

Out of the darkness Dillon came up the verandah steps. Even Myra, who had been watching the road, hadn't heard him or seen him.

The four men sat still, looking at him. Then Gurney said, "This is Dillon."

Butch got to his feet. He moved round the small table, on which stood a bottle and glasses. He held out his hand. "So you're Dillon, the fight-fixer?" There was a faint sneer in his voice.

Dillon looked him over, looked at his hand and ignored it.

Butch moved his great paw impatiently. "Gimme your hand," he said. "I wantta see what kind of a guy you are."

A gleam came into Dillon's eyes. He put his hand in Butch's. Then Butch squeezed. The tremendous muscles of his forearm swelled as he put all his strength into a crushing grip. The sweat suddenly jumped out of Dillon's face. He shifted his feet, then swung a punch at Butch with his left, coming up and hitting Butch in his thick throat. It thumped into Butch like a cleaver into beef. Butch reeled back, making a croaking sound. Gurney sprang to his feet and saved him from going over.

Dillon stood flexing his fingers. "That's the kind of a guy I am," he said evenly.

Butch put his fingers to his throat. He sat down a little heavily. No one had hit him so hard since he left the resin. He said, when he got his breath, "This guy's okay; he can punch."

Dillon came a little nearer. "Suppose we get inside where I can see you."

They went inside without a word. Dillon stood by the window. He said, "Sit down."

Gurney said, "There's some booze outside, want any?"

Dillon looked at him. "I don't use it. Forget it! This is important. Franks has got your boy on the run. You're all backing Sankey for a win. Sankey ain't goin' to win unless Franks is so bad that a child could push him around. That right?"

Gurney nodded. "I guess that's about it."

"Any of you guys got any dough?"

They looked at Morgan, a thin, cruel-faced little man who looked like a jock. He said, "Maybe I could find some."

"I'll fix this fight for five hundred bucks," Dillon said.

A little sigh went round the room. Gurney shook his head. "That's too much," he said.

Dillon rubbed the back of his neck. "You mugs dumb?" he said. "I said I'd fix this fight, and I mean fix it. Your man'll win. You can back him for any money. You can't lose."

Morgan leant forward. "I guess I'd like to know just who you are, mister," he said.

Dillon looked at him under his eyelids. "Maybe you'd like to know a lot of things... you ain't got to worry about me. I've done this sorta thing before. What's it to be?"

Morgan looked at the other three. Butch nodded. "We'll come on in with you," he said.

Morgan shrugged. "Okay," he said. "I'll pay the money when Sankey's won."

Dillon showed his teeth. "You'll bet that five hundred bucks on Sankey for me. An' you'll lay the dough when I tell you."

Morgan thought a moment, then said, "Fair enough." The four men began to catch some of Dillon's confidence.

"Dig down," Dillon said, spreading a fin on the table. "I want some working expenses. This is all I got. Dig down."

Each contributed. Between the five of them they put up a hundred dollars. Dillon put the bills in his pocket. Gurney went out on to the verandah and fetched in the drinks. They all had a shot except Dillon.

Butch said, "How you goin' to handle this?"

Dillon tapped on the table with his fingernails. "I'm goin' to tell Franks to take a dive."

Butch said, "He'll knock your guts out."

Dillon shook his head. "He won't." He pushed back his chair. "I guess that's all." The others, except Butch, got to their feet. Dillon said, "Suppose you boys blow, I wantta talk to Butch."

Gurney moved to the verandah. "Maybe we'll get together some other time," he said.

"Yeah." Dillon nodded his head. "You might look around tomorrow."

Butch sat waiting until the others disappeared into the night.

Dillon came back from the verandah. He stood looking at Butch thoughtfully. Then he closed the door and came over. Butch said, "Who taught you to punch like that?"

Dillon shrugged. "Never mind that. I've got things to talk to you about. Anyone else in this dump?"

Hogan shook his head. "My gal's upstairs in bed. That's all."

"I'm goin' to make some dough out of the town," Dillon said. "You can come in on the ground floor if you want to."

Butch stroked his nose. "Suppose you put the cards down an' let me look at 'em," he said at last.

Dillon lowered his voice. "I carried a gun for Nelson," he said.

Crouched outside the door, Myra shivered a little.

Butch looked a little uneasy. "He was a hard guy," he said.

"He was a mug," Dillon said bitterly. "I've been under cover now some time. The heat's off. Okay, I guess it's time to move into the money again. How's it feel?"

Butch said, "You ain't tellin' me this unless you knew right off I'd agree."

Dillon nodded his head. "I thought you were a bright guy. Maybe you have lost your peepers, but you still got some brain."

Butch said again, "You want the house, huh? Near the State line. Me as a cover?"

"You got it." Dillon relaxed a little. "I ain't working anythin' this side of the border. Just quick raids. Nothin' very big; that'll come later. Then back under cover here. How do you like that?"

Butch brooded. "What's it worth?" he asked at last.

"Twenty-five per cent cut on everything."

Butch nodded. "Okay."

Dillon asked abruptly: "This guy Gurney—is he all right?"

Butch nodded. "He'd come in, I guess," he said. "Gurney's after the big dough. He ain't particular how he makes it."

"I'll have a word with him later. Now this guy Franks. There's only one way to deal with him. He's gotta have a scare thrown in him, see? He's got to be tipped off that he gets it if he doesn't take a dive. The first thing is to square the Town Marshal. How'd you stand with him?"

"He's an old bird. Sell his soul for a buck. He can be squared."

"Then see him an' fix it. I gotta keep out of this. Tip him off to put his money on Sankey an' tell him the fight's rigged. If Franks puts up a squawk for protection, he won't get it, see?"

Butch nodded.

Dillon took out the hundred dollars and counted out fifty of them. "Give him that to bet with."

Butch fumbled with the money and put it in his pocket. "I guess you're goin' to fix this fight all right," he said. "I'm putting everything I've got on this."

Dillon said, "It's goin' to be okay. You see."

He moved over to the door. Outside, Myra crept away, not making a sound. She climbed the ladder leading to the loft which served for her bedroom; and safe in the darkness of familiar surroundings she slipped out of her dress before going to the window. Dillon was standing in the road, looking cautiously up and down, then with a quick shuffling step he disappeared into the darkness.

Myra stood by the window some time, thinking, her face lit by the moonlight, the hot air of the night touching her skin. Even when she got into bed she could not sleep. The clay-like face of Dillon hung before her like the dead face of the moon. His voice still rang in her ears, scorning her. The blow that he had struck her still burnt her body, making her squirm on the sagging mattress. Sleep would not come to her, to blot out mercilessly the pain of her bruised pride. She suddenly began to cry, the hot tears running down her face unchecked. Her two fists, clenched, beat on the bed. "I hate you! I hate you!" she sobbed.

Gurney drove carefully. He had to nurse the car over the rough road. One good pothole would sure bust the axle. Dillon sat beside him, his hat over his eyes. Every now and then Gurney shot him a quick look. Dillon had him guessing. He couldn't place him. Something told him that Dillon would get him somewhere, that he would lead him to the money class, but, fascinated by the thought, he still hung back a little, not trusting him.

It was the evening following the meeting of Dillon and Butch. Dillon had picked Gurney up after the store had closed for the night. They were on their way across the border to the hick town where Franks lived. They were going to call on Franks.

Dillon said suddenly: "You gotta tackle this guy; I'll just be around. You know what to say. Don't let him start anythin'. Talk tough. He won't take a sock at you. I'll be right with you."

Gurney brooded, staring at the road, white and dusty in the headlights. "This guy can hit," he said uneasily. "He'll get mad if I shoot off too much"

Dillon shifted. "You do what I say," he said; "I can handle any mad guy."

He pulled a heavy Colt automatic from the inside of his coat, turned it in his hand so that Gurney could see it, then he put it back.

"For Pete's sake"—Gurney was startled—"where did you get that?"

Dillon looked at him, peering at him from under his hat. "You ain't scared of a rod?" he asked.

This was too tough for Gurney, but he didn't say so. He licked his lips uneasily and drove on.

After a while he said, "You ain't goin' to pop this guy?"

"Sure I'm goin' to, if he gets mad," Dillon said. "This ain't the first guy I've popped."

The old car swerved a little. Gurney found his hands trembling. "I guess I ain't standin' for a murder rap," he said suddenly.

Dillon reached out and turned off the switch. The engine spluttered and went dead. Gurney trod on the brake. "What's the idea?" he asked nervously.

Dillon pushed back his hat and leant towards Gurney, crowding him into the corner of the car. "Listen," he said, "you're goin' to get this straight. From now on I'm givin' the orders and you're takin' 'em, see? We're gettin' into the dough, an' no one's stoppin' us. If they get in our way it's goin' to be so much grief for 'em—get that? In a little while I'll be running the town. You can get in on the ground floor or you can stay out. You stay out, an' one dark night someone's goin' to toss a handful of slugs in your guts; you know too much—get all that? Butch's on, so get wise to yourself."

Gurney went a little yellow. He didn't have to think much. "Sure," he said, "I get it. Sure, you go ahead. You're the boss."

Dillon raked him with his cold eyes. "There was one bright boy who talked like that an' changed his mind. Someone gutted him with a knife. Hell! You ought to have seen that guy."

Gurney said, "You ain't goin' to have any trouble with me." He said it in a weak voice, but he meant it.

They drove on.

A clock somewhere struck the half-hour after ten when they pulled up outside Frank's house. It wasn't much to look at from the front, but then Franks was only a small-time fighter, just making his way. They walked up the short path and stood outside the screen door. Gurney pulled at the bell, hearing it jangle somewhere at the back. Behind a yellow blind a light gleamed. Someone was up all right.

Through the screen door they could see a woman coming. Dillon nodded to Gurney and stepped back a little.

The door opened outwards, and the woman stood on the step looking at them with a little puzzled frown. She was young and plain. Her black hair was done up in a coil, a few ends straggling untidily. When she spoke, her voice was soft and carried a southern accent. "What is it, please?" she said.

"Len in?" Gurney said.

The woman nodded. "Sure he's in," she said. "Who shall I say?"

Gurney took a step forward, pushing the woman back. Followed by Dillon, he walked into the house. The woman retreated, her face suddenly frightened. "What is it?" she asked breathlessly. "You can't come busting in like this."

Gurney walked into the sitting-room. Franks was sitting in an easy chair holding a child awkwardly, a bottle of milk suspended in his hand. Franks was a big, smooth-faced guy, young and free from the usual mashed features of a fighter.

The woman brushed past Gurney and ran over to Franks. She was badly scared. Franks pushed the baby into her arms, getting to his feet quickly. He was startled. His eyes showed it; they were a little wide, but he wasn't losing his head. If there was going to be trouble, his confidence in his great flat muscles was unshakable.

"You can't come in here like this," he said to Gurney. "I see guys like you at the gym."

Gurney grinned uneasily. He was a little nervous of Franks. "We're in, buddy," he said. "Get the dame outta here; we want to talk to you."

Frank said, "Beth, take the kid."

She went out without a word. She was only gone a second or so. She came back alone, and stood just behind Franks. Her eyes were big and scared. Franks said to her patiently, "Keep out of this, honey."

She didn't say anything, but she didn't move. Dillon's thin lips set in a sneer.

Franks was calming down. He said, "You sure startled me," there was a foolish little smile on his big, rubbery lips, "bustin' in like that. You're crazy. I might've pushed you boys around."

Gurney said, "Don't talk big, Franks, you're in a spot."

Franks' eyes opened. He knotted his muscles. Gurney could see them swelling under his coat. "Not from you I ain't," he said. "What is it?"

Gurney pulled a chair round and sat down. He was careful to put the table between them. Dillon leant against the door. Beth watched him the whole time. She was dead scared of Dillon.

"We're tippin' you off," Gurney said evenly. "Sankey's gotta win this brawl."

"Yeah?" Franks' breath whistled through his nose. "He'll win okay if he ain't flattened before the last round."

"You don't get it," Gurney said patiently; "you're throwin' the fight."

Franks stood very still. "Like hell I don't get it," he said. "Who said?"

Dillon said quietly from the door, "I said so."

Franks turned his head; he looked Dillon slowly up and down. "Who're you?" he said. "You're nuts. You two'd better get outta here before I toss you out."

There was a pause, then Dillon said, "You're goin' to run into a lotta grief if you don't take a dive."

Franks went a little pale. "Okay, you two rats; here it comes." He jerked aside the table. Gurney scrambled to his feet, his face white. Beth gave a sudden short scream as the big Colt sprang into Dillon's hand. Franks saw it. It stopped him just like he had banged his face against a brick wall. "Hey!" he said.

"That's it," Dillon said viciously. "Don't start anything; you'll have trouble if you do."

Beth put her hand on Franks' arm. "Don't let him shoot you, Harry!... Don't let him shoot you!"

Dillon crouched a little by the door. His face was drawn, his lips just off his teeth. "I'll give it to you, sucker," he said; "just one move outta you an' you get it."

Franks was scared of the gun. He'd never run into a gunman before. It unsettled him. "Are you bugs?" he said, keeping his voice steady. "You can't do this."

"Forget it," Dillon said savagely; "you listen. You're takin' orders, an' you're likin' 'em. You're throwin' that fight, see? Sankey's gotta win in about the fifth. You can fix it how you like, but he's gotta win. We got too much dough on that boy to fool around makin' mistakes."

Beth began to cry. She made a little shuddering, jarring sound that got on Gurney's nerves.

Dillon went on talking. "When you get in there, you put up a good show, but no heavy work; just rough around, see? Then let Sankey haul off an' sock you. Just one. Make it look a lucky punch. Right, you go down, an' you stay down. Now listen, you punk, you double-cross me an' see what you get. I'll get this dame first, an' I'll get the little 'un as well. Then I lay for you. This ain't a bluff—you see."

For a moment Gurney thought Franks was going to rush Dillon, and he braced himself. Franks could see that he'd get nowhere doing that. Dillon could have fired three or four times before he caught up with him. So he just stood there, his head lowered, his eyes gleaming, and his great hands working at his sides. He said at last, "Sankey'll win okay." His voice came out of his throat in a strangled croak. Beth slipped to her knees, holding his hand. They stood like that for a long time, with Dillon staring at them. Then Dillon jerked his head at Gurney, and together they backed out into the night.

Gurney sat in the car, smoking. He had left Dillon at Abe's store and had driven out of town. The night was still and very close. Big black clouds, looking like lumps of coal, hung sluggishly in the sky. The moon rode low, just skirting the black tree-tops.

His mind excited, Gurney sat smoking hard. The red tip of his cigarette glowed in the smothering darkness of the car. His brain was crawling with thoughts. It was the gun that excited him. He could see Franks' face now. He could see how that gun stopped his rush, turned him from toughness to dough. Any guy could give orders with a rod in his hand. It was the rod that did it. Gurney shifted in his seat. Dillon was a hard guy, but without a gun Franks would have squashed him—made a smear of him on the wall. That showed you how powerful a gun was.

A big, silent car flashed past. Gurney saw the dame sitting in front with a well-dressed guy, looking as if he owned the earth. The dame was glittering in a white dress that sparkled. She looked a honey all right.

With a gun, Gurney thought, I'd have the last word with that punk. A gun would level things up mighty quick. Thinking about the dame, his mind went on to Myra. If there was ever a broad asking for it, there she was. What was he waiting for, anyway? He leant forward and turned the switch.

It did not take him long to run out to Butch's place. He stopped the jalopy a few hundred yards from the shack under a clump of trees and turned off the lights. It was off the road, and it would be safe there. He got out, and walking on the grass border of the road approached silently.

One solitary light was burning in the downstairs room. Silently moving his feet with care, he walked towards the window. He had a great respect for Butch's ears. He put his fingers on the window-ledge and pulled himself up.

Myra was standing quite close to him, pressing a dress with a flat-iron. She was alone.

Gurney lowered himself to the ground and walked round the front. He rapped on the screen with his knuckles. He waited a minute, feeling his heart beating jerkily against his ribs. Then Myra's silhouette blotted out the screen and she said, "Who is it?"

"Hyah, baby," Gurney said, speaking very low; "you alone?"

She pushed open the screen and came out on the step. "Nick!" There was a little catch in her voice.

It didn't get by Gurney. He grinned in the darkness.

"Sure," he said. "Butch in?"

She shook her head. "He went down to the gym. He won't be so long, though."

"Lemme in, baby, I gotta talk to you."

"No—no, it's late, Nick. You can't come in now."

Gurney reached out his hands, taking her arms just over her elbows. "Get goin'," he said gently; "you don't want to be seen yappin' out here."

At his touch her resistance sagged. She let him push her back into the house. She broke away from him when they entered the room, standing with her back against the wall, her eyes fixed on him.

"You gotta be careful," she said. "He's coming back. You know him. He'll be right in on us; he comes so quietly. Not now, Nick, I'm scared he'll come. Nick, please... "

Gurney, his hat still at the back of his head, pulled her away from the wall. She struggled to get away from him until his mouth reached hers, then she clung to him, beating his shoulder-blades with the flat of her hands.

Down the road Butch came, his great body throwing a bloated shadow that stumbled and lurched just ahead of him. He made no sound, walking in the grass. He kept his ear cocked for motors. Butch had got to watch out for himself. Skirting the bend, he hastened his steps; he knew that he was nearly home. Walking, his head bent, he was puzzling about Dillon. Sankey also worried him. He'd got a lot of dough on Sankey. If Dillon didn't get that brawl rigged he was going to be down a lot—a lot too much.

He silently padded up the mud path, pausing on the top step of the verandah to have a last smell of the night air. He didn't like it. It came hot and close to him. He thought maybe a storm would get up.

Myra slid from the settee to the floor when Butch walked in. Gurney sat up, his face going a little green with his fright. Butch would break his back if he caught him in here.

Myra stood quite close to Gurney, her face set, and the first shock ebbing away. She said, "I was just going to bed." Her voice was steady.

Butch remained by the door. Something told him that things weren't right. "It's late," he said, listening with his head on one side.

Myra motioned Gurney to stay where he was. Gurney was sitting propped up on his elbow, one leg on the floor. Sweat ran down his face, making him look ghastly in the bright naked light.

Butch moved forward a little, shutting the door.

"Sankey all right?" Myra asked.

"Yeah," Butch said; he passed his hand over the top of his bald head. His eyes looked straight at Gurney. The two yellow clots bored into Gurney's brain. "Seems quiet here," Butch went on.

Myra stooped and picked up her dress. Butch heard the rustle of the material as she gathered it into a ring to slip over her head. "What you doin'?" he said sharply.

Myra shook a little, the dress slipping out of her hands. "I told you, I'm going to bed." She began to walk heavily about the room, taking up the ironing-board and putting it against the wall. "Sankey going to win?" she asked, for something to say.

"You're interested in that guy, ain't you?"

Gurney's muscles began to ache, sitting like that. He was too scared to move. He just stayed there, his eyes fixed on Butch.

"Why not?" Myra's knees were beginning to shake. The old geezer guessed there was something wrong, she thought. She walked carelessly over to the couch again and picked up her dress. Neither Gurney nor she looked at each other.

Butch moved quickly. He almost trod on Gurney's foot as he went by. He snatched Myra's dress out of her hands. Myra skipped away and flattened herself against the wall. Her eyes sprang open wide.

Butch felt the dress in his hands. His big, rubbery face darkened. "What are you doin'?" he growled. "Why've you taken this off?"

Steeling her voice, she said, "What's the matter with you tonight? I was hot... can't a girl take her dress off?"

"Come here."

Gurney stopped breathing.

Myra said, pressing herself against the wall, "Not likely!"

Butch walked slowly to the door and locked it. He took the key and put it in his pocket. "There's something phoney goin' on here," he snarled at her. "Let's see what it is."

Gurney thought, "With a gun I could blast the old devil."

With a sliding shuffle Butch came at Myra. He came so quickly that she only just escaped him. Slithering along the wall, out of his reach, she stood, by the door, breathing in short, jerky gasps.

Butch stood, his hand on the wall, his sightless eyes turned on her. "You'd better come here," he said.

Myra said in a small voice, "You're scaring me. Open the door, I tell you, I want to go to bed."

Butch caught her this time. Gurney didn't think it possible for him to move so quickly. His great hand caught her arm as she fled from him. He jerked her to him. His hot breath fanned her face.

She said, "Let me go!... Let me go!... Let me go!" Her voice went up a tone, mounting to a scream.

Gurney swung himself to the floor and stood up. Swiftly, Butch jerked his head round. "What's that?" he said harshly. He shook Myra. "What was that? There's someone else here.... Who is it?"

"You're crazy," she gasped. "There's no one here."

His hand, swinging down, slapped her. Then he stiffened. Holding both her wrists in a crushing grip, he touched her quivering body.

Gurney was creeping inch by inch towards the open window. Myra, seeing him, began to scream, covering any sound that he made.

Butch reached up; his hand, closing on her throat, nipped her screams short. Gurney swung himself forward, falling head first out of the window, his feet jerking the curtains from the rod. Picking himself up, he began to run drunkenly down the road, swaying from side to side.

Butch said, "So that's it, is it, you little devil?"

Myra felt her knees buckle. If Butch weren't holding her she would have slipped to the floor.

"Who was it?" He shook her. His great arms flung her this way and that, banging her legs against the wall. "Do you hear, who was the punk?"

"You'll... never make... me tell," she gasped, trying to tear her hands away.

"Yeah? Just wait an' see."

He dragged her across the room, until his legs struck the settee, then he flung her down on it. She lay there, her eyes wide with terror. He kept a grip on her arm, muttering to himself and fumbling at the buckle of the broad belt at his waist.

As he pulled it off, she twisted and turned over on her face, her arms protecting her head, screaming deep in her throat.

The belt curled through the air and hit her arched body. Myra screamed, "I'll kill you for this!..."

It was only when his hand was slippery with sweat that she escaped him. She rolled off the settee, her arm sliding from his grip. They stood there, facing each other. Butch, his rubbery face hideous with cruel rage; Myra, her body streaked with red weals, murderous in her fury. Her hands closed on the back of a chair and, swinging it high, she hit Butch across the head with it.

Butch half guessed what she was doing, and he swerved, but she had anticipated the move. The chair crashed on his bald head, shattering itself. The legs of the chair flew across the room. Butch fell on his knees, roaring as his brain reeled. She came at him again, battering down his upraised arms, beating him again and again with the thick chair-back. He tried to save himself, his defense becoming more and more feeble, until he reeled over and fell on his side, like a stricken elephant. She drew off. Swinging the chair-back over her head, she gave him one final crushing blow that made his battered head jerk up and then flop on the floor. Then, with a frightened look, she snatched up her dress and ran blindly up to her attic.

They pushed their way down the aisle. Gurney came first, then Dillon, and then Morgan. The house was so full they had difficulty in getting to their seats. They were right on top of the ring.

A preliminary was just commencing. The arc-lights overhead dimmed as they arrived at their seats. Gurney squeezed past a slim blonde, pulling her skirts to her knees. "Don't mind me," she snapped.

Dillon stood waiting to pass. "If your arches ain't broke," he said, "suppose you stand up; I ain't so likely to strip you that way."

Two fat guys sitting behind her went off in loud, explosive sniggers.

The blonde took a look at Dillon and figured he was too tough for her. She stood up and let him through. Morgan crowded past her quickly. They sat down.

Just above the ring lights a heavy haze of tobacco-smoke lay like a mist rising from damp ground. The hall was as hot as hell. Dillon wrenched his collar undone and pulled his tie down a little.

The two lightweights were slamming into each other murderously. Gurney leant toward Dillon. "You seen Sankey?" he asked.

Dillon shook his head. "Sankey ain't worryin' me," he said. "I guess I'll give Franks a call."

"We got him scared," Gurney said; "you see."

The crowd suddenly gave a great sigh, that sounded like a groan, as one of the fighters began to buckle at the knees. Morgan shouted, "Go after him, you little punk—nail him."

The gong saved him.

Dillon got to his feet; he pushed past Morgan, climbed over the blonde and walked up the aisle again. At the head of the corridor leading to the dressing-rooms a little runt in a yellow-white jersey stopped him. "This is as far as you'll get," he said.

"I'm on business," Dillon said, and went on.

The little runt had to let him go; he was just swept aside.

Dillon wandered into Sankey's room. Hank was sitting on a stool beside the table. Sankey was lying on the table, a bright-red dressing-gown covered him. They both looked up as Dillon came in.

Hank said, "He's on next but one."

Dillon pursed his lips. "You okay?" he said.

Sankey half sat up. "Sure I'm okay. This guy's goin' to take a dive, ain't he?"

Dillon nodded. "That don't mean you ain't gotta try," he said evenly; "you gotta watch this guy, Sankey."

Hank said heatedly, "Sure he'll watch him... what you think?"

Dillon nodded. Then he wandered out again. He walked softly down the corridor until he came to Franks' room. He put his hand inside his coat, feeling the cold butt of the Colt. Then he opened the door and went in.

Franks was staring moodily at his feet. His trainer, Borg, was sitting despondently on a wooden chair, cleaning his nails with a small knife. He looked up sharply as Dillon came in. "Wrong room, buddy," he said crisply. "On your way."

Dillon didn't even look at him. He said to Franks, "We're outside watching."

Franks looked up. "Get out and stay out!" he said.

Dillon didn't move. "Don't get this thing wrong," he said. "We don't want to start anythin'."

Borg got off his chair. He came over to Dillon fast. He was only a little guy, and fat, but he'd got plenty of guts. "What are you blowin' about? Scram; you ain't wanted here."

Dillon looked down at him, sneered, and wandered out. At the door he turned his head. "In about the fifth, Franks," he said, and pulled the door to with a sharp click.

A sudden burst of ironic cheering came to him from the hall. He passed the little runt again, who glowered at him but said nothing.

At the entrance of K Section he saw Gurney and Morgan pushing through to the saloon. Dillon forced his way through the crowd and caught up with them.

"Those two little punks are scared sick of each other," Morgan said, as he came up. "They're just sleepin' off time in each other's arms."

Gurney said, "Did you see Franks?"

Dillon nodded. He leant against the counter, his thumbs hooked in his belt. "He'll be okay," he said.

Gurney poured himself out a shot of bourbon and pushed the bottle over to Morgan. "And Sankey?"

"Sankey's got his nerve back. He's a big shot now the brawl's rigged. That guy's got a yellow streak somewhere."

Morgan didn't like that, but he kept his mouth shut. He wasn't sure of Dillon. "Too bad about Butch," he said, pushing the conversation into safer channels.

Dillon raised his eyebrows. "I ain't heard," he said.

Gurney looked uncomfortable. He hurriedly filled his glass. Under his eyelids, Dillon watched him.

Morgan gave a tinny laugh. "Ain't you heard? Say, it's rich! That little kid of his nearly knocked his block off."

"You're crazy," Dillon said, frowning.

"It sounds like that, but it's on the level. Old Butch comes back from an evenin' out, and catches her with some guy neckin' in the front room. Gee! I'd like to've been there. The guy blows his top an' lams through the window. I guess it must've been a scream." Morgan hit his thigh, bending forward, laughing in a hoarse burst.

Dillon eyed him contemptuously.

"Then Butch takes his belt to her and raises a few blisters. Just what's been comin' to that little broad. After he's half skinned her she breaks loose, an' damme if she don't bounce a chair on his dome. I tell you, that dame is sure hot an' wild. She goes on bouncin' that chair until Butch takes the count. He's lying up now, sore as a bear with a boil, an' the kid's runnin' the house, givin' herself airs."

Dillon said, "Who was the guy?"

He knew, by just watching Gurney.

Morgan shrugged. "Butch can't find out," he said. "He figgered the strap would make her talk, but it didn't. She kept her mouth shut. I guess it was a lucky break for that runaway. Butch would've twisted his neck for him."

Gurney mopped his face with a silk handkerchief. Dillon looked at him, but Gurney shifted his eyes.

Dillon said, "We'll go back. They'll be comin' in soon."

The hall was ablaze with light when they walked in. A buzz of talk hummed round the walls. The ring was empty. As they took their seats the lights began to dim.

The fat men behind them were talking in loud, hoarse voices. "There ain't enough business goin' on tonight," one of them complained. "I'm layin' three to one on Franks. The suckers ain't taking me."

Dillon turned his head. "I'll take five hundred of that," he said.

The two fat men looked at each other, a little startled. Then one of them said, "Sure," but they stopped talking after that.

Gurney nudged Dillon, jerking his head. Beth Franks was coming down the aisle. She slipped into a vacant seat near one of the corners. Her face had a bony, scraped look, and her eyes glittered as if she had a fever.

Gurney whispered, "She's nuts to come here."

Dillon shook his head. "It'll keep Franks' mind right," he said.

The crowd began to yell. Sankey was coming in. The spotlights followed him down the aisle, reflecting on his red dressing-gown. He climbed through the ropes, holding one hand above his head.

Gurney said, "He thinks he's Louis."

Sankey plodded round the ring, keeping his hand up, while half the house groaned at him, and the other half yelled. He had four handlers in white, who stood self-consciously in the corner, waiting for him to get through with his stuff. He came back at last, and stood in his corner, flexing his knees and worrying the ropes.

Morgan cast a look at Dillon. "He's got his nerve back, ain't he?"

Dillon sneered.

Franks came down now. The crowd got to their feet for him. The roof trembled at their roar. The three twisted their heads to watch him come. Franks looked a little fine-drawn, and there were smudges just under his eyes. He had to walk past them to the ring.

Gurney called, "Don't get too tough with him, Harry."

The crowd liked that, and they hooted. Franks didn't look, he kept on.

Beth heard Gurney and she stood up, looking with wild eyes at the three of them sitting on her left. She stared at them for several seconds, then she sat down again.

Morgan shifted uncomfortably. "She'll know us again," he said.

The other two didn't say anything.

Sankey bounced out of his corner and pushed the rope down for Franks to get through. Franks paused, looking up at him. "Be yourself," he snarled. "Get to hell out of it!"

The crowd thought Sankey was being sporty. They gave him a yell. Franks took the ropes like a hurdle, leaving Sankey still holding them. The crowd liked that too. They hooted and clapped.

They couldn't keep Sankey out of Franks' corner. He went over there and patted Franks' shoulder. The crowd thought it was wonderful.

Franks said, "If you don't keep this jerk away from me, I'll start on him now."

Borg said to Sankey, "Give us a little air, brother, you'll be seein' him too much soon."

Sankey wandered back to his corner, his two fists together, waving to the crowd.

Gurney said, "This punk'll drive me barmy."

Hank went over to Franks' corner while Borg bandaged his hands. Hank said, "You got enough tape."

Franks looked up at him. "Don't be dumb," he said, "it's soft enough."

A little guy with a hand-mike got into the ring and started blowing. He got the crowd worked up all right. The only thing worth noting was Franks went six pounds heavier than Sankey. Gurney was conscious of a dryness in his throat and his heart's heavy thumping. He pushed his hat to the back of his head and rubbed his glistening forehead with his hand. Dillon sat like a rock, his hands limply on his knees and his jaw moving slowly, clamping on the gum.

Gurney watched the referee call the two men in the centre of the ring. Sankey came out, his dressing-gown like a cape on his shoulders. Frank had only a towel across his back. They stood there listening to the referee giving them the same old line. Gurney wished they'd get on with it.

They went back to their corners. Cigar-smoke spiralled slowly to the ceiling. The crowd was tense, silent and waiting. Sankey shed his dressing-gown, holding on to the ropes, rubbing his shoes in the resin. The handlers bundled themselves out of the ring as the gong rang.

Franks came out cautiously, his chin on his chest. Sankey almost ran at him. He swung a left and a right, but Franks went under them, socking Sankey in the body. Sankey didn't like it; he went into a clinch, roughing Franks round, cuffing his head with half-arm punches that didn't worry Franks. He hung on until the referee smacked his arm, then, as he was going away, Franks caught him with a right swing to the side of his head. The crowd howled with joy. Sankey came back at him, but Franks tied him up in a clinch. They wrestled some more and again Franks caught him as he broke.

Gurney shifted, crossed his legs and uncrossed them. "What's he playin' at?" he asked.

The other two didn't say anything.

Franks was coming in fast again; Sankey backed against the ropes, smothering most of what Franks was handing out to him. Sankey sent over a tremendous right that caught Franks as he was coming in. It caught him too high up to hurt him, but it stopped him, and Sankey got off the ropes and danced away. Franks bored in and they both exchanged short jabs to the head and body. The gong went just as Sankey was getting going. It was Franks' round all right.

The crowd buzzed and buzzed all around them. Gurney sat back, conscious of the sweat that was running down his back. He said to Dillon, "You said the fifth, didn't you?"

Dillon said, "Don't get into a spin. It's in the bag. That punk's got to put up a show."

Sankey lay back in his corner, his face sullen.

Hank flapped a towel over him, telling him to take it easy. The gong went for the second round.

It was Franks who came out fast this time. He was almost into Sankey's corner before Sankey got his hands up. The crowd roared at them. Sankey's left jumped into Franks' face, jerking his head back, but he was coming in with such steam that it didn't stop him. He banged Sankey into his corner, bringing both hands hard into his body. You could hear those two blows out in the street.

Sankey jerked up with both of them, his mouth going slack. A wild look came into his eyes, but he' kept his hands up. Gurney screamed at him, "Push him off! Get away from him!"

Franks brought over a round-house swing. It landed on Sankey's head. Sankey went down on his knee. Franks was keeping cool. He immediately walked away to a neutral corner, letting the referee start a count. The hall shook with the noise. People stood up on their chairs, yelling themselves hoarse.

Morgan's shrill yell drifted to Sankey. "Wait for it! Stay where you are!"

Sankey got up at nine. He seemed all right. Franks came at him, just a little reckless. Sankey saw an opening and lammed in. Franks didn't like it. He was shaken. They were both glad to clinch. And this time Franks missed Sankey when they broke. Sankey kept Franks away with left jabs, running backwards all round the ring, poking with his left. Franks just wanted to get in and sock. Towards the end of the round Franks got in. Sankey tried to tie him up, but it was like holding on to a buzz-saw. Franks let go four hooks one after the other. They sank into Sankey's ribs, making the crowd give a sighing groan. Sankey's knees went. He was in trouble, trying to keep his hands up when the bell went.

Dillon got to his feet. "Go to his corner," he said to Gurney savagely. "Tell him to fight. He won't last to the fifth at this rate. Let that palook Franks see you. Give him a signal or something."

Gurney pushed his way to the aisle and made his way to Sankey's corner. Hank was working on him desperately. He was looking worried. Gurney said, "You gotta watch that fella."

Sankey glared at him. Great red blotches on his ribs showed the beating he was taking. "A rigged fight, huh?" he snarled. "This punk's killin' me."

Before Gurney could say anything the gong went. Out came Franks, weaving and bobbing, with Sankey back-pedalling, snorting heavily through his nose. Gurney put his elbows on the canvas, watching closely.

Sankey tried a left, but Franks' head moved, then Franks caught him with a left and a right. Sankey began to bleed from his mouth. He drew his lips off his gum-shield, snarling at Franks. He kept circling until the crowd began to yell at him. He flung over another left that landed as Franks was going away, and tried to follow it up with a terrific right swing. It whistled over Franks' head, who came in close and socked with both hands. Sankey pushed him off and jabbed away, landing too high up to do any damage.

Sankey was getting sore. Every time Franks came in he belted Sankey in the ribs. They were landing solid. Sankey just couldn't keep him out. He was taking an awful beating in the body. The round finished with a flurry in the far corner. Sankey managed to uppercut Franks with the heel of his glove, cutting Franks' nose.

Sankey came back to his corner flat-footed. Gurney could see the muscles in his legs fluttering. He flopped on his stool and his handlers went to work on him.

Gurney said, "Keep him off this round. He's goin' to dive in the fifth."

"I can't stay," Sankey said; he was almost crying. "He's spillin' my guts."

Gurney snarled, "You'll stay all right, or you'll run into more grief outside." He looked across at Franks, who was lying back taking in great lungfuls of air. They weren't even working on him.

The gong went for the fourth.

Sankey went out with a little more spring. He was desperate. He drove a right at Franks, connected, and followed it with a left. Franks went back on his heels, covering up. The crowd rose to their feet, howling.

Gurney shouted, "Get after him... beat the hell out of him!... "

In went Sankey, swinging punches from all angles. Franks rode the dangerous ones and smothered the wild swings. Then he suddenly jabbed a left in Sankey's face, bringing him up short, and crossed with his right. It caught Sankey between the eyes. There was a sharp silence when Sankey went down on his hands and knees, then the crowd screamed with excitement. Franks went to a corner, opposite Gurney. He was breathing slowly, his great chest rising and falling without effort.

Gurney shouted, "Next round, or you get it!"

Franks showed no sign that he heard.

The referee was standing over Sankey, shouting the count in his ear. Sankey's muscles were fluttering as he tried to drag himself off the canvas. They were all shouting at him. The gong stopped the count at eight.

They got Sankey into his corner by dragging him. Hank gave him a shot of rye, tugging his ears and pouring water on his head. Hank was scared stiff. Dillon came up and leant over the ropes.

"Get a grip on yourself, you big slab of —," he snarled. "Y're goin' to win in this round. If you don't go out and tear that punk to bits I'll give you the heat."

Sankey fought down the nagging tiredness. "My left's like lead," he whined.

"Then use your right," Dillon said. "Remember, hit that guy all over the ring. He'll go down."

The gong went for the fifth.

The crowd expected Franks to come out and finish it, but he didn't. He, seemed to have suddenly lost his steam. Sankey went straight into a clinch. He hung on, leaning his weight on Franks, until the referee had to shout at him. Franks caught him as he went away, but there was no snap to it. Sankey was breathing like an escape of steam. He jabbed Franks as he came in, and Franks hit him in the ribs, three light blows that didn't even make Sankey flinch. He danced away from Franks, coming down on the flat of his feet. Franks shuffled after him, his hands low. Sankey saw his opening. He'd have been blind if he hadn't seen it. In went his left and across went his right. It was with an open glove, but they both sounded good. The crowd heaved to their feet. Franks went down on his side.

Gurney gave a little hiss of relief. The crowd screamed and rocked, yelling to Franks to get up. The referee, slightly startled, began to tick off the seconds.

Sankey leant against the ropes, his knees buckling and his face smeared with blood. He couldn't even look pleased. Franks didn't move, he just lay there.

Beth Franks fought her way to the ringside. She beat on the canvas with her hands. "Get up and fight!" she screamed. "Don't let 'em get away with it! Harry... get up and fight! ..."

Franks took his time, but he got up at nine. The crowd, backing Sankey now, screamed to him to go in and finish Franks. Sankey tottered out of his corner, swearing. Franks stood waiting for him, his lips in a thin line, looking like a killer. There was nothing the matter with him. He was as strong as when he started. As Sankey came on he called Franks every obscene name he could lay his tongue to.

Franks brushed aside his feeble guard and belted him in the ribs. It was an awful punch, landing solid in the church roof of Sankey's chest. Sankey's eyes rolled back. His mouth formed a large "O"; then, as he fell forward, Franks whipped up a punch that came from his ankles to Sankey's jaw.

It was a waste of the referee's time to count. The crowd went mad. They yelled and hooted as the little guy's arm ticked off the ten. Then, when he threw his arms wide and ran over to raise Franks' glove, they stood on their seats and rattled the roof.

Dillon turned his head and looked at Gurney. His eyes smouldered. "The dirty, double-crossin' rat," he said through his teeth.

They all crowded into Butch's shack. There was Gurney, Hank and Morgan. Sankey had gone home, too sullen and furious to come. Dillon shuffled along behind the others, savage and silent.

Butch was sitting in a dirty dressing-gown. His head was wrapped in a bandage. He sensed at once that Sankey had flopped when they came in.

Overhead, Myra could hear the uproar that was going on, and she came down the ladder to listen.

Dillon sat on the table, picking his teeth, while the others shouted and cursed. Butch was so mad, Gurney thought he'd have a stroke. He beat the arms of his chair again and again. "I put all I had on that punk!" he bawled; "now where am I?"

Dillon suddenly came to life. "Shut up, you rats!" he snarled.

"Franks's got more guts than the bunch of you rolled into one. What does it matter if you lost a little dough?"

There was a terrible silence, each man glaring at Dillon murderously. Butch said in a strangled voice, "You fixed that fight, huh? You ain't losing any dough... an' you talk like that?"

Dillon looked him over contemptuously. His eyes went round the others. They began to edge a little towards him, except Gurney. Gurney knew about the gun.

Butch climbed out of his chair. "Bring him to me," he said savagely, flexing his fingers. "I'll teach the bum somethin'."

Dillon's thin lips smiled. His eyes were stony with contempt.

"Forget it," he said. "You little punks don't know where you get off."

Butch said, "Leave him to me."

He began to weave forward, his great hands questing. Dillon, sitting on the table, watching, just hunched his shoulders in his coat. Then, when Butch was within a foot of him, the Colt leapt into his hand.

Hank screamed, "Get back, Hogan, he's got a gun!"

Dillon shot Butch low down. The crash of the gun made Myra scream out. She stood outside the door, her hands to her mouth, shuddering.

Butch's blind eyes closed, blotting out the two yellow clots from Dillon's sight. He put his hands over his belly and squeezed. The blood ran through his fingers. Dillon watched him, his smile a little fixed.

Butch went down on his knees with a thud.

Hank and Morgan fought each other to get out of the room. Dillon let them go. He didn't even turn his head. They went out through the verandah, and Gurney heard them running down the road.

The door opened and Myra came in. She stood in the open doorway, her face bony, holding herself upright against the woodwork. She made no move to go across to Butch. She just stood and watched.

Butch died like that; on his knees. He gradually slumped over like a limp sack of wheat.

Dillon eyed Gurney, then put the gun away inside his coat. "He was crazy to start on me," he said.

Gurney said hoarsely, "You'd better get outta here."

Dillon showed his teeth. "You're comin' with me, pal," he said. "Don't make a mistake about that."

Gurney gulped and said hastily, "Sure... I didn't blow like those other palooks."

The two of them looked at Myra. She was suddenly conscious of them, aware that she was now alone, that Butch was finished, and she had to look after herself.

Gurney went over to her. "Shove some things together," he said. "You're comin' with me."

She didn't say anything, but turned and went out of the room with trembling knees.

Dillon said, "Yeah, she'll be useful."

Gurney nodded, "Sure," he said, "I guess she'll be that."

There was a long pause, both men remaining still, their eyes away from

Butch. Then Gurney said, "Where we goin'?"

"Over the State line quick," Dillon said. "We'll see when we get there after that."

Myra came in, holding a small leather case.

Gurney said, "Go out an' get into the car."

She turned on her heel and went out.

Dillon went over to Gurney. "We gotta have a little dough before we start," he said. "Maybe you know Abe's got a wad salted away. We're goin' to lift that. I know where it is."

Gurney licked his lips. "It ain't safe," he said nervously. "The sheriff'll be along pretty soon."

Dillon said, "I'm tellin' you... not askin' you."

They went out into the darkness, climbing into the old car. Myra was sitting at the back. She was holding on to her nerves, but she couldn't stop herself shivering. The car lurched on to the main road, and the gears grated as Gurney changed up.

It didn't take them long to get to Abe's store. The place was in darkness. Dillon climbed out of the car. He leant forward and took the ignition key. Gurney watched him, feeling trapped. Then Dillon said, "You stay here. I ain't goin' to be long."

He walked round to the back, opening the door with a key. Silently he moved down the dark corridor, until he came to the shop.

Abe was adding figures in a ledger, a skull-cap on his head, and his face alive with intent satisfaction. He glanced up when Dillon came in. "Was it a good fight?" he asked, keeping one bony finger on the ledger page, nailing down a figure, as if he were frightened that it would escape him.

Dillon said, "Stay where you are. Don't start a squawk." He held the Colt so that Abe could see it.

Abe laid down his pen. His old fingers trembled a little. "My Rose was wrong," he said sadly.

Dillon walked to where Abe hid the day's takings. They were in a coffee-tin, up on a shelf. He reached up and took it down. Abe sat with his hands in his lap, quite crushed.

"I guess I want this more'n you," Dillon said, emptying the tin on the counter. There were just over a hundred dollars in small bills in the tin. Dillon scooped them into his pocket. He said, "I guess I'll take your wad too... maybe you'll use a bank after this."

Abe gave a groan. "You ain't givin' me a break," he said. "That money took some earning."

Dillon opened the till, pulled the drawer right out, and put his hand in the gap. He felt round the wood carefully, found the wad of notes in the false drawer, took them out and put them in his pocket. "Two grand, ain't it, Goldberg?" he said. "I've watched you count it enough times."

Abe said, "I guess this is the last time I'll help any bum."

Dillon sneered. "Aw, can that," "he said. "Suckers like you go on givin' a hand till they're buried."

While he was speaking Dillon moved round the store putting some tins of food together. He shoved them roughly into a large paper carrier. "We're makin' a trip," he said. "I'd hate to steal this stuff from you... see, I'll pay you for it." He tossed three dollars on to the counter.

Abe said nothing. He just wanted Dillon to go away. He kept thinking how he was to tell Rosey. She'd never forgive herself.

Dillon picked up the carrier and walked over to the door. "Maybe, when I get the breaks, I'll remember you, Goldberg... then maybe I won't... you see."

He walked out into the night, tossed the carrier into the car and climbed in. He gave the key to Gurney. "State line, fast," he said.

Gurney started the engine and engaged the gears. They pulled out of Plattsville as the street clock struck two, and headed for the border.

PART TWO

The Boss, the Molls,
and the Mob

Myra swung her legs off the bed and sat up. The sun came through the open window, burning her feet. The cheap clock on the mantleboard indicated 8:10. She sat there, sniffing the crisp air. She fished about with her feet, hunting for her shoes.

Finally, with a little gasp of annoyance, she went on hands and knees and dug them out from under the bed.

She knelt there staring at the shoes. "By heck," she said, "I'm getting a regular bum." The shoes were just about handing in their checks. Two large cracks gaped like little mouths at her from the top, and the soles were as good as a sieve.

She sat back on her heels, scratching her thigh, thinking. It wasn't from choice she was almost in rags. She just hadn't anything to wear.

Three long weary weeks had crawled by since Butch had been knocked off. The cabin, hidden in the hills, was just held together by its paint. Dillon had been glad to move into it, and now he was in he just stuck.

The last owner had been an Okie, who had taken his family with him on the futile search for work in the California invasion. He had left the cabin pretty well as it stood. Even the bedding had been left. The Okie had certainly been in a hurry to get away.

Taking the car to the nearest small town, Dillon had got in enough stores to last for some time, and the three of them had dug themselves in. The cabin was lonely, off the beaten track, and they didn't see anyone from dawn to dusk.

Dillon spent most of his time lying in bed, brooding. He got up around midday, had some food, and sat on the step of the cabin in the sun. He got on the other two's nerves. The work was shoved on to Myra. Gurney cut the wood and got the water, but he didn't do much else. He hung around the house, treading on Myra's heels, keeping his hands off her with an effort, and generally eating his head off with boredom.

Myra was getting sick of it. She wasn't taking any chances on getting laid up, so she kept Gurney out of her room. This made Gurney sore, but Myra's waspish temper stood between them like a wall.

She got to her feet and put on the shoes, wriggling her toes inside them, feeling the rough boards through the soles. She splashed water into a tin bowl and began to wash. Slapping the water on her body, she rubbed herself briskly. All the time she was doing this her mind was busy. It was time to shake these bums up a bit, she thought. Dillon would have to be handled carefully. Up to now he had ignored her. That irritated her. He just didn't know she was there. She thought he was a cold-blooded fish. She walked over to the stool where she had dropped her clothes. She turned them over, her nose wrinkling with disgust. Every garment was in holes. Even her dress was patched heavily under the arms.

Pulling the dress over her head, she smoothed the creases with her hands. Then she walked into the living room.

Gurney was standing in the open doorway, fixing his belt. He nodded to her sourly. He thought he was having a swell break bringing her along, and then to have her lock herself in every night. His chin was covered with a stubbly beard, and his eyes, still puffy with sleep, peered at her hungrily.

Across the way was another little room, where Dillon slept. The door was shut. They didn't expect to see him for some time.

Myra said, "Suppose you get the fire goin'." She spoke shortly.

Gurney said, "Sure." He wandered outside and came back with a handful of wood. He sat down in front of the small stove and began to poke at the ashes.

Myra filled the kettle and began to lay the table. When the wood in the stove was crackling Gurney got up and put the kettle on. He walked round the room, scratching himself under the arms, yawning. His eyes were on Myra. She didn't take any notice of him.

He came up behind her, slipping his arms round her waist. He hugged her to him.

Myra stood quite still. "Get away, will you?" she snapped. "There's work to do."

Gurney forced her round. "I'm sick of this," he said savagely. "I ain't goin' to stand it."

He lifted her off her feet and ran her into her room. Myra made no effort to resist him. In the room, he set her down and stood holding her, his chest heaving.

She said, "You're gettin' wrong ideas, Nick."

"Yeah?" He shook her a little. "That's what you think. You're enough to drive a guy nuts.... What's the idea? You're hot enough when Butch might've killed you... but now..."

She kept her face cold. "The kettle's boiling," she said. "Suppose you come down to earth."

Gurney took his hands off her. "By heck!" he said angrily. "You can't treat me like this."

A furious wave of rage shot through her like a flame. "And what d'you think this is?" she screamed at him. "Look at me! how d'you think I like this? There's not a rag to my back. All you think is gettin' into bed. Well, you got another think coming. That lousy punk out there's got a roll of dough, and he just sits on it. How long d'you think we're goin' to stay in this sty? Who are you to get sore?"

Gurney backed away uneasily. "Pipe down," he said surlily. "I can't help it, can I?"

"You can't help it!" She beat her hands together. "I'll show you something."

She pushed past him and burst in on Dillon. Dillon was sitting up in bed. He was wearing a shirt and trousers, a splinter of wood between his teeth. He looked at her suspiciously. "What do you want, bustin' in like this?" he snarled.

"I'll tell you what I want," she stormed at him. "I want to get out of here. I want some dough to buy things with.... I'm sick of messing around working for a couple of ragged bums like you for nothin'. Look at me... look at this dress..."

Dillon swung his legs over the edge of the bed and got up. Gurney stood in the open doorway. He was scared. Dillon hunched his shoulders. "Listen," he said. "You just get out quick or I'll toss you out. I'm the boss of this outfit, see?"

Myra sneered at him. She stood with her legs planted wide and her hands on her hips. "You couldn't be a boss of any outfit, you small-time gunman," she said. "Get that into your thick dome. Now come on, let's have some dough."

Dillon swung his fist and hit her on the side of her head. It was a solid punch. She hurtled across the room, banging her shoulder against the rough wood, and falling in a heap.

Gurney said feebly from the door, "Hey! You can't knock her around like that."

Dillon looked at him. His cold eyes were glittering. "Keep out of this," he said; "she had it comin' to her. She ain't goin' to get anywhere with that line of talk."

Myra scrambled to her feet. She held her hand to her head. The ground rose a little under her feet. She focused Dillon with difficulty. "You devil!" she said.

Dillon hitched his trousers up and walked over to her. "Get out an' put some food together. You're here to work, see? I ain't havin' any hot air from you."

She looked over his shoulder at Gurney. "Think I'm going to play with you after this, you yellow rat... you've got some chance."

Dillon said, "You shut up!"

Gurney turned and went into the front room. He guessed Myra would give him hell for this. Dillon didn't take his eyes off Myra. He remembered the way she bounced Butch around. This dame was dangerous. Myra looked at him, her eyes hating him. "You ain't going to get away with this," she said through her teeth. "I'll fix you, you dirty heel!"

Dillon said, "Aw, can it!" He moved away, still keeping his eyes open.

Myra hesitated, then walked into the front room. Gurney gave her a scared look, but she took no notice of him. She began to prepare the meal. She cut the ham into thick hunks, savagely sawing at the salty meat, and slapping the slices into the pan.

Gurney expected her to cry. He guessed most dames would have folded up from a smack like that. Myra's face was white and set. A livid mark, where Dillon had hit her, burnt on her temple, and her eyes were stormy.

Gurney said uneasily, "You ain't goin' to get nowhere, startin' to fight that guy."

Myra said nothing. She served the food, banging the plates on the table. Then, pouring herself out a cup of strong coffee, she went out into the sunshine and sat away from the cabin.

Dillon came in, looked at the food and grunted. He sat down at the table and began to eat. Gurney sat down gingerly.

"You gettin' sick of things?" Dillon said. There was a tense threat in his voice.

Gurney slopped his coffee. "Me?... I ain't squealin'," he said hurriedly.

Dillon jerked his head to where Myra was sitting. "I figgered maybe you put her up to that."

Gurney was round-eyed with innocence. "You got me wrong," he said hurriedly. "You ain't got to worry about her. She's just mad at havin' nothin' to wear."

Dillon cut the ham up in small squares. "You have a talk with her... she'd better watch her step. I ain't standin' any buck from her—get it?"

Gurney pushed his plate away and lit a cigarette. The food stuck in his throat. "Sure," he said, "she's just a kid... you know, she don't mean a thing."

Dillon said evenly: "You tell her... unless you want me to give her a rubdown. You want to handle that broad... what you scared about? Why don't you teach her who's boss?"

Pushing back his chair, Gurney got to his feet. He mumbled something and went over to fix the stove.

"I'm goin' to take the car out," Dillon said, finishing his food and getting up. "I've a little job I wantta case. Maybe you can do somethin' with it later."

Gurney looked at him uneasily, but said nothing.

Myra watched the two men come out of the cabin and walk over to the shed where the car was garaged. She got up and went in, clearing the table and stacking the plates. She was still trembling with suppressed rage. She heard the car drive off, and she ran to the window. Dillon was sitting at the wheel.

Gurney came in. "He's gone downtown," he said.

Myra sat down on the wooden bench under the window. "I want to talk to you," she said, her words coming tense and harsh. "It's time you got wise to this guy."

Gurney scratched the back of his head. "I don't get this," he said.

"You ain't goin' to get anything from him. Don't you think it. He's got that scratch from Abe Goldberg... has he given you any? Not a chance! You're running around with him, an' he's tied an accessory rap on you. He's the boss, an' you jumpin' in circles. You're just a crazy sucker, scared by a bum like that."

Gurney shifted. "That guy totes a rod," he said. "What can I do?"

Myra's eyes glittered. "I'm goin' to tell you what you're goin' to do. You're goin' to 'yes' that guy until you get the run of his game, then you're goin' to turn him in. You're goin' to have a gun, an' you're goin' to shoot better than he shoots. You're goin' to do everything better than he does. Then he goes."

Gurney stood looking at her. Then he nodded his head slowly. "Sure," he said thoughtfully. "That's an idea."

The sun was falling behind the hills when Dillon got back.

Gurney heard the old engine faintly in the distance, and he went out, standing by the well, looking down the rough road. He wondered where the hell Myra had got to. She had slipped off after the midday meal, and he hadn't seen her since. Restless and bored with his own company, the sound of the car chugging up the hill came as a relief.

He had spent most of the afternoon wandering round the cabin, brooding. He felt that Myra had a good idea, ditching Dillon. He was scared of the guy. He couldn't bring himself to think how Dillon was to be ditched. Unconsciously, he left that for Myra to fix. Sitting on the step in the sunshine he had gone over everything Myra had said. That dame had a head all right. She'd got Dillon pinned down. Yeah, she was right. Dillon was a mean guy. He'd run them for a while, then leave them flat. Gurney's hands ached for the feel of a gun. Just give him a gun and he'd fix Dillon okay.

Dillon drew up outside the cabin. He waved his hand to Gurney. His sullen face seemed more animated. Gurney came over.

"You been away some time," he said. "You get the breaks?"

Dillon climbed out of the car and went round the back. He reached in and dragged out a bulky object covered with a blanket. "Come inside," he said, "I got somethin' to show you."

Gurney followed him in. Dillon dumped the bundle on the table and carefully unwrapped it.

Gurney stood quite still, his heart beating hard. "Well, by heck!" he said.

Lying on the table was a Thompson riot gun, a heavy .45 Smith & Wesson, and a large case of shells.

Dillon patted the Thompson, his thin lips curving a little. "A guy who's got a thing like that can get most places," he said.

A shadow fell across the table. They looked up sharply. Myra stood in the doorway, her eyes fixed on the gun. The two men took their eyes away from her, and forgot her in the gun.

"How did you get that?" Gurney asked. He picked up the .45 and caressed the cold butt. It felt good.

Dillon was in an expansive mood. He wandered over to the bench under the window and sat down. "Once you know the tricks," he said, "it's easy."

Myra went over to the table and stood looking. She cautiously put her hand on the cold barrel of the Thompson.

Dillon watched her. His triumphant mood included her. "Pick it up," he said. "It ain't goin' to bite."

She held the Thompson, the butt tucked under her arm. The long barrel pointed to the stove. She let her hand run over the smooth drum.

Gurney watched her. His mouth was dry with excitement. Maybe this guy wasn't such a bum after all, he thought. "You didn't find that growin' on a tree," he said.

Dillon shook his head. "These guns don't get picked up easy," he said, hooking his thumbs in his belt. "Know how I got it?" His thin lips grinned at them. Myra watched him, her face blank, but her eyes hated him. Dillon didn't feel her. He was big-shotting himself to death.

"I went into the sheriff's office an' bought it off him," he said.

"That's a hell of a tale," Gurney said. The admiration in his voice pleased Dillon.

"Listen, bozo," Dillon said. "This country's nuts. Every single flatfoot has to buy his own rod. They give him everything else, but not his gun. He has to lay down cash for it. Okay; there comes a time when a sheriff gives over, see? Maybe he gives over 'cause he's too old, or maybe he's sick or somethin'. Well, that guy wants to buy a business or a farm or live on his savings. What the hell does he want with a gun? What's he to do then?

Some guy blows in an' makes him an offer. He gets an offer twice as good as he'd get if he turned the rod over to a gunsmith. It ain't legal sellin' Thompsons to anyone, but what the hell? He's out for good, so he should worry."

Gurney said, "You got this from a sheriff?" His voice was incredulous.

Dillon nodded. "Sure I did." He reached forward and picked up the .45. "I went into town today an' got talkin'. Some guy said the sheriff in the next town was closin' down, so I grabbed the car an' went out to see him. That little lot set me back a good few bucks, but that ain't goin' to worry me. A Tommy talks any time."

Myra recognized this much. Dillon knew the ropes. Gurney wasn't in the same street with him for ideas. He knew where to get things and how to get them. This guy could teach them something.

She said, making her voice soft, "I guess that's smart."

Dillon looked at her hard, but Myra's eyes were wide with admiration. He grunted. "I guess I know my way around," he said.

"Can you work this?" Gurney said, tapping the Thompson. Dillon stood up. "Can I work it?" He picked it up and walked outside. "You watch me."

Myra and Gurney followed him out. They did not look at each other, but Myra put her hand on Gurney's arm, gripping his muscle. Gurney nodded his head, still keeping his eyes on Dillon's back.

Dillon looked round thoughtfully, selecting a target. "You ain't got to worry about aimin' this gun," he said; "you spray it, see? You just gotta hold it steady an' bring it round slow in a sweep... like this."

He raised the gun, levelling it at the garage door, then he pressed the trigger. The shattering roar of the gun made Myra take an involuntary step backwards. Chips of white wood flew from the door. From where they stood they could see the holes spring up in the woodwork in an even line.

Dillon stopped firing and turned to look at them. "See?" he said. "That's the way. This gun's goin' to stop anythin' on two legs."

Myra came over to him. "I bet I could do that," she said.

Dillon looked down at her, hesitating. Then his good humour overcame his caution. He gave the gun to her. "You gotta hold her."

Myra pressed the butt into her side, her finger curling round the trigger, then she squeezed. The gun jumped about in her hand as if it were alive. The dry mud puffed up and the leaves from the trees overhanging the garage fell in a shower; she winged the door twice.

Dillon said, "Take it easy... you gotta hold that gun."

Gurney was itching to try. He looked at Dillon, trying to catch his eye. Myra held the gun, looking at it thoughtfully, then she shoved it in Gurney's hands.

Dillon scowled. "Hey," he said, "those shells cost dough!"

Gurney was not to be put off. He raised the gun and fired off a round. The wood splinters again spurted. He could see he'd drawn a line of holes almost as well as Dillon.

Myra said, "You ain't so good as this guy."

That pleased Dillon. Anyway, that's why she said it. He took the gun from Gurney and walked back to the cabin. Gurney followed close behind him.

They both sat and watched Dillon clean the gun. Every now and then Myra would ask a question. She asked it in a way that touched Dillon's vanity. He talked all right. They learnt a lot about that gun while he was cleaning it.

Gurney helped Dillon hide the case of shells, and they put the gun under Dillon's bed. Then they came back to the sitting-room.

Dillon sat on the edge of the table and looked at Gurney. "There's a small bank down there that might be worth workin' over. I'd do it if I'd someone to drive the car."

Myra said quietly, "I'll drive the car."

Dillon jerked his head round. "What do you know about a car?" he said shortly. "A getaway is the main thing in a bank stick-up. The guy who handles the wheel's got to use his head. He's got to drive like hell an' keep on drivin' like hell."

Myra shrugged. "I guess nobody's goin' to drive like hell in that old jalopy," she said.

"Who said I was going in her?" Dillon demanded. "You don't know a thing about this business. I'll knock a car off when I'm ready. A real fast job, with enough steam under the hood to shake anythin' on four wheels."

"Get a bus like that," Myra said, "an' I'll drive it."

Dillon began to get angry. "Will you keep your nose outta this?" he snarled. "This ain't for you, so shut up."

Myra got up and walked to the door. "Yeah?" she said. "Then watch this."

She ran over to the old car outside, slipped under the wheel and started the engine. She had that old bus going forty before she was out of sight. She had changed up, one—two—three—almost in so many seconds. Back she came, swinging the wheel so that the wheels on the offside lifted and slammed back, nearly jerking her out of the car. She pushed the old bus right up to the cabin, making Dillon and Gurney jump to their feet before she nailed it dead. She got out of the car and walked into the cabin again.

Dillon looked at her. There was a look of astonishment in his eyes, but he kept his face blank.

"She can handle a car all right," Gurney said to him. "I guess she wouldn't lose her nerve."

Dillon hesitated and then he nodded. "Sure," he said. "I guess we'll knock that bank tomorrow."

Behind his back the two exchanged glances.

The big Cadillac settled down to business. Myra kept the pedal on the boards, holding the car to the crown of the road. Gurney was beside her, and Dillon sat at the back. He held the Thompson by his side, covered with a blanket.

It was just after three o'clock, and the afternoon sun was hot. It reflected on the white road and shimmered across the green fields.

They'd had the breaks all right. It was not just chance. Dillon had gone over everything with a thoroughness that surprised the other two. First he made a map on a piece of white card. The bank was plotted right in the centre. He had made arrangements for getting away in three different ways. "It's like this," he explained. "We come out with the dough. Maybe some guy puts up a squawk. Okay. The sheriff might've grabbed himself a car and come beating down here." He traced a line on the map. "We gotta go this way. Maybe he'll come from this direction. We ain't got time to swing the bus round, so we beat it to the right. With this map we got three getaways." He had pinned the map just above the windscreen, over Myra's head. He'd taken Myra through that map until she was sick of it.

"You gotta keep your nut," he had told her. "I'll be right with you, but you gotta go where I say, an' go quick. You ain't gotta argue… you gotta drive."

When Dillon was through with her, he started on Gurney, He showed Gurney how to pull the gun, and how to shoot.

Dillon said to him, "You ain't to pop that heater. You leave that to me. There's only two punks in that bank, an' those guys ain't goin' to cause trouble. They got wives, an' maybe they got kids. All you gotta do is to collect the dough and get out quick."

Gurney had the .45 under his coat. It made him feel good. He was excited, and he wasn't scared any more.

The jalopy had been hidden in a wood some twenty miles from the bank. Dillon hadn't any trouble knocking off the Cadillac. It just stood in the main street asking to be knocked off. Even the engine was running, while some guy did his weekend store buying. That bus certainly could move.

They began to run into the town. Dillon edged himself forward, so that his head came between the two in the front. "Take it easy," he said. "Just run up and stop without any fuss."

Myra said, between her teeth, "What you think I'd do? Turn the damn' thing over, and push it down the street on its roof?" Her heart was banging against her ribs.

Dillon sat back. "You keep your nut," was all he said. Taking the blanket off the Thompson, he pulled the gun across his knees, his left hand on the car door.

Gurney pulled the .45 from inside his coat. He held it in his lap. His mouth was very dry.

They pulled up outside the bank.

Myra shoved out the clutch, put the gear in bottom, and revved the engine hard. She said, "Don't take all day."

Dillon put his Colt automatic beside her. "Maybe you better have that."

Myra slipped the gun under her, and sat on it. The butt was just under her hand.

Swinging the door open, Dillon ran across the pavement and entered the bank. The Thompson was under his coat. Gurney came in at his heels. There was a fat woman wedged against the grille, arguing with the teller. Gurney could hear her voice putting up a squawk. His brain was stiff. He couldn't get what she was saying.

A thin, lanky man got off a stool at the far end of the bank and wandered down when he saw Dillon.

"Stand by the door," Dillon said to Gurney.

The lanky guy said, "We're closin' down right now"; he sounded as if he were bored to hell with the bank.

"Grab some air!" Dillon yelled, pitching his voice high. "This is a stick-up." The Thompson showed its black barrel.

The two guys behind the counter stiffened into waxworks.

The fat woman turned her head. Dillon was right behind her. She took one look at him and her big mouth opened. Gurney nearly dropped his gun. "That dame's going to yell the roof off," he thought.

Dillon shifted the gun a little and swung his fist. He hit the woman across her mouth with his knuckles. There was a lot of steam in that punch. She was right up against the counter, so she couldn't ride the punch. It made a real mess of her face. She flopped down on her knees and then spread out. A whistling sound dribbled from her throat. Without taking his eyes from the other two, Dillon kicked at her head. He kicked her just once. The woman's head bounced away from his boot. She stopped making any noise.

The lanky guy suddenly went green, and vomited on the floor in front of him. He didn't lower his hands, but just bent his head forward.

Dillon said to Gurney, "Hey! This crum's been eatin' ice cream."

Gurney wasn't feeling so good himself. He scrambled over the grille. The two watched him with wide eyes. They were scared to death.

Gurney went through the drawers, piling the notes on the counter. Dillon stood watchful, holding the Thompson ready. He said, "Get the safe open." He looked hard at the teller.

Gurney grabbed the teller's arm. "Get it open!" he snarled, pushing the .45 into his ribs. "Get goin', you lug."

The teller staggered across to the vault, his knees buckling. Gurney could see the sweat running down behind his ears into his collar. The teller pulled open the door. It wasn't even locked. He tried to say something, but he was so scared he couldn't get his tongue working.

Gurney grabbed the money, done up in neat packets. There wasn't a lot, but he took everything he could see. He left the coin. Then he ran back to the counter and shoved all the money into a small flour-sack he'd brought with him. He vaulted over the grille again.

Dillon said, "Get goin'." He stood by the door until Gurney was out, then he began to back out. "Don't start anythin'," he snarled at the lanky guy. "This typewriter'll cut you to hell."

He turned and ran. Myra was already rolling the car. As he sprang on the running-board the Cadillac shot forward with a jerk that nearly threw him loose.

The car lurched with screaming tires as she pulled into the centre of the road. Dillon tossed the Tommy into the back seat and clung to the running-board, trying to get in. "Gimme a hand, you punk!" he yelled at Gurney.

Gurney grabbed Dillon's arm, pulling him forward. Another lurch tossed Dillon head first into the car. He scrambled to his knees, swearing savagely.

Myra gritted her teeth. At the back of her mind she had hoped to lose Dillon. She had not consciously tried to ditch him, but now he was safe she knew that she had tried to shake him.

The Cadillac went down the main street with a rush. The quivering needle of the speedometer swung to seventy. Faintly above the swish of tires and the scream of the wind they could hear people shouting.

Myra gripped the wheel, her eyes fixed on the road that seemed to jump up from the ground and rush to meet her. Another car coming from the opposite direction crowded on brakes as the Cadillac hurtled down on it. Myra touched the wheel and swept by. The open road lay in front.

Dillon glanced through the rear window. The road was deserted. He sat back on the seat and wiped off his palms. He was tossed about in the back as the car tore down the rough road.

Gurney twisted his head and grinned at him. "Just like that," he shouted.

Dillon didn't say anything. He was looking murder. He wasn't sure if Myra had tried to ditch him. He knew it was a mighty close thing. Gurney was still clutching the sack. Dillon leant forward and took it from him. Gurney looked round, a little startled, but Dillon's cold eyes made him flinch. "Take it easy," Dillon shouted to Myra, "we ain't goin' to turn this can over."

Myra eased the pressure on the pedal and the Cadillac dropped down to fifty.

Gurney said, "It was a cinch."

Dillon sneered. "Sure, but it could've been tough."

They drove in silence for the next few miles. Gurney was feeling uneasy. He knew that if he'd let Dillon alone he'd have been shaken off the running-board. He knew Dillon knew it. What was Myra playing at? This guy Dillon was too tricky to double-cross.

Myra ran the Cadillac off the road when they came to the wood where the jalopy was hidden. They all got out, leaving the Cadillac hidden from the road.

Dillon took two quick steps away from the other two. His face was hard and threatening. He slightly raised the Tommy. "Put your rod on the ground," he said to Gurney. "You keep away from the car," he went on to Myra.

The two stood very still. Myra found her voice. "What's the big idea?" she said, her voice suppressed.

"I want those rods... maybe you didn't try to hang it on me in the car, but I ain't takin' any chances with you. Snap into it. Drop that gun, Gurney."

Gurney let the gun fall on the grass. He stepped away from it. His face was a little white. He was scared.

Dillon picked the gun up and shoved it down the waistband of his trousers. He walked over to the Cadillac and took the gun lying on the seat. "Okay," he said. "I guess that's all. We'll run back to the cabin now in the jalopy."

The two didn't say anything. Gurney got under the wheel and Myra got in beside him. Dillon climbed in at the back. They drove away, leaving the Cadillac.

When they reached the cabin Dillon went straight to his room and shut himself in. They heard the bar fall in its socket, bolting him in.

Myra stood very still, looking at Gurney. "We ain't gettin' anywhere with this guy," she said, keeping her voice low. "He's gotta lot comin' to him."

Gurney slouched over to the bench and sat down. He rubbed the back of his neck thoughtfully, looking hard at his feet. Myra stared at him for a moment, then she began getting a meal together.

They didn't see Dillon until supper was on the table. He came out of his room, a cold, triumphant look on his face. He was conscious of the hard glances from the other two. Sitting down at the table, he began to shovel the food into his mouth. The other two just sat and watched him. After a moment he looked up irritably. "What's the matter with you?" he demanded fiercely. "Ain't you hungry?"

Myra said, "Did we get much outta that bank?"

Dillon sneered at her. "You ain't gotta worry about that," he said. "You're here to work, see?" He took some notes out of his pocket and tossed them across the table to Gurney. "That's your split," he said evenly, and went on eating.

Gurney looked at the notes as if he couldn't believe his eyes. He poked at them with his finger.

Myra said, her voice very brittle, "Count 'em."

Gurney couldn't count them. He just sat and stared at them.

Myra leant forward and snatched up the notes. She counted them out on the table, slapping them down and counting aloud. She made it a hundred dollars.

Dillon went on eating, his eyes on his plate. There was a little circle of white round his mouth. He was getting mad all right.

Myra said with a little hiss of breath, "What's this?"

Dillon looked up at Gurney. "You let this chippy talk too much," he said. He tossed the knife and fork on to his plate with a clatter and sat back. His hands lay on the table, his fingers tapping.

Gurney said with a little rush, "A hundred bucks ain't much."

"Don't you stand for this," Myra shrilled, pushing the notes away from her. "He's double-crossing you."

Dillon stood up, kicking over his chair. His eyes glittered. "I've told you," he snarled at Gurney, "I ain't standin' any more of it. That dame gets outta here, see? You're crazy to have her here... well, this finishes it... she's out!"

Gurney looked up at him, his face drawn and glistening, but he knew he was up against Myra. "Say, listen," he said, "somethin' is wrong. You don't mean this's all I get out of the stickup?"

Dillon eyed him. "You gone nuts?" he demanded savagely. "What the hell d'you think you're goin' to get out of it?"

"A hundred bucks is peanut money."

Dillon sneered. "Sure it's peanut money. What of it? You didn't case the job, did you? You didn't fix the plans, did you? You didn't know where to find the bank, did you? Like hell you didn't. You just went in there and picked the dough outta the safe. A monkey could've done it."

Gurney dropped his eyes. Dillon had him.

"I'm givin' you that hundred bucks, an' you can like it. When you've used that nut of yours an' pulled somethin' good, then we'll split even, but not before."

"You double-crossing rat!" Myra screamed at him. "What do I get out of it? Didn't I drive the car?"

Dillon looked at her.

"You ain't nothin' to me," he said, his lips grinning. "That punk brought you. It's up to him to give you somethin'."

He turned his back and walked into his room. They heard the bolt slam in the socket.

The moon floated high.

From his bed Gurney could see every object clearly in the room. The window was wide open, but no air came to him. He was feeling hot and uneasy, lying there. He knew he couldn't sleep. His mind dwelt on Dillon. He thought of the hundred dollars, and he sweated with fury. When Dillon had gone into his room, Myra had disappeared into hers. She hadn't said a word to Gurney.

Sitting up impatiently, Gurney glanced at the battered clock on the mantelshelf. It was just after one. He sat up and swung his legs to the ground. His mind, restless and frustrated, made his body uneasy. He wanted Myra. He wanted her so badly that it made him feel weak.

There she was, just across the room, behind that door.

Then he lay back on his elbow, savagely gnawing at his lip. He knew he hadn't the nerve to go in there and start anything. She was too well guarded by herself. She was too strong for him.

He sat up again, his eyes wide. Her door was opening quietly. He felt his heart hammering against his ribs, and he began to breathe unsteadily. He could see the flicker of the candle behind her, making her shadow dance before her. She raised her hand and beckoned him. He slid across the room quickly, without a sound. She took his arm and pulled him into the room and shut the door.

He was surprised and disappointed to see that she was still dressed. Her white face, and her eyes, hard and bright like glass, frightened him. He put his back to the door and stared at her.

"What is it?" he said, keeping his voice down.

"Don't you know?" she said. "We ain't takin' any more from that lousy heel. He's gotta go."

Gurney stared at her, his mouth going dry.

"But how?" he whispered.

"You gotta get into that room an' knock him off," she said.

Gurney recoiled.

"You're nuts," he said. "That guy's got three guns in there."

Her face was close to his. "He's got a lot of dough in there as well. We gotta do it, Nick, can't you see? We won't get anywhere unless we do."

Gurney walked round her and sat on the bed. "I tell you it can't be done," he said, slamming his fist down on his knee. "What you thinking about?

I tell you that guy's got three rods, and he'll just fall over himself to put some slugs into both of us."

Myra came over to him and sat close. She put her arms round his neck. He could feel the warmth of her body pressing against him. He could feel the curve of her breast against his arm. He turned, dragging her over his knees, gripping her tight, his blood singing in his ears. She let him kiss her, then she broke away from him and stood up.

He sat there, shaken with desire for her.

Myra's voice came like a cold douche. "Get a grip on yourself, Nick... Dillon first... you'll never have me if you don't get that rat... and you've got to get him now."

Gurney got to his feet. He leant forward. "Do you mean it?" he said, his voice harsh.

She stood there looking at him. "I mean it all right," she said.

"What've I gotta do?" He relied on her.

Myra moved round the room, thinking. Gurney could only watch her. His brain refused to work. He had eyes only for her, raking her from head to foot.

She said at last, "We mustn't slip up on this, Nick."

Gurney didn't say anything.

"Give him a chance, an' he'll finish both of us." She moved to the door. "Wait, I'll be right back."

Gurney wiped his sweating palms on the sheet.

She came back into the room again. He caught the flash of steel. "What've you got there?" he said, his voice just a croak. She showed him. The short blade of the knife flashed in the candlelight. He looked at her, his eyes popping. He started to say something, but stopped.

She sat down on the bed beside him.

"Listen," she said, "we'll do it this way. When we're set, I'm goin' to start yellin'. I'm goin' to bring the roof down. He'll come in quick enough to see what's wrong. I'll give him the line that you attacked me, an' you've gotta get tough. When he's talkin' to you, I'll come up behind him an' stick him with this. As soon as the knife's in, you slam him one from the front. Watch his gun—he'll bring that out all right. He might start shootin' unless I kill him on his feet."

Sweat ran down Gurney's face.

"I don't like this."

Myra jerked impatiently. "It's goin' to work—you see."

"A knife ain't goin' to stop this rat," Gurney said; "don't you think it will."

Myra hesitated. She guessed maybe Gurney was right about that. Then she said, "We'll give it to him like he gave it to Butch."

She slipped into the outer room and came back almost immediately. She gave Gurney a small tin of pepper. Gurney looked at the tin and twisted his mouth into a grin.

"Yeah," he said, and stood up.

"Wait for a break," Myra warned him, "then toss the lot in his face. You make a mess of that, an' you an' me won't last long."

Gurney nodded his head. His hands were shaking, but he was cooling down.

Myra pulled off her dress. She ran her hands through her hair, mussing it. Gurney pulled her to him. She pulled his head down to her mouth, forcing herself against him. They stood like that for several moments, straining to each other. Then Myra broke away from him, and stumbled over to the bed.

Gurney said between his teeth, "Start squawkin'." He wanted to get this over.

Myra began to scream—high-pitched screams that jarred Gurney's nerves. She stopped for a moment, then, when they heard the bolt slide back with a crash in Dillon's room, she started again.

Gurney shouted, "Shut up!"

"Get out... get out!" she screamed at him.

Dillon said from the door, "What the hell's goin' on?"

Gurney jerked his head. "She's gone nuts!"

Dillon advanced into the room. His face was cold and suspicious. Myra saw the gun in his hand. She sat up in the bed, her eyes wild. "Get him out of here!" she screamed to Dillon, "I won't have him here!"

Dillon said with a little snarl, "Pipe down... what do you think this is?" He turned his head and looked at Gurney. "You better get out of this. Suppose some car passed an' came up to see what was wrong? You two screwy or somethin'?"

Myra got off the bed. She kept the knife behind her back. She said in a frightened voice, "You must help me. Please keep this heel out of my room. I know you ain't got much use for me, but I guess you ain't lettin' him get away with this?"

Dillon turned his head to look at her, and Gurney tossed the pepper in his face. Myra threw herself flat. Dillon gave a strangled scream and the gun exploded at his side. Gurney made a dive for the door. He wanted to get the Thompson. He blundered into Dillon's room. It was dark in there, lit only by a flickering candle. He couldn't see the Thompson anywhere. He swore as he rushed round the room, feverishly turning things over, pulling out drawers, and groping in dark corners. Every moment he expected to feel the cold barrel of the gun, and his terror grew as his questing hands found nothing.

There was a fearful commotion of Dillon's screams and the gun going off outside. Gurney, sobbing with panic, ran back to the door again. He almost ran into Dillon, who was stumbling across the outer room, one hand over his eyes, the other holding the gun waist-high. Gurney ducked back, hastily squeezing himself behind the door. Dillon fired once. The bullet sent a spurt of splinters from the wall. He came into the room and stood listening.

Gurney held his breath. He was scared all right. Dillon groped his way across to the bed. Gurney let him go past, then he leapt forward, driving his knees into Dillon's back. The two went down with a crash. Gurney screamed for Myra to come.

The gun shot out of Dillon's hand and slid under the bed. Gurney could feel the heat from Dillon's body. They were both sweating with fear.

Arching his back, Dillon shot Gurney over his head, and then grabbed him round the body. He hit Gurney twice with his fists, as if he were driving a nail into wood. They both caught Gurney on the chest, driving the wind out of his body. Gurney lashed out with his feet, but in his terror he kicked wild. Dillon came at him again, his lips off his teeth, and a horrible sobbing noise coming deep down from his chest. Gurney took another punch that made him jerk convulsively, and then he slammed his right into Dillon's face.

Myra came running in. She stood in the doorway, the knife held before her, waiting for a chance to get at Dillon. The two men rolled over, away from her, into a dark corner. She sprang forward and caught up the candle, holding it above her head. "Kill him, Nick!" she shrilled. "Get after him... don't let him get away!"

Gurney made a desperate effort to break away from Dillon, but Dillon was too strong for him. They crashed against the wall. One of Dillon's hands groped for Gurney's face, hooked fingers questing for his eyes. Gurney yelled and jerked his head back. Pinning Gurney with his knees, Dillon heaved up. Myra saw the broad shoulders suddenly coming up out of the shadow. She ran forward, holding the candle in her left hand, and drove the knife down hard.

The light warned Dillon. He let go of Gurney and threw himself backwards, crashing into Myra. The candle fell to the floor and went out. Myra went over heavily. The breath in her body rushed out of her throat as she hit the boards. She felt a hand close round her ankle. Screaming wildly, she kicked out furiously with her free foot. Twice she kicked Dillon's head, but he kept on. He dragged her close and his hands gripped her thighs, his fingers like steel hooks, driving into the flesh and muscle. The agony of his grip made Myra scream again. She twisted forward, her fists beating him like flails. Still he kept that grip, digging his nails deeper and deeper into her.

"Nick... for Pete's sake...!" Myra screamed.

Gurney heaved out of the darkness and smashed down on both of them. Myra got a hard knock from his arms as he came down. The paralyzing grip on her legs loosened as, swearing in great gasping breaths, Dillon grabbed at Gurney again. Myra rolled clear. The cold blade of the knife touched her hand and she seized it by the handle.

Gurney yelled, "I got him... quick... Myra... quick!" She ran into the darkness towards the sound of the struggle.

Her shins struck their bodies and she fell on top of them. Gurney panted out of the darkness, "Get him... Quick... I can't... hold him!"

Myra kept her head. She lay flat on the two struggling bodies. Her hand groped in the dark and touched a face. The two men heaved up, nearly throwing her clear.

A muffled voice mumbled, "He's underneath... get him." And blindly she thrust down with the knife. She heard a sigh and the struggling suddenly ceased.

"Don't leave him... Nick..." Myra gasped to Gurney. "Hold him." Her hand still held the horn shaft of the knife; she pulled it out, and then, moving the point a little way up, she shoved down hard again on the handle.

She stabbed four times before she was satisfied. Then she rolled away and got shakily to her feet. There was a heavy silence in the darkness. She said uneasily, "You all right, Nick?"

A burning, claw-like hand gripped her wrist, twisting it sharply, so that the knife fell with a little clatter on the boards. "You've killed him, you silly little fool," Dillon said in her ear.

Myra screamed once. Then her body stiffened with terror. "Don't touch me!... Don't touch me!" she moaned, trying to free her wrist.

She heard Dillon's foot touch the knife and kick it away. Then he let go of her and struck a match. With red, streaming eyes he looked at her in the dim flicker of the light.

"Stay still," he said through his teeth. "You make a move an' I'll smash you."

She remained motionless, one shaking hand at her mouth, while he walked stiffly to the lamp and lit it. Her eyes left him and turned slowly to Gurney, lying in the shadow. A narrow ribbon of blood ran from Gurney towards her, twisting like a snake across the rough boards. Still she could not move. The blood ran close to her feet, and she followed its course with eyes wide with horror.

Dillon pushed the door closed and mopped his eyes with his shirtsleeve. His chest still heaved a little, and his face was set in granite-like lines.

"You dumb little fool," he said, "what you think's goin' to happen to you now?"

Myra jerked her eyes from Gurney. She looked at him, suddenly sensing her danger. "He made me do it..." she began; "he made me—"

Dillon sneered. "That hick wouldn't've started anythin' like that. He ain't got the guts. You put him up to it; ain't that the way it went? You said 'Kill him', an' the louse just went ahead. I got you lined up. You bashed Butch. You're a little hell-cat. Well, I guess you an' me are goin' to understand each other."

He walked over to her slowly. She backed away, throwing out her hands and shaking her head at him in her terror.

"Don't kill me!..." she implored. "Don't... do... it!..." Her voice went shrill.

He reached out and grabbed her wrist, jerking her close. His inflamed eyes made her shrink back. "I've changed my mind about you," he said. "You've got what it takes, so I guess you can string along with me. I always could use a broad like you. When I pick a moll she's got to be tough, an' I reckon that goes for you. Now do you get it? You an' me are goin' to work together. You're doing what I tell you. I'm the boss, and you're liking it."

Myra said quickly, "I'll do anythin'."

Dillon took her arm and led her out of the room. She went with him, keeping her eyes from the still body that had now ceased to bleed. Dillon took her into her room again. He said quietly, "Wait here." He went out, leaving her standing shivering by the bed. There was something terrifying in his cold, ruthless face. She just stood, her hands hanging at her sides, and her eyes blank.

Dillon came back again. He brought with him the thin steel rod they used to clear the stove. Myra looked at it and then suddenly came to life. Her hands shot up to her face. "What are you doin' with that?" she gasped, pushing herself against the wall, as if trying to force her body through the plaster.

"You gotta learn some sense, ain't you?" Dillon said, moving softly towards her. "I guess this will get your ideas workin' right."

Myra screamed, "Don't!... Don't!... Don't!..."

Off Bunker Avenue, within smelling distance of the Kansas City Stockyards, Miss Benbow ran a dress shop. It was the kind of shop you'd go to if your last nickel was a phony, and you were anxious to have some excuse to scratch yourself.

Miss Benbow was a big Negress. She'd got a smile like a split pumpkin, and if you looked hard enough at her when she pulled that grin you'd see it never reached her eyes. She made a lot of money, but not from the shop. If you asked her when her last sale had been she couldn't have told you. Her memory wasn't that long.

At the back of the shop, up a flight of dirty narrow stairs, she ran a flop-house. At one time or another she had given guys like Karpis, or Barker or Frank Nash a shakedown while the cops were looking for them.

Miss Benbow was safe. The cops left her alone. Some said she'd got a hold on the Police Commissioner. Anyway, the police let her alone, and that was good enough.

The two, Myra and Dillon, came to Miss Benbow at night. The rain fell lightly on the glistening pavements, and the soft mist from the river was for the moment washed away. They came out of the night, Dillon walking softly, looking over his shoulder suspiciously from time to time. He was conscious of his new clothes, and the weight of the Thompson lying at the bottom of his big grip.

Myra stepped down the wet flags, her wooden heels tapping their challenge. She held her head up, delighting in the soft caress of silk against her skin.

Dillon had done things to her in a short time. For the first time in her life she knew what it meant to have a man around. She no longer had to urge or suggest. She was told what to do and she obeyed blindly.

She glanced at Dillon, seeing his powerful shoulders and his thick, muscular neck. A little flame flickered through her.

They had been two nights on the journey, moving cautiously forward towards Kansas City. She had spent two nights of sick disappointment with him. He had treated her coldly, sharing the same room with her, but not touching her.

Dillon disturbed her thoughts abruptly. "This is it," he said.

They stopped outside the dress shop. The place was in gloomy darkness.

"This joint is good," Dillon said, speaking out of the side of his mouth. "All the boys come here."

He located a bell-push at the top of the door and pressed. They could hear the sharp whirr somewhere at the back of the building. They waited there in the rain like statues.

Miss Benbow came and opened the shop door herself. She blocked the entrance with her great body. "My!" she said. "Ain't you made a mistake?"

Dillon said distinctly, "It's mighty hot round here. I guess it's cooler inside."

Miss Benbow looked at them suspiciously, "Where you from?" she snapped.

Dillon growled. "Suppose we come in an' talk? I'm gettin' wet."

The Negress hesitated, then stepped to one side. "Come in," she said.

They stepped into the dark shop and waited in the darkness until Miss Benbow had shot the bolt, then she turned on the electric light, and they blinked at her.

"Now then," she said suspiciously, "where you from?"

"Plattsville," Dillon said.

"Who sent you here?"

Dillon said softly, "You heard of a guy called Nelson?"

Miss Benbow nodded. "Sure," she said, "I knew Nelson."

Dillon pushed his hat back. "Okay; I toted a rod for Nelson. I'm Dillon."

Miss Benbow moved uneasily. "I guess most of Nelson's boys are dead," she said.

"This one ain't." Dillon grinned mirthlessly. "We want a room an' some grub."

Miss Benbow hesitated, then she said, "Ten bucks a day."

Myra said, "For Pete's sake... this ain't the Belmont Plaza."

Dillon broke in sharply. "Shut up! We're floppin' in this joint... who's payin', anyway?"

"Let's see your money." Miss Benbow held out her hand. There was a cold look in her eyes.

Dillon grinned wolfishly. He pulled out his roll and let Miss Benbow feast her eyes on it. She drew her thick lips off her teeth. There was plenty of grease in that smile of hers. "Like the look of that?" he said.

Miss Benbow said, "You can have a room all right. I guess I want a week's rent now, mister." Her voice was well shot with oil.

Dillon stripped some notes off the roll and slung them on the table. Miss Benbow picked up the money and counted it carefully. Then she jerked her head. "I'll take you up," she said.

They followed her up a narrow stairway to a big landing that could have been a lot cleaner. There were four doors leading onto the landing. She plodded over to the farthest one and unlocked it.

"How's this?" she said.

The room was big. Two beds divided by a small table faced the window. The carpet was thick, and the chairs overstuffed. It looked good to Myra after Butch's shack.

"This'll do fine," she said.

Miss Benbow shot her a contemptuous look. Her eyes rolled inquiringly at Dillon.

"Yeah," Dillon said, dumping the suitcases down. "What about some chuck? My belly's flappin'."

Miss Benbow put another pound of grease in her smile. She could well afford to feed these two. "I'll send somethin' up right away," she said, "you bet."

When she had pulled the door to after her Myra shot a look at Dillon. "You're playin' a fancy hand, ain't you?" she said. "Ten bucks a day! That's some dough."

"Pipe down," Dillon said coldly. He gave her a hard look. "Can't you use your head? This joint means a lot to me. I can meet the big shots here.... I gotta hunch I can pull somethin' big... ain't that worth payin' for?"

He tossed his fedora on a hook on the door and walked over to Myra. They looked at each other.

"I've been out of this game too long," he said, speaking very slowly, choosing his words. "I gotta get an in before I get goin'."

Myra put her hand on his sleeve. "You're goin' to be the biggest shot of them all." There was a soft yielding tone in her voice.

Dillon curled his lip. "Yeah?" he said. "Who says?"

Her face, no longer the face of an adult child, was hard with determination to the point of ruthlessness. "I say so. You're goin' to show all these little mobsters just where they get off. You're gonna think and act big. No one must get in your way... you understand that? *No one must get in your way*." She spoke slowly, emphasizing every word.

Dillon reached out and gripped her arms. His steel-like fingers bit into her muscles and she suddenly went weak inside for him.

"You got it right the first time," he said. "And you're trailin' right along behind me." He paused, then went on, "Thought of the cops?"

She laughed at him. "What did Nelson do with the cops? He'd enough dough to straighten things. Didn't he get protection? Okay, that's what you're goin' to get."

Dillon shook his head wisely. "Sure he got protection—an' look at him now. They dug twenty-four slugs outta that guy when they put him on the slab."

"G-men," Myra said tersely. "You ain't got any worry. You keep clear of the G-men an' you'll be okay."

"Yeah, I'll keep clear of the G-men." There was a hard note of menace in his voice.

A knock sounded on the door. They stiffened, then Dillon said crossly, "Relax, can't you?" He went over to the door and jerked it open.

A tall, thin girl, with heavily rouged cheeks, was standing there holding a large tray, covered with a cloth. "Miss Benbow sent this up." She had a nasal whine that put Myra's teeth on edge.

Dillon stood back and let her in.

Myra looked her over. The girl glanced at Dillon wide-eyed, and put down the tray. She again looked at Dillon, a sly side-look with a strong line of "come hither" in it. She went out, swinging her hips a little.

Dillon kicked the door shut. "I guess that woman thinks she's good," he said.

Myra took the cloth off the tray. "I guess dames don't mean much to you," she said, trying to keep her voice steady.

Dillon shrugged.

Myra put her hands on the table and examined her nails. She said, without looking up at him, "They could give a guy like you a pretty good time."

Dillon turned and stared at her. "That's what you think," he said, a faint sneer on his mouth. "I think different."

He sat down at the table and began to eat hungrily.

Across the landing, behind a locked door, Roxy was having breakfast. The *Kansas City Times* was propped up against the coffee-pot, and he read it carefully as he ate.

Fanquist still lay in bed, her flaxen hair spread out on the pillow, a cigarette in her lips. She watched Roxy sleepily.

"A blue-nosed senator is puttin' up a squawk about the number of unfortunate women he's been runnin' into lately on Main Street. Says it's a disgrace," Roxy announced with a grin. "What you think, Fan?"

"Search me," she said with a Southern drawl. "Maybe he forgot his dough."

Roxy shook his head. "Those guys never forget anything," he said. "I guess he hadn't any dough. And listen to this, Fan: Some guy found his wife two-timin' and set about her with a meat-cleaver. There's a picture of the guy here... wantta see it?"

Fanquist shook her head. "I don't like horrors... lay off it, will you?"

Roxy tossed the paper on the floor. He finished his coffee and lit a cigarette. "Got any ideas for today?" he asked hopefully.

"I'm havin' a finger-wave." Fanquist stretched her arms and yawned. "Ten o'clock. It'll take the best part of two hours... meet me for lunch?"

Roxy nodded. "Yeah, I'll do that," he said. "I'll pick you up at Verotti's."

A tap came at the door. Roxy looked over at Fanquist, his eyebrows raised. Then he put his hand inside his coat and loosened the gun in its holster. "Who is it?" he asked.

"It's okay," came Miss Benbow's hoarse whisper.

"What does she want?" Roxy said, walking to the door and jerking it open.

Miss Benbow came in. Her white teeth glittered like piano-keys. Roxy shut the door and turned the key again. "What's the trouble?" he asked, tossing the cigarette-butt into the fireplace.

Miss Benbow nodded to Fanquist. "You've got neighbours," she said. "They're new... I ain't seen 'em before."

Roxy looked a little startled. "They okay?" he asked sharply.

"I guess so," Miss Benbow said. "They knew how to get in. He's called Dillon."

"Dillon? Why, that guy's been out of the game for a long time. You remember Dillon?" Roxy looked over at Fanquist. "Sure, I remember hearin' of him. A mean guy. A guy who don't smoke or drink or have a girl is a mean guy."

Roxy grinned. "That's what you say."

Miss Benbow moved a little restlessly. "There's something about those two I don't like. The broad is just a kid, but she's bad. She's got a cold little face that I wouldn't like to wake up an' find on my pillow. The guy's big an' tough. He makes me uneasy."

Fanquist looked interested. "This guy, is he handsome?"

Roxy laughed. "You oughtta have a cold bath, Fan," he said. "Ain't she a hot momma?"—to Miss Benbow.

Miss Benbow grinned some more. "I like to see it," she said. "There're too many cold-blooded broads around to please me."

Fanquist pouted. "Come on, you big lump," she said. "Don't keep a girl waitin'. What's he like?"

Miss Benbow nodded her head. "Sure, sure," she said. "He's got it all. Dressy kind of a guy. Big, strong and hard."

Fanquist looked over at Roxy. "Ain't you jealous?" she asked.

Roxy grinned. "Sure I am... I'm burnin' up."

"I'd leave that guy alone," Miss Benbow cautioned. "That little bag don't look like she'd stand for much interference."

Fanquist shrugged. "Aw! To hell with her," she said. Then, glancing at the clock, she dragged off the bed-clothes. "My Gawd!" she said. "I gotta get my hair fixed at ten."

Miss Benbow moved to the door. "I figgered you'd like to hear about those two," she said.

Roxy nodded. "I'll look 'em over."

He sat down in the overstuffed chair and watched Fanquist dress. "You ain't in such a hurry you can't wash," he said, when she started to pull her clothes on.

She took no notice. She adjusted the straps of her hold-up. Roxy looked with raised eyebrows. "You be careful," he said. "Some guy's going to trip over your chest one of these days."

Fanquist giggled. "The things you say," she said, doing things to her face.

Roxy switched his mind. "I guess I'll take a gander at those two," he said, picking his teeth with a match-end. "Maybe they'll be interestin'."

"Watch yourself with the broad," Fanquist warned him, "I'll hook her eyes out if she starts on you."

"Okay." Roxy waved his hand. "You know me. I ain't got the strength to take on two dames at once. You watch Dillon."

She paused at the door. "Say, if these two ain't dumb, bring 'em along to Verotti's. They might amuse me."

Roxy nodded. "Yeah," he said, "if they are bright I'll do that." Fanquist shut the door behind her and ran downstairs. Roxy picked up the paper again and studied the police news.

Roxy was a heistman. He wasn't very spectacular, but he made a nice living on the side. He specialized in car holdpups. Gangdom considered him smart, and they had a certain respect for him. He had kept clear of the cops, he'd never been mugged or fingerprinted, and he wasn't a killer. His stick-ups brought him in on the average a grand a week, and he was doing pretty well for himself.

Fanquist helped towards the weekly contribution by dipping pockets. She seldom came back without a piece of jewellery or a pocket-book in her bag.

Roxy and Fanquist had teamed up about eighteen months ago. They liked each other well enough, but there was no real affection there. Fanquist thought he was a bit of a wop, and Roxy considered she was a little tramp. They kept their opinions to themselves and broke no bones. They slept together as a matter of physical convenience, and they ate together for company. They shared a room for economy, and they got on pretty well.

When Roxy had finished the newspaper he got up, put on a black fedora, looked himself over in the long wall-mirror, and sauntered on to the landing. He took a packet of gum from his pocket and peeled off the wrapper, then he put the gum in his mouth and clamped on it thoughtfully. All the time he did this he was listening.

He knew it would be dangerous to tap on the door; he remembered hearing things about Dillon. He'd seen a guy take some hot lead through his belly, just tapping on doors. He leant up against the doorway and waited, hoping someone would come out. He waited some little time, then he shrugged his shoulders. He went back to his room, leaving his door open.

The big Spanish guitar gave him an idea. He reached over and began playing. He went right into the Prologue to *Pagliacci*. Roxy had a smooth voice; a nice rich tenor. With the Prologue he knew he was good. He could reach the E Flat and he could swell up on it until the windows rattled. He liked tossing this high stuff off, but Fanquist wouldn't stand for it.

He guessed no dame would remain long behind a door with this hot Italian stuff going on, and he was right. Myra put her head round the door and came out.

Roxy wallowed in the sobs, made himself miserable with the last bars, then closed down hurriedly with a few showy chords.

He grinned at Myra. "I bet you thought it was a cat-fight."

She stood looking at him admiringly. "Say, that was swell," she said.

"You like it?" He tried to look surprised. "That's just classic stuff. Wantta hear me do 'Stormy River'?"

She nodded, her hands clasped in front of her. Roxy thought she was easy on the eye. Her figure was subtle, not like Fanquist's curves that reached out and tried to snap at you. Her big eyes made Roxy glad that she couldn't read his mind. He ran his fingers over the strings. Roxy could certainly handle that guitar.

Out came Dillon. His face was cold and suspicious. Roxy nodded to him, but kept on playing, then he began to sing. It wasn't for nothing he had listened to every record Bing Crosby had ever made. Roxy hadn't enjoyed himself so much for years.

He finished off with a real tricky ending, and put the guitar down on the couch. "Come on in," he said; "I guess I owe you two a drink."

Myra walked in quite at ease. She sat down on the arm of the couch and looked round the room. Dillon leant against the doorway. He watched Roxy closely.

Myra thought Roxy looked like George Raft. She liked him. He didn't strike her as being a big shot, but she thought he'd do to be getting on with.

Roxy fixed three highballs and passed them round. Dillon put his glass on the table, shaking his head.

Roxy raised his eyebrows. "What's wrong with it?"

Dillon said sourly, "I don't use it."

Myra said, "Come on in an' shut the door—there's a draught."

Dillon came in and shut the door. There was a second's silence. Then Myra and Roxy started to speak. They looked at each other and laughed. "I'm Myra... this is Dillon," she said.

Roxy nodded. "I'm pleased to know you both. I guess you two wouldn't be here if you weren't in the game."

Dillon said coldly, "What's your racket?"

Roxy took a pull at his glass. He glanced at Myra. "I'm known as Roxy around here," he said. "Maybe we'd better get more acquainted before we get down to rackets."

Dillon shrugged. "That don't suit me," he said. "You may act dumb, but I bet you know who I am, so I guess a little info' from you might ease things."

Roxy tipped his hat over his eyes. This guy had a mean look, he thought. He tried to remember some of the things he had heard about him. It was too long ago. He could only remember he was a killer.

"Sure," he said at last, "I know you. I guess I'm just in a small way. My line's stickin' up cars. I make a little dough now an' then. My girl's a dip."

A sneer went across Dillon's face. Real small-time stuff, he thought. "I gotta get back into the racket," he said. "I've been out too long."

Roxy went over and lay on the couch. He studied his cloth-top boots. He had very small neat feet, and he liked to admire them. "Yeah," he said, "I guess you're forgotten."

Dillon flashed a look at Myra—signalling her to be quiet. He said, "I wantta contact someone big."

"I like you two," Roxy said thoughtfully, "so I'll deal it off the top deck. You don't stand a chance musclin' in on anything big in this burg until you got yourself a reputation again. The old mobs are washed up and the new crowd just think there's no one who can show 'em anythin'. You try to horn in there an' you're goin' to run into plenty of grief."

Myra said in a quiet voice, "Well, that's talkin'."

Roxy looked up and grinned. "Sure, that's the way it is, sister. You gotta go slow, see? I can give you an openin' here and there. I'd be glad to, but you gotta build your set-up slow."

Dillon said, "We're as good as the rest of the punks in this dump." The cold light in his eyes escaped Roxy.

Roxy rambled on: "You ain't met the big shots yet," he said. "I've been in the racket for ten years, an' I'm glad not to know them, see? The big shots stick out, an' they're the first to get their ears slapped down. You gotta get protection, an' you've gotta pay for it, if you're a big shot. You get G-heat smeared over you. Look at Floyd an' Bailey an' Nash or any of 'em. They're on the run an' they'll keep on the run. I ain't got anythin' to worry about; I'm smart." Again he missed the look in Dillon's eyes.

The telephone whirred suddenly, startling them. Roxy got off the couch and took the receiver off the cradle. A husky voice came over the wire. "There're a couple of hard-lookin' guys casin' the street. I guess they're Feds. They're headin' your way."

Roxy said, "Thanks, pal," and put the receiver back. He looked at the other two. "You better park your rods," he said quietly. "A couple of Federal dicks are on their way up."

Dillon got to his feet quickly and silently. "They got nothin' on me," he said.

Roxy pulled his coat away from his shoulder-holster and undid the buckle. He slipped off the harness. "If you got a rod, you better park it," he said; "these guys get tough if they catch you toting a gun."

Myra said in a little flurry of panic, "Where can we hide them?"

Roxy walked over to the fireplace and, knelt down. He pushed the tiled hearth back like a drawer and dropped his gun into the narrow hollow beneath. "The old girl's got this in every room. Use it."

Dillon left the room and went to his apartment. He collected his two guns and the Thompson and stowed them away. He came back silently. "What's the idea?" he snarled. "I thought this place was okay?"

Roxy nodded. "Sure it's okay. You can't keep the Feds outta any place. The bulls leave it alone, but not the Feds. You ain't wanted by no G-man, are you?" There was sharp anxiety in his voice.

Dillon didn't say anything. He stood by the table, a little tense. With eyes like chips of ice he stared at Roxy. The expression in his eyes quite startled Roxy.

Myra broke in. "I guess not," she said.

Roxy relaxed. "Okay, just you go on drinkin' an' say nothin'. I'll do the talkin' if there's any talkin' to be done."

"Hell!" Dillon said savagely. "That black dame's goin' to lose some of her rent. She's nuts thinkin' I'm payin' all that dough when the Feds can come in here."

Roxy nodded his head. "Sure," he said. "I guess she's been stringin' you along. You fix her. It's been comin' to her for a long time."

Suddenly they heard a commotion going on downstairs. They stiffened involuntarily. "Here they come," Roxy said, putting his feet up on the couch. "Now don't let those guys stampede you. They'll try all right."

They could hear Miss Benbow protesting on the stairs.

They heard her say, "You dicks ain't got anythin' on me. You can't come bustin' in like this. I tell you this is a respectable house."

Someone said in a gritty voice, "Take it easy, Coon, we're just lookin' the place over."

A heavy step sounded outside, then the door was kicked open. The three in the room turned their heads and looked. Dillon was cool, but Myra's nerves were jumpy. Two big men stood in the doorway, their eyes watchful. Dillon thought they looked a couple of real tough birds.

"Hello, boys," Roxy said from the couch. He kept his hands in his lap. "I guess you ain't lookin' for me?"

One of them wandered into the room, leaving the other by the door. He said, "Get up when you talk to me."

Roxy got up quickly and took off his hat. He looked hard at the Federal and grinned a little uneasily. "Why, if it ain't Mr. Strawn," he said. "Ain't seen you for a long time."

Strawn went over to him and patted his pockets. "Where's your rod?" he asked.

Roxy shrugged his shoulders. "You got me wrong," he said. "I don't tote a rod. You know me, boss; I wouldn't do a thing like that."

Strawn said, "That line don't get you nowhere, so lay off it."

He looked at Dillon. Then he glanced over to the other dick. "Seen this monkey before?" he asked.

The other dick shook his head.

Strawn walked over to Dillon. "Who're you an' what you doin' around here?"

Dillon looked at him impassively. "Just havin' a drink with a pal of mine," he said. "What's wrong with that?"

Strawn looked him over, his face hardening. "Where you from?" he snapped.

Dillon shot a look at Myra. Strawn swung his fist. He smacked Dillon on the jaw. Dillon was off balance—he went over with a thud.

Roxy yelled, "Don't start anythin'!" His eyes were popping.

Dillon looked up at Strawn, his eyes black with hate. He came slowly to his feet, rubbing his jaw with his hand. Beyond the look in his eyes he remained impassive.

Strawn said, "Listen, you melon-headed monkey, when I ask you somethin' you answer quick. Where are you from an' what's your name?"

The other dick looked bored, but he had got a gun in his hand.

Dillon said between his teeth, "I'm from Plattsville. Name's Gurney... Nick Gurney."

Myra stood very still. She put her hand to her mouth.

"Just a big farmer's hick, huh?" Strawn sneered. "Well, listen, hayseed, you better keep outta this town. We don't like punks like you. You better go right back to Plattsville an' stay there. Do you get it?"

Dillon just stood there hating him with his eyes. Strawn clenched his fists. "Answer me, will you? By heck! You get snotty with me, you bohunk, an' I'll tear your guts out an' beat you to death with 'em!"

Dillon said, "I get you."

Strawn looked Myra over. "Well, sister, an' who're you?" he asked, eyeing her thoughtfully.

"I'm his wife," Myra said quietly. She put a lot of personality into her look.

Strawn shook his head. "This ain't no place for a kid like you to be in. You better get out an' go home. You'll lose a lotta time goin' round with a bum like this." He jerked his head at Dillon. "Forget him, an' go home to your Ma."

Myra lowered her eyes. She thought, "The big dumb-mouthed hick."

Strawn shrugged. "Okay, watch yourselves, you three." He stepped outside the door and pulled it shut. He said in a low voice to the other dick, "We'll watch that Gurney, he's a bad guy."

Roxy held his hand up for silence. They sat there staring at the door listening. It was only when they heard them go downstairs that they relaxed.

Dillon said evenly, "Some day I'll fix that heel. He's got it comin' to him!"

Verotti's was a dive off Twenty-second Street, near the Union Station. Fanquist had a table in the corner. She was drinking a rye highball.

When Roxy came in with Dillon and Myra she waved excitedly to them. Roxy came up to the table and waved his hand.

"This is Myra and Dillon," he said. "They've got a room across the way."

Fanquist had eyes only for Dillon. "What a hot-looking man!" she said. "Am I pleased to meet you, or am I?"

Myra's face was cold. She sat down next to Fanquist, trapping her against the wall. Dillon sat opposite, with Roxy at his side.

Myra said, "It's grand to run into a guy like Roxy. He's been a real pal."

Fanquist shot her a quick look. "Say," she said, swivelling round so that she faced Myra, "what are you doin' away from your Ma? Hey, hot man, you're baby-snatching. That ain't right."

Myra's eyes glinted. "Don't embarrass him," she cut in quickly. "He likes 'em young. This guy ain't got time for broads who've seen their best days... you ask him."

Fanquist leant against the wall. "Smart kid, huh?" she said, two bright red spots on her cheeks. "Seen their best days, huh? That's a nice crack from a kid."

Myra turned her head. "Don't we do anythin' around here but talk?"

A waiter shuffled up and they ordered drinks. Roxy sat with his hat over his eyes, grinning to himself. Nothing pleased him more than to listen-in to two women clawing each other.

Fanquist leant over the table towards Dillon. "I bet you know some hot spots in this town," she said.

From where he sat Dillon could look down the neck of her dress. He lifted his eyes and gave his hard stare. Fanquist suddenly felt a little cold. She sat back hurriedly.

Dillon said, "We thought maybe we might see some of 'em. We've just blown in."

Roxy said, "That guy over there's Hurst."

They looked across at a table in the middle of the room. A big blond man was drinking by himself. He wore his neat dark suit well. There was an air of money and importance about him.

Dillon said, "Who's Hurst?"

Fanquist laughed. "You do say things!" she said. "That guy's tops just now. He runs most of the big rackets round here."

"That so?" Dillon looked Hurst over again. "A big shot, huh?"

Roxy nodded. "Yeah, he's a big shot all right."

Myra said, "Maybe you know him?"

Roxy looked blank. "Hey!" he said. "What you think? I said this guy was a big shot. He don't mix with guys like you an' me."

Fanquist said in her slow drawl, "Maybe the kid fancies her chance."

Myra said, "Why not? He's just a guy, ain't he?"

Fanquist sneered. "Hurst don't play with kids," she said. "When that guy takes a woman he takes a woman."

Myra pushed back her chair. "I'll show you how I take a guy like that," she said.

Roxy said quickly, "Don't you start anythin' like that. Hurst's a tough bird. He don't like stunts like that."

Myra paused. "I'm interested in that guy," she said.

"You're interested because he's got somewhere. But the trouble with those guys is they don't stay that way long."

"No?"

"No. Hurst won't stay much longer. He's been in the racket too long."

Myra took a sip from her glass. Her eyes were cloudy. "He looks big enough to take care of himself," she said.

Roxy shook his head. "You wait an' see. Little Ernie's gunnin' for him. An' Little Ernie'll get him all right."

Myra moved restlessly. "Maybe he'll get Little Ernie first," she suggested.

"You ain't got the lowdown to this burg." Roxy spun his glass between his finger and thumb. "Hurst runs the Automatic racket. He's been makin' a pile of dough for some time. Little Ernie runs the women. He's in a big way too. That's the set-up. For years these guys ain't overlapped. They've made their pile outta their rackets an' kept to their side of the town. These guys are never contented, see? Maybe they pick up a couple of million bucks a year. Good money? Not to these guys. They want more. They've got big overheads. They've got a long list of retainers to pay off. So they always want more."

Myra said softly, "A couple of million bucks?"

Roxy nodded. "Sure, that ain't so much to guys like that," he said. "Hurst is startin' somethin'. He's expandin'. He's pushin' into Little Ernie's territory. That guy won't stand for that. Hurst says it's okay. Automatics can't hurt Little Ernie's joints. So he pushes ahead." Roxy shrugged. "One day, mighty soon, Hurst's goin' to get a handful of slugs tossed into his guts. Then his million bucks ain't goin' to mean a thing."

Myra lit a cigarette. "Maybe he'll get the wop first," she said. "Yeah, maybe he will."

Fanquist said, "So you ain't taking Hurst after all?"

Myra shook her head. "I'll take him a little later on," she said.

Fanquist got up. "I guess we'd better get goin'," she said to Roxy. "I gotta job of work to do."

Roxy pushed his chair away and nodded to Myra. "We'll be seein' you."

Fanquist turned to Dillon and gave him one of her 'any-timeyou-say-so' smiles. "'Bye, big boy," she said. "Don't let this babe get too many big ideas."

Dillon grunted.

Myra watched them go. "That little curdle-puss thinks she's smart," she said furiously. "She'd better keep her claws off you."

Dillon sat back. "You've got a lot to worry about, ain't you?" he sneered.

Hurst snapped his fingers, calling the waiter. He paid his check and got up. Myra watched him walk across the room and go into the street. Two tough-looking birds, sitting by the door, got up and followed him. Through the doorway she saw them get into a big powerful car and drive off.

Dillon said, "That guy might get me somewhere."

Myra said softly, "You don't need guys like that. You can get sky-high playin' solo."

"Yeah?" Dillon sneered. "Suppose you get wise to yourself. We ain't nobody here. Look how that Federal dick shoved me around. Think we're goin' to get anywhere without an in? Not a chance. You keep your trap shut an' let me do the thinkin'. When I run outta ideas I'll give you a buzz. An' believe me, it'll take a long time before I'm screwy enough to take ideas from a dope like you."

Myra flushed. Her eyes grew stormy, but she didn't start anything. She said, "Maybe a smart chippy like that Fanquist moll could give you ideas."

Dillon stared at her. "Your mind runs on one track," he said. "She don't cut meat with me. You dames are all alike, ain't you? There's nothin' new about you, is there? I've seen it all before... so what the hell?"

Myra thought savagely, "I'll get under his skin one day. I'll fix him."

Dillon got up. "I'm takin' some air," he said. "This line of talk gives me a pain."

She followed him into the street. The sun was hot, and they walked along, keeping in the shade.

Dillon said, "I gotta get me a car—I guess I'll get it now."

"A car?" Myra was startled. "Where's the dough comin' from?"

"Suppose you keep your mind on your bed and your nose outta this?" Dillon snarled at her.

Off the main street they found a large garage with a dilapidated showroom, full of second-hand cars. A tall, thin guy, with a bobbing Adam's apple, came out and nodded to them.

"I'm pleased to meet you," he said. "Mabley's the name, an' if you're lookin' for a good bus you've come to the right joint."

Dillon said, "We're lookin', brother, but maybe we won't buy; then, maybe, if we find somethin' good an' cheap, we will."

Mabley put his thumbs in his trousers pockets and raised himself on his toes. "That's fair enough, mister," he said. "You look around." He leant up against the wall and watched them.

Dillon spotted the car right away. It was a big, shabby-looking Packard standing in a corner by itself. It was the only car of the lot that looked as if it could hit a wall at sixty and not dent its fenders.

He didn't go over to it at once, but made a pretence of looking at the others first. Myra followed him around, not saying anything. She left it to him. At last he walked over to the Packard and examined it carefully. He opened the door and got in. The springs were good.

Mabley came over and dusted off the hood with a flick here and there. "You like this one, I bet," he said.

Dillon got out of the car and leant against the fender. "Maybe we could use it."

Mabley opened his eyes wide. "Listen," he said earnestly, "that car's got guts. There's plenty under that hood. Suppose you come for a run an' see?"

Dillon nodded. "Sure," he said, "I don't mind givin' you a break if it will hold together."

Mabley ran his hands through his hair. "If it will hold together... you'll see."

Dillon got under the wheel. "I guess I'll drive," he said.

The Packard was good. Dillon knew it would be. Out on a good stretch of road he worked it up to eighty-five. It held the road without a roll, and he guessed with a little tuning he could squeeze some more speed out of it.

They drove back to the garage in silence. Mabley was smug with certainty. When Dillon nailed the Packard, and they got out, Mabley said, "Didn't I tell you?... That bus can move."

Dillon said, "You're right. She's a bit too fast, if anythin'."

Mabley raised his hands. "Gee!" he groaned. "Ain't you ever happy?"

Dillon broke in. "Now, come on, we ain't got all day. How much?"

Mabley leant against the fender. "Two thousand bucks, an' it's cheap at the price," he said.

Dillon stared at Myra. "Did you hear him?" he gasped. "Two thousand bucks for that old heap?"

He turned to Mabley. "We don't want your garage, we want the car, see?"

Mabley shrugged. "I tell you it's cheap," he said firmly. Dillon said, "That old can ain't worth more'n eight hundred bucks, an' you know it."

Mabley said, "Two thousand."

Myra shrugged. "Let's go," she said. "This guy's crazy."

"Maybe he doesn't know his game right. Listen, I'll stretch a point an' buy it from you for a grand."

Mabley shook his head. "No use to me, mister. It's givin' it away at two."

Myra wandered away. "Come on, you can see he won't be reasonable."

Dillon said, "You're right. I guess we'll leave it." He walked over to where Myra was pretending to examine another car.

Mabley hesitated. "Well, seein' you're sold on this bus, I'll let you have it for nineteen hundred. That's rock bottom."

Dillon took Myra's arm and walked her to the door. "These small-time traders are nuts," he said. "Nineteen hundred! What a crack!"

Mabley came after them. "Wait a minute. Don't you be in such a hurry."

Dillon said, "Forget it. We ain't interested no more."

Myra cut in sharply, "Fourteen hundred. That's flat."

Dillon shot her a hard look, but didn't say anything. Mabley scratched his head. "I'll split the difference. I'm cuttin' my own throat, but I guess business is busted to hell these days."

Dillon wanted that car. He nodded. "Sixteen hundred if you fill the tank an' oil her."

Mabley looked at him. "You sure are a hard guy," he said. "But I'll do it."

"Get her ready in an hour," Dillon said sharply. "We'll be back."

They walked out of the garage. Myra started a moan. "This is goin' to knock a hole in our dough."

Dillon said, "Where do you get this 'our' stuff? We're fillin' the hole up again tonight, so what do you care?"

The Conoco service station at Bonner Springs was floodlit at night. Two tired attendants relaxed in the office, their ears unconsciously cocked for the sound of a car, ready to snap to attention and come out at a run.

George, a fair-haired boy, thought of his girl-friend. When he wasn't busy his mind dwelt on her, when it wasn't dwelling on how he could make more money. George was a simple hick. He was like thousands of other guys. Two things came uppermost, his girl and money.

Hank, his fellow attendant, lolled across the table. "What's bitin' you, pal?" he asked. "You been lookin', like a bad dream for a coupla hours."

George heaved a sigh. "Say, you know Edie... What you think's the matter with her?"

Hank scratched his head. "How should I know what's the matter with her?" he said impatiently. "She ain't in trouble?"

George shook his head. "Not a chance," he said gloomily. "Maybe we'd get married if it was like that."

"Then what's biting you?"

"She keeps away from me now... she's cooled off. Now what you think's come over her?"

Hank said with a sudden rush of inspiration, "Suppose you try this soap they're always croakin' about."

George scowled. "Don't you start to rib me," he said coldly. "I guess it's the dough that's the trouble. Edie was always keen to have dough. I ain't had a raise for two years now. I guess that's what's makin' her sore."

Hank said, "It'd be nice to own a joint like this, wouldn't it?" He wandered over to the cash register and rang up "No Sale." He peered into the drawer, poking the money around with his finger. "I figger we take five hundred bucks a day here."

"There's more'n that in the can," George said. "We had a few odd bills settled today."

"You think it out. I guess a joint like this would be mighty nice to own."

George nodded. "You're right," he said.

Outside, a car pulled up. The two jumped to their feet and ran out. The big shabby Packard was parked near the gas-pumps. Dillon got out. "Any more of you guys inside?" he asked. The two looked at him in surprise. "Just the two of us,"

George said. "We'll take care of the bus all right."

Dillon raised his hands a little. He was holding the two guns. "Grab some air," he said viciously, "and get inside."

The two attendants raised their hands. George went a little wobbly at the knees. He said, "Don't let that gun off, mister."

"Get inside!" Dillon snapped. "Jump to it!" He backed them into the office. "Stand over there by the wall, and keep your traps shut."

Myra came in and went over to the register. She rang it open and began scooping the money into a small bag. "Watch closely, boys," she said. "You're seein' history bein' made."

Dillon said, "Much there?"

Myra nodded. "It's worth while." She went through the two drawers and then slammed them to. "Maybe they've got a can round here."

Dillon said, "Where's the safe?"

Hank nodded miserably. "It's behind the desk," he said.

"Okay, get it open."

George unlocked the battered safe, and Myra walked over and peered inside. She scooped up a small wad of notes, pulled two or three ledgers out of the way, and glanced behind them. She straightened up. "That's the lot," she said.

Dillon went round to the telephone and jerked it away from its cable. "I don't want you boys to start yellin' just yet. We wanta get home safe, see?" He was feeling mighty pleased.

Myra looked them over. "I guess this is your first stick-up?" she said.

George mumbled, "Sure."

"You're havin' the breaks." She took a cigarette from her handbag and paused to light it. "You're in swell company. Know who this is?" She jerked her head towards Dillon. "I bet you don't. That guy set fire to the Middle West. He's the original twenty-five minute egg. There'll come a time when you'll tell your grand-kids how you were stuck up by this guy. I sure envy you boys; you gotta story to blow."

Dillon said, "Get goin', you big-mouthed doll."

She walked over to the door and Dillon crowded her into the darkness outside. The two attendants stood against the wall, their hands held high.

The Packard shot away and ripped into the darkness.

Dillon shoved his gun away.

"Suppose you keep that trap of yours shut?" he said from the blackness.

"You ain't got to worry... I'm buildin' you up."

"If there's any buildin' up, I'm the guy to take care of that," Dillon returned.

Myra held the wheel. She didn't say anything. Her eyes were intent on the road. As the car lurched to the bends she let her body swing against Dillon. She could feel the hardness of him under his coat, and it sent a flicker through her that made her blood sing in her ears.

This guy was tough, she thought, but he was a man.

Dillon, suddenly sensing her physical feeling for him, moved away, leaning well into the corner of the seat. She went limp with her frustrated longing for him.

Back at the apartment, they mounted the stairs silently and shut their door. Myra flicked on the light, walking slowly into the centre of the room, pulling her hat off as she did so, shaking her hair free.

Dillon stood by the door, rubbing his chin. He felt a vague urge towards her, but he ignored it. That urge made him a little uneasy.

Myra emptied the sack on the table and turned the money over with her finger.

"Ain't a great deal here," she said, "but it'll do to get on with."

Dillon came over and sat down. He counted the money and stacked the notes neatly before him. Myra stood behind him, watching him. When he had finished she reached out and put her hands on his shoulders. The heavy muscles of his back contracted under her touch.

He got abruptly to his feet, throwing her hands away. "Cut it out!" he said savagely. "You keep your tricks for some other punk."

She moved towards him. "We can't go on like this," she said; "you can't share this room with me—"

Dillon reached out his fist and shoved her away. "You heard me," he said. She caught the unevenness of his voice. "Get into bed, an' shut up!"

She said softly, "Sure, I guess I was only thinkin' of you."

Dillon turned from her and went over to his bed. He sat down and began to pull off his shoes. Myra stood in the middle of the room and undressed. She took her time. She let each garment fall to the floor. She stood looking at Dillon, then she turned and got into bed.

For the first time since she had known him she knew that she had made an impression on him. She knew that he was aware of her and she was content to wait for him.

Early next morning they woke with a start. Someone was drumming on their door. Dillon shot out of bed, making a grab for his gun. For a moment Myra was startled and she made to follow him, then she relaxed back on the pillow.

Roxy called from the other side of the door, "It's me."

Swearing softly, Dillon opened the door. "What the hell do you want?" he said. "You got me thinkin' the bulls were here."

Roxy eased his way into the room. He looked a little startled at the sight of Dillon's gun. "I guess I'm sorry about that," he said, "but you two seen the paper?" His eyes were popping a little.

Myra said from the bed, "Let me see."

Roxy tossed the paper on to the bed. "Got a big write-up there," he said. "I guess you two've started already."

Dillon went over and took the paper from Myra. He read through the account coldly and then tossed the paper back to Myra. "What makes you think that was me?" he asked Roxy quietly.

Roxy didn't like the look in his eyes. He said uneasily, "Why, I just guessed it. None of the mob round here talk big when they pull a job. I just figgered that maybe you had started a new line."

Dillon walked over to the mirror and examined his beard in the glass. Both Myra and Roxy watched him. He turned his head, so that he could look at them. "It ain't goin' to be the last those rags are goin' to print about me," he said. "They'll have plenty to print before I'm through."

During the two weeks that followed Dillon pulled three more hold-ups. He purposely kept them small—a service station and two out-of-the-way stores. He made enough money to be sure of living well for the next few weeks.

Although they shared a room, he did not again give Myra any opportunity of expressing her feelings. He was cold and ruthless to her. She was there to do what he said, and nothing more. Myra was sure of herself. She accepted his indifference and waited. She knew now that he had feelings, and she knew that it was only a matter of time.

Acting on Roxy's suggestion, they moved out of Miss Benbow's and took a small apartment off Grand Avenue.

Roxy thought Strawn might get a line on Dillon. Strawn was no fool, and he was just aching to push someone around. Dillon, one day, would over-step the line and start shooting, Roxy reasoned, and Roxy was not going to be there when Strawn called with the wagon. He reasoned it out carefully with Dillon. "This guy Strawn likes gettin' tough. He ain't got any-thin' on you, but that wouldn't stop him lookin' you up an' slapping your ears down if he hadn't anything better to do. I guess you'd be a lot safer away from this joint."

Through Roxy's efforts they got another apartment. It had one big ad-vantage of being near the Union Station and having two entrances, and con-sequently two exits. Also, Roxy pointed out, they were just a block away from the General Hospital, so what more could they want!

A week after they had moved in Roxy surprised them by a late visit. It was just after eleven o'clock, and Dillon was sitting by the radio reading the newspaper. Myra was practising dance steps at the other end of the room. She broke off to let Roxy in. She had only to take one look at Roxy to see that he was seriously worried. "What's your grief?" she asked him sharply.

Dillon swung round in his chair and stared at him with his hard eyes.

Roxy wandered in and sat on the arm of a chair. He pushed his hat to the back of his head. "I gotta load on my mind," he said. "You know Hurst?"

Dillon said impatiently, "I know Hurst all right. What's the matter with him?"

"Little Ernie's crowd is after him. He's asked for it an' he's goin' to get it."

Dillon shrugged. "Why get low? You ain't got to worry about Hurst. Sup-pose they do iron him out?"

Roxy said, "You don't get it. If Hurst gets knocked there's goin' to be a stink. The cops'll crack down on everyone they can lay their hands on. Hurst pays 'em plenty, and it's sure goin' to make them mad to have a meal-ticket like that shot to hell."

Myra said, "What do you mean, crack down?"

Roxy moved a little impatiently. "This guy's a big shot. The papers'll play it to the sky. The cops won't touch Little Ernie... he's too big for 'em. They'll go after the small guys like us. They'll hang every frame on us to make a pinch, get it? We'll be the mugs who'll get tossed in the can."

"You mean all this?" Myra asked.

"For Pete's sake, of course I mean it! There's only one thing to do, an' that's to take a powder, quick."

Dillon got up. His face was cold and set. "No bull's goin' to frame me," he said. "How the hell do you know they're after him?"

Roxy said, "I heard it from Archer, one of Ernie's boys. He took Fan out last night an' got a little plastered. Fan keeps her ears open; she kidded him along, an' he blew the set-up. They're fixin' him tonight."

Myra took a step forward. "Tonight?"

Roxy nodded. "Hurst's got a dame he's nuts about. She's the wife of some high-pressure guy in the City. She's scared sick her old man'll get the low-down on her two-timing. Right; she meets Hurst in an apartment every now an' then. Hurst is crazy enough to go there on his own. I guess he's scared his bodyguard might get talkin'; anyway, when he goes on these out-ings he goes alone. Ernie's been watching him for weeks, an' he's got this business taped. They're callin' on Hurst and they'll give it to him at the apartment.

Dillon sprang to his feet. "Get the Tommy," he said, his words tumbling out of his mouth, "We're certainly goin' to surprise those bums."

Myra stared at him. Roxy put in quickly, "You goin' to pull Hurst out of this?"

Dillon swung round. "Sure I'm goin' to pull him out of it. It's the chance I've been waitin' for. Listen, Roxy, you use your head. *You* ain't gettin' any-where as a solo stick-up artist. You want to get in with Hurst. You come with us. We're gettin' in on the ground floor."

Roxy shook his head. "Yeah, it's a grand chance all right—for a swell funeral. Little Ernie's mob know how to handle a rod. I ain't riskin' my hide for a punk like Hurst."

"He's right," Myra said. "Forget it, can't you?"

Dillon went over and took the Thompson gun out of the cupboard. "Where's this guy meet the dame?" he asked.

"It's a corner place on Seventeenth and Central. Apartment 964." Roxy moved to the door. He seemed anxious to go. "I guess I'll be movin' along. Take my tip; pack your bags and scram. This burg ain't goin' to be too healthy after they've put this Hurst guy in a wooden overcoat."

Dillon waited until he had gone, then he wheeled round on Myra. "You're comin'," he snarled at her. "This is our big break. We let Hurst get knocked off an' the bulls either make a pinch or run us out. We go down there an' pull Hurst outta this jam an' he's goin' to take notice."

Myra shook her head. "Forget it," she said stubbornly. "If you think I'm goin' to stick my neck out an' get it snapped you're crazy."

Dillon jerked up the Tommy. The thin barrel pointed directly at Myra. "Listen," he said evenly. "This is the chance I've been waitin' for. If you think I'm goin' to let a rotten-gutted monkey like you get in my way, you got another think comin'. You back out of this an' I'll make a sieve out of you. Get it? I can go into the street an' get some other punk who's got enough guts to work with me any time I want to. So get this right, now and for keeps. You play ball the way I want it or else…"

The vicious look in his eyes made her mouth go dry. "You ain't got to get mad," she faltered. "I'll come. I didn't think you felt that way about it, that's all."

Dillon lowered the gun. "Maybe you'll get into your skull one of these days that when I tell you what to do you do it quick." His eyes were hard and suspicious.

Myra walked to the door, snatching up her hat and putting it on. "Come on," she said, "I'm ready."

In the car, Myra drove rapidly past the George Washington monument, past Union Station and into Main Street. She kept the car steady, threading her way through the traffic, but taking no risks. This was no time to get into an argument with a traffic cop. Dillon sat beside her, the Thompson between his knees, covered by his raincoat.

Myra said, "For Pete's sake don't wait for these guys to start anythin'. Blast 'em as soon as you see 'em." She eased the Packard past a tumbledown jalopy, then went on, "Hurst'll see there ain't a murder rap hangin' on to this."

Dillon said out of the darkness, "One of these days I'm goin' to shut that trap of yours for good. You talk too much."

Myra said nothing. Her lips tightened a little, but she kept her temper with an effort. She swung into Eighteenth and stopped the Packard at the corner of Eighteenth and Central Streets. She spilled out of the car quickly. Seventeenth was just a block ahead.

Keeping the Thompson under his coat, Dillon hurried after her. The apartment house was one of those discreet places with everything automatic and no attendants to check who came in or went out.

Myra went over to the row of mail-boxes. She looked over her shoulder at Dillon. "It's on the fourth floor. Suppose we take the elevator to the third an' walk?"

Dillon said, "We walk from here."

Silently they mounted the stairs. On the third floor two tough-looking birds were lounging against the wall. They looked at Dillon hard, but the two kept on. Myra gave them just a casual glance. Dillon didn't even look at them, but he saw them all right. On the fourth floor no one was about.

A little breathless from the climb, Dillon said, "I guess those two guys are waiting for him down there."

"What are we goin' to do? Go back an' give it to 'em?"

Dillon shook his head. "Maybe we can tip Hurst off first," he said. "I'll go up the next set of stairs an' you ring up Hurst. If they come up I'll start somethin'. Mind you drop flat."

With her heart jumping a little, Myra watched him disappear round the bend of the staircase, then she walked over to the apartment door and rang the bell. Faintly she could hear the bell ringing. No one came.

She waited there impatiently and rang again. A faint sound behind her made her look round quickly. The two men had come up and were standing at the head of the stairs watching her. She kept her thumb on the bell and looked at them coolly.

One of them, a dark man, took two steps forward. "Get away from that door, sister," he said.

She said, "I don't know what you mean." Her thumb dug the bell flat.

The punk came over to her quickly and knocked her hand away. "If you squawk I'll kick your mug in," he said softly.

Myra backed away a little until her shoulder touched the wall. She stood looking at him, not saying anything.

The other guy moved a little round the bend of the staircase, sliding the gun from his holster.

Dillon, watching them through the banisters, couldn't start anything because of Myra.

The dark one said, "Who are you?"

The other guy broke in. "Where's the punk who came in with you?"

That startled the first one, who had forgotten about Dillon. He jerked out a gun quickly.

Myra screamed, "Give it to them!" and flung herself flat.

Dillon squeezed on the trigger and the Thompson roared. He held the muzzle high. The stream of lead caught the two like a whip-lash across their faces. Dillon gave them just a short burst, but it was enough.

The dark one stood for a moment, his hands groping out before him. The front of his face had disappeared, leaving just a horrible spongy mess on his shoulders. Myra caught her breath and turned her head quickly.

The mobster fell near her. His body twitched and jerked. The other guy curled up in a corner, the top of his head blown off.

Dillon came down the stairs like a cat. He stood looking at the two incuriously. "You all right?" he called to Myra. She got to her feet, keeping her eyes away from the two. Her face was pale, but her eyes glittered with suppressed rage.

"I rang an' rang," she said, keeping her voice low. "An' that yellow rat inside didn't come. Those two might have killed me but for you."

Dillon straightened a little. He went over and beat on the door with the butt of the Thompson. He made a lot of noise. "Open up!" he shouted. "The war's over."

The door opened an inch or two, and the face of a terrified woman peered at him. She was dressed in an orange wrap, which she clutched tightly to her. Dillon could see her figure sharply outlined beneath the silk. Behind her, his face twitching with terror, stood Hurst. He was holding a heavy gun in his hand. His hair was standing stiffly and his complexion was a dirty muddy colour.

Dillon said, "We've just knocked off these two killers." He jerked his head to the two bodies. "They're Little Ernie's mob."

"Who are you?" the woman stammered.

"The name's Dillon—"

"Let him in, can't you!" Hurst snarled. "We'll have the cops up here in a minute."

The woman said, "Come in."

Dillon walked into the apartment, followed by Myra, and the woman hastily closed the door.

Hurst covered Dillon with his gun. "Put that Thompson on the floor," he said.

Dillon stared at him, shrugged, and put the gun down. He walked a little way past Hurst.

"Come on," Hurst snapped. "What the hell's going on?"

Dillon said, "Little Ernie's gunnin' for you. He sent those two punks up here. I heard about it and came down quick. That's all."

Hurst hesitated, and then he said, "Wait." He went over to the telephone and dialled. He stood there, the gun still menacing, waiting for his line to connect. They heard the faint "plop" as someone answered the ring at the other end. Hurst said, "McGovern? Listen, there's been a fight up here an' two of Ernie's boys have run into a lot of grief. Send a wagon an' pick 'em up. This has got to be covered up, see? Just come up quick and get these birds out of here. I'll be along an' do some talking later. I don't want your men asking questions here, do you get all that?" He listened for a moment and then hung up.

He put the gun on the table and lit a cigarette. Myra could see his hand was still shaking. He looked at the woman and jerked his head. "Get dressed quick," he said. "Maybe the newshounds'll start buzzin'."

The woman went into the other room and shut the door. Hurst pushed his fingers through his hair and looked at Dillon. "What's the idea of butting in on my fight?"

Dillon showed his teeth in a mirthless smile. "I guess you ain't so good at lookin' after yourself. Anyway, I figgered it's time you an' I got together."

"You're the guy who's been stickin' up all those service stations, aren't you?" Hurst was watching him closely.

Dillon nodded his head. "Sure," he said. "I'm figgering to get in with a mob like yours and doin' somethin' in a big way."

Hurst stared at his fingernails, thinking. He looked up at last. "I guess we might talk this over some time," he said. "Suppose you look me up tomorrow?"

Dillon said, "Sure, I'll do that."

Hurst jerked his head to the other door. "I gotta get this girl out of here. I ain't got time to talk to you now. You've done a swell job... don't think I ain't mighty obliged."

Dillon moved over to the front door. "I'll see you tomorrow," he, said. Myra followed him out.

Coming up the stairs with a rush were two cops. They waved their guns at Dillon. Hurst heard them and came out quickly.

"Let these two through here," he said. "Those are the stiffs you gotta look after." He pointed to the two bodies lying on the floor.

The cops stared at Dillon and Myra as they walked past them. Their looks were curious. They hadn't seen these two before.

Dillon kept the Thompson under his coat and walked quickly. He was glad to get into the street. In the car, on the way back, he said, "I guess we're movin' in the right direction. This Hurst bird will get us just where we wantta get... you see."

Leaving the car in the basement garage, they groped their way upstairs to their apartment. Dillon went first. Half-way up, her heart beating hard, Myra made a deliberate false step. She stumbled up against Dillon.

He cursed as her weight struck him, and to save himself he twisted and caught at her. She felt his hard hands gripping her waist. The feel of his hands for the first time made her go limp. They stood in the dark like that, his hands digging into her flesh.

He said at last, "Can't you watch your feet?" He did not take his hands away, but shifted them a little so that they were just under her arms.

She said nothing. His touch paralysed her. The fire that had burnt inside her for him blazed up so that she could only lean limply against him, willing him to stay there.

He suddenly took his hands away and took a step from her. "Come on up, can't you?" he said thickly. "You goin' to stand there all night?"

They moved on again. He kept just one step ahead of her. She could feel the heat from his body, and she could hear his breath coming jerkily.

In the apartment he flicked on the light. She could see his face glistening, and a wild look she had not seen before in his eyes. She leant against the wall, her mouth a little slack, looking at him through half-closed eyes.

They stood facing each other, then without moving she said, "Now..."

PART THREE

Wholesale Murder

Outside, the rain beat on the windows. Below, the streets were empty and glistening in the yellow lights of the street lamps.

Myra paced the room restlessly, a cigarette in her mouth. No word from Dillon. She looked impatiently at the clock. Then she turned and, pulling back the curtain, looked into the empty street.

Her mind was alive with doubts. She went over to the telephone, lifted the receiver, hesitated, then put it back on its cradle. Where was Dillon? she kept asking herself. He said he'd be there at nine o'clock; it was just after eleven.

She walked into her bedroom and switched on the table-light. The room was well furnished, looking rather like a movie set. She stood looking round, seeing nothing.

Six months had gone by since the day they had got Hurst out of a jam. Six months of unrest and feverish activity. Hurst had paid them back for what they had done. Dillon was his right-hand man now. They were no longer petty gangsters. They were in the money now. Dillon's job was to see Hurst's racket ran smooth. He had a tough mob to work for him, while Hurst was content to sit in the background and collect the money as it rolled in.

Hurst's racket was this. He manufactured automatic machines of every description. He had gambling machines, moving-picture machines of a doubtful kind, food machines, cigarette machines and even prophylactic machines. On the face of it, a good sound business. It was where he put the machines that made his game a racket.

His mob went round with a truck planting the machines on small shop-keepers, or hotels, apartment houses and suchlike. These people were forced to take them. Those foolish enough to resist were either beaten up or had their windows smashed. They got no rake-off from the machines and Hurst had no overheads. He sent men round weekly to clear the money, and he made a big thing out of it. His gambling machines were fool-proof. Foolproof for Hurst. A sucker simply could not win anything from them, but still they tried. Hurst had over six thousand automatic machines in operation.

It was Myra who suggested the schools. Hurst was nervous that there would a row, but Myra had planned carefully. Nearly every school had a favourite candy shop, and it was in the candy shop that the automatic was planted. They put a smut movie automatic and a gambling automatic, and the kids flogged all their candy money in these machines. It brought in a new and pretty big revenue.

Dillon kept all the shopkeepers on the jump. He had to find fresh fields to plant the automatics, and he had to supervise the collecting of the money. Hurst gave him a ten per cent cut on what he turned in.

It was not quite the big job Dillon had planned but it was bringing them in fifteen hundred dollars a week. Also, Dillon was running a mob, and it was a mighty tough mob at that.

Myra had money to burn. She kept away from Dillon's headquarters, and lived the life of a rich business man's wife.

For six months Dillon had been coming back each night around nine o'-clock, and they would go out some place and eat. And now there was no sign of him.

She wondered if he'd run into trouble. After his one attempt to get rid of Hurst, Little Ernie had sunk into the background. Myra began to think maybe Dillon had got himself knocked off in a gunfight.

The bell whirred suddenly, making her start round. She ran to the front door. Roxy was standing there, his black fedora tilted over his eyes and his hands in his pockets.

Myra said, "Why, Roxy!" She was pleased to see him.

"H'yah, baby." Roxy stood smiling at her. "Ain't seen you for a long time."

"Come right in." She stood aside to let him pass.

Roxy wandered in, his eyes roving round the room. He raised his eyebrows a little. "Swell joint you got here," he observed.

"Do you like it?" Myra led him over to the leather couch.

"Sure, I think it's class. You two must be knockin' the berries off the bush all right."

Myra nodded. "We get along," she said. "And you, Roxy, how are you makin' out?"

Roxy shrugged. "About the same," he said. "I'd like somethin' more steady, but I ain't moanin'."

Myra said, "Maybe Dillon'd fix it for you."

"You think he would?" Roxy sounded eager.

Myra nodded. "I guess he'd be glad to. I'll speak to him when he blows in." The look of uncertainty came back.

"Ain't he around?" Roxy sounded disappointed. "I hoped to see that guy."

Myra shook her head. "I'm worried," she said. "He ain't given me a buzz or nothin'."

Roxy leant back. "Well, he'll be along... you see."

Myra moved about the room. "What'll you drink, Roxy?" she asked.

"A rye if you've got it," Roxy said. "You sure have moved up in the world." He watched her mix the drinks, then he said casually, "You heard about Fan?"

Myra came over and gave him the rye. She shook her head. "No," she said. "What's Fan been doin'?"

Roxy held the glass up to the light and looked at the liquor thoughtfully. "She pulled out about three weeks ago. Left me flat. I miss that dame."

Myra raised her eyebrows. "What she want to do that for?" she asked.

"You know how it is. I guess we got along all right, but we just didn't think much of each other. She ran into some bird who'd got a lotta dough, and she joined up with him."

Myra said, "Who's the bird?"

Roxy shook his head. "She didn't tell me that," he said, stretching his legs out and looking at his feet. "Went off kind of mysteriously. Didn't even leave an address. She just said she'd found some guy who was goin' to stake her for a good time, and off she went."

Outside they heard the front door click, and Dillon walked in. He stood in the doorway looking at Roxy, a little startled. Roxy put his glass on the table and stood up. "Hello, Bud," he said. "I guess it's good to see you."

Dillon came over and shook hands. He didn't look at Myra. "For the love of Mike," he said, "this is a surprise."

Myra said, "Where've you been? I'm starvin'."

Dillon looked at her. "Yeah," he said, "I guess I've dealt you a raw hand. I got held up by Hurst just as I was leavin', and that guy jawed until right now. I'd've given you a buzz, only you know how he is."

Myra relaxed a little. "I was gettin' the jitters. I thought maybe you had been in a fight."

Dillon grinned. "I don't get into fights," he said. "This was just business."

Roxy thought he was lying, but he wasn't sure.

Myra said, "Look, honey, can you work Roxy in your outfit?"

Dillon hesitated a moment, then he nodded. "Sure, I'd be glad to. Suppose you come down to the office tomorrow an' let's talk it over."

Roxy was impressed in spite of himself. This Dillon was certainly a big shot now. He nodded. "I guess I'll blow," he said. "You two want to eat."

Myra saw him to the door. "Good night, Roxy," she said. "Don't you worry. He'll find you a job. We owe you somethin'."

Roxy tipped his hat and grinned, then he let himself out of the apartment.

Myra came back. "Suppose we have somethin' to eat right here?" she said. "It's too late to go out."

Dillon was lying back in a chair, his eyes half shut. "You go ahead, I've had somethin'."

Myra stood looking at him, her mind suddenly suspicious. She started to say something, but changed her mind. She went into the kitchen and cut a meat sandwich. She stood leaning against the kitchen table, thinking. When she had finished the sandwich she went back into the other room.

Dillon had gone into the bedroom. She could hear the bath-water running. She finished her rye and lighted a cigarette. She stood waiting until she heard him go into the bathroom, then she walked over to the telephone and dialled a number.

Hurst came on. He sounded irritable. Myra said, "I'm worried about Dillon, Mr. Hurst. You ain't seen him, have you?"

"Hasn't he come in?" Hurst sounded bored. "No, I don't know where he is.... I haven't seen him all day."

"Wasn't he with you tonight?"

"I tell you I haven't seen him all day," Hurst snapped. "He'll be along," and he hung up.

Myra dropped the receiver into its cradle. Her eyes were stormy. There was only one reason why Dillon had lied to her. So the heel was two-timing. Who was the woman? Her hands clenched at her side, wave after wave of rage ran through her. For a moment she played with the idea of shooting Dillon there and then, but she knew he was now in too strong a position to be cast aside. Myra knew that without Dillon she would have to start all over again. No longer would she have an apartment or money.... No, Dillon must not be touched. It was the woman she'd have to go for.

Her rage subsided as she turned the problem over. The more she thought about it, the more she realized the danger she herself was in. Let Dillon find someone who really pleased him, and there was nothing to stop him from ditching her. He had Hurst and a tough mob at his back, and although she had given him ideas, and had helped him, she knew he was ruthless enough to toss her aside if she tried to make trouble for him.

She walked into the bedroom and began to undress. Dillon came out of the bathroom, humming to himself. She caught a glimpse of his face in the mirror. His eyes were dull; dark rings under them gave him a tired, heavy look. She caught her breath sharply, sitting there, her heart beating hard.

Dillon got into bed and snapped off the lamp at his side. "Come on," he said, "I wantta go to sleep."

She stood up, passing the comb through her hair. "You *are* tired tonight," she said, keeping her voice steady with an effort.

"Yeah," Dillon grunted, "I'm damn' tired. Get into bed for Pete's sake."

She put the comb down on the dressing-table and came over to him. She sat on the bed, looking at him with glittering eyes. "Shall I come in with you?" she almost snarled at him.

Dillon's heavy face hardened. He sat up on his elbow. "Didn't I tell you

I'm beat?" he snapped. "Get into bed. I wantta sleep."

"Too tired?" The gritty, suppressed rage startled him into wakefulness.

"What the hell's this?" he said. "Can't I get tired sometimes?"

"I'm on to you—"

Dillon pulled back the bedclothes and swung his feet to the floor. He reached out and gripped her throat in his hand. She struck at him wildly, but his arm was too long. He held her away from him.

"That's the way it is, huh?" he said softly. "You're gettin' too big for your pants. Jest because you've been this and that you think you can talk big. Okay, sister, here it is."

He smacked her across her face hard with his open hand, at the same time releasing his grip on her throat. She fell off the bed and rolled on the floor. He kicked her hard in her ribs with his bare foot. She slid away with the force of the kick across to her own bed.

"Now get to sleep an' shut your trap. You ain't got anythin' more than any other woman... get it?"

He pulled up the bedclothes and snapped out the light. She remained sobbing with rage on the cold floor.

Dillon used Jakie's Poolroom on Nineteenth for his headquarters. The boys spent a lot of their time pushing the balls around, waiting for something to turn up. Dillon had a little office at the far end of the poolroom. It was quite a place. He had a roll-top desk and several modern chairs of chromium and leather. The door had a ground-glass panel with 'AUTO-MATICS, INC.' painted on it, and in smaller letters at the bottom right-hand corner, 'Manager.' Dillon liked that, it made him feel good.

When Roxy blew in during the early afternoon the poolroom was full. Dillon's boys were drinking, talking and playing snooker. They glanced up when Roxy came in, looked at him suspiciously and glanced at one another.

Roxy stood in the doorway, his hat tipped over his eyes. "Mr. Dillon around?" he asked.

One of them jerked his thumb to the door. "In there," he said briefly.

Roxy started across the floor. A big bird suddenly got in his way. "Hey!" he said. "Where the hell do you think you're goin'?"

Roxy said patiently, "I wantta see Dillon."

The big bird said, "Wait." He ran his hands over Roxy, feeling for a gun, then he knocked on the door and put his head round. He withdrew after a moment and nodded at Roxy. "Go ahead," he said. "You're okay."

Dillon was thumbing through a newspaper, half hidden by the top of the desk. He glanced up and looked at Roxy thoughtfully.

"Jeeze! Quite the big shot," Roxy said.

Dillon said coldly, "Come on in, an' shut the door."

Roxy closed the door and sat down. He ran his fingers over the stove-pipe furniture. "Hot, ain't it?" he said admiringly. "This is some joint."

Dillon opened a drawer and took out a box of cigars. He pushed them over to Roxy. "You wantta join up?" he said.

Roxy selected a cigar, bit the end off and spat it from his mouth. "Yeah," he said. "I'd like to get into somethin' steady. My racket is gettin' shot to hell."

Dillon looked at him thoughtfully. "What I'm goin' to tell you ain't to go further," he said, keeping his voice low.

Roxy looked a little startled, but he nodded. "Sure, I don't talk," he said. "You should know that."

Dillon hitched his chair closer. "I'm figgerin' you're the guy I've been lookin' for," he said. "Maybe I'm wrong, but I don't think so. Listen. At the moment I'm runnin' this automatic racket an' I'm picking up around fifteen grand a week. Nice, but nothin' to rave about. Hurst's got a grand organization. He's got protection. He's got a real tough crowd workin' for him. This Hurst guy gets so far, but he don't go the limit. With his organization, he could go the limit."

Roxy drew on his cigar, letting the heavy smoke slide from his mouth. "What's the limit?" he asked.

Dillon said very quietly, "Little Ernie's the limit."

Roxy's eyes narrowed. "I don't get that," he said.

"I want to take over Ernie's part of the town. Hurst won't stand for it, but I guess if I did it he'd have to stick by me an' like it."

"What's that to me?" Roxy asked cautiously.

Dillon looked at him hard. "The whole town'd be too big for me to handle. I gotta have a guy I could trust. You'd get in on this on the ground floor."

Roxy said, "Maybe Hurst wouldn't stand for it."

Dillon got up and walked to the door. He opened it and glanced outside, then he came back and put his head close to Roxy's. "Maybe what Hurst says won't count any more."

Roxy looked up into his black eyes. He shifted uneasily at the malevolence there. He hastily turned his eyes, and studied the grey ash of his cigar. "Got the mob at the back of you?" he asked.

Dillon nodded. "Yeah," he said. "Those guys out there see me all the time. I tell 'em to do this an' that an' they do it. Okay. When the time comes, an' Hurst fades away, those guys ain't asking questions. They'll just go on takin' orders from me... get it?"

Roxy thought a little, then he said, "You've got somethin' there."

Dillon nodded. "Yeah, I guess I got somethin' there all right."

Roxy said, "I bet Myra thinks that's a good stunt."

Dillon scowled. "That dame don't count," he said coldly. "She's gettin' big ideas, an' she's goin' to get a surprise one of these days."

Roxy looked startled. "I like Myra," he mumbled. "She's got what it takes."

Dillon shrugged and stood up. "When I'm ready, I'll tell you," he said. "Can I count on you?"

Roxy said, "Sure, you can count me in. I've been waiting for a break like this for some time. I guess I was too cautious when I was runnin' around with Fan. You seen her, by the way?"

Dillon shot him a quick, suspicious glance. "I ain't seen her," he said.

Roxy sat down on the edge of the table. "Listen, Bud," he said evenly. "Don't let's start this game with a double-cross. I ain't sore you pinched Fan from me. I miss her just like I'd miss a deck of cards I got used to, but that's all."

Dillon clenched his fists. His eyes gleamed at Roxy. "You been checkin' up on me?" he said, a gritty sound in his voice.

Roxy said hastily, "Hell! I wouldn't do a thing like that. I just heard—"

Dillon said, "It'd better get no further. I don't want that little bag Myra gettin' ideas about Fan."

Roxy shook his head. "She ain't dumb," he said thoughtfully. "You watch her. She'll get on to it."

Dillon began pacing the small office. "I'm gettin' rattled with that dame. I guess she's about washed up with me. She'll have a get to hell out of it."

Roxy touched the ash off his cigar into the tray. "You'll have a little trouble," he said, "I'd be careful how you handle that bird."

Dillon shot him another cold look. "I can handle her," he said. "You keep your nose clean on this. Anyway, suppose you get to work an' wise yourself up on Little Ernie's territory? What I want is a list of all the small-time stores, hotels an' suchlike who could take on automatic machines. You walk around an' take a look at the ground. You're on the pay-roll now, so you might as well get used to a little work."

Roxy grinned. "I get it," he said. "What you payin'?"

"I'll give you a couple of hundred bucks an' ten per cent on he take when we get goin'."

Roxy shrugged his shoulders. "I guess you're right about getting' rid of the big shots. I could do with a little of their share."

When he had gone, Dillon went over to the telephone and rang Fanquist. Her slow drawl floated to his ear. "Listen, baby," he said, speaking close to the mouthpiece, "I've just had a word with Roxy. He knows, but that guy is shootin' on the level. I've fixed him up to work for me; an' he ain't goin' to start trouble."

Fanquist started her old beef. "When are we really goin' to get together?"

Dillon said sharply, "It ain't time yet. Myra wants handlin'…"

Fanquist said, "Why don't you toss that little chippy out on her can?" Her voice was suddenly strident and furious.

"I tell you it ain't time for that yet," Dillon snarled. "Suppose you leave this to me?"

"Am I seein' you today?"

Dillon looked round his office, a harassed expression on his face.

"You gotta have patience—" he began.

"That's another tune I'm getting sick of," Fanquist said bitterly. "You make me tired. I guess I'm a sucker to stand for it. All right, if that's the way you feel I guess you can stay away." She hung up.

Dillon slammed the receiver down on the prong and mopped his face with his handkerchief. Women were hell, he thought. Before Myra had come along and he had started fooling with her he just kicked women around; now they had him crawling. What had come over him?

The door opened and Hurst walked in. For a moment Dillon was startled. Hurst never came to this place. He got to his feet. Hurst looked at him thoughtfully, then nodded. He walked over to a chair and sat down. "I was passing, so I thought I'd look in and hear how things were going," he said.

Dillon sat down. "They're all right."

"No trouble?"

Dillon shook his head. He gave a bland smile. "Why, no, Mr. Hurst, I guess things are goin' mighty smooth just now."

Was Hurst looking at him in an odd way, or was he imagining things?

Hurst said abruptly, "What's wrong with your girl-friend?"

Dillon raised his eyes. A muscle in his jaw twitched. "Myra? I don't get it."

Hurst shrugged. "She pulled me from a game last night asking where you were."

Dillon suddenly went cold. "Aw, she's always like that if I'm a shade late," he said carelessly. "I'll tell her not to worry you."

Hurst got to his feet. "That's okay," he said. "I just wondered." He moved to the door. With the handle in his hand, he glanced back over his shoulder. "You ain't causin' Little Ernie any worries?"

Dillon knew now why he had come in. Since Little Ernie had sent two gunmen after him, Hurst was scared sick of any other trouble starting.

Dillon shook his head. "We're leavin' 'em alone," he said quietly, and grinned to himself. This punk would have a fit if he knew what was going to happen.

Hurst nodded. "That's it," he said. "You leave those guys alone. We can get along without treading on their corns."

Dillon watched him go, and when the door had closed he stretched his neck and spat viciously into the brass spittoon by the desk.

The news that Myra knew that he wasn't with Hurst the previous night infuriated him. He sat back in his chair and tried to reconstruct the scene between them. Myra was no sucker. She knew there was another woman. His brows came down. Just let her start something, he told himself. If she thought she could push him around she'd got a surprise coming. Hurst and Myra. They both knew too much for his comfort. Maybe... He sat there thinking. Yeah, maybe.... He'd have to watch those two. It looked like he'd have to do something.

His cold, sullen face became grimly set.

Myra waited until Dillon had left the apartment, then she began a systematic search. She knew Dillon had no head for addresses. Somewhere, she was sure, she would find a clue that would lead her to this broad. Her face hard and set, and her hands impatient, she went carefully through Dillon's wardrobe. She turned out every pocket, but she found nothing. She went through his drawers, careful not to disturb anything, but again she was unsuccessful.

She sat back on the bed thinking. This was getting her nowhere. He must have written the address down. She was certain of it. The only hope was he would be carrying it on him. That would make things difficult. She went once more to his wardrobe. Three soiled evening shirts caught her eye, hanging up on a peg. He'd been too lazy to throw them out for the wash.

On the cuff of one of them she found what she was looking for. Scribbled in pencil was an address—158 Sunset Avenue.

She stood there, holding the shirt in her hand, a cold fury sweeping over her. "You see, you two-timin' heel, this chippy of yours is goin' to get a shock."

Putting the shirt carefully back in the cupboard, she went to her drawer and found her gun. It was a toy affair with a mother-o'-pearl handle, exceedingly unpleasant at close quarters. She put on her hat and coat and shoved the gun in her handbag. Then she stood hesitating. Maybe this wasn't quite the job for a gun. A hard little smile reached her mouth. She took from Dillon's drawer a length of solid rubber hose. She balanced it in her hand thoughtfully. Then, winding the thong round her wrist, she forced the hose up her sleeve.

Slamming the front door behind her, she took the elevator to the street level. A yellow taxi shot to the curb and she nodded briefly. "Sunset Avenue," she said. "An' flog your horse."

The taxi jerked away. The driver said, "This is a hell of a town. I never run into any guy who ain't in a hurry."

Myra wasn't in the mood to talk. She said nothing. The taxi-driver studied her in the mirror, thought she was easy on the eye, and let it go at that.

Sunset Avenue was at the far end of the town. It took them a good half-hour's run to make it. The driver suddenly crammed on his brakes. "Here it is, lady; what number jer want?"

Myra said, "Stop here... this'll do." She got out of the cab and paid him off. Then she walked slowly down the Avenue looking for 158. Her fury was smouldering by the time she found it. The place was a neat little villa, standing in a fair-sized garden. A place like this would cost money to keep up, she thought, and for a moment she hesitated. Maybe she had made a mistake. This place might be where one of Dillon's business associates hung out. Her step faltered. Then she thought that as she'd come this far it wouldn't take long to check it up.

She walked up the crazy pavement and rang on the bell. She stood waiting, uncertain of herself. The door jerked open and Fanquist gaped at her.

It was certainly a shock to Myra. She saw it in a flash. Dillon was the rich guy who was staking this floosie to a good time. She said quietly, "Hello. I bet this is a surprise."

Fanquist got her nerve back. She said, "My Gawd, it's the kid again! What you doin' here?"

Myra said, "Dillon told me you had moved, so I thought I'd look you up."

"Dillon told you?" Fanquist's eyes hardened.

Myra nodded. "Sure. May I come in? I'd love to look around."

Fanquist stood squarely in the doorway. She said in a hard voice, "Scram... go on, get to hell out of here!"

Myra could see two men wandering down the street. She had to get inside quick. Still keeping a smile on her face, she said, "Why, Fan, that ain't the way to talk. I gotta message for you." She opened her bag casually. Fanquist watched her, a puzzled look on her face. She wondered what all this was leading to.

Myra took the gun out of her bag and showed it to Fanquist. "Get inside quick, you bow-legged broad," she said with a rush.

Fanquist's eyes opened very wide, and she went white under her rouge. She took a step back, and Myra stepped in and shut the door.

A big living-room opened out from the hall, and Myra drove Fanquist in there. The room was expensively furnished.

Myra said between her teeth, "So this is the love-nest, is it?"

Fanquist stammered, "You're going to be sorry for this. Wait until he hears about it."

"Sit down, you jerk," Myra said. "I've got a lot to talk to you about."

Fanquist sald harshly, "You ain't throwin' a scare into me. You'd better get out, an' get out quick."

"Sit down," Myra repeated. She held one hand behind her back, jerking the rubber club down from her sleeve.

Fanquist was getting her nerve back all right. She sneered. "That rod ain't gettin' you anywhere.... Get out!"

Myra swung the club round and hit Fanquist across her face with it. Fanquist staggered back, the chair struck her behind her knees, and she collapsed into it. She held both her hands over her face, the pain striking her dumb. Myra stepped back a little and waited.

"Maybe you'll jump to it next time," she said.

"You're goin' to pay for this," Fanquist gasped. "You are goin' to pay for this!"

"Listen, you bohunk. You're goin' to clear out of this town quick, an' you'll stay out. I'm just givin' you a warning."

Fanquist took her hands away from her face. Her eyes glittered murderously. She screamed suddenly, "You can't make me get out!... Dillon's mine now.... He's mine—do you hear?"

Myra's face was hard. She took a step forward. The .25 was pointing directly at Fanquist. "That's what you say," she snapped. "You're goin' okay, and you're goin' for good."

Fanquist moved like a snake striking. She smacked Myra's hand away, sending the gun flying across the room. At the same time she sprang forward, her head down, and her hands grasping Myra's waist.

Myra went over with Fanquist on top of her. They both hit the floor with a crash that jarred the room. Fanquist shifted her hands quickly, trying to catch Myra round the throat. Myra got her chin down, so Fanquist only got a grip on her jaw. Swinging the club up, Myra hit Fanquist on the shoulder. It was a glancing blow, but it made Fanquist squeal. She made a grab at Myra's hand, but missed and got another sock from the club.

Myra was twisting like an eel, trying to get from under Fanpquist, but she was too heavy for her. She kept beating Fanquist with the club, but there was no weight behind the blows. They hurt Fanquist, but not enough to shake her off. All the time she was lunging to get Myra's arm pinned down with her knee.

Myra got in a lucky one, hitting Fanquist on the side of her head. Fanquist went crazy with the pain. She grabbed Myra by the hair, banging her head twice on the floor. Myra stiffened her neck, checking the force, but even then it half stunned her.

Letting go of the club, so that it swung by its thong, she reached out, catching Fanquist's ears. Fanquist was wearing big pearl stud earrings.

Myra wrenched them away, splitting the lobes as she did so. Fanquist let go of her and put her hands over her ears, screaming like a train going through a tunnel. Blood ran through her fingers, down her neck.

Myra hit her across her eyes with her open hand, sending her reeling backwards. A sharp kick got Myra in the clear. Fanquist crawled up on her hands and knees. Myra stiffened, then launched herself at her again. They went over in a heap, upsetting a small table and sending two chairs flying with a crash. Myra's clutching hands ripped Fanquist's dress down the front, and as Fanquist, screaming wildly, tried to roll clear, Myra clawed her down her bare back, making four long deep grooves.

Fanquist was terrified. She was half-crazy with pain and panic. She just wanted to get out of the room, away from those claw-like fingers. Somehow she managed to wriggle loose and get to her feet. She ran with unsteady steps to the door. Myra heaved up and collared her round the knees, bringing her crashing down on the floor again.

"Let me go... let me go... let me go!..." Fanquist screamed, twisting and kicking.

Again Myra clawed her, ripping her clothes, stripping her to the waist.

Fanquist tried to fight back, making a lunge at Myra's eyes with her nails. Myra jerked her head away, and hit her across both wrists with the club. She put a lot into that blow. Fanquist fell on her knees, her head swimming with pain.

"Now, you two-timin' floosie," Myra panted, "here's what's comin' to you." She kicked Fanquist in her side, sending her over hard. Fanquist was past squawking. Her eyes wide with terror and pain, she crouched there, moaning. Blood glistened on her body like paint.

Myra said, "Get up before I start on you again.... Go on, get up... you heel!"

Fanquist dragged herself off the floor, her breath coming in great heaving sobs. "Don't... hit me..." she whined. "I'll... play ball...."

Myra sneered. "I ain't finished with you," she said. "I've got a long way to go before I'm through with you."

Fanquist, giving a strangled cry, turned and stumbled to the door. Myra threw a chair in her way. Fanquist banged her knees against it and went forward, falling across the chair with a thud that shook the breath out of her body.

Myra sprang forward, and driving her knee into Fanquist's shoulders, she pinned her.

Fanquist screamed, a real terror gripping her. With one hand pushing her face into the carpet, Myra swung the club with the other. "Go on," Myra said, "you yell...."

She began to beat Fanquist's arched back with all her strength. Fanquist wriggled and screamed, but Myra held her. She tried to protect herself with her hands, but the club beat them away, sending waves of pain up her arms as well as through her body. Myra beat her until she drooped over the chair, limp and silent.

Standing there breathless, Myra said, "I guess that's all."

Fanquist didn't move. She was past hearing anything. Myra dragged her off the chair and turned her over on her back. She stood over her, a hard little smile on her mouth. "I guess you won't pull any more tricks with me," she said.

Leaving Fanquist lying there, Myra went into the bathroom. Her dress was stained with blood and her hair was like a woollen rug. She poured some water into the hand-basin and bathed her face. She carefully washed her hands and sponged the blood from her dress. All the time she was doing this her mind was active.

Would Dillon start something now? she wondered. She guessed Dillon would be mad about this. A pair of electric hair-tongs caught her eye. She stood looking at them, hesitating. She picked them up and turned them over in her hand, then she took the plug and plugged it into the socket. She turned the switch.

Going back into the outer room again, she stood over Fanquist. Fanquist was lying there, her arms thrown wide and her breath coming in a whistling sound through her open mouth.

Myra said between her teeth, "I guess you ain't goin' to have any looks in a little while. He's kind of fussy about the broads he takes around, an' a bag with marks on her mug like you're goin' to have ain't getting to the first base with him."

She turned and walked with vicious determination back to the bathroom and to the red-hot tongs.

The next two days Dillon was very quiet. Myra expected him to say something, but he didn't. Sometimes she caught him looking at her thoughtfully, but he always shifted his eyes when she looked up.

He came back from the poolroom at his usual time, and Myra began to believe that nothing would be said. She made a few enquiries and learnt that Fanquist had disappeared. The villa was empty and deserted. Myra thought she'd done a nice job of work, but Dillon was still quiet and he still looked at her as if he wasn't quite sure what to do.

Sitting in his office, Dillon brooded about Fanquist. He had gone down in the evening and found her. Even his brutal mind was shocked. But as he looked at her, any feeling he might have had for her went away. The two deep burns across her face sickened him. Her sobbing whine gave him the jitters. He had said brutally and bluntly that she'd better get out of town.

Myra scared him a little. She was getting too dangerous. When he had put through his plan of fixing Little Ernie he'd have to do something about her. She had served her purpose, and now he felt he had outgrown her.

Outside in the poolroom, the buzz of talk suddenly stopped. Dillon stiffened. He cocked his ear, a frown on his face. The sounds from outside were no more to him than the ticking of a clock. He was used to them, and suddenly to have a heavy silence made him think something was wrong.

Before he could move from his chair the office door pushed open and two men wandered in. Dillon looked at them, his mouth going to a thin line.

Strawn pushed his hat to the back of his head and rubbed his thick nose with the side of his finger. "Well, look who's here," he said, speaking out of the side of his mouth.

The other man looked Dillon over with distaste.

Through the open doorway Dillon could see the others standing like waxworks. He could see Sam Vessi holding a cue, as if he were going to make a shot, his head turned to the office, motionless. Jakie McGowan had his hands resting on the table, his thick features glistening with sweat. The others just stood or sat about motionless.

Dillon said, "You got no right bustin' in here, an' you know it." His black eyes glittered.

Strawn wandered farther into the room. "Ain't you the guy I told to get out of this town?" he asked.

Dillon stood up. These birds weren't going to push him around any more. "Maybe you think you're smart with this line of talk," he snarled. "But it don't wash with me. You ain't got anythin' on me, so you can get the hell outta here."

Strawn said evenly, "So you're a big shot, huh? Well, listen, Big Shot, I still don't like you, an' I still say get out of this town. What do you think of that?"

Dillon shrugged. "You ain't causin' me any grief," he said. "I know where I am, an' you can't do a thing."

"One of these days," Strawn said quietly, "you an' me are goin' to take a ride. Smart guys like you always come unstuck... you see."

Dillon sat down again. "Okay," he said. "Maybe I'll take a ride with you. Maybe a lot of things. But right now you're using too much air around here."

Strawn nodded briefly. "I've heard a lot about you an' your girl-friend. You two are getting big. But you can't last. None of you guys can last. You think you can, but you can't."

He nodded to the other guy. "Take a look at him," he said. "I'll lay you ten to one we fix him in six months."

The other guy shook his head. "You just want to make money outta me," he said. "I've been caught like that before."

Dillon sat glowering at them, a blazing hatred surging through him.

Strawn nodded to him. "Okay, Big Shot," he said. "Don't keep us waiting too long." He jerked his head to the other guy, and they went out of the room.

When they had gone, Dillon got up and began to pace the office. Smart punks, he thought savagely. If they thought they could pin anything on him, let them try.

Vessi, a thin little guy, put his head round the door. "You sure pushed 'em around," he said admiringly. "These Federal dicks are gettin' too big for their pants."

Dillon looked at him irritably. "You've gotta watch those guys," he said. "They're just waitin' a chance to crack down."

Vessi propped himself up against the door. "Sure," he said. "They've been on the look-out for us for a long time…. It ain't gettin' them anywhere."

Just then the telephone rang, and Dillon nodded to him. Vessi went out, shutting the door. Dillon scooped up the phone. "Yeah?" he asked. His temper was short.

Hurst said, "Who the hell is that guy you got looking over Little Ernie's territory? Listen, Dillon, I told you to lay off that part of the town. Conforti's just been on, complaining we've got a man askin' questions in Little Italy. What's it all about?"

Dillon grinned a little. "Search me," he said. "How should I know?"

Hurst said furiously, "You know all right. Get that man out of there and keep him out! I know your ideas, Dillon, and I don't like them. I've told Conforti to take the matter into his own hands if that guy ain't out by to-morrow."

While he was speaking, Roxy came in. Dillon looked at him and jerked his head to the 'phone. He winked at Roxy and said "Hurst" with his lips, not speaking. Roxy grinned and sat down quietly. He put his cloth-top boots on the desk.

Dillon said, "They're crazy. I don't know a thing about it."

Hurst said, "You see to it, Dillon, or I'll come down and start something." He slammed down the receiver.

Dillon put the telephone down on the desk. His face was thoughtful. "You ain't been careful enough," he said to Roxy.

"What's that? A squawk?" Roxy tilted his chair back.

"Yeah!" Dillon took a quill from his vest pocket and began exploring his teeth. "Quite burnt up he was. I guess he figgered Little Ernie would start on him again, the yellow rat."

Roxy smiled. "I wasn't careful," he said. "I got right down to things."

He took a sheet of paper from his inside pocket and tossed it on the desk in front of Dillon. "Take a gander at that," he said.

Dillon looked through the long list of names. "What the hell's this?" he asked.

"Look at 'em."

Dillon snarled. "Come on, cut out the mystery act. What is it?"

Roxy wasn't to be hurried. "All those guys there've got swell joints for your automatics. They've all got big corner stores and they've plenty of space. Suppose we persuade them to take six machines instead of one. That would be gettin' somewhere."

"Six? Are they big enough?"

"Sure they're big enough."

Dillon got to his feet. "Little Ernie's got to be fixed first," he said.

Roxy examined his finger-nails. "I got him tied up." Dillon stood still. "What was that?"

"I got him tied up. You've only to take the boys along an' there he is waitin' for you."

"What's this, Roxy? Let's have it fast."

Roxy took his feet off the table. "Little Ernie and his mob will be at the Hot Rhythm Club tonight. They've got some big night on or somethin'; anyway, the gang will be there. Suppose we go an' join 'em? It would be a fine time to meet all the mob together."

Dillon demanded, "Is this straight?"

"Yeah, it's straight all right. I've been usin' my ears around that part of the town."

Dillon stood hesitating, then he said, "Wait here." He went to the door and beckoned. Vessi and McGowan put their cues down and wandered over. Dillon shut the office door. Vessi and McGowan ran the mob for Dillon.

He said, "Sit down, you two, I want to talk."

They pulled up chairs and sat down. "What's up?" Vessi asked.

Dillon sat on the edge of his desk. "I'm puttin' my cards on the table," he said shortly. "We ain't expanding like we should. That's not your funeral; it's Hurst's an' mine. Hurst is scared of the other mob; I ain't. Okay. Suppose we expand an' not worry about Hurst?"

The two looked at each other, puzzled. McGowan said ponderously, "Say, we gotta do what Hurst says, ain't we?"

Dillon shrugged. "Why?" he asked. "Who the hell's Hurst, anyway?"

Vessi scratched his head. "Ain't he the boss any more?"

"Wait a minute," Dillon said. "I want you to get the layout of this. If we expand, we'll have to get rid of Hurst an' we'll have to get rid of Little Ernie. Tough job, but ain't impossible. If we expand we make twice as much dough as we're making now. For instance, you two guys will be holding down a couple of grand a week."

Vessi's eyes opened. "Sure," he said. "I guess we'll expand."

"Don't rush it," Dillon warned him. "If you come in on this there's goin' to be a lotta grief for someone.... Maybe it'll be you an' me. If you want the dough, I guess you gotta earn it, so it's up to you."

McGowan said, "What are you goin' to do?"

The door opened and Hurst walked in. The four men swung round, blinking at him. Even Dillon was startled.

Hurst stood there, a heavy frown on his face and his lips twitching with rage. "What's going on here?" he demanded harshly. "Get these guys out of here, I want to talk to you."

Vessi and McGowan hastily scrambled to their feet. They slid past Hurst as if they expected he was going to land them one.

Roxy sat where he was. He didn't look at Hurst.

Dillon pushed hack his chair and drummed his fingers on the desk top. He stared at Hurst with blank eyes.

Hurst said, "Get this other guy out." He jerked his head at Roxy.

Dillon shook his head. "He won't be in the way."

Hurst stiffened. "You heard what I said," he barked.

Dillon nodded. "Sure," he said; "but this guy ain't in the way. What's on your mind, Mr. Hurst? You seem sorta steamed up."

Hurst stood hesitating, then he sat down. "Look here, Dillon, this game of yours has gotta stop. I've told you before you gotta leave Little Ernie's ground alone."

"Can't you take it, Mr. Hurst?" Dillon sneered.

Hurst sprang to his feet. "What the hell's this?" he snapped. "You take your orders from me, and when I say leave off you leave off!"

"I've been getting some ideas that'll get us somewhere in this organization," Dillon said, speaking slow. "Suppose we push into that ground you're so scared about? Suppose we give Little Ernie the works? How do you like that?"

Hurst was speechless. His face turned a dusky red, and his big hands clenched on his knees. "By heck!" he blurted out at last. "This finishes it. You're out, Dillon! Do you hear? Out!"

Dillon pursed his heavy lips and shot a side look at Roxy. Roxy sat in a heap, his hat tilted over his eyes.

Hurst went on, "You're crazy to think of such an idea. A thing like that would blow the town to hell. I ain't having you around my mob any more.... You get out."

Dillon leant forward, his eyes like ice chips. "Where did you get that 'my mob' stuff?" he snarled. "You ain't got a mob no more, you yellow fourflusher. I got it, see? An' what I say goes with the mob. I've given you a chance, an' you're too damn' yellow to take it. All right, from now on I'm runnin' this outfit, an' you're likin' it... get that?"

Hurst got to his feet. He controlled himself with an effort. "You're drunk," he said. "You haven't the brains to run any business. You want protection, an' you ain't got it. You're nobody. The cops would close you up damn' quick without me right behind you."

Dillon sneered. "Do you think I've been in this game an' not got the low-down to it? You ain't got any pull; you've got dough. I know how much you give the cops to lay off you, an' I'll give 'em more. The guy that pays the most gets the best service."

Hurst turned to the door. "You're washed up," he said shortly. "Get out and stay out!"

Dillon jerked his gun from inside his coat. "Just a minute, Mr. Hurst," he said between his teeth.

Hurst stood, frozen. Then he put out his hands like a blind man grop-ing. "What are doing with that gun?" he gasped, his face going suddenly flabby.

Dillon didn't bother to get to his feet. "You talk too much," he said. "If we're goin' to break, I guess we'll break the way I want it."

While he was speaking, his finger curled on the trigger, gently squeezing. The gun suddenly boomed, jerking a little in his hand.

Hurst took a step forward, his hands pressed to his chest. Then his knees gave, and he sank down. Leaning forward over the desk, Dillon shot him again. The heavy slug made a big hole in Hurst's head.

Dillon stayed there, leaning over the desk, his gun still pointing at Hurst, his lips off his teeth. "Now, you jerk," he said, "you can stay dumb!"

Roxy tipped his hat back and stared. "Hey," he said, "you've spoilt your rug."

Myra sat before the dressing-table, a loose silk wrap across her shoul-ders. Her skin was faintly red from the hot water of the shower. A ciga-rette dangled from her full red lips and the spiral of smoke rose over her head. She took time fixing her nails.

Dillon jerked open the door and walked in. Myra looked at him and glanced at the clock. It was not seven o'clock.

"You're early," she said, laying down the file. She pulled the wrap on and fastened the sash.

Dillon was very thoughtful. He went over to the window and, raising the blind a little, peered into the street. Myra watched him. She had an uneasy feeling that something had happened. "What is it?" she asked.

Without looking round, Dillon said, "Plenty." He stood there a moment, then he dropped the blind and came back to the middle of the room. With his hat at the back of his head, he stared at Myra with blank eyes.

She said, "For Pete's sake... what is it?"

"Hurst's washed up," he said abruptly.

"Little Ernie?" Myra got to her feet.

Dillon hesitated, then he shook his head. "I did it."

Myra put her hand to her mouth. She took a step back, pushing the stool away. "You did it?" she repeated. "Did what?"

Dillon moved restlessly. "I gave him the works," he said. "The yellow rat came in shootin' off his mouth, so I gave it to him."

Myra's eyes flashed. "Are you crazy?" she screamed. "You've killed Hurst, you fool?"

Dillon went over to her with two quick strides. His hand shot out and gripped her wrap, twisting it in his fist. He jerked her forward, so that their faces were close. "Shut up!" he snarled. "Shut your trap. I'm runnin' this outfit. I ain't standin' any yap from you. If you don't watch out, I'll' knock you off."

Myra stiffened.

"Yeah, I mean that," he said, his eyes glaring at her.

She put her hand on his wrist. "Let me go," she said. "I won't start any-thin'."

Dillon gave her a shove, sending her backwards. She sat down in the chair, her hands limply at her sides. "What are you goin' to do?" she asked.

Dillon, satisfied that he had fixed her, went over to an armchair and sat down.

"I've got the mob," he said, picking his words. "I've got the racket. I guess I'm goin' to be the big shot... the only big shot around here."

Myra said, "But the cops?"

Dillon sneered. "Hurst paid the cops. Okay, I'll pay 'em. They ain't to have any beef. I'll pay 'em better, see?"

Myra didn't say anything. She sat staring at the floor.

Encouraged by her silence, Dillon went on, "Tonight I'm goin' after Ernie. We've got him sewn up tight."

Myra jerked up her head. She just stared at Dillon, speechless. Dillon nodded at her, his triumph making him expand. "Yeah," he said, "I've got the whole layout fixed. First Hurst. Okay, he's gone. Then Little Ernie.... He goes tonight. Then I got this burg to play with. It means plenty of dough, baby, and I'm gettin' the lot."

Myra beat her hands together. "For Pete's sake... can't you see where you're headin'? Little Ernie's got everything. He's got a bigger mob... he's got protection... the cops are behind him.... I tell you he's got everything."

Dillon grinned. "Okay. When he's washed up, I get it, so what?"

The telephone began to ring shrilly. Myra got up and answered it. Dillon saw her suddenly stiffen. She said, "Sure he's here." She turned round. "Roxy wants you quick," she said. "Something gone wrong."

Dillon scowled, but he got up fast and took the receiver out of her hand. "Yeah, what is it?" he snapped.

Roxy said, "Listen, Bud. Vessi's blown the gaff. He's tipped Little Ernie off about tonight. You gotta get out fast. They're after you with rods."

Dillon went a dirty white. "After me?" he said, his voice rising. "What do you mean, they're after me?"

"Sweet grief," Roxy raved at the other end, "don't stand there yappin'. Get out quick. They've taken two cars and are on their way right now."

"Sure, I'll scram," Dillon said evenly. "Listen. Come on over, with a fast car. I ain't gotta car here. I'll meet you at the corner."

Roxy said, "I'll do that."

Dillon slammed down the receiver and swung round. His face was twisted with fury. "Come on," he said, "we gotta get out of here quick."

Myra sprang to the cupboard and snatched out a dress. Tearing the wrap off, she pulled the dress over her head. She put on a pair of shoes. She was dressed under thirty seconds. Her eyes were like two glittering pebbles.

"The Thompson," she said.

Dillon ran into the other room. As soon as he had gone, she hurriedly returned to the cupboard and took from an inside pocket of a coat hanging there a roll of money. She hastily slipped it into her bag, looking over her shoulder while she did so.

Dillon returned, carrying the riot gun. He went over to the door and opened it, looking into the dark passage. Then he jerked his head at her and walked out.

Myra heard a car draw up with a squeal of brakes. She ran over to the window and peered round the blind. Four men came bundling out of the car and ran across the pavement into the house.

She shouted to Dillon: "Come back... quick... they're here!"

Dillon slipped into the room again, and shut the door. He turned the key. For a moment he stood hesitating, then went over to the cupboard. "Give me a hand," he said. "Get this across the door."

They jerked and pulled the cupboard into position. Heavy footsteps came thudding down the passage and someone knocked on the door.

Dillon raised his hand to Myra. They stood looking at the cupboard, waiting.

Myra suddenly spun round and ran to the telephone. She hastily dialled. Dillon made as if to stop her, then shrugged.

The desk sergeant at the other end of the line listened to her incoherent whispering. "You're nuts," he said at last. "Things don't happen like that in this city. Take a pill… that's what you want." As he hung up, she heard him say, "Ernie's goin' for 'em now."

Myra dropped the receiver into its cradle. She turned round to Dillon, her eyes wide with fear. "It's a frame-up," she said jerkily. "The cops won't come."

A sneer went over Dillon's face. "Yeah?" he said. "I don't want the bulls to pull me outta this."

Again someone knocked on the door.

Dillon said softly, "Out the back way."

Quietly they left the room and went through the kitchen. The back door led down a long flight of steps to a dark alley. Dillon went first, holding the Thompson close to his side. Myra followed him. They went down the stairs slowly, watching the door at the bottom. Myra expected it to fly open any moment, and she felt her body cringing.

They got to the bottom without anything happening. Dillon snapped off the light before opening the door. He put his hand on her arm. "Get down flat," he said.

Myra crouched on the floor. Dillon knelt, reaching for the door-handle. His hand was steady as he quietly turned it. The door came towards him very slowly. As the aperture widened he sank lower on the floor. Outside was black. It was just as if a heavy curtain hung in front of him. There was not a sound.

At last he got the door wide open. Faintly, he could hear them smashing the door down upstairs. He touched Myra's arm, and they began to crawl forward. Without warning a gun exploded above him. He heard the bullet smack against the wall, and the faint sound of the plaster as it ran down.

Raising the Thompson, he suddenly opened fire, sweeping the gun round in a half-circle. Above the roar of the gun he heard a strangled cry. He stopped firing and crawled on. The damp pavement touched his outstretched hand. Faintly, now that he was outside, the reflected lights of the city glowed over the high wall. The alley was still dark, but he could see a little. Drawing his breath sharply between his teeth, he stood up slowly, keeping the Thompson ready.

Nothing happened. Myra stood up, her heart pounding, and came close to him. They began to walk slowly down the alley. Almost immediately Dillon stumbled over a body. He didn't take his eyes off the exit to the alley. He carefully stepped over, raising his feet and feeling before he put his weight on them again. He kept on. The open street ahead of him, the deep shadows, and the knowledge that somewhere death was waiting for him made his nerves tingle. He told himself if Roxy wasn't there he was sunk.

Myra said in little gasps, "Watch out... for Pete's sake watch out!"

Dillon said nothing. He went on, getting slower as the end of the alley crept towards him. When he was a few yards from the street he went down on his hands and knees.

Myra's nerve cracked. She leant against the wall, letting him go on ahead. She was ready to spring after him if nothing happened, but she could go no farther until she knew.

Quite suddenly two men sprang into the alley. Dillon could see them outlined against a street light. He started firing before his brain telegraphed to his hand. One of the men tossed up his hands and fell forward, but the other ducked out of sight.

Swearing softly, Dillon dived forward into the street. Excitement sent caution overboard. A gun exploded in his face, and he felt a little hiss of air as the bullet went past. He swept the gun round in an arc, firing wildly. The hideous roar echoed through the deserted street. The man who had fired at him was caught in the blast of lead. He crumpled up, lying with his head in the gutter.

Dillon saw a big closed car shoot over from the other side of the street. As he jerked the gun up, Roxy screamed his name, waving his hand frantically. He nailed the car just where Dillon stood. Myra sprang out of the darkness and scrambled in. Dillon got in as Roxy released the clutch with a bang. The car shot down the road. Behind them they heard a burst of gunfire. A bullet coming through the rear window smashed the windscreen.

Myra crouched on the floor, her head between her hands.

Dillon snapped, "Get into a side road... quick!"

Roxy shoved the pedal down to the boards, holding the car to the road. As a turning loomed up, he threw out the clutch, slammed on his brakes and swung the wheel over. The big car went into a skid, lurched up against the curb and righted itself as Roxy released the brake.

"We've done it!" he said excitedly, as the car pounded down the road. "We've beaten 'em to it!"

"All right, all right," Dillon said.

They had been driving furiously for a short time. Roxy glanced at him and eased the pressure on the pedal.

"Stop her," Dillon snarled. "Where do you think you're rushin' to?"

Roxy drew to the side of the road. "We gotta get outta town," he said nervously.

"Wait a minute... wait a minute." Dillon shifted the Thompson off his knees on to the floorboards. "Now what is all this? Come on, spill it.... What is this riot?"

Roxy started to splutter, saw the hard gleam in Dillon's eyes and stopped. Then he took hold of himself and said, "Vessi ratted. You shook his nerve rubbin' Hurst. Somehow he didn't see you bein' boss long, so he runs to Ernie. McGowan didn't like the set-up, but he came along and blew it to me. I went after Vessi an' got him to talk. He said Ernie wasn't wasting time. He tipped the cops that you had knocked Hurst off, and then sent his boys after you."

Dillon said, "Vessi?" There was a lot of hate in his voice.

"I took care of Vessi." Roxy sounded satisfied. "He won't worry about his dinner any more."

Myra said from the back, "Get goin'... that smashed windscreen'll make the bulls curious."

"Shut your trap!" Dillon said, without looking round; then to Roxy, "You know where Ernie hangs out?"

"Sure.... You ain't...?" Roxy twisted his body round in the car. His eyes suddenly widened with surprise.

"No yellow heel's runnin' me out of this burg," Dillon said between his teeth. "I guess we'll go an' call on that guy."

"Don't... no... don't be crazy." Myra struggled up from the floor. Her hands resting on the back of the seat, she again said, "No... no...."

Dillon shifted round and hit her with his open hand across her face, sending her back into the darkness with a crash. "I'll settle with you in a little while," he said. "Get goin'," to Roxy.

Roxy hesitated, then he started the engine. Swinging the car round, he headed back to the East side.

Dillon picked up the Thompson and examined it carefully, then he laid it down. "I guess this gun's too big for the job," he said thoughtfully.

Roxy said uneasily, "You'll never get in with that."

Dillon pulled his .45 from its holster and made sure that it was ready for use. He shoved it away again, and relaxed, watching the dark road. At the back, Myra sobbed quietly, now completely terrified.

Roxy said at last, "It's down on the left. I'll drive past it."

They went slower. Dillon kept well back in the darkness of the car.

"See? By that light. That's the joint."

As the car went past, Dillon looked the house over. Bright lights gleamed in most of the windows. It was big.

Dillon said, "Seems like there's goin' to be plenty of company."

Roxy didn't say anything. He was scared.

"Okay. Stop her over the way. We'll go an' look at the place."

Roxy ran the car into the shadows and switched off the engine. Dillon opened the door and got on to the street, looking cautiously up and down. The street was empty. Roxy came and stood at his elbow.

"You stay here," Dillon said to Myra. "Get in the drivin' seat an' wait till we come. You gotta be ready to get goin' quick."

Myra got out of the car and climbed into the driving-seat. She sat there, hunched up over the wheel, silent.

Dillon leant into the car, his face quite close to hers. "Watch yourself, sister," he said softly. "You try to pull a quick one on me an' you're goin' to have a bad time... get it?"

"It'll be all right," she said.

"Sure it'll be all right," Dillon said, and he jerked his head to Roxy. They walked slowly down the street, keeping on the opposite side of Ernie's place.

"We'll go round the back," Dillon said. "Maybe he's got a fire-escape or somethin'."

Roxy nodded. He was feeling bad.

At the end of the street they crossed over and cut down an alley. They came down along the back of the buildings. Dillon counted each building carefully; then he stopped. "This is it," he said.

They stood in the darkness and stared up. Dimly they could see a fire-escape straggling up into the darkness.

Dillon moved forward cautiously. He could see the swing-up several feet above his head.

"If I give you a back, you can reach it," he said to Roxy. Roxy came forward reluctantly. "You're goin' to start somethin' in this joint," he said uneasily.

"Yeah!" Dillon leant against the wall. "You're right I am." Roxy put his small shoe in Dillon's hands and Dillon hoisted him up. The swing-up came within reach of Roxy's fingers. He pulled gently, bringing the escape down slowly. It made no noise.

Dillon began to walk up the escape quietly. Roxy followed him. Dillon peered into each window as he passed. Three rooms were in darkness, but on the fourth landing of the escape there was a blaze of light. Dillon shifted his gun from its holster and moved forward more slowly. Roxy stayed between the landings, waiting.

Dillon edged his way closer to the window and glanced in. There were a number of people in the room. Dillon's eyes fixed on a small apeish-looking man who was sitting in a big overstuffed chair in the centre of the room. He guessed that must be Ernie. He raised his hand and beckoned to Roxy.

Although the evening was close, the window was shut. Dillon could hear the buzz of talking faintly through the glass, and now and then the shrill high-pitched laugh of one of the women came to him with startling clearness.

Roxy crawled up on hands and knees. Dillon said, keeping his head close to Roxy's, "That Ernie, the little mug sitting there?"

Roxy took a quick look into the room and nodded. "Yeah," he mumbled, "that's him."

Dillon watched the scene in the room thoughtfully. He fingered his gun, but he knew it would get him nowhere if he did start shooting. He had got to go down four flights of escape, and by that time he'd be as dead as a pork chop.

One of the women, a tall, brittle blonde, was making a big play at Ernie. She was holding a long glass full of Scotch, and by the way she giggled and swayed, Dillon guessed she was getting plastered fast.

Ernie was watching her under his hooded eyes. His face was expressionless, but his little black eyes never left her.

Dillon thought: In a moment or so something will blow up there.

Someone started a gramophone and faintly Dillon could hear the rhythmic pulse of the music. The blonde began to swing it. She stood in the middle of the room swaying her hips at Ernie, the others grouped round the walls, clapping their hands and shouting to her. She stamped round the room, contorting her body and snapping her fingers in time with the rhythm.

Ernie sat like a stuffed monkey, his eyes gleaming a little brighter. She lifted her long skirts to her knees and pulled off a pretty fair high kick. Ernie took his hand out of his lap and scratched the side of his face. He got out of the chair and she swayed over to him, wrapping her long arms round his neck.

Dillon thought they looked bad. She was a head taller than Ernie, and with her back turned to the window, Ernie disappeared from sight.

The others in the room watched with interest. One or two of the other women giggled, but they didn't get smart. Dillon reckoned that Ernie wouldn't stand for much, and he was right.

Maybe Ernie was a little guy, but he was right in the right places. He took the blonde by the arm and shoved her out of the room. The door closed behind them.

Dillon cursed softly. He turned his head and looked at Roxy. "Now what?" he said through his teeth. "Where the hell's that guy gone to?"

Roxy shrugged. He felt relieved. "I guess he's got a date with that dame," he said thoughtfully. "Maybe we'd better take it on the lam."

"I'm goin' to get that guy if I have to stay here all night," Dillon returned. "Shut up, an' let me do the talkin'."

Roxy relapsed into gloomy silence. He glanced down into the dark street, but he couldn't see anything. Dillon suddenly clutched his arm. Roxy turned his head quickly. A light had sprung up on the next landing.

"They've gone up there," Dillon said. "Ain't that a break?"

Without waiting for Roxy to say anything, he climbed up on to the next landing.

The blonde was sitting on the bed trying to take off her dress. She was so drunk that she couldn't quite make it. She sat there struggling and giggling. Little Ernie was not in the room. Dillon could see a light coming from a half-open door leading off the room, and he guessed he was in there.

The blonde got to her feet and lurched through the door, leaving the room empty. Dillon put his fingers under the window-frame and quietly lifted the window. He had a little struggle, but he managed it. The window slid back without any noise.

Roxy came up, a gun in his hand. His eyes were popping out of his head.

Dillon said quietly, "Stay here. If there's any trouble, shoot."

He put a leg over the window-sill and slid into the room. He stood listening in the middle of the room, his gun held by his side. Faintly he could hear the two in the other room. They were not talking, but he could hear the blonde giggle and Ernie's grunts. He stepped quietly to the door and looked in.

Little Ernie was dressed in a salmon-pink dressing gown. He was standing with his back to the door. The blonde had got rid of her dress and she was facing Dillon. She was wearing a cloudy piece of chiffon that didn't cover her much. She saw Dillon standing in the doorway and she stiffened. The liquor died on her, leaving her sober and terrified.

Dillon said, "Don't move, you two. I'm itching to blast you."

Little Ernie didn't bat an eyelid. Dillon had to hand it to him. He just stood looking inquiringly at the blonde. She folded her hands across her breasts and moaned softly.

Dillon moved into the room, stiff-legged, like a cat about to fight. He circled slowly round until he was behind the blonde, facing Ernie.

"I guess you didn't expect to see me?" he said evenly. Little Ernie licked his lips. His small monkey-like face turned a little green.

"I'm the guy you tried to rub out tonight," Dillon said. "I guess this burg's too small for both of us. I guess you're comin' for a ride, Ernie... a one-way ride."

Ernie said, "Don't be a fool. You an' me can do things together in a big way." His voice was thick, as if he'd a clot in his throat.

Dillon sneered. "Yeah?" He shook his head. "You're too late on that stuff, Ernie.... It's curtains for you." While he was speaking, he shifted his gun a little, so that he held it by its barrel. Then with a quick savage swing, he struck the blonde behind her ear with the butt of the gun.

She went down like an inanimate doll. Dillon had Ernie covered in one movement.

Ernie looked down at the blonde and shook his head. "That was a lousy one to pull," he said.

Dillon said, "Get goin'… you an' me are goin' for a ride."

Ernie looked at him, hesitated, then he turned and walked into the other room. He paused then. "I guess you'll let me dress?" he said.

Dillon said, "Get outta the window… quick." He rammed the gun into Ernie's back.

Ernie climbed out of the window. He started back against Dillon when he saw Roxy. Dillon shoved him forward roughly. "Get goin'," he said.

Roxy stood aside. Ernie began to move to the stairs. Dillon quietly slipped the gun into its holster and bent down quickly. He caught Ernie by his ankles and with a great heave threw the little man over the rail. It was done so quickly that Roxy couldn't believe his eyes. Ernie was there one second and vanished the next.

Just one terrified squeal sounded in their ears, then a heavy dull thud as Ernie hit the flags down below.

Dillon gripped Roxy's arm. "Get goin'," he said viciously. "We gotta get out of this quick."

They pelted down the escape and blundered into the dark alley. Dillon didn't pause to look at Ernie, but ran on to the street.

Myra started the engine as she heard them coming. Dillon swung himself on the running-board. "It's okay," he said. "You get into the back. Roxy can drive."

She clambered over the seat and Roxy got in under the wheel. His teeth were chattering, but he managed to engage the gear.

Myra said, "Did you get him?"

"What do you think?"

Roxy said, "There's a guy in Springdale who'll hide us up until this blows over."

"Yeah?" Dillon said. "That's a good idea. You know this bird?"

"Sure…." Roxy spun the wheel at Twenty-third Street and headed the car up Kansas Avenue Bridge. "I know him all right. He's safe and they won't look for us there."

They shot across the bridge fast. Suddenly Myra leant forward violently and gripped Roxy's shoulder. "Stop!… stop!… stop!" she screamed.

Roxy was so startled he nearly piled the car into a wall. He crammed on his brakes, throwing Dillon forward. "What the hell's wrong?" he demanded.

Myra's face was livid in the street light. "Quick… where did you get this car?" she gasped.

Roxy twisted and looked at Dillon. "She gone nuts?" he asked angrily. "Jeeze, I nearly crashed this heap."

Dillon didn't like the look on Myra's face. He demanded harshly, "What is it?"

"Where did you get this car?" Myra repeated, pounding Roxy's arm with her fist.

"Where do you think I got it?" Roxy said surlily. "I knocked it off."

Myra turned wildly to Dillon. "The fool's finished us," she shouted. "Can't you see... we've taken this heap over the State line!"

Dillon suddenly turned on Roxy, his fist clenched above his head. "You punk!" he snarled. "You've got the Feds on to us."

Roxy stiffened. "Hell! You'll have a crowd round us. What do you mean... got the Feds on us?"

Dillon said furiously, "It's a Federal offense to take a stolen car over the State line.... Didn't you know that, you crazy fool?"

Roxy engaged his gear. His face had gone the colour of putty. "They'll hang Hurst on to us now," he said unsteadily. "They're sure goin' to get us now."

Myra said, "Get on... get on... quick!... We gotta get under cover."

The big car quickened. Dillon said, "When that heel Strawn hears about this, he'll come arunnin'."

Myra said between her teeth. "See what you've done, you lug." She beat her fists on her knees. "We had it all an' you must get smart. I'm finished with you, do you understand?... I'm washed up. We're through."

Dillon said, "You're through when I say so, an' not before. You know too much, an' what's more, Strawn will pin somethin' on to you... don't you think he won't."

Roxy called, "We gotta switch cars... this broken screen'll stop us. I'm goin' on a bit further, then we'll have to walk."

They drove on in silence. The night was very dark. There was no moon, and heavy threatening clouds hung low. Once in the open, the big beams of the car lit up the dirt road and they lurched and jolted as Roxy tried to keep up speed.

Dillon said in an undertone to Myra, "You got any dough?"

She said quickly, "What you think? I came away in a rush." She put her hand cautiously on her bag that hung on her wrist. Dillon leant forward and ripped the bag from her. For a moment she hesitated, then she flung herself forward. Dillon was expecting her to start something, and he swung a backhand, knocking her into the corner of the car. "Cut it out!" he said viciously. "You ain't got no dough, so what you gettin' sore about?"

He put his hand inside the bag and felt the big roll of money. He grinned to himself in the dark. Taking the roll out, he transferred it to his own pocket. He tossed the bag into her lap.

She said feverishly, "Give me that dough."

Dillon said, "Be careful." There was such an ugly threat in his voice that she shivered.

Roxy slowed down. "Springdale's just ahead," he said. "I guess we'll ditch this heap an' walk."

He ran the car off the road and stopped. The three climbed out. Dillon said, "I'll look good carrying this Thompson."

Roxy said, "Suppose you wrap it in your coat?"

Dillon took off his coat and did as Roxy suggested. They began to walk down the dark road. Round the bend they could see lights.

Roxy said, "This guy we're goin' to has big ideas. You'll have to pay him plenty."

Dillon said coldly, "We'll see about that."

They walked some way, Myra between the two men. Her mind was busy as she stumbled along the dirt road, not seeing where she was going. Dillon had got her money; without that she couldn't leave him. The Feds wouldn't stop until they got Dillon. Especially a guy like Strawn, who was just laying for him. Somehow or other she had got to get the money away from Dillon and get out quick, before anything happened. The Feds hadn't the same ideas as the cops when handling a woman.

"That's it," Roxy said suddenly.

Just ahead of them they could see the outline of a building. One solitary light gleamed through the window.

They hastened their lagging steps. Roxy said, "We'll go in the back, quiet."

They left the road and worked their way to the back of the building. It was so dark Myra kept stumbling, but the two men didn't offer to help her. She gritted her teeth furiously. She was on her own against these two, but she wasn't scared. She had plenty of confidence in herself.

Roxy rapped on the door with his knuckles. After a short wait the door opened. A tall, thin form of a man peered at them.

"That you, Joe?" Roxy said. "Gee! Joe, it's nice to see you. These are a couple of friends of mine.... Can we come in?"

The man stood aside. "Sure," he said, without enthusiasm, "come on in."

They entered a small, poorly furnished room, lit by an oil lamp. Roxy said, "This is Joe Chester, the guy I told you about."

Joe had a thin skull-like face, and his big yellow teeth stuck out, giving him a foxy look. He glanced at the three furtively, rubbing his hands on the seat of his trousers. "I guess I'm glad to know you," he said.

Dillon grunted. He glanced at Roxy and jerked his head.

Roxy said, "Listen, Joe. We wantta lie up here for a little while. Can you fix it? You know how it is."

Joe said, "I'll get a drink. I guess we can talk better with a drink."

He went out of the room.

Dillon said, "I don't like that guy."

Roxy shrugged. "He's okay. He'll fix us, you see."

Joe came back with a bottle and glasses. He put them on the table. The others sat down. Myra sat away from them by the window. She glanced out into the dark night from time to time.

When the drinks were fixed, Joe said, "How long?"

"Maybe a couple of weeks, not more," Roxy said.

"It'll cost you a grand a week," Joe said, sniffing at his whisky.

Dillon moved jerkily, but Roxy put out his hand. "Wait a minute," he said.

Dillon shook his hand off. "This guy ain't goin' to start skinning me," he snarled. "A grand? You're crazy!"

An oily smile went over Joe's face. "It came over the radio ten minutes ago," he said softly. "You three are wanted by the Department of Justice for pinching a car, and the State police are after you for the murder of Hurst."

There was dead silence in the room. Myra ran her fingers through her hair. She shot a look of hatred at Dillon, but she said nothing. He started it and it was up to him to see it through.

Dillon stood up. "So what?" he said.

Joe spread his dirty hands on the table. He nodded his head. "You three are hot. You're too damned hot. I know Roxy.... I'm a friend of his, so I take risks, but I guess I gotta get well paid for takin' em."

Dillon wandered over to Joe. "You'll get well paid, but you ain't gettin' a grand a week. You'll take five hundred bucks an' like it, get it?"

Joe shook his head. "That ain't any use to me, mister..." he began.

Dillon reached out and gripped Joe's shirt. "Listen, punk," he snarled. "I'm booked to sit on the end of a stream of hot juice—one more guy to get knocked off don't help me, anyway, see?"

Joe turned a dirty white. "You're the boss, mister," he said hoarsely. "My ma'll look after you. We gotta farm in the hills. Roxy knows it. They won't find you there."

Dillon took his hand away and glanced at Roxy, who nodded him. "Sure," Roxy said, "it's a good place."

"We want another car," Dillon said.

Joe said, "I'll sell you mine. It's old, but, by heck, it goes all right!"

Dillon turned his back so that Joe couldn't see the size of his roll. He pulled off some bills and put the rest in his pocket. "I'll give you twelve hundred bucks. That's for the car an' two weeks' rent."

Joe took the money and counted it carefully. He couldn't keep the pleasure off his face. He just gloated at the sight of so much dough.

Dillon walked over to him. His face was hard. "Listen, bozo," he said. "Get the car an' get some drink on board. I want a pile of grub too. That comes outta the dough I've just slipped you."

Joe looked at him and cringed a little. "Sure," he said; "I'm glad to help you folks."

When he had gone out, Dillon said to Roxy, "You think you're smart? Pushin' me on to a chiseller like that."

Roxy didn't say anything. He just shrugged. They stood there waiting.

Joe came back. "The car's ready," he said. "You've got plenty of gas. I've put in the things you want."

Dillon said, "Can you find this dump, Roxy?"

"Sure, I know where it is."

"Well, come on, can't you? We ain't got all night to hang about."

Joe saw them to the door. "I'll be over in a few days. I'll let you know how things go."

Dillon grunted and got in the back of the car with Myra. Roxy took the wheel. The car shot off into the night.

Roxy kept the pedal down. The car tore down the rough road, jolting them violently.

"This place far?" Dillon shouted to him.

Roxy shook his head; then remembering that Dillon couldn't see him, shouted, "No. It'll take us about a couple of hours."

They drove on in silence after that. The car jolted on and on, its beams lighting the rough road, making the potholes look like craters.

Myra raised her head suddenly. She put her arm on Dillon's arm. He had been cat-napping and jerked up. "What the hell?" he growled.

"Listen," she said.

He thought he could hear something above the roar of the old engine, but he wasn't sure. He jerked round and looked through the rear window. In the distance he saw a single beam of light, jerking behind them.

He listened again and faintly he heard the wail of a siren. Instantly his mind came alive.

"There's a cop behind us," he snapped to Roxy.

Roxy was so startled that he nearly ran off the road. The flickering light was coming up fast.

"Shove her along," Dillon snarled. "He's comin' up like hell." Roxy pressed the pedal down hard, and the car drew away a little. That seemed to get the cop. They could hear the roar of his engine as he forced his machine forward. The siren screamed in their ears.

Dillon jerked out his gun and smashed the rear window. "Not yet... don't shoot yet!" Myra cried.

Dillon took no notice. He fired twice at the light, but the jolting of the car spoilt his aim. The cop swerved a little, but kept on. Dillon flung the gun down on the seat and groped for the Thompson. "I'll settle this punk," he said viciously, jabbing the nose of the Thompson through the broken window.

Just as he was squeezing the trigger the cop started firing. He fired four times, and each time the bullet smacked into the back of the car.

Dillon dug the butt of the gun into his shoulder and fired back, sweeping the gun in a half-circle. He kept the barrel down. The light of the pursuing machine went out.

"I got him!" he shouted to Roxy. "Get on... he's finished."

He put the gun down and sank on to the seat. "I guess we're gettin' a little hot," he said.

Something touched him and he jerked away. Something hot and sticky was on his hand. For a startled moment he thought he had been hurt, then he knew he couldn't have been. He peered into the darkness.

Myra was lying back in the corner of the car.

"What is it?" he said. "You hurt?"

She gave a sudden cough.

Dillon said to Roxy, "Stop... she's been nicked."

Roxy hesitated. "Anyone behind?" he asked.

Dillon looked back, then he said, "No... stop now."

Roxy pulled up and turned the spotlight round, switching on the beam. They both looked at Myra. She was huddled up. Her hand was pressed to her right side. Dillon could see the blood oozing through her fingers.

He swore softly. "You hurt bad?" he said.

She raised her head slowly. Her mouth was screwed up and he could see the marks of her teeth on her lip, where she had bitten the pain silent. The glaring light made her look ghastly. Her hair had gone limp and beads of sweat made her look as if she had just come out of rain.

Roxy leant well forward, gaping at her. "We gotta get a doctor to her," he said. "She looks bad."

Dillon looked at him hard. "Sure she looks bad," he said slowly. "Yeah, we better get a doctor."

Roxy swung round and started the engine. Dillon put his hand on his shoulder. "Wait," he said. "We can't drive into a town with her like that.... It would start something. I'll stay here an' look after her." He put a lot of meaning in the last words.

Roxy started to argue, but a look that had come into Dillon's eyes stopped him. "Okay," he said huskily.

He reached forward and turned off the engine, then he opened the door and got into the road. Dillon said under his breath, "I'll sound the horn."

Myra raised her head. "Roxy... where... are... you... goin'?"

Roxy said, "I'm gettin' a croaker... you'll be okay... just you stay quiet."

A sudden wave of panic swept over Myra. "Roxy... don't leave me... don't leave me... with him!"

Roxy was already walking quickly down the dark road, his shoulders arched as if he expected a violent blow.

Dillon reached up and shoved the light out of her eyes. "You're goin' to be okay now," he said.

Myra crouched back against the seat. "Give me a break," she implored him. "I know what... you're goin' to... to do. Don't... please—"

Dillon leant forward. "You nuts or somethin'?" he said. His face was glistening. Two deep lines ran from his nose to the corners of his mouth. "What you squawkin' about?"

"You wouldn't... treat... me like a dog?" she gasped.

Dillon threw off pretence. "You didn't give Fan a chance, did you?" he snarled. "You burnt her, didn't you, you little heel? You took all that dough an' I wasn't to see any of it. You know too much, sister—"

"Look, I'm bleedin'.... It hurts so... don't hurt me any more." She took her hand from her side and tried to reach him. He shied away from her blood-encrusted fingers. Quietly he groped for his gun. His fingers closed on the cold barrel. He got a grip and drew it off the seat, holding it behind his back.

"Sure I'll give you a break," he said, grinning at her.

She was dazed with the pain and loss of blood. She could only see his outline bending over her, and his words came to her faintly. She began to cough again, and a sudden rush of blood to her mouth terrified her.

"I'm scared..." she whimpered. "I'm scared...."

Dillon brought his hand from behind his back. His arm flashed up and then down. He hit her on the top of her head with the gun-butt with all his strength. In the silence of the night he heard her skull crack. Blood came out of her mouth again as she fell forward.

Dillon scrambled out of the car. He ran round to the other side and opened the door. Then, cautiously, he fumbled for her in the dark. His hand touched her head and he drew back, catching his breath a little. His hands were slippery with her blood.

He stood there, glaring at her dim outline, suddenly frightened to touch her. In a fit of insane panic he began to beat her head and shoulders with the gun-butt. At last he stopped and stood panting, his chest heaving and his mouth slack. Her two legs hung from the car door. The rest of her was hidden in darkness. Moving forward slowly he reached down and wiped his hands on her stockings. He did it in little jerks, as if he expected the legs to come to life.

The moon suddenly swung above the clouds, lighting the road. Roxy sat on the grass farther up the road, his head in his hands. He swore continuously, refusing to let his brain dwell on what was going on. Two short blasts from the horn of the car made him get unsteadily to his feet.

Ma Chester was a small, mean-looking woman, with hard eyes and a thin pinched mouth. She stood on the stoop of the farmhouse and looked down on them. Round her waist was a piece of sacking that did for an apron. Her gnarled hands were folded across her withered breasts and Dillon could see her black broken nails clawing at the cotton stuff of her dress.

The farmhouse was well hidden in the hills. It was several miles from the main road, and stood entirely alone. It was well off the beaten track.

The sun was just up. Dillon and Roxy had spent the night in the woods, fearing to call at the farmhouse at night. They were both tired and irritable. Dillon's nerves seemed to stand outside his body, so that the slightest movement or sound jarred him.

Roxy handled Ma Chester. She seemed to know all about it. Joe had got her on the telephone.

She said, "I guess you two want to see your room."

They followed her into the farmhouse. There was a smell of dirt and cooking in the place. Dillon twitched his nose a little.

The main living-room was bare and dirty. An old man who looked old enough to be Ma Chester's father sat in a small rocker in front of the kitchen stove. In spite of the growing heat from the sun, he seemed to be cold, shivering every now and then. He was bald, unshaven and rheumy. He didn't bother to look up as they came in.

Ma Chester led them through to a door at the far end. The room would have shamed an Eastside tenement. Dillon looked round, his face showing his disgust.

"I'll bring you some breakfast," the old woman said. She said it as if she expected a refusal.

Dillon said, "Yeah, and make it a big one."

When she had gone, pulling the door behind her, Dillon wandered round the room. "A thousand bucks for this!" he said. "I'll wring that chiseller's neck."

Roxy sat on the bed gingerly. "They'll never find us here," he said. "I bet Joe won't turn in much dough to the old girl. He'll keep it for himself."

Dillon went over to the window and looked out. Roxy watched him cautiously. Roxy was scared of Dillon. The horror of last night was still with him. Sitting there on the bed, he could relive everything he had done. They had found a big gravel dump off the road and had shoved her body into it, pulling the gravel down on top of her. Roxy shivered a little. Maybe they wouldn't find her for weeks, maybe they'd find her tomorrow.

Dillon said, "Snap out of it!"

Roxy jerked up his head. Dillon had turned and was watching him. "That broad never was no good," Dillon said. "She had it comin' for a long time. What could we do with her? If we'd left her, she'd've squawked. I know."

"Sure, sure," Roxy said hastily, "we'll forget it."

Dillon said in a threatening voice, "You better."

Just then Ma Chester put her head round the door. "You can eat now," she said.

The two men wandered into the other room. The table was covered with a soiled newspaper. Old man Chester was already eating. Dillon looked at him with disgust. The old man glanced up and grunted. Ma Chester said, "Don't take any notice of him... he's deaf."

Dillon jerked a chair out and sat down. The food was poor and coarse.

Roxy said, "You gotta radio here?"

Ma Chester stood over the stove, watching the coffee. She shook her head. "Nope," she said. "We ain't got a radio."

Dillon cut the salty ham angrily. "I thought every farm had a radio," he said.

"Well, we ain't," Ma Chester snapped. "We're poor, see?"

"You're tellin' me," Dillon snarled.

The shack door opened and a girl came in. Both Roxy and Dillon stopped eating and stared at her. She was big. Her straw-coloured hair hung down to her shoulders. Her dirty cotton dress barely concealed her over-ripe figure. She was as tall as Dillon, with big hands and feet. Her features were regular and good, but the expression on her face and in her eyes was that of a child of seven.

She stood there shifting her feet, looking with scared eyes at the two at the table.

Ma Chester said, "Sit down, Chrissie; these two gentlemen ain't goin' to worry you."

There was a long awkward silence as she shuffled over to the table and sat down. Then with a burst of confidence she said, "Did you come in that big car?"

Dillon glanced over at Roxy. Roxy said, "Yeah, that's right."

Chrissie smiled timidly. "We ain't got a car," she said, reaching out a large hand for some bread. "Can I go for a ride?"

Ma Chester snapped, "Don't you worry these gentlemen. You get on an' eat."

Chrissie began to bolt her food. She had an enamel mug of milk by her plate, and when she drank Dillon could see the milk running down her chin on to the front of her dress. He was suddenly aware of a sour smell coming from her; the same sort of smell small children have if they're not looked after. He felt a little sick and pushed his plate away. Then, muttering something, he got up.

Ma Chester said, "Here's the coffee." She banged a pot on the table. Dillon reached out and poured himself a cup and took it to the window. When Ma Chester went back to the stove Chrissie leant forward and scooped the ham Dillon had left on to her plate.

Roxy laid down his knife. "You're hungry?" he said, for something to say.

She looked at him and gave a pleased little smile. "Yes, I am," she said. "Will you give me a ride, Mister?"

Roxy nodded. "Sure I will."

"You be quiet," Ma Chester said from the stove.

A sudden blank look came over Chrissie's face and she began to mumble. A little saliva ran down her chin. Ma Chester walked over to her and rapped on the top of her head with her knuckles, just like she was rapping on a door. Chrissie pressed her head against the old woman's breast, a look of contentment coming over her bovine face.

Ma Chester said to Roxy, "She's simple, but she's a good girl. There's something wrong with her head. She gets like this sometimes. I rap her nut like this, an' it helps her." The old woman's face had softened while she was speaking, and she looked down at the girl with a rough tenderness that quite altered her face.

Roxy sat there staring with a morbid fascination. "She's quite a big girl, ain't she?" he said at last.

"She's eighteen," Ma Chester told him. "But I guess she's never grown up."

Dillon couldn't stand any more of it. He went outside. The hot sun was fast drying the heavy dew. The ground was steaming a little, and a faint white mist, extending as far as the eye could see, hovered just above the ground. The air smelt good and he was glad to get away from the staleness of the shack.

He walked over to the car and glanced inside. The back seat was stained dark with Myra's blood. He wrinkled his nose a little. This was a hell of a morning.

Over the way he noticed a well, and he went over and drew a bucket of water. Then, finding some rags under the front seat, he began sponging the mess away. He had just got through and had got rid of the water when Roxy came out.

Dillon looked at him. "I'm goin' to go nuts in this dump," he said. "Just wait until that chiseller comes out here... I'll kill him."

Roxy sat on the running-board of the car and lit a cigarette. "Hell," he said. "It's somethin' to be safe, ain't it?"

"That loony gives me the creeps," Dillon muttered, shoving the back seat into place.

"Aw, she's okay…. She's just a kid really…. You look on her as a kid. She ain't goin' to worry you."

Chrissie came out just then. She edged over to them. "You've made the seat all wet," she said, looking into the back of the car. "Why have you done that?"

Dillon turned away. He spat on the ground. As he moved off, Chrissie said, "I don't like him," to Roxy.

Roxy grinned at her. "He's all right," he said. "I guess he's got somethin' on his mind."

Chrissie looked puzzled. "What?" she said. "How do you mean, somethin' on his mind?"

Roxy scratched his head. "You know," he said; "he's worried about something."

"Is that all?" She lost interest. "When are you taking me for a drive, Mister?"

Roxy said "I can't take you now. Maybe tomorrow. But not just now. What do you do with yourself all day?"

She stood looking longingly at the car. "Aw, not much," she said. "I play… I like playing best."

Roxy eyed her over. He thought it was tough for a fine looking broad to be so simple. "Well, let's play at somethin', shall we?" He felt a little embarrassed, but he was sorry for her.

She looked at him as if making up her mind whether he'd be worth playing with. Then she nodded.

Dillon had made a circuit of the shack and was standing watching them. A curious gleam came into his eye. "Take her down to the river," he said. "Get her to swim." He said out of the corner of his mouth, "Get her goin'. She might be worth lookin' at."

Roxy's face went a deep crimson. "You lay off that," he said angrily. "This kid's simple, see? I ain't standin' for any of that stuff."

Dillon stood looking at him, his face sullen. "Aw, go an' play dolls," he sneered. "You give me a pain."

He stood looking after them they wandered away into the woods.

After two days on the farm Dillon was nearly crazy. He was nervous of walking too far from the thick woods. He was sick of sitting inside watching old man Chester, or listening to Ma Chester singing her son's praise.

Roxy, for something better to do, had turned his attention to the farm. Dillon was too lazy to do that. Chrissie followed Roxy about like a dog. She had got over her first shyness and Roxy quite liked her. She was amused at most things he said, which flattered him, and she helped him with the work on the farm.

He was quite startled at her strength. She would think nothing of shifting heavy sacks or logs of wood that made Roxy sweat to move. Under his directions, put in the simplest way, she carried out quite a programme. Sometimes she got bored and began to fool, then Roxy took her off for a walk.

Dillon watched them contemptuously. He made no attempt to join them. Roxy never discussed her when they were alone. Chrissie went to bed around eight o'clock, and Roxy and Dillon played cards monotonously into the night.

It was Sunday, and Dillon was jittery. Joe Chester was coming out, and he'd have news. Cut away from the radio and the newspapers, neither of the men knew what was going on. Even Roxy couldn't get up any enthusiasm to play with Chrissie. He hung around the shack doing odd jobs, his eye on the dirt road.

It was after ten o'clock when Joe turned up. He came bumping along the dirt road in a new car. He looked mighty pleased with himself.

Chrissie was the first to spot him, and she lumbered down the road to meet him. Joe stopped the car and let her get in.

Dillon and Roxy watched them. Dillon said, "We gotta get this punk alone."

Roxy said, "Sure... we'll get him all right."

It was some little time before Joe could get round to them. Ma Chester and Chrissie were all over him. Even old man Chester wakened up and had something to say. By the time Joe shook them off Dillon was in a vile temper.

The three of them walked into the wood and when they were some distance from the shack they sat down on the grass.

Dillon said, "Now come on, for Pete's sake. What's been goin' on?"

Joe gave him a worried look. "I don't like it," he said, wagging his head. "The Feds are raising hell."

"What you mean, raising hell? Got a newspaper with you?"

Joe shook his head. He seemed quite surprised at the idea. "No, I ain't got no newspaper," he said.

Dillon looked at Roxy, his face dark with fury. "What a guy!" he snarled. "Came from town an' ain't got the sense to bring a newspaper."

Even Roxy was put out. "Why, Joe," he said, "I guess that's dumb."

"Dumb?" Dillon snarled. "Why..." he broke off, spluttering.

Joe looked concerned. "If I thought you guys wanted a paper, I'd've brought it."

Dillon nearly struck him. He clenched and unclenched his fists. "Listen, you bohunk," he said at last. "We gotta have a radio up here, see? I gotta know what's goin' on. I'll go nuts in this dump if I don't get some information through."

Joe nodded. "Sure, I'll bring one up when I get round again."

Dillon said, "You'll bring one up right away."

Roxy said hastily, "Well, come on, Joe, what's been happening?"

Joe looked glum again. "The Feds have been in to see me. They've been everywhere. They found the car you ditched not far from my place.... I guess that was a smart thing to do."

Dillon demanded, "Do they know you've got this dump up here?"

Joe shook his head. "Nope," he said. "I guess they don't. Look here, Mister, it ain't goin' to be good for me or my folks if they catch you here."

"What do you think I'm payin' you a thousand bucks for?" Dillon snarled.

"I was comin' to that." Joe shifted his eyes. "I guess I had a bad bit of luck the other day. I lost that dough in a crap game."

Dillon stiffened. "What the blazes has that got to do with me?" he demanded.

Joe picked at the grass, keeping his head turned. "Why, I guess maybe you're right. It ain't got a lot to do with you, but I just told you."

Dillon said, "See here, Chester, I gave you that dough to keep us under cover. If you've lost it, that's too bad, but it ain't our funeral, see?"

Joe shifted the conversation. "Ma tells me you've made a swell job of work with the old fence," he said to Roxy.

Roxy shrugged. "I'd go nuts tryin' to pass the time. I enjoyed doin' it."

Dillon said between his teeth, "Suppose you skip this an' tell me what's been goin' on."

"Sure I'll tell you." Joe leant back on his elbows, raising his skull-like face to the sun. "Well, you know how it is, the newspapers have been playin' the Hurst murder up. The Feds have been lookin' for you. Comin' round asking questions. Huntin' around; you know how it is."

Dillon said, "They don't suspect you?"

Joe shook his head. "Did I tell you they're offering five grand reward for you guys?"

Both Roxy and Dillon stiffened. "Five thousand bucks?" Roxy said unsteadily.

"That's right," Joe said; "I guess they sure want you guys bad."

There was a heavy silence while the two turned it over. Joe went on, "I figger to some people five grand would come very nice."

He got to his feet. "I gotta get back to Ma. She gets mad as hell if I don't hang around when I'm up here. I'll be seein' you boys before I go."

He went away, his long thin legs moving stiffly through the grass.

Roxy said in a low voice, "Did you get it?"

Dillon clenched his fists. "He ain't gettin' another dime outta me," he said. "The double-crossin' rat."

"Listen, Nick, don't do anythin' foolish. If we don't square this guy, he's goin' to squeal. He said as much, didn't he?"

"How do we know they're offerin' a reward?" Dillon raved, "Suppose they ain't lookin' for us an' this is a frame to skin me?"

Roxy shook his head. He was nervous. "I'd hate to call his bluff," he said. "We don't stand much chance if the Feds come up here."

Dillon took his roll of money out of his pocket and thumbed it through. He had two thousand dollars and two fifty notes.

Roxy watched him. "Maybe he'd take the two grand an' call it square."

Dillon's hand shook with fury. "We give him this dough an' he can still turn us in," he said.

Roxy shook his head. "I guess he ain't that low. I know Joe, he wouldn't do that."

Dillon got to his feet. "I do the payin' and save your hide," he snarled. "Ain't you got any dough?"

Roxy looked uncomfortable. "Hell, Bud," he said, "I ain't gotta nickel. I'm in this with you.... Didn't I tip you what was happenin'?"

Dillon shrugged and walked towards the house. Joe saw them coming and came out walking to meet them.

Dillon said slowly, "Listen. This five grand reward comes tough on a guy like you. We wouldn't like you to lose by it."

Joe's eyes glistened. "You got me wrong, Mister," he said hastily. "I ain't hankerin' after the reward. I guess I'm glad to hide you guys up. I only said I'd lost the dough you gave me an' was a bit short."

Dillon's eyes hated him. "We figgered maybe two grand would set you up."

Dillon saw Joe hesitate. He saw the look of doubt in his eyes. He thought: The punk's going to turn it down. He went on hastily: "Two grand can buy plenty."

Joe said, "Sure, it's mighty fine of you guys." His long bony hand came out. Dillon gave him the small roll of notes. Joe counted them, his hand shaking a little. The greed in his eyes scared Roxy.

Dillon watched him. "I expect some work for that," he said, keeping the rage out of his voice with an effort. "Don't go makin' mistakes, will you? We got your ma an' pa up here, Joe."

Joe's eyes opened. "You ain't got nothin' to worry about," he said quickly. "You've fixed me up fine.... The Feds won't bother you if I can help it."

"You'd better see to that," Dillon said viciously.

"Sure, sure," Joe said hastily, "I'll see to that okay." He seemed in a sudden hurry to leave. He ran towards his car and drove off rapidly down the dirt road.

Ma Chester came out and stood on the stoop. Her face had a sly expression as she watched Joe drive away. Chrissie came round the side of the house, calling to Joe loudly. Joe didn't look back.

Chrissie said, "Why's he gone like that? Ain't he comin' back?"

Ma Chester stepped down and went over to her. Roxy heard her say, "Joe's got business on... he'll be along in a little while. You oughtta be mighty proud of your Joe, he's a smart guy."

Her little pebbly eyes mocked the two as they stood watching her uneasily.

Dusk was falling. Dillon sat on the stoop. His eyes were watching the sun sinking behind the trees. He was seriously worried. One hundred bucks was all he had left. One hundred bucks was as useful as a horse's tail.

He got to his feet restlessly. This dump was driving him crazy. He looked around for Roxy, but could see no sign of him in the thickening dusk. It was still very close, and a faint hot breeze fanned his face.

He wandered round the shack, glancing in the windows. He saw Ma Chester busy with a flat-iron. For a moment he stood looking at her, then his eyes shifted to old man Chester hunched up over the stove. Shrugging, he wandered on. The next window was a little higher, and he had to stretch to see in. One look made him stiffen to attention.

Chrissie was moving about in the dim light of a flickering candle, undressing. She pulled her clothes off with difficulty, her fingers fumbling awkwardly with the buttons.

Dillon remained there watching, until she blew the light out. A primitive animal feeling for her gripped him, so that he could only stay there staring into the blackness of the room. The sudden realization that he had been cooped up in this shack for so many days without a woman came upon him with paralysing violence.

He was still standing there peering into the darkness when Roxy found him. Roxy said quietly, "What the hell you doin' here?"

Dillon started round. He looked at Roxy uneasily. "I've been lookin' for you," he said, his mind still far away with his thoughts.

Roxy looked up at Chrissie's window. His face hardened. "You didn't think I was in with the kid?" he said softly.

"Kid?" Dillon sneered. "She ain't no kid... she's a woman."

Roxy stretched out a hand and took Dillon's coat front. "Lay off that, Dillon," he said. "Don't you start anythin' with that girl. She's good an' she's simple.... I won't stand for it."

An overwhelming rage mounted inside Dillon. He flung Roxy's hand away. "Listen, you louse," he said. "You do as I tell you... If I want that broad, I'm havin' her—get it? You ain't stoppin' me, or any heel like you."

Roxy stood very still. "If that's the way you feel..." he said.

Dillon couldn't quite see his face in the light, but he didn't like the threat in Roxy's voice.

He suddenly saw the danger of making an enemy of Roxy and he retreated hastily. "Forget it, will you?" he said surlily. "I guess the heat's worryin' me. I guess I was crazy."

"Sure." Roxy's voice was relieved. "I know how it is. This place gives me the jitters. Suppose we take the heap and get into town?"

Dillon nodded. "We'll take the Thompson. I guess they won't be lookin' for us to drive in." He was eager to get away. "An' say, I guess we can check up on that punk Joe. Maybe we'll hear somethin'."

Roxy said, "Let's go.... We won't tell the old woman."

They walked quickly over to the shed where the car was hidden and quietly pushed her out. Dillon went back to the shack, passed through the room where Ma Chester was working, nodded to her briefly and went into his own room. He picked up the Thompson, then, gently pushing the window up, he climbed out, dropping to the ground. He ran round quickly to where Roxy was waiting with the car.

"I guess we're nuts not to have done this before," Dillon said, sitting beside Roxy. "Suppose we stick up a service station? We want some dough badly enough."

Roxy said, "Sure. Why not?"

They drove on into the night. Dillon sat with the Thompson on his knees, his eyes searching the dark road ahead for the sign of a light. He was nervous, but it felt good to get away from that shack.

After some time Roxy said, "Round the bend is one of those Conoco stations. We'll drive up an' get a tank full.... If there ain't any excitement, we might surprise 'em."

Dillon nodded. "Yeah," he said. "You do that."

Roxy slowed down, and they ran round the bend. The station was about a couple of hundred yards down the road. A big car was just pulling away, heading towards them. Dillon's fingers tightened on the gun, but the car swept past.

An attendant was going back into the office when he spotted their lights. He stopped and stood waiting at the petrol pump.

Roxy drew up beside him. The attendant was a fair-haired youngster, his eyes heavy for want of sleep.

"Give her ten," Roxy said.

Dillon pushed open the door and stepped into the road. The darkness and the shadow of the car hid him. He saw the office was empty.

Roxy said, "Get a move on.... We ain't got all night."

The attendant called "It's in, Mister." He screwed the cap home and came round to Roxy.

Roxy said, "Gotta paper I can look at?" He gave the boy a bill.

"Sure. It's in the office. I'll get it for you."

Roxy opened the door of the car and got out. "I'll come in with you," he said. "I guess I could stretch my legs."

He followed the attendant into the office. Dillon walked quietly behind them and waited just outside the door.

The attendant went to the till and rang the drawer open. Dillon walked in and rammed the Thompson into his back. "Take it easy," he said.

The attendant looked over his shoulder and gasped. He tossed his arms above his head. Roxy stepped past him and emptied the till. There wasn't much there.

"This all there is?" Roxy demanded.

The attendant was utterly terrified. He nodded his head.

'Sure... That's all... Mister... honest, it is."

Roxy grunted. "Like bashin' a kid's money-box," he said.

Dillon took the attendant by the arm and spun him round. He shoved him into a chair. "Know who I am?" he demanded. "I'm Dillon... the guy the cops are after."

The boy's face was blank. "I don't know you, boss," he said with a gulp.

"Didn't you know there's a big reward out for me?"

The boy shook his head.

"Where's that paper?" Dillon snarled.

Roxy had already found it and was looking through it. Finally he tossed it down. "Not a word," he said.

"Didn't I tell you?" Dillon raved. "It was a frame to skin me." He pointed furiously to the door. "Get out!" he shouted to Roxy. "Get in the car an' wait."

Roxy gave him a quick look, then he went out into the darkness and climbed into the car. As he settled himself he heard a sudden terrified scream. He put his hand on the car door, then hesitated. His hand fell to his side.

Dillon came running out. His face was like stone. "Get goin'," he snapped.

"What was that?" Roxy asked uneasily, as he engaged his gears.

"What you think?" Dillon snarled from the darkness. "Think I could let that punk run around and yap his head off?"

Roxy said nothing. He moved a little way away from Dillon. He said at last, "I guess we'd better get back."

"Get back nothin'," Dillon said, his voice gritty. "I'm goin' to see Joe. Keep her goin'."

They reached Joe's place after a long run. The road carried little traffic, and the cars that swept past them didn't bother them.

At Joe's, Dillon got out quickly. "You stay here," he said. "I'll handle this rat. Sound your horn if anythin' starts."

Roxy opened his month to say something, but thought better of it. He sat still, watching the road.

A light still burned in Joe's room. Dillon walked quietly up the path. He tried the door, but it was locked. He rapped on the door with his knuckles. Roxy could hear him from the car. After a pause, Joe came out. He stood in the open doorway, his mouth hanging slack.

Dillon moved the Thompson so he could see it. "Get inside," he said through his teeth.

Joe fell back, his eyes glued to the gun. He couldn't say a word.

Dillon forced him into the room and shut the door. "I'm on to you, you double-crossing jerk," he said. "Hand over that dough."

Joe fumbled in his pocket and brought out the roll. He said in a quavering voice, "You got me wrong.... I know you've got me wrong."

Dillon snatched it from him. "Where's the rest of it?" he demanded. "You know, the thousand you said you lost?"

Joe's eyes widened. "I did lose it," he gasped. "I don't get this... what's it all about... ain't you stayin' at Ma's no more?"

Dillon said, "Give me the rest of the dough or I'll blast you. My finger is itching.... Snap to it!"

The Thompson was pointing at Joe's vest. He gave a strangled gasp. "I'll get it for you, Mister..." he whined. "Don't you shoot... I'll, get it."

He stumbled over to the table and took another roll of notes from the drawer. Dillon made him count it. "I got the car—" Joe began explaining.

Dillon cut him short. "Come on out," he said. "I still got somethin' for you to do. You play ball, an' you'll come outta this okay, but you gotta watch your step."

Joe went with him to the car. Roxy stared, but didn't move. Dillon pushed Joe into the back of the car, then he said to Roxy in a low voice, "Get to the river... quick." He got in beside Joe, and Roxy sent the car shooting forward.

They rode in silence for a mile or so, then Joe said, "Where... where you takin' me?" He was suddenly uneasy.

Dillon looked for Joe's face in the darkness, saw the white outline and swung his fist. Roxy heard the soft spat as his fist crushed into Joe's face. Joe gave a muffled groan and slid forward in his seat. He ducked his head, holding his hands over his nose.

Dillon pulled his arms from his face slowly. He had to exert a little strength. Joe sobbed, "No... no..." Dillon said, "Here it is, you heel!" and swung his hand again.

Roxy slowed down. He peered ahead until he saw the glitter of water in the moonlight, then he stopped the car. "This is it," he said.

Dillon got out of the car. He said to Roxy, "Get him out of there.... I don't want to wash that heap again."

Joe gave a scream. Roxy put his arms round him and half dragged, half pulled him out of the car. Joe couldn't stand. He put his legs down, but they folded up, so that he fell down in the road.

Dillon said, "Move the car up a bit."

Roxy got in the car and moved it forward. Joe lay in the red circle of the tail-lamp. Complete and awful panic seized him.

Dillon shot him with the Thompson. Just one harsh roar of the gun and Joe was nearly cut in two, the slugs, like a steel knife ripped across his chest, killing him instantly.

Dillon said, "We gotta get him into the river."

Roxy leant out of the car. "I don't like touchin' him," he said, "I guess I just hate touchin' that guy."

"Get goin'... We might get company pretty soon." Even Dillon was slow off the mark. He put the Thompson in the car and they both walked slowly to Joe. They got him into the river. Standing on the bank, they watched the water close over him. The current was strong. They could see the rush of water in the moonlight. Joe would be taken care of for a little while.

Dillon reached forward and washed his hands in the river. He wiped them dry on the grass.

"I guess he ain't goin' to talk no more," he said, staring out across the swiftly moving river.

Roxy stood just behind him. In spite of the close night, he felt cold. His eyes were on Dillon's back. He suddenly shivered a little.

The next two days drifted by. Both Roxy and Dillon were on edge. They did not talk about Joe, but he was on their minds all right. On the morning of the third day it came as a little stabbing shock when Ma Chester said during the morning meal, "Joe's comin' out today. He promised to bring me some stores. I guess he'll be along pretty soon." There was a lot of pride in Ma's voice when she said it.

Roxy glanced up and looked across at Dillon. Then he pushed his plate away and got up. "Maybe he'll bring a newspaper," he said with difficulty.

Ma Chester began clearing the table. "If Joe said he'd bring a newspaper, he'll bring a newspaper. Joe is that sort of a guy. I always say you can rely on Joe."

A thin, mirthless smile went over Dillon's face. He followed Roxy out into the open. They wandered away together. "Think the cops'll come on out here?" Roxy said quietly.

Dillon shook his head. "Don't seem like Joe talked about this place.... We gotta keep an eye open, but I guess they won't."

Roxy sat on the side of the well. He lit a cigarette. Dillon could see his hands shaking. "We're takin' an awful risk stayin' here," he said at last.

Dillon put his foot on the edge of the well. "Where else can we go?" he asked irritably.

Roxy shrugged. He didn't know. They remained there some little time discussing things but getting no further, then impatiently Roxy got up. "I guess I'll go an' fix that fence. I'm almost through."

Dillon watched him go. When Roxy had disappeared round the side of the shack Dillon saw Chrissie come out. She stood looking round for Roxy. Dillon kept his eyes off her face, and eyed her over from her neck down. A sudden tightness gripped him across the chest. He wandered slowly over to her, going slow so as not to startle her. She looked at him without interest.

"I'm goin' shootin'," he said when he reached her. "Suppose you come along an' watch."

Her face brightened a little. "I want Roxy," she said. "Where's Roxy?"

Dillon said as patiently as he could, "Roxy's fixin' the old fence somewhere." He took his gun from his holster and pretended to look at it. The gleaming barrel attracted Chrissie's attention. She moved forward, peering at it.

"Some gun, ain't it?" Dillon said, showing it to her. Chrissie had forgotten Roxy. She stood with her head on one side, her eyes longingly fixed on the gun.

"Suppose we go into the woods... you can pop this if you want to," Dillon said thickly.

Chrissie's eyes opened, "Don't it make an awful bang?" she asked.

"Sure, but it won't scare a big girl like you.... Come on an' try it."

He turned and began to move away. Chrissie hesitated. She didn't like Dillon, but the lure of the gun was too much for her. She followed him. "Can I carry it?" she asked pleadingly.

Dillon took the clip out of the gun and jerked the bullet from the chamber. He wasn't having her fool around and shoot him. He said, "Sure you can.... You be careful with it."

She took the gun, holding it gingerly, her big hands nursing it like a doll. "Ain't it heavy?" she said. "I bet Roxy's got a bigger gun than this."

Dillon kept walking. He said, "Roxy ain't got a gun. When you can pop this good, we'll surprise Roxy... that'll be an idea."

Her face brightened. "I'd like that," she said, moving forward at a faster pace. "I'd like to surprise Roxy."

Dillon looked at her. He walked closer to her, the sleeve of his coat touching her arm. He put out his hand and touched her shoulder. The contact sent a little white-hot flame shooting through him. She shied away, her eyes suddenly nervous.

Dillon smiled. His breath whistled through his nose. "We got to get away from the house. They'll hear us shootin' an spoil the surprise," he said.

Her mind switched back to Roxy, and her nerves quietened. Dillon didn't touch her again. The thick woods opened out into a clearing. Dillon stopped. "I guess this'll do," he said.

He sat down on the grass. "Come on down," he said, the pulse in the side of his head pounding. "I'll show you how to fix the gun."

She stood looking at him and Dillon tried to smile at her, but his face only grimaced. The look in his eyes frightened her. She moved back a pace.

Dillon took the clip out of his pocket. He tried to sound casual. "Gimme the gun."

She leant forward, holding the gun out to him but keeping away. There was a tense frightened look on her face which made Dillon think of some timid animal, not sure of itself. He took the gun, his hand touching hers. Again she took a step back.

Dillon slipped the clip in and jerked the lever, bringing a slug into the chamber. He said, "Sit down.... I wantta show you how it works."

She didn't move. Dillon had the impression she was about to run away. He quickly turned from her. "Look over there," he said, pointing across the clearing to a broken branch of a tree. It hung like a withered arm.

"Watch me pot it." When he brought the gun up his hand was shaking. The gun-sight flickered up and down, and he cursed softly. "Don't you get scared with the row," he mumbled. He knew if he didn't start shooting and hold her interest she would go. He could feel the panic that was mounting in her.

The gun cracked. In the stillness of the wood the noise was startling. Chrissie sighed. Although the roar of the gun had made her flinch, she wanted to try.

Dillon said, "I guess I ain't so hot.... I missed it." He tried again, gripping the gun until his hand sweated.

He drew his breath in hard, holding it, then he squeezed the trigger. Again the gun cracked. This time a shower of splinters flew from the branch.

Chrissie clapped her hands. "Oh, it's good!" she said.

Dillon didn't say anything. He fired once more. The branch dropped a little. "Now you have a go," he said, getting slowly to his feet.

Chrissie came up to him, her eyes fixed on the gun. She had forgotten him. Her mind was only for the gun.

He said with difficulty, "You stand here."

She was quite close to him, her face intent and excited. Dillon turned a little sideways, slipping the clip out. He wasn't taking any chances. He put the gun in her hand, then he moved a little behind her.

She stood, her eyes fixed on the branch of the tree.

"You hold the gun like this." He put his hand on her wrist, raising her arm and pointing the gun. Her firm flesh burnt in his hand. He felt a little shudder run' through her, but she was so anxious to fire the gun that she let him hold her.

The blood pounding in his ears, he gripped her round her waist with his other hand. He said thickly, "Don't get scared.... I ain't goin' to hurt you."

The gun slipped out of her hand. It was forgotten immediately. The terrifying, tightening pressure of his hands sent her into a blind panic. She stood trembling, her eyes going wild. She began to mumble.

Dillon snarled, "Stop that row!"

He jerked her close to him. Her weak, idiotic face sickened him, but her womanness got him. He turned her slowly stiffening body and crushed her close to him.

Then suddenly, like a released spring, she was gone from him. Her strength completely staggered him. He had had her gripped tightly, then his arms were powerless against the sudden heaving twist of her body. She sprang away, without looking back; she ran mumbling into the woods.

Dillon made no attempt to follow her. He just stood watching her, a feeling of sick frustration creeping over him. When she had vanished and the last sound of her flight faded away he moved a little uncertainly, as if to pursue her. Then he stopped. Roxy was standing in the clearing, his face white, and his eyes gleaming dangerously.

"I saw you," Roxy said. "You rotten louse."

All Dillon's pent-up fury became centered on Roxy. Here was someone on whom he could wreak his rage. He began sliding across the grass, his eyes gleaming.

Roxy slipped off his coat. He let it fall at his feet. "I warned you once about that," he said through his teeth. "Now I guess I gotta hammer it home."

He came at Dillon with startling speed. Dillon didn't bother to protect himself. He had too much confidence in his own strength. He swung a long raking left at Roxy's head as he came in, but Roxy shifted a little, not stopping his rush, and Dillon's fist sailed over his shoulder.

Roxy got in close and hit Dillon in the body with two heavy blows. Dillon went crazy and missed with his wild swings.

Roxy kept stepping in and out. Every time he stepped in his fist thudded into Dillon, and when he stepped out Dillon missed him with a swing.

Dillon tried to get in close and wrestle, but Roxy kept going away, letting him have it as he rushed in. Dillon was getting a fearful lacing, but he didn't feel much; he was too mad to feel anything. Roxy hit him twice on the jaw as hard as he could. The blows sent Dillon's head back, but it didn't stop him.

That scared Roxy, and gave Dillon confidence. He began to get a grip on himself. He swung his usual wild left which Roxy was waiting for, and then he sent in a right which caught Roxy. The blow made Roxy sag at the knees. In went Dillon, taking Roxy's feeble left in his face, but getting two sledgehammer punches to Roxy's ribs.

After that Dillon began to get it his way. He kept hitting and Roxy couldn't back away fast enough. He caught his heel in a tuft of grass and went over backwards. Dillon dropped on him, his great weight pinning Roxy flat.

Neither of them said anything. Roxy reached up and caught Dillon by the neck. He couldn't quite get under Dillon's chin. Roxy began to lose his head. His legs kicked wildly as he tried to shift Dillon. He could see the cold merciless face close to him and his strength began to ebb.

Dillon raised his fist and smashed it down on Roxy's upturned face. The heel of his hand caught Roxy across his nose. Roxy's hands fell away limply. Dillon shifted a little and had Roxy by the throat. He flung his weight on his hands. Roxy kicked a little. His eyes opened very wide, and his hands plucked futilely at Dillon's wrists.

Dillon panted, "You were always a smart guy."

He stayed there until Roxy died.

The two of them remained so still in the clearing that a small bird dropped from a tree and hopped towards them. With bright, suspicious eyes it watched them, its small head a little on one side. Then, as Dillon got slowly to his feet, the bird hastily took wing.

Dillon stood over Roxy, one of his hands touching his bruised face. Then he turned and stumbled back to the farmhouse. He cautiously approached, but no one seemed to be about.

Lying near the old barn was a pick and shovel. He carefully took them and turned back to the woods again.

The grave he dug for Roxy was a shallow affair, but it was away from the path and it would be difficult to find. He patted the soil flat and covered it with branches of trees. Then he stood up, beads of sweat on his face.

From behind a big clump of bushes Chrissie watched him with puzzled eyes, and when he had gone away she came out quietly and stood looking down at the grave. She knelt down and scratched at the loose soil with her hands.

When Dillon had put the shovel and pick back he wandered into the fields. He wanted to think what he had to do. Would it be safe to take the car and blow? Would Chrissie put up a squawk? He guessed maybe she wouldn't. She might have forgotten what he had tried to do. She was crazy enough to forget anything.

He had got money and he had the car, but could he take the risk and go now, or would it be better to wait? He couldn't make up his mind. He wandered on, untroubled at the death of Roxy. When guys got in his way he just trampled on them. He had got to live, he told himself, and the others had got to look after themselves.

Farther down the fields he ran into Ma Chester. She was working on the land, a long hoe turning up the brown soil. She paused, pushing back a grey strand of hair that hung over her eyes.

Dillon said, "Roxy's skipped."

She stood, leaning her weight against the shaft of the hoe. "What's he skipped for?" she asked. Her face showed her impatience to get on with her work.

Dillon shrugged. "I guess he was tired of bein' in this dump," he said indifferently.

"You ain't goin'?" she asked.

"I ain't goin' yet," he returned. "But I'll go all right."

Ma Chester wagged her head. "Joe ain't come," she said. "It ain't like Joe to say one thing an' do another."

Dillon made to move on. "Maybe he's busy," he said. That decided him, he'd go soon. He told himself he might even go that night. He went on, leaving her with her work. He didn't look back.

It was decided for him not to go that night. On a telegraph pole, several miles from the farm, he saw a notice. It carried his photograph. He stood there, his mouth going dry, reading the notice. They offered five thousand dollars for him dead or alive.

A faint feeling of panic crept into him as he read. Here in the wilderness of hills was a picture, calling attention to himself. Anyone he met might recognize him. Anyone who suspected him could bring the Federal agents in their airplanes or their cars to seize him. He turned hastily and almost ran back to the farm.

He spent the rest of the day in his room, sitting by the window, watching. His nerves got so bad that the slightest noise made him stiffen.

He began to brood about Roxy. He couldn't bring himself to think that Roxy was dead. It would have seemed quite natural if Roxy had opened the door and come in. There was no one to grumble at, and he suddenly realized that there was no one to play cards with. That was serious. He had the long hours of the night before him with nothing to do, and sleep far off.

Well, Roxy had asked for it, he thought savagely. That guy certainly had narrow ideas. This brought his mind back to Chrissie again. He leant against the wall and thought about her. What went through his mind made him restless. He got to his feet and paced the room. He was nervous of going out in case he ran into her and she raised a squawk. Maybe the old woman would get mad. He couldn't afford at the moment to have trouble with her.

He remained shut in his room until after sundown. Then, guessing that Chrissie had gone to bed, he went outside.

Ma Chester was dishing up the evening meal. She shot him a hard look. "What's up with Chrissie?" she asked.

Dillon turned a blank face in her direction. "What's up with her?"

The old woman shrugged. "She's got a mood on, I guess," she said a little wearily. "Ain't said a word since she came back."

Dillon breathed gently with relief. "Maybe she's upset that Roxy's gone away," he suggested, sitting down at the table.

The old man hobbled from the stove and sat down too. Ma Chester shook her head. She brought over a dish of food from the oven and put it down in front of Dillon. "I ain't told her about Roxy," she said. "She might get excited."

Dillon helped himself and shoved the dish over to the old man. "She's gotta know some time," he said.

"Ain't Joe come yet?" the old man piped suddenly, not stopping his eating.

Dillon glanced up quickly. He didn't say anything.

"I reckon Joe's sick," Ma Chester said uneasily.

Dillon ate in silence. He felt they would be glad to see him go to his room. After the meal was finished he got up and went outside. He sat on the stoop. The evening was very warm, and fluffy white clouds still drifted in the darkening sky.

He sat there brooding. The thought of his room without Roxy was unbearable. Every now and then Chrissie loomed up in his thoughts, and he hastily shifted, trying to push her image away.

He heard the old man going to bed. The old man had fixed habits. He took himself to the outhouse and then hobbled slowly back. He grunted at Dillon as he passed.

Dillon got to his feet and went back into the shack.

Ma Chester was washing up. He didn't say anything to her, but shut himself in his room.

The dim flickering light of the candle made the shadows oppressive. He stood looking round the room, his nerves starting a little at every moving shadow. His eye fell on a bottle of Scotch that Roxy kept by him. He went over and took the bottle in his hand.

Dillon didn't use any hard drink. He had disciplined himself years ago. Now he didn't hesitate. He splashed the whisky into a tumbler and tossed the fiery stuff down his throat. He stood there coughing and spluttering, trying to get his breath.

The whisky did things to him. He felt a sudden rush of courage and his jumping nerves relaxed. He filled the glass again and sat down by the open window. Outside, he could hear Ma Chester locking up. He could hear her plodding about the other room, then, listening carefully, he heard her blow out the lamp. The sound of her stumbling movements across the dark room came clearly to him. Then a door shut.

He got up and took his candle from the mantelshelf and put it on the table. Then, for something to do, he checked his money. He put the pile of notes in front of him and counted them carefully. He made them into two separate rolls and put them in his pocket. Then he reached forward and blew the candle out. The moonlight made the room dim, and he went back to the window again and sat down.

His hand closed round the tumbler and he took a long pull at the Scotch. He held the liquor in his mouth for a second before swallowing it. His head began to feel a little light.

Chrissie came out of the dark shadows and peered at him. Chrissie called to him from the shadowy path outside. Chrissie sat at his elbow stroking his sleeve. Chrissie was everywhere in the room.

Still he sat there, letting the hours crawl past, the small glowing ember of horror of what he wanted to do slowly dying in his mind.

Then he got up. He leant down and took off his shoes. The hot darkness of the room lay heavily on him. He took a slow step forward, and then another. His progress was silent. Opening the door, he stepped into the outer room. A faint gleam came from the stove, and the coal hissed a little. He moved on, trying each board carefully with his stockinged foot before putting his full weight on it.

His hands touched the rough wood of Chrissie's door. He turned the handle and went in.

He could see nothing. It was as if he were blind. He closed the door gently behind him, his fingers easing the door so that it shut without a sound. Then he put out his hand and moved forward again, groping for the foot of the bed. The whisky fumes were tight round his brain, and he felt his legs lurch as he came forward. It seemed to him that he must have moved right across the room, and it startled him when his hand touched the cold rail of the bed.

He waited there listening. Faintly he could hear Chrissie breathing. Very faintly, as if she were a long way from him.

He moved on, pressing his leg against the side of the bed to guide him. His hand touched the rail of the head of the bed. He crouched a little, his hands moving down, feeling very gently for Chrissie's throat. Hands that were ready to nip any cry that she might make.

His hands touched something. Something cold came to his touch. Something he didn't like. He drew his hands away. A little shiver ran through him because the thing he had touched was like nothing he knew. It scared him.

Angry with himself, he put his hand out again. His fingers encountered a face. He knew he was touching a face. He could feel the nose, and the eyebrows were rough to his touch. But the face was cold and leathery, not the warm soft face he expected.

With a catch in his breath, he snatched his hand away, and with trembling fingers he fumbled for a match. The sweat ran down his face. He struck the match, which flared up with a little hiss.

He saw the outline of a body lying under the soiled sheet and, bending forward, he looked into the dead face of Roxy. In the faint flickering light he could see the mud in Roxy's hair and nostrils. The light reflected in the glassy protruding eyes; across one of them a fly was moving with slow intentness.

Dillon's cry woke Chrissie, who had been sleeping in a corner away from the bed. She started up, terrified at the sight of Dillon standing there; and as she saw him, the match went out. Roxy's gun, that she had cuddled to her breast, went off in her twitching hand, and the bullet smashed into Dillon, sending him to the floor.

He had only a few seconds of pain before life went away from him.

The End

JAMES HADLEY CHASE
BIBLIOGRAPHY
(1906-1985)

No Orchids for Miss Blandish
   (1939; reprinted as The Villain
   and the Virgin, 1948)
The Dead Stay Dumb (1940;
   reprinted as Kiss My Fist!, 1952)
Twelve Chinks and a Woman
   (1940; reprinted as 12 Chinamen
   and a Woman, 1950, and as The
   Doll's Bad News, 1974)
Miss Callaghan Comes to Grief
   (1941)
Get a Load of This (1941; stories)
Miss Shumway Waves a Wand
   (1944)
Eve (1945)
I'll Get You for This (1947)
Last Page (1947; play, filmed as
   Man Bait)
The Flesh of the Orchid (1948)
You Never Know With Women
   (1948)
You're Lonely When You're Dead
   (1949)
Lay Her Among the Lilies (1950;
   reprinted as Too Dangerous to be
   Free, 1951)
Figure It Out for Yourself (1950;
   reprinted as The Marijuana Mob,
   1952)
Strictly for Cash (1951)
The Double Shuffle (1952)
The Fast Buck (1952)
I'll Bury My Dead (1953)
This Way for a Shroud (1953)
Tiger by the Tail (1954)
Safer Dead (1954; reprinted as
   Dead Ringer, 1955)
You've Got it Coming (1955)

There's Always a Price Tag (1956)
The Guilty are Afraid (1957)
Not Safe to be Free (1958;
   reprinted as The Case of the
   Strangled Starlet, 1958)
Shock Treatment (1959)
The World in My Pocket (1959)
What's Better Than Money (1960)
Come Easy Go Easy (1960)
A Lotus for Miss Quon (1961)
Just Another Sucker (1961)
I Would Rather Stay Poor (1962)
A Coffin from Hong Kong (1952)
Tell it to the Birds (1963)
One Bright Summer Morning
   (1963)
The Soft Centre (1964)
This is for Real (1965)
The Way the Cookie Crumbles
   (1965)
You Have Yourself a Deal (1966)
Cade (1966)
Have This One on Me (1967)
Well Now, My Pretty (1967)
An Ear to the Ground (1968)
Believed Violent (1968)
The Whiff of Money (1969)
The Vulture is a Patient Bird
   (1969)
There's a Hippie on the Highway
   (1970)
Like a Hole in the Head (1970)
An Ace Up My Sleeve (1971)
Want to Say Alive? (1971)
You're Dead Without Money
   (1972)
Just a Matter of Time (1972)
Knock, Knock! Who's There?
   (1973)
Have a Change of Scene (1973)
So What Happens to Me? (1974)
Goldfish Have No Hiding Place
   (1974)

Believe This, You'll Believe
  Anything (1975)
The Joker in the Pack (1975)
Do Me a Favour Drop Dead
  (1976)
My Laugh Comes Last (1977)
I Hold the Four Aces (1977)
Consider Yourself Dead (1978)
Can of Worms (1979)
You Must be Kidding (1979)
Try This One for Size (1980)
You Can Say That Again (1980)
Hand Me a Fig Leaf (1981)
Have a Nice Night (1982)
We'll Share a Double Funeral
  (1982)
Not My Thing (1983)
Hit Them Where it Hurts (1984)

Omnibus Editions

Three of Spades (1974; includes
  The Double Shuffle, Shock
  Treatment and Tell It to the
  Birds)
Meet Mark Girland (1977;
  includes This is for Real, You
  Have Yourself a Deal and Have
  This One on Me)
Meet Helga Rolfe (1984; includes
  An Ace Up My Sleeve, A Joker in
  the Pack and I Hold Four Aces)

As Raymond Marshall
(reprinted as by Chase except *)

Lady Here's Your Wreath (1940)
Just the Way It Is (1944)
Blonde's Requiem (1945)*
Make the Corpse Walk (1946)
No Business of Mine (1947)*
Trusted Like a Fox (1948;
  reprinted as Ruthless, 1955)

The Paw in the Bottle (1949)
Mallory (1950)
In a Vain Shadow (1951; reprinted
  as by Marshall as Never Trust a
  Woman, 1957)
But a Short Time to Live (1951;
  reprinted as The Pick-Up, 1955)
Why Pick on Me? (1951)
The Wary Transgressor (1952)
The Things Men Do (1953)
The Sucker Punch (1954)
Mission to Venice (1954)
Mission to Siena (1955)
You Find Him—I'll Fix Him
  (1956)
Hit and Run (1958)

As James L. Docherty
(reprinted as by Chase)

He Won't Need it Now (1939)

As Ambrose Grant
(reprinted as by Chase)

More Deadly Than the Male
  (1946)

As René Raymond
(reprinted as by Chase)

The Mirror in Room 22 (1946;
story, appeared in Slipstream: A
Royal Airforce Anthology edited
by René Raymond and David
Langdon)

For further info on the works of
James Hadley Chase, visit
www.hadleychase.co.nr, compiled
by Dr. P. C. Sarkar. This is the
definitive Chase website.

Crime classics from the master of hard-boiled fiction...

Peter Rabe

The Box / Journey Into Terror $19.95
978-0-9667848-8-6
"Few writers are Rabe's equal in the field of the hardboiled gangster story." –Bill Crider, *Twentieth Century Crime & Mystery Writers*

**Murder Me for Nickels /
Benny Muscles In $19.95**
978-0-9749438-4-8
"When he was rolling, crime fiction just didn't get any better." –Ed Gorman, *Mystery Scene*

**Blood on the Desert /
A House in Naples $19.95**
978-1-933586-00-7
"He had few peers among noir writers of the 50s and 60s; he has few peers today." –Bill Pronzini

**My Lovely Executioner /
Agreement to Kill $19.95**
978-1-933586-11-3
"Rabe can pack more into 10 words than most writers can do with a page."—Keir Graff, *Booklist*

**Anatomy of a Killer /
A Shroud for Jesso $14.95**
978-1-933586-22-9

"*Anatomy of a Killer*...as cold and clean as a knife...a terrific book." –Donald E. Westlake

**The Silent Wall /
The Return of Marvin Palaver $19.95**
978-1-933586-32-8
"A very worthy addition to Rabe's diverse and fascinating corpus."—*Booklist*

**Kill the Boss Good-by /
Mission for Vengeance $19.95**
978-1-933586-42-7
"*Kill the Boss Goodbye* is certainly one of my favorites."— Peter Rabe in an interview with George Tuttle

**Dig My Grave Deep / The Out is Death
/ It's My Funeral $21.95**
978-1-933586-65-6
"It's Rabe's feel for the characters, even the minor ones, that lifts this out of the ordinary." –Dan Stumpf, *Mystery*File*

**The Cut of the Whip / Bring Me Another
Corpse / Time Enough to Die $23.95**
978-1-933586-66-3
"These books offer realistic psychology, sharp turns of phrase, and delightfully deadpan humor that make them cry out for rediscovery."—Keir Graff, *Booklist*

In trade paperback from:

**Stark House Press
1315 H Street, Eureka, CA 95501
griffinskye3@sbcglobal.net
www.StarkHousePress.com**

Available from your local bookstore, or order direct with a check or via our website.

HE WON'T NEED IT NOW

Bill Duffy is a tough newsman but he finally pushes too hard and is canned. That's when he decides to take a photo job for a rich fat man named Morgan who wants Duffy to get some pictures of his ex-wife. Blackmail is involved, and Morgan wants the guy caught with the goods. But the set-up isn't what it seems, and someone sticks a gun in Duffy's back and makes off with the camera. Nor is the ex-wife who she appears to be. She's Annabel English, a slumming society dame. And pretty soon Duffy is helping her get rid of the body of the dead blackmailer. Now Duffy is being followed by Morgan's boys. It's a toss-up who plays it harder, Morgan's goons or red-headed Annabel, the most kill-crazy lady Duffy has ever met.

THE DEAD STAY DUMB

Dillon is as ruthless as they come, brutal and tough. When he wants something, he takes it—with a gun or with his fists, it doesn't matter to Dillon. When he first blows into town, he hooks up with Nick and his girl, Myra. First they try to fix a fight, then Myra joins them as driver for a few heists. But Dillon isn't satisfied with the penny-ante jobs. He's got bigger plans. So he joins up with a local mob boss. Pretty soon, Nick realizes he's out of his depth, but by then it's too late. Now Dillon's got Myra, and Myra's got a taste of the high life. If only that were enough. Because Dillon's got a tiger by its tail, and its name is Myra. And all Myra's got to do to survive is stay out of the way of those iron fists.

"The king of all
thriller writers."
Cape Times